ON THE BATTLEFIELD

On the night following Ed Sullivan's blistering attack in the *Graphic* on other Broadway columnists, Sullivan was in Reuben's restaurant and ran into Walter Winchell. Winchell at first didn't say a word, but he was obviously sulking. Sullivan turned to talk to Holtz and then Winchell cut in savagely. "Did you mean me in what you wrote in your column?" he asked.

"No, not exactly," Sullivan said. "You know, the stage axiom of a big entrance."

"Well, Ed, as long as you've apologized to me, it's all right," Winchell said.

"I got so mad," Sullivan told the reporter doing a profile of Winchell for the *New York Post*, "I grabbed him by the knot of his necktie and pulled him over the table, right on top of the cheesecake.

" 'Apologize to you?' I said—'You sonofabitch, I did mean you, and if you say one more word about it I'll take you downstairs and stick your head in the toilet bowl.'

"Winchell didn't answer me," Sullivan said. "I got up and left."

The feud was to simmer for some thirty-five years, with occasional flare-ups that made national headlines.

THE
GOSSIP WARS

*An Exposé
of the
Scandal Era*

Milt Machlin

1.

"A man's reputation is not in his own keeping, but lies at the mercy of the profligacy of others. Calumny requires no proof. The throwing out of malicious imputations against any character leaves a stain, which no after refutation can wipe out. To create an unfavorable impression, it is not necessary that certain things should be *true*, but that they *have been said*. The imagination is of so delicate a texture that even words wound it."

William Hazlitt
Selected Essays

"Slander is worse than cannibalism."

St. John Chrysostom
Homilies III Ch. 388

The era of the gossip column was born on the day when Walter Winchell was hired by New York's *Evening Graphic*, the sleaziest daily newspaper in the history of American journalism. The year was 1924 and Winchell had been working for $50 a week on a weekly publication financed by the Keith-Albee vaudeville circuit where he was employed to write a lively chatter column about the vaudevillians and their acts. He was also expected to solicit advertisements for the publication and take a camera with him to grab a few shots from time to time of actors, actresses and other people associated with vaudeville.

Generally he would take up a stand at Broadway and 47th Street near the Palace Theater, and there he would take pictures and assemble news and chatter from the professional passers-by for his column which was called "Stage Whispers." The Albee paper was called *The Vaudeville News* and though its circulation was limited, interest ran high in the relatively tame tidbits of personal trivia Winchell assembled—usually details of births, marriages, divorces and so on, interspersed with bits of light poetry and jokes. In a publication otherwise devoted to rather boring trade news, Winchell's column became the liveliest feature.

Although Winchell later took credit for inventing the format of short, gossipy items, in fact Louella Parsons was already doing a similar column about Hollywood for the *Daily News* and its syndicate. But Winchell, a former vaudevillian himself, was already showing a gift for clever neologisms, occasionally witty *mots*, and snappy anecdotes. "Seen outside of Cleveland movie theater: Geraldine Farrar supported for the first time by her husband"—a typical item.

Winchell's column had started when he was in vaudeville with an act called Winchell and Green featuring skits, songs and dances. The young couple managed to make a living with it but were not exactly setting the world on fire. A review in *Variety* said: "The turn isn't one to bring forth any volume of applause, but it's pleasant . . ." Winchell, whose name was originally spelled Winchel, added the second "l" somewhere during his vaudeville days. Some say it was an error on the part of the typesetter but he liked it.

Winchell, at the age of 22 years, began to get the feeling that his life wasn't going anywhere. To pass the time, he began to type out a one-sheet bulletin of gossip gleaned from actors on tour with him in the Pantages road show number 151. He called the column "The Merciless Truth" and he would tack it on the backstage call board where the whole company would be sure to see it. Shortly afterward he created his first portmanteau word when he began to call the typed gossip sheet "Newsense."

In 1920, he married his partner Rita Green, but change of marital status did nothing for the act—if

6

anything, bookings began to get fewer and fewer. Meanwhile, people were beginning to notice the gossip column, feeding him items and talking about the gossip sheet enough that several people outside the vaudeville circuit began to hear about it. Ultimately one of the theatrical managers on the circuit sent a copy of "Newsense" to Glenn Condon, managing editor of the *Tulsa World*. Condon on the side was a contributor to the *Vaudeville News* and he asked Winchell to contribute items for that. When a number of his offerings were accepted, Winchell began to see the possibility of actually making something out of his writing, and he tried to get a job on *Variety* as a correspondent. But Sime Silverman, the editor, turned him down. *Billboard*, however, did take an occasional piece, for which they made nominal payment. As small as the money was, Winchell was thrilled to have his own feature appearing in print with his name on it. The columns began to appear more regularly under the title "Stage Whispers" and carrying the initials W.W. Here's a typical entry:

"Most actors are married and live scrappily ever after.

"In New York, recently the snow tied up traffic severely. A gang hired to remove same struck at the crucial moment, carrying banners which read 'You took away our beer, now take away the snow.' "

(The country was beginning to really suffer under the recently passed alcohol prohibition law.)

"Did you ever see the little brass tablet on the door in the room of your hotel which reads: 'Stop! Have you left anything?' Apropos of the h. c. of l., it should read: 'Stop! Have you anything left?' "

Meanwhile Green and Winchell, unable to make it as an act or a couple, headed for splitsville and Walter, returning to the big city from the circuit, decided to look up his editor Glenn Condon, who had now become

7

editor of *Vaudeville News*. Condon, pleased with the work that Winchell had been doing as a stringer, hired him as a reporter at $25 a week. In addition, he would be expected to sell ads, but he could take a 20 percent commission on these.

The paper actually had been formed by the National Vaudeville Artists, a company union which was part of the Albee organization and had been designed to oppose the White Rats, a vaudeville union which was the predecessor to Equity and was trying to improve working conditions on the circuit. The policy of the *Vaudeville News* under the direction of NVA (which somebody said meant "Never Vex Albee,") was to make the status quo seem pleasant and to encourage vaudevillians to continue working under poor conditions for small pay with run-down dressing rooms and martinet managers. To be fair, Winchell was hardly aware of the editorial undercurrent of the newspaper. In fact, Winchell saw the new job as an opportunity to realize a long-felt ambition. He wrote to his friend Howard Langford just after getting the job: "My dear Howard, I am writing to tell you that a wonderful proposition has been made to me from the Keith Exchange to be assistant editor of the *Vaudeville News*. I have accepted, believing that the future of such a position holds remarkable things for me (if I show 'em what I'm made of) and has unlimited possibilities.

"You no doubt don't blame me, because you have heard me mention that I would like to become a figure in the world, preferably the news game. I have always had an inclination toward it and at last I have had my wish granted . . .

"I also realize that when I tire of this (if I do), I can always go back to being an ordinary actor, can't I . . .?"

With Condon's guidance, he was learning to dig up the dirt and present it in a glib and readable fashion. And in fact, Winchell's impact on the *Vaudeville News* soon began to be felt, to the point where they were actually able to charge for the newspaper instead of giving it away. At the end of his six months' trial employment,

Winchell's salary was doubled to $50 a week and with the additional money he got from selling ads, he actually was soon making more money than his editor.

With the confidence gained from his burgeoning success, Winchell found the courage to woo and marry June Magee, a pretty young redhaired dancer from Mississippi who was—at least at first—impressed with the fast-talking fledgling journalist. June was then appearing with the dance team Hill and Astor and one of the first things Winchell did to impress the young dancer with whom he had become enamored was to give a free inside cover of *Vaudeville News* to the team. After a courtship of two years, June Magee finally gave in to Winchell's salesmanship and agreed to marry him in 1923. June felt that young Winchell definitely had a future, and her hunch shortly afterward proved to be accurate.

2.

In his new job, Winchell met a great many people on and off Broadway, including Jimmy Walker in the days before he became Mayor, and Herbert Bayard Swope, who was then executive editor of the *World*. Swope recalled his meeting with Winchell vividly.

"I was impressed at once with his energy and efficiency." Winchell had also made the acquaintance of Fulton Oursler, a journalist who had frequently submitted poetry unsuccessfully to *Vaudeville News*. Winchell's job had been to send the rejection slips. Oursler, not otherwise noted for his humility, somehow felt that the rejections were a sign of Winchell's innate good taste.

In 1924 Bernarr Macfadden, an enormously wealthy eccentric who had made his pile with such magazines as *Physical Culture* and *True Story*, decided the time had come to put himself on the map by publishing a sensational new daily in New York which he called the *Graphic*. New York, already host to more than ten dailies, hardly needed another paper, but Macfadden was a man with a whim of iron. Earlier in life he had been the traditional 90-pound weakling who had built himself up through exercise and various diet regimes as well as self-denial, into a magnificent figure of a man. He attributed his health and manly vigor to a variety of health fads and eccentric theories. He walked barefoot whenever possible because he believed that he got magnetism from the earth. In his sixties Macfadden conceived a publicity stunt for his magazines. He planned to walk barefoot from 66th Street to City Hall and to present the Mayor with a photograph of his newborn baby girl as proof of the effectiveness of his physical culture theories. However, he was dissuaded from this particular stunt by his p.r. man, Edward L. Bernays, one of America's first great press agents. Bernarr Macfadden was so in love with his theories and his physical being that he was certain he was destined to become the President of the United States and that founding the new evening paper would help him to achieve this goal.

To launch the new venture, Macfadden picked two experienced journalists, both destined to achieve greater reputations: Fulton Oursler, who went on to write *The Greatest Story Ever Told*, and to become a noted right-wing ideologue, and George Sylvester Viereck, later to win fame as a novelist and a convicted German spy. For managing editor, he hired Emile Gauvreau, a tense, frenetic French-Canadian who had gained a reputation for energy and brilliance on the *Hartford Courant* in Connecticut. The *Graphic*, Macfadden told his staff, was to be a crusading, fighting journal, standing up for health and fitness against medical ignorance. But the unorthodox appearance and approach of the paper hardly impressed the readers as the proper framework for a crusading journal. Ultimately Macfadden was to pour $11 million into the paper before giving it up.

One of his first stunts was a contest to find the perfect physical and mental specimens of a man and woman. "We want perfect mates for a new human race, free of inhibitions, and free of the contamination of smallpox vaccine." Macfadden had many strong views on health, and one of them was that vaccination was one of the scourges of humanity. This statement led a local wag to comment that the *Graphic* was for fornication and against vaccination. Certainly the newspaper itself was uninhibited in its treatment of news. It was the *Graphic* that originated a feature called "Daily Photo-drama from Life," which depicted news items in a comic-strip style similar to the Italian *Fumetti*. Models would pose as the news figure and act out the item in photographs taken in the *Graphic's* studios. Another photo feature

11

was called "Composograph," in which the heads of famous people were superimposed on the bodies of models in a reenactment of news events.

Composograph was actually invented during a lurid trial. A wealthy New Yorker had forced his wife to leave him because he claimed that she had concealed alleged Negro blood. The wife, in an effort to prove that she was white, stripped to the skin in the judge's chambers. Since cameras then and now were limited in courtroom use, the *Graphic* simply assembled a photograph showing a half-naked model standing beside a photograph of the husband in the case. The posed photograph had such a sensational impact that it soon became a regular feature, which included such items as composite photos of the final operation of Rudolph Valentino, the bedroom cavortings of Daddy Browning and his fifteen-year-old bride, Peaches and other lurid and usually sexy news items. Some people began to call the paper the *"Porno-Graphic."*

None of this bothered Winchell, who saw his chance to make it from a small trade weekly to a New York daily. He approached Oursler who remembered him well from his own *Vaudeville News* days, and asked for the job. "What do you think you can do for us?" Oursler asked. Even then Winchell had a ready tongue and an earnest convincing manner. "I've got enormous experience in the theater and I know everybody in the game," he said. "I could be a drama critic and I could write a Broadway column, too."

Oursler was aware of Winchell's already wide contacts in the entertainment world and saw instantly that Winchell could be valuable as a tipster to some of the juicier stories in New York. He agreed to hire Winchell at double his *Vaudeville News* salary, but insisted that, besides writing reviews and the Broadway column, he would have to act as drama editor, amusement editor and advertising salesman for the amusement section. He did agree to pay a 15 percent commission on the amusement ads.

Winchell got right to work feeding in items that had

been too hot to publish in *Vaudeville News* and which had accumulated in his files, as well as new stories that came to his attention. With a brash and crusading newspaper like the *Graphic* behind him, he was sure that his reputation would soon be made. But the *Graphic* was strangely schizophrenic. Winchell had been told by Oursler to pass along to the city desk any hot news tips he received, and Winchell was eager to comply. But every single story he passed along to Gauvreau, the city editor, was turned down. The newspaper had a divergent view toward sensational news. If a scandal was actively in the court, it was flashed all over the front page and photo features. But until the principals had made statements in court that were libel-proof or otherwise authenticated the story, it was hands off. Winchell took an instant dislike to the feisty Canadian editor. "That sonofabitch won't ever print anything I give him," he commented to a fellow reporter.

With his five jobs, he had to cover 220 Broadway openings during the 1924–25 season alone, as well as turning out the column which he called "Broadway Hearsay." The column appeared only on Mondays. As yet, it didn't evidence the Winchell panache which was yet to come. In fact, Winchell was so impressed with his advancement into a major New York daily that he actually began to tone down his naturally flamboyant style. Columnists then popular, such as Franklin P. Adams who wrote "The Conning Tower" in the *World*, and O. O. McIntyre, featured literary verse, quips and gossip of the publishing world, rather than stories of people's private lives and show business scandals.

One day, Winchell brought still another hot tip in to the city editor. Gauvreau, looking over the story, conceded that it might have some merit. "Why don't you run it down yourself, Walter?" he said generously. But Walter felt a bit overworked to take on the assignment. "Listen," Walter answered, according to his biographer Bob Thomas, "I've got five jobs now. My feet are worn off up to the ankles. If you got a tip over the phone from some half-witted schoolboy you'd rush ten reporters out on motorcycles."

The editor insisted that Walter take on the assignment, but Walter insisted that he had no time. The next day, the *Daily News* broke the story. Bitterly, Winchell threw the opposition paper across the city desk. "That's the last item you get from me," he muttered. It was only the beginning of a long and bitter feud with Gauvreau, which often degenerated into wild shouting matches in the newspaper office, overheard by the entire amused or appalled staff. Winchell decided to keep his news tips to himself and began to accumulate a file of gossip items which were deemed by the city desk too hot to handle. It was the best move Winchell ever made in his long and flamboyant career.

One day he sat down to write his Monday column of quips and poems and found that his folder was empty. Winchell in the end was certainly no F.P.A., and the *Graphic* was certainly not the *World*. Voluntary contributions to the *Graphic* from the literati were few, far between, and usually anonymous. Winchell idly leafed through his "hot file" and had an inspiration. He began to type out the items, abbreviating them as much as possible, trying to liven up the copy and separating them with three dots:

"Helen Eby Brooks, widow of William Rock, has been plunging in Miami real estate . . . It's a girl at the Carter DeHaven's . . . Lenore Ulric paid seven dollars income tax . . . Fannie Brice is betting on the horses at Belmont . . . S. Jay Kaufman sails on the 16th via the Berengaria to be hitched to a Hungarian . . . Report has it that Lillian Lorraine has taken a husband again . . .

It was the birth of the modern gossip column.

3.

"*The Evening Graphic* had lowered its standards without knowing it and modern gossip writing had been born." St. Claire McKelway was later to write of Winchell in *The New Yorker*.

"The journalistic taste of the ex-hoofer, Winchell, was to bring about within the next few years the only significant change in American journalism produced by the postwar generation. Emile Gauvreau, the managing editor who, like his assistants, had never thought it was possible to print such things, saw instantly that they looked all right in Winchell's column. Gauvreau was a man of originality and imagination. He instructed Winchell to write 'more of that kind of stuff.' Winchell did."

Probably the reason Winchell's column met with such instant success is the eagerness, new enthusiasm and brash iconoclasm with which he attacked his subjects. But even his most vociferous enemies had to admit that Winchell had stumbled on something new in journalism.

And oddly, Winchell seemed to catch on very quickly with New York's smart set among the literati. Alexander Woollcott, whom Winchell met first in his days as a drama critic and who had snubbed him then, suddenly became a great enthusiast of Winchell's and introduced him to people like Heywood Broun, George Jean Nathan, Dorothy Parker and even the poet Alice Duer Miller. Woollcott later described his reaction to this early Winchell:

"It was his contribution to go on strike against the

vast impersonality which at the time of his advent was deadening the American newspaper to a kind of daily *Congressional Record*. Beginning with the War, the mighty journals became such consciencious purveyors of international events, blessed or otherwise, that only episodes like war, famine, flood, bank failures, or legislative investigations seemed fit to print. If a story involved fewer than 50,000 people, it could not make the front page.

"Only when some discontented cow would make so striking a gesture as doing in her husband with a sash weight, let us say, or when some nameless avenger would stretch a parson and his choir singer dead beneath a crabapple tree, was the reader reminded at breakfast that there were, after all, individuals as well as groups astir on this planet.

"Soft-shoeing into this dreary phase of American journalism came Master Winchell, his eyes wide with the childlike interest all newcomers have, his nervous staccato pace as characteristic of his day as are the rhythms of George Gershwin. His success reminded a generation of columnists who were mere jokesmiths, after all, there is nothing so richly entertaining as a fact, and also reminded a generation of despondent city editors that, after all, people, as such, are interesting too."

Other prominent New York writers were also impressed. In 1927 Robert Benchley wrote in *The New Yorker*, "Within a year Mr. Winchell has become an institution, both as a personal reporter and a compiler of folk sayings. People buy the *Graphic* who never knew it existed. His words and the words of the people he quotes are taking their place in the national language."

Winchell developed all sorts of techniques for finding his scoops. His informants included doormen, show-girls, bartenders, elevator operators, and often the subjects themselves—as well as the ubiquitous press agents who increasingly gained favor with him by feeding him gossip items on a three-for-one trade basis. That is, if Winchell ran three items submitted by the press agent, he would, in turn, run one plug for one of the press agent's clients. Winchell referred jocularly to these press agent informants as "field representatives." Ziegfeld himself once asked Winchell a year or so after his column had gotten its start, "Where do you get your news, Mr. Winchell?"

"All you do is keep your nose to the grindstone and pick up particles of dust," Winchell replied, "like the story I just picked up today. It'll probably interest you. It's about Hazel Forbes, one of your outstanding beauties. Do you know she got married yesterday to some small-time booking agent without telling anyone? Then she returned to the Follies for the show last night, and some stage-door John, who was crazy about her, slipped a bracelet, a diamond bracelet, over her graceful arm. What a fool he must be!"

Ziegfeld's face reddened and he abruptly changed the subject and walked away from Winchell. Winchell later told a friend, "That guy can really put on the chill. All I did was report the facts. I could have been unkind and named the sucker who dished out the bracelet, but why should I embarrass Ziggy and tell him I knew *he* was the guy?"

As the Winchell column gained more and more clout, prominent men and women, some of them surprisingly distinguished, would vie for a mention in it. It became a tradition that anybody expecting a baby must give Winchell the news first. According to one of his closest associates, Winchell was once seated at his table in the Stork Club, when a proud parent rushed in, and, seeing the reporter, shouted, "I just had a baby!"

Winchell eyed him coolly, and then asked, "Who do you suspect?"

Herbert Bayard Swope, the editor of the *World*, quickly recognized the appeal of Winchell's column and asked him to bring it to his distinguished newspaper. Winchell jumped at the chance, but unfortunately the *Graphic* had tied him to a five-year contract. Heywood Broun commented that as fas as he was concerned, Winchell's column was the only thing worth reading in the *Graphic*. Circulation began to pick up as people bought the paper to read Winchell's newest effusions, and because of the popularity of the column, the *Graphic* syndicate, which was run by Louis Sobol, was able to find more and more newspapers to sign up for "Your Broadway and Mine."

Mark Hellinger, later to become a movie producer, was then a columnist on the *Daily News*, writing short novelettes along the lines of Jimmy Breslin on New York happenings, especially on Broadway. He found the eager young columnist amusing and often took him on his prowls of the Great White Way.

Gauvreau, admittedly no fan of Winchell, described him at this time as "a hunched figure with a lean, white face of deceptive humility . . . looking up occasionally, startled. He pecked the typewriter nervously."

Not everyone agreed with Gauvreau's sour assessment. The *New York Post*, no friend of Winchell's, said of him: "Winchell had an attractive presence. Lean, alert, with regular features and a nervous energy that kept him vibrating even while theoretically idling. He spoke vividly, if ungramatically. Never shy or retiring, he had a forthright aggressiveness that was even then more disarming than intimidating."

Meanwhile, despite Gauvreau's disapproval, the column grew in popularity and Winchell was getting offers from all over. The prestigious publisher Simon & Schuster gave Winchell a contract to write a book (the advance was only $150) but he was too busy to write it. However, he was turning out articles for the sophisticated *Vanity Fair* and the literary *Bookman*. Here's a description of the Broadway he was coming to love that he wrote for the *Bookman*:

". . . (Broadway) is a sublimated Coney Island or county fair or street carnival, with its mummer plays and catch-penny devices, its cacophony and gaudy lights, its peep shows and wax museums, its skating rinks, hootch dances, freaks and fol-de-rol—brought to a degree of refinement and dignity and yet still, in essence, only the merry-go-round with the steam calliope on which the adult infant spends his nickels away from his school books and other serious activities of life.

"As a standard of moral comparison it is at once an enticement and a hell, a Circe's cavern of lascivious and soul-destroying delights, an unholy place where producers are the seducers of women, where stars without talent are made meretriciously overnight, where pure girls succumb to rich admirers for diamond brooches, furs, imported automobiles, apartments and other luxuries—a Babylon, a Sodom and Gomorrah, all within the confines of a garish district extending from just below 42nd Street to Columbus Circle at 59th . . ."

Even his admirers along the Broadway beat found it curiously un-Winchell-like in style and some actually felt that it might have marked an early example of the help Winchell got in actually writing his column. His biographer, Bob Thomas, wrote, "Either Walter had been studying the dictionary given him by his Aunt Beatrice, or he was getting help in some of the writings that bore his name."

It is true that by this time, Winchell had met a brilliant, near-sighted young press agent named Irving Hoffman who offered some help in the styling of his column and apparently soon was writing paragraphs and whole columns in return for plugs for his clients.

Another who gave Winchell quite a bit of help was Sime Silverman, the editor of *Variety* who had once turned him down for a job. Now Silverman would make available advance copies of his weekly theatrical paper so that Winchell could scoop *Variety* itself. Silverman had a theory that this kept his own staff on their toes. It also got publicity for *Variety*. Silverman introduced Walter to Texas Guinan, the flamboyant blonde known as the Queen of the Speakeasy, an endless source of column items, one of which was to ultimately get Winchell into a lot of trouble. And also through Silverman, Walter met Damon Runyon at Billy La Hiff's Tavern. Runyon had an austere appearance and could be very chilly on first meeting. He was not impressed with the upstart columnist. Runyon had a good background as a hard news reporter and in fact had been Hearst's star reporter in New York. He had a respect for facts and didn't feel that someone who checked his stories as carelessly as Winchell was to be taken seriously. However, Winchell had great respect for the older man and felt that Runyon was such a good writer that he should try his hand at fiction.

"I can't write that stuff," Runyon said when Winchell suggested it. "I wouldn't know where to start." But a year or so later, faced with a stiff doctor bill for an appendectomy, he turned out a short story called "Romance in the Roaring Forties" and sold it to *Cosmopolitan*. The story, ironically, was about a Broadway columnist named Waldo Winchester who fell in love with a tap-dancer. The dancer was the girlfriend of a gangster named Dave The Dude. When Dave found out about Winchester's romance with his girlfriend, he slugged him and then kidnapped him, with the intention of forcing him to marry the tap-dancer. But in Runyon's story, it turned out that Winchester was already married to an acrobat named Lola Suppola, so Dave The Dude married the dancer instead. It was Runyon's first story and the beginning of a long friendship which later became very close. Winchell didn't mind the thinly disguised alias in the story and was pleased that Runyon had added to his growing legend.

But Winchell was even then beginning to gain some of the egregious self-esteem which marked his later character. In only the second week of his column, he listed famous Walters such as Walt Whitman, Walter Reuther, Walter Scott, Sir Walter Raleigh . . . and Walter Winchell. A reader wrote in to ask Winchell if he knew that there was a town in Texas called Winchell. "What!" Winchell commented. "Already?"

One of his sternest critics, St. Clair McKelway, who wrote a scathing series on Winchell in *The New Yorker* in 1940, said of him:

"Winchell introduced to New York journalism . . .

20

the same sort of personal item which is the cornerstone of country journalism and has been since the birth of newspapers, with the difference that Winchell was governed neither by taste nor a sincere respect for accuracy. If a personal item in a country newspaper says that Elmer Higgins is getting his roof painted, the item is written with taste and a sincere respect for accuracy. It doesn't go on to tell what is happening or what people *say* is happening, in the rooms under Mr. Higgins' roof. This is not gossip writing because gossip, by definition, is irresponsible and intrusive. Winchell wrote personal items which were gossip. He first began to gossip in the *Graphic* about what was going on around him. What was going on around him was the boom, with the effects of Prohibition thrown in. There was a spirit of lawlessness, of revolt both from unreasonable reform and from Victorian convention, reasonable or unreasonable; there was the hysteria of elation which precedes a depression, and a tolerance everywhere which amounted to abnegation. He was encouraged in his work by . . . numberless members of New York society and by the gangsters who ruled the nightlife of the town. Almost any man would have been tempted to go on writing gossip on an even larger scale, no matter what his equipment for the task happened to be. Winchell's equipment happened to be an inordinate yearning for public recognition and for riches, a staunch disregard for the feelings of others, a lack of instinct for privacy in his own life, a highly developed opportunism, an ability to get along without friends, a shrewd intelligence, a facile literary style of some merit, and a physical and nervous energy which is maniacal."

In fact, in the beginning almost everybody in New York seemed impressed by Winchell's style and verve, except his city editor Gauvreau, who was somewhat underwhelmed by his energetic fledgling columnist. The feud with Gauvreau, whoever started it (and nobody seems to quite know this), was the first of many. For Winchell's insecurity made him extremely thin-skinned to any criticism or fancied rejection. Old *Graphic* veterans believe that Winchell's trademark, wearing his snap-brimmed fedora indoors and outdoors in-

21

discriminately, began when he wore the hat into the city room, flouting a long-standing journalistic tradition, just to get Gauvreau's goat.

Thin-skinned or not, Winchell's manner as well as his success was making him as many enemies as friends and his personal flamboyance was often the subject of laughter on the part of his fellow journalists. There are Graphic veterans who still remember the day when Winchell, who had just been given his first raise, burst into the *Graphic* office attired in a new camel's hair coat and exclaimed, "Look, a belt in front and behind!"

Winchell's sometimes ignorant but often acerbic and waspish drama reviews were not making any friends for him, either. In fact, he stung the powerful Shuberts, Lee and J. J., so severely with some of his flippant comments that they finally barred him from all of their many theaters. He had just about convinced them to allow him back into the first night openings when he threw another bomb. "A certain critic," he wrote, "barred from Shubert openings, says he'll wait three nights and go to their closings."

That did it. From then on, Walter was on the outside looking in as far as opening nights were concerned. But according to Louis Sobol, of whom more later, Winchell found an amusing way to get around the Shuberts' ire. When his pals the Marx Brothers were opening in "Animal Crackers," Winchell decided that, come what may, he was going to get in. Sobol was then second-string dramatic critic on the *Graphic* and he was actually assigned to do that show. But Winchell and Sobol had an agreement that if Winchell got in, he could write the review.

On opening night, Sobol had neither heard from Winchell nor seen him at the theater so he went back to the office and pounded out quite a favorable review of the Marx Brothers' epic. Just as he completed the piece, Winchell popped into the office and told Sobol not to bother, he would write the review. "It appeared," Sobol says, "that he had walked in boldly—disguised in a dripping beard!" (Others say he was actually made up

. ˙ Groucho) The managing editor, however decided to use Sobol's review instead, insisting that Walter should first straighten himself out with the Shuberts.

Sobol is under the impression that it was this incident that started Winchell's problems with Gauvreau, but according to other witnesses this hardly seems to be the case. Later on, when Al Jolson was to open in "Wonderbar," he stipulated that he would not go on unless Winchell was admitted and this, in the end, made peace in his feud with the Shuberts.

Sobol also described another feud that arose between the abrasive columnist and a British critic named St. John Ervine, who had succeeded Alexander Woollcott on the old *Morning World.* "St. John, or Sinjin, as the boys called him," Sobol remembers, "was an aloofish gentleman who scorned the speed of the American fraternity and saw no earthly reason why he, too, should make a hasty exit before the final curtain in order to write his piece in time for the city edition. The reviews of St. John, it was announced, would appear, not the following day—but the day after."

New York critics began to poke mild fun at Ervine's leisurely pace, but Winchell, probably only because he thought it was a clever pun, called him "St. Yawn Ervine" and ridiculed him until the Britisher struck back, criticizing him for his gossip-gathering and calling him "Little Boy Peep," an expression which, perversely, Winchell later on chose to regard as a compliment. When he returned to England, Sinjin made only a passing reference to this spat with Winchell, writing that his visit to America had been most pleasant, marred only slightly by "the incessant buzzing of an insignificant gadfly."

A daily column has an enormous appetite and now that he had to turn out five times as much copy as before, Winchell had to expend perhaps ten times as much energy gathering his material. He would often appear in speakeasies and grab people by the arms or coat lapels and say, "Got an item?" or even beg them "Come on, gimme a gag." Arthur Caesar, a movie writer, used to watch with considerable venom as Walter made his rounds. "Look at him," he would say when Winchell came up to his table at Tony's speakeasy on West 49th Street, "the literary mendicant."

In those days the institution of press-agentism in regard to columns was still not fully developed to the point it reached in later years when often Winchell's entire column would be written by some press agent eager to get bartered items of publicity for his client. In fact, one of his early columns stated under the headline "WE HATE TO BRAG":

> "In justice to the followers of this pillar of gab we regret that limited space forces us to crowd out 1,500 items of press agent material. Apologies to the *Times* and *News.*"

This suggested, of course, that the *Times* and *News* were using press agent material and Winchell wasn't. This was somewhat deceptive, because even then Winchell was building the army of accommodating press agents he needed for his voracious column.

Shortly after Winchell signed up with the *Graphic*, a muscular young sportswriter and athlete named Ed Sullivan was hired to beef up the growing staff, and it wasn't long before Sullivan, still just a sports writer, had somehow gotten himself into a feud with Winchell which was to last for most of the rest of both of their lives. Ironically, the feud, according to Sullivan, started when he tried to make peace between Winchell and his dyspeptic editor, Gauvreau. Sullivan at the time had a friend high up in the Macfadden organization named O. J. Elder, who was one of their top advertising executives. Elder and Sullivan used to play golf and go fishing together and it was well known that they were close friends. In fact, it was Elder who had first suggested Sullivan for the job of sports writer. One day, Winchell cornered Sullivan in his office and said, "Look, you're a pal of Elder's; can't you get him to get Gauvreau to stop picking on me?"

Walter Winchell on the air

"I was surprised," Sullivan said, "that he asked me, but I agreed. The following week I went on a fishing trip with Elder and remarked to him, 'It's too bad Winchell and Gauvreau don't get on.' Elder said he didn't know about it—he worked in a separate building—but he said he'd try to straighten it out."

About six days later, Sullivan said in an interview in the *New York Post*, he got a phone call from Gauvreau, who invited the sportswriter into his office and asked if Sullivan realized who was the editor of their paper. Sullivan said sure, Gauvreau was. Then Gauvreau said: "If you know so damn well, why did you go over my head and talk to Elder?" Sullivan tried to explain that he had simply remarked that it was a shame Winchell and Gauvreau were always feuding, but Gauvreau could not be pacified and raged on about Sullivan's interference in the newspaper's affairs. When he finally cooled down, he said to Sullivan, "All right, now who do you think told me about going to Elder?"

"Elder, of course," Sullivan said.

"No," Gauvreau said, "it was Winchell."

Then he called in Winchell. Winchell's face was white when he walked into the office and was asked whether it was true that he had told Gauvreau, Sullivan said.

Winchell admitted it, but he said it was Gauvreau's fault that he had told, that Gauvreau had forced it out of him.

"Imagine," Sullivan told the *Post* interviewer, "Winchell first asked me to do it for him, and then he went and told Gauvreau himself. How do you like that for a guy who's always bragging about the way he protects his sources?

"I remember saying afterward to Winchell: 'Walter, what can I do with a cringing coward like you? If I hit you, you might get hurt; if I spit in your eye, it will be coming down to your level.'

"After that incident, we didn't talk to each other for several years."

The feud with the editor was making Winchell gray before his time, or at least *something* was. In what would have otherwise been the most satisfying and exciting part of his life, Gauvreau was the principal fly in Winchell's ointment and the feud even erupted into print. Once Winchell in his column asked, "Who called that piccolo player a managing editor?" And Gauvreau actually wrote an editorial which seemed to be a denunciation of Winchell.

In any event, Winchell was more than eager when he was approached after the first few years of his column by the Hearst organization and asked if he would be willing to work for the *Evening Journal* when his contract with the *Graphic* expired. Since everybody knew that the *Graphic* was losing a fortune, Winchell was glad to accept the offer and possibly had reason to believe that the paper might fold before his contract ran out. The *Journal* money was good, too. He was offered $500 a week to start.

At this point, Gauvreau seemed to actually give Winchell's career a boost. He had been arguing day in and day out that he could not continue to exist on the same paper as Winchell. Bernarr Macfadden, who had taken a strong personal dislike to Winchell himself, particularly because of Winchell's obvious involvement with the world of drinkers and smokers, finally gave in to Gauvreau's pleas, despite the fact that Winchell was the most valuable asset that the paper had.

Gauvreau himself gave an unverified version of the reason that Macfadden finally decided to let Winchell go. According to the *Graphic* editor, Winchell had got into the habit of irritating Macfadden by telephoning him at three o'clock in the morning and shouting imprecations.

"According to a report which I never verified, Winchell, in one of his telephone tirades, at four a.m., accused the physical culturist of having eaten a planked steak floating in worcestershire sauce while he was supposed to have been on a diet," Gauvreau reported.

According to the editor, he received word from Macfadden to release Winchell on the day following that phone call.

Bernarr Macfadden himself challenged Gauvreau's version of Winchell's firing. He didn't remember any calls about beefsteaks slathered with worcestershire sauce. He had an entirely different memory of it, as he told one reporter.

"Gauvreau sold me out," he said. "We were negotiating to buy the *Mirror* from Hearst. It had already lost a couple of million. Then Gauvreau sold me out. He talked me into firing Winchell."

The reporter asked Macfadden about the beefsteak rumor.

"I don't remember that," Macfadden said. "If Gauvreau hadn't sold me out, we would have been the second paper in New York . . . Gauvreau fixed it so that I'd fire Winchell. . . Then Gauvreau quit and went to the *Mirror*. We didn't have much chance after that at the *Graphic* . . ."

While this maneuvering was going on, A. J. Kobler, the publisher of Hearst's morning paper, the fairly new *Mirror*, spoke to Hearst and got permission to ask Walter if he would object when he left the *Graphic* to working for the *Mirror* instead of the *Journal*. To sweeten the pot, Kobler said he would give Winchell a $500 bonus in addition to his $500 a week salary when he left the *Graphic*.

4.

Winchell's thralldom to Gauvreau ended suddenly and somewhat mysteriously in May 1929. Louis Sobol, who had been toiling away in the syndication section of the *Graphic*, selling Winchell's column to an increasing number of papers, among other duties, was called to Gauvreau's office. When Sobol arrived, Gauvreau didn't ask him to sit down. He simply stared at the newsman a while, grinned weakly for a moment and then, according to Sobol, snapped: "Do you think you can handle Winchell's job?"

Sobol was floored. Winchell was the number one star of the *Graphic* and practically its only attraction. Before he could answer, Gauvreau continued in his staccato manner: "I want you to write the column for a few days. If it goes over you've got the job—permanent."

Sobol was completely flummoxed. He had filled in on rewrite and often was called on to ghostwrite pieces for various celebrities. His style was facile, fluid and at times verged on elegance, but in no way resembled the driving, electric and exciting tone that Winchell had brought to the Broadway column. However, before he could even voice a protest, Gauvreau spoke again. "Winchell in?" Sobol nodded. (Winchell occupied a tiny, windowless cell adjoining Sobol's.) "Okay, you tell him he's to go on vacation tomorrow. Tomorrow, get me? Now go tell him."

In a daze and considerably confused over these orders, Sobol stumbled toward Winchell's office. He came in just as Winchell was finishing a phone conversation with Alexander Woollcott. "Ever meet Alec?" Winchell asked Sobol.

Sobol answered that he'd seen him during various opening nights and dramatic occasions, but he had not actually met him.

"Good guy," Winchell said. "I get great stories from him."

Sobol nodded distractedly, still somewhat stunned by the task that had been set for him. "Walter," he said, "Gauv just told me to tell you you can start your vacation right away—tomorrow. He said to tell you I'm going to take over your spot, and if I do all right, he's going to let you go to Hearst. That's what the man said, Walter."

Winchell stared at him in stunned disbelief, turned slightly in his chair and stared thoughtfully at some of the autographed celebrity photographs tacked to the wall. Then he turned back and in a tone that Sobol thought was notably subdued, asked, "When did he tell you that?"

"Why—just now. I've just come from his office. He told me to tell you just what I've told you."

Winchell kept his feelings bottled up for not more than a few seconds and then he exploded. "Why, the little sonofabitch!"

He lapsed back into silence. Obviously he was shocked by the news and had no intimation that it was coming. For a moment he seemed to lose that assertiveness and vehemence of tone for which he was noted around Broadway. Then, in a voice that Sobol says was almost boyishly timid, he asked: "Do you think I ought to go and see him about this? What do you think?"

"Sure, Walter," Sobol answered. "Sure, why don't you?"

Winchell left the office to see Gauvreau, but returned within five minutes. He seemed subdued, but far from depressed. After all, if Sobol made good, it meant that Winchell would be able to go to the *Mirror* at more than double the salary he was making, plus the $500 bonus he was promised. He started to try to break Sobol in to the job.

"Look," he said, "here's some releases just in—you

30

can use them if you want to for the column tomorrow. See you later.'' Winchell cocked his ever-present hat at a slightly more rakish angle and, with a slight bow, left the office, never to return again.

For the moment Sobol, whose salary was up from $90 to $200 with innumerable additional perks about which he was shortly to become informed, was thrilled at the new assignment, but extremely puzzled at Gauvreau's way of handling the situation. He knew, of course, as did everybody in the newspaper business, about the editor's fierce hostility to Winchell. Once in the heat of a screaming argument in the city office, Winchell had even hurled a sneering remark at the editor about his crippled leg, something for which Gauvreau never forgave him.

On May 31, Sobol took over the column "Your Broadway and Mine" and also the dramatic critic's chores, technically as a substitute. He was to be the first clone of Winchell's new-style Broadway column. More were to follow shortly. Underneath the column, the newspaper placed a box which said simply, "Walter Winchell is holidaying for two weeks. Until Mr. Winchell returns, his department here will be conducted by Louis Sobol."

On the following day, without any further comment, Sobol's name replaced Winchell's on the column. The paper might be lurid, lowbrow and poorly regarded in the trade, but Sobol was in seventh heaven. Winchell was the keystone of the paper whose only other feature of note was the sports column written by Ed Sullivan.

Sobol was awed by his promotion and not at all certain that he was the right man for the job. Prior to coming to the *Graphic* he'd worked on small town papers such as the *Waterbury Republican* and the *New London Day*. He'd come to New York to become eventually city editor of Macfadden's trade paper the *Automotive Daily News*. While with the syndicate that distributed the *Graphic*, Sobol was given a chance to ghost several pieces by Queen Marie of Romania and had revised several short pieces of Helen Keller's for the

31

feature syndication. He had also turned out ghost-written, first-person stories in the Peaches and Daddy Browning scandal and what he calls now some "allegedly first-person revelations" by two of the figures in the Hall-Mills murder case.

He had also taken the time to hit Broadway with a farce called "The High-Hatters" which starred an unknown young actor named Robert Montgomery and a supporting player of no reputation at the time, Brian Donlevy. Fortunately for the history of Broadway columns, but perhaps not unfortunately for the theater, the play was hardly a vast success. Burns Mantle said that he thought that while the author was carrying "The High-Hatters" around the theater district looking for a place to lay it down "it is rather to be regretted . . . he did not pass a manhole at the time of explosion." Richard Watts, Jr. did not demur: "What is easily one of the lowest points reached by the current—or for that matter any past dramatic season, was achieved by the Klaw Theater."

The day Gauvreau handed him the exciting news of his appointment happened to be Sobol's tenth wedding anniversary. Sobol rushed home to tell the news to his wife Lee and they decided that they would take some of their $400 bankroll and splurge on a celebration.

"Buy yourself some fancy duds," Sobol told his wife. "The Sobols are beginning to ride."

However Lee, in the tradition of all good and pessimistic wives, settled for wearing her one good dress and no jewelry, since she had none. Sobol decided to go along with her in hedging their splurge, deciding to wear the better of his two blue serge suits, the less shiny one. The Sobols were about to learn one of the great lessons concerning the job of Broadway columnists.

5.

In 1929 America was still basking in the specious glow of the tremendous boom that followed World War I. That was the year the big stock market frenzy reached its peak, with everyone from shoeshine boys and chorus girls to the producers that funded their shows investing in the great bull market of Wall Street. It was also the year that the stock market crashed, but that wasn't to be until late October.

There had been a vast revolution in manners and morals in the country since the passage of the Prohibition Amendment in 1919, the same year, incidentally, that women got the vote. When the dry law was passed, women wore skirts down to their ankles, were never seen to drink in public and rarely did so in private, were hardly a factor on the work market and were expected to have no sex life outside of marriage and not much there, if popular literature were to be believed. Within five years after the ratification of prohibition, women were wearing skirts halfway up their thighs, patronizing speakeasies catering particularly to women, and drinking publicly from hip-flasks in the back of open cars. The age of Freud had come in, along with the dry era and the women's vote, and now it was considered fashionable not only to have sex, but to flaunt it. The speakeasy era had come to stay, and with it the dominance of the gangsters who controlled the liquor traffic.

Before the war, saloons were not only strictly masculine, but very utilitarian affairs. Lots of dark mahogany, sawdust on the floor, free lunches and soup—and strictly male. But in this new era, women emerged from behind Victorian and Edwardian beaded curtains into

33

the bright spotlight of the Roaring Twenties. Since most of the fashionable eating and drinking spots—Tony's, the Stork Club, 21, El Morocco and the rest—operated with no legal franchise, no holds were barred, in a sense. There was no official closing hour. There were no laws or regulations to be observed, and a spirit of wildness and frenzy swept the land. New York certainly was the hottest of all the hot spots.

The gangsters who ran midtown Manhattan, Owney Madden and Big Frenchie LaMange (a. k. a. Frankie DeMange and Frankie LaManche) needed publicity and plenty of it. After all, most of them could not advertise for customers and how else could they bring in their clientele? This atmosphere served as the perfect incubator for the development of the gossip columns. The columns gave free publicity to these glamorous, if illicit, drinking spots, and the gangsters who backed or had a piece of practically every major spot going (with the possible exception of 21) were glad to pick up the tab for the chroniclers of night life.

Curiously enough, 21 barred most columnists. Jack Kriendler, one of the owners of 21, told Sobol once why his club was the only place during the speakeasy era that barred Winchell, Hellinger and the others: "Suppose something happened," he explained to the columnist, "like someone starting a fight or some prominent married customer out with a girl or someone else's wife? There was always the danger that one of you fellows would have it in the column, and that certainly would not do us any good. Besides, Charlie and I (Charlie Berns his partner) thought it was a mistake to have any publicity at the time—we always thought the owners were out of their minds to let you fellows in and write about their places."

The mob did try to muscle in on 21 several times, but for some reason, Berns and Kriendler were able to hold out, and threats from the Madden group had no effect on the stalwart partners. In fact, on one occasion, two of Madden's henchmen showed up and there was indeed massive mayhem. But the victims were the two hoodlums.

Things were at their frantic height the night that Sobol started his first club- and pub-crawl as a columnist. Ornate mansions had been converted into opulent, illicit night haunts. Landlords were getting five to ten times their normal rental on any hole-in-the-wall that consented to sell liquor. Many of the places operated as chartered, supposedly private, clubs, and when prohibition agents raided them, they flashed their club charters and membership lists. A few, among them the Artists and Writers Club, the Stork and the Embassy, used the private membership gimmick as a way to keep undesirables out also. Only a few of the big, preprohibition restaurants were able to survive under the law. Luchow's on 14th Street kept going, but it was known that the waiters all had private supplies of liquor they could make available to the cognoscenti.

"By the time I became an authorized Broadway reporter," Sobol remembers, "it had become definitely chic to be illegal and one could be illegal in the embrace of luxury such as New York had never encountered before. Broadway itself degenerated into a street of cafeterias, electric shoeshine stands, soft-drink and hamburger kiosks, physical culture demonstrators and street-corner demagogues, ten-cents-a-dance halls—while the gates to an invisible paradise in the Fifties suckered away the silk-hat and ermine crowd.

"The speakeasy, indeed, had traveled quite a distance in those intervening years, when you contrast the first bars—a few planks across a pair of sawhorses—with the silver and chromium masterpiece at the Park Avenue Club, for instance, which enforcement wreckers chopped up one day and carted off to the government warehouse . . .

"In this luxurious set-up, host (George) LeMaze served dinners that put old man Lucullus back into the Automat class. The feet of his chickens and guinea hens had never touched the ground; his baby lamb came from a special farm in Ohio; every morning the express brought from Florida 30 pounds of pompano bonne femme, served with a mustard sauce that only a chef knew how to mix.''

But though it was boom time, prices were still fantastically low by present standards. Lunch at the Park Avenue Club was a dollar and the table d'hote dinner was $2.50. Of course, even in those cheap times, LeMaze knew he couldn't make money at those prices, but he made a fortune from the booze.

The elite of all America, judges, senators, generals, admirals, executives, poets, artists, authors, musicians, college professors, stage and screen stars, explorers and Broadway columnists all showed up at the doors of these elegantly furnished, illicit boites and nobody was ashamed of it. In fact, anybody who wasn't known in all of the most elegant upholstered sewers was considered a nobody, including the Mayor of New York, Jimmy Walker. West 52nd Street between Fifth and Sixth Avenues became a veritable carnival show of speakeasies. Private residents who still occupied the few brownstone mansions that had not been converted to speakeasies had to put up signs saying "Do not ring. This is a private residence." Robert Benchley once tried to drink in every saloon along the street and gave up when he counted thirty-two. He was only able to count that many because he had kept notes, which gradually degenerated into an illegible scrawl.

Tony's was considered the most elegant and intellectual of the saloons along that street and catered to most of the members of the Algonquin Round Table— Dorothy Parker, Heywood Broun, Edna Ferber, Alec Woollcott, Catherine Brush, James Thurber, Ernest Hemingway (when he was in town), Michael Arlen, Ben Hecht, Charles MacArthur, E. Phillips Oppenheim, George Jean Nathan, to say nothing of members of the Society set. It was here that a young drinker and matinee-idol-type leading man named Humphrey went to sulk when nobody paid much attention to him, and to stand on his head to attract attention. Tony the owner liked actors and tolerated his behavior. When it got too much he would say: "Humphrey? Humphrey Bogart, stop standing on your head and act like a gentleman."

(In fact, Tony was not too opposed to head-standing, since he was, himself, an avid practitioner of yoga.)

If you went to another popular speak called the Five O'Clock Club, you might be lucky enough to arrive when Flo Ziegfeld hove into view almost nightly just before midnight, usually accompanied by at least half a dozen of his famed Follies beauties. Sometimes on the same night you might also see George White and Earl Carroll, both of them producers of fabulous girl shows too, each accompanied by beauties from their respective productions, the "Scandals" in George White's case and the "Vanities" in Carroll's.

The Napoleon Club catered to illustrious and accomplished guests such as illustrator James Montgomery Flagg, Bob "Believe It or Not" Ripley, Sir Hubert Wilkens the explorer, Floyd Gibbons the newsman, and others.

All in all, a thriving swamp into which a tadpole columnist could launch himself. The many speakeasies and nightclubs gave rise not only to gangster dominion, hoodlum hosts and hard-nosed bouncers, but to a profession that had really only started after the war, that of press agent. On Sobol's first night out on the town, he was taken in hand by Irving Strouse who offered to show him the ropes. He introduced the Sobols to celebrities they had only read about to that date: William Gaxton, Ed Wynn, Will Rogers, George Jessel and one fellow columnist, Sidney Skolsky, shortly to depart for the glamour of movie land, and finally to the owner of the famed theatrical restaurant, Vincent Sardi, Sr.

Suddenly Sobol realized that everybody was falling all over him, glad-handing him, vying for his attention. Jessel told him a joke and swore that it was exclusive and that he could be free to use it in his column. Skolsky invited him to join a luncheon group at Sardi's for laughs and for copy.

"And the big moment came at the dinner's end," Sobol recalls with a smile. " 'Compliments of Mr. Sardi,' the captain of waiters announced as I asked nervously for the check, hoping I had sufficient funds to cover.''

Prior to this inaugural outing, a big night for the Sobols would be a trip to a Second Avenue restaurant where they might spend a total of two dollars for their entire dinner and leave a generous tip of fifty cents. Now in his new station, Sobol wondered what he should tip. He called Strouse over and frankly explained his problem. Strouse told him, ''Leave two dollars for the waiter and a buck to the captain. That'll be plenty.'' Louis sighed and caught his wife's eye, shrugging in resignation. The three-dollar tip was already more than they had ever spent on an entire night out, and this was only their first stop.

Their second stop, with Strouse as their guide, was Texas Guinan's, the rowdy night club where the expression ''Hello, suckers'' was originated by the brassy fast-talking hostess, a former star of western movies. Tipped off to Sobol's arrival, Guinan called for a spotlight.

''And now, suckers, I want you to meet someone you'll get to know better soon—you *better* get to know him better soon. The fellow who's taken over Walter Winchell's column on the *Graphic*. Give Louis Sobol a nice, big hand—make him feel at home. Get up, Louis, let all these suckers see what you look like. Go on, get up!''

Embarrassed at the attention, Sobol raised himself slightly in his chair and sat down quickly. There was a spattering of applause and from a nearby table he could hear someone chuckling in amusement. ''He's taking Winchell's place? Oh, no!''

Here again, when Sobol asked for the check, everything was on the cuff and the hostess even came over to their table, chatted affably with Sobol and his wife, and offered him a couple of gags that he could be free to use under her name in his column. She swore that they were brand new, just off the main stem. (Sobol says he later learned they were old chestnuts, but he had never heard

38

them before.) Again the columnist left two dollars for the waiter and a dollar for the captain, which were accepted somewhat disdainfully.

Their next stop was Reuben's, where Strouse, who had other fish to fry, abandoned them. But in this case, he left without introducing the new columnist and explaining his function. As a result, the Sobols got a check this time for three dollars and according to his briefing, Sobol dutifully left two dollars for the waiter and a dollar for the captain, except this time both the captain and the waiter seemed astounded and thanked them profusely.

Still celebrating, the Sobols decided to go whole hog and take a taxi back to Jackson Heights that night, instead of their usual subway. Lee Sobol, who had been adding up the evening's expenses, turned to Louis in some concern and said, "Do you think we will be able to afford this new job of yours?"

But the life of a columnist, for good or for bad, as they were shortly to learn, was not the life of your ordinary citizen or even your journeyman journalist.

6.

Walter Winchell, taking to heart the tip that he was about to be released from his contract to the *Graphic*, got hold of the Hearst organization and told them he was ready to go to work on the *Mirror*.

As far as Winchell was concerned, as long as he got the $500 a week, he didn't care which Hearst paper he worked for, and he was so, so happy to be out from under the thumb of Emile Gauvreau.

As soon as Winchell was settled at the *Mirror*, Irving Hoffman, who had already established himself as one of Winchell's major press agent contributors, had a suggestion: "Listen, Walter," he said, "now that you're working for Hearst, why don't you have them print your column in red ink?" (Hoffman was not referring to the financial status of the *Mirror* which was, in fact, shaky, but to the fact that the Hearst papers had a habit of emphazing their hot stories with headlines printed in red.)

"I'll think about it," Winchell said. And in fact the next day he approached the publisher to ask if red ink was possible. Brisbane didn't feel it was a good idea, but suggested instead that he use bold face type in alternate paragraphs with light. Winchell took the suggestion, and it gave the column an even more breathless and startling format.

However, two months later Winchell stepped into the offices of the *Mirror* to find some shocking news. Emile Gauvreau had been hired as managing editor of the *New York Mirror* and it was to be another round of shoot-outs in the city room.

Later, sitting in his office and making a few phone

40

calls, Winchell finally figured out what had happened. Gauvreau, convinced that the *Graphic* would never make it in New York, had simply made a deal with the publisher Kobler to fire Winchell, let the *Mirror* hire him, and then quit himself to go over to the larger and more successful paper.

Winchell's column had first appeared in the *Mirror* on June 10, 1929—on page one. Winchell was actually concerned about this. "Will it really look like a column on page one?" he wondered. Walter Howey, the tough and cynical editor of the *Mirror*, explained: "It'll be the only news in the paper." Howey was the model for the fire-eating city editor in Hecht and MacArthur's play, "The Front Page." He was cynical about the tabloid which, although less racy and unconventional than the *Graphic*, was barely a few steps ahead of the *Police Gazette* on a general taste level. Designed to compete with and imitate the *Daily News* visually, the *Mirror* never quite caught the quality of the older and larger paper. However, the page one spot was only an introduction and Winchell was later to move to page ten, where he remained for the rest of his career on that paper.

An observer of the newspaper scene in later years remarked, "The *Mirror* is a mess of newsprint built around page ten." For Winchell's column soon became the tawdry tabloid's chief asset. His friend Woollcott commented: "Recently a *New Yorker* cartoon pictured a formidable matron as saying that all she needed for breakfast was orange juice and Walter Lippmann. I know a great many lighter creatures who can get along on just Winchell—with perhaps a dash of gin."

Winchell should have been deliriously happy with his new salary, his increased readership, and his added clout. But, as ever, Gauvreau was the bane of his existence. Winchell was developing the technique of getting good tips from press agents and speakeasy owners in return for praise in his columns. Gauvreau made it a habit to knock out anything that could be interpreted as free advertising or a plug. Winchell's ploy was to inaugurate a department called "Orchids" in which he

41

would praise those selected for his kudos or payoffs.

Gauvreau resented everything about Winchell, from his appearance and style to his morals. He complained bitterly about Winchell's open friendship with the notorious gangsters who supplied him with much of his material as well as a number of perks in the form of presents, bar tabs, free suits and hats. Of course, it was impossible to have access to the kind of information a columnist needs without being intimate with some of these gangsters, and the relationship was somewhat symbiotic. Winchell claimed that he knew every important gangster in New York except Dutch Schultz. According to Bob Thomas, his biographer, he almost met Schultz one night when he was visiting the Polly Adler's house that was not a home with comedian Lou Holtz. As the two men walked down one of the corridors of the bordello, they glanced through the open door of one of the bedrooms, and there they saw supine the unmistakable figure of Dutch Schultz. Schultz at that time had declared a war to the death on another vicious killer, Vincent "Mad Dog" Coll.

Winchell took a look and grew pale. "Let's get the hell out of here," he said. Holtz had already made it to the door and Winchell wasted no time in following him.

Polly Adler later said that Dutch Schultz had actually recognized Winchell and Holtz, and felt hurt that they didn't join him for a social drink.

In the late twenties, the most important gangster on the Broadway beat was Owney Madden, and since most of the action Winchell wrote about revolved around or was talked about in the night clubs, it was important for him to be able to establish and maintain a friendship with Madden. It was a strange union, to say the least. Madden was raised in the slums of Liverpool and left there as a boy to settle in the slums of New York's Hell's Kitchen. He was prococious and it took him no time at all to learn the ways of America and particularly Manhattan. By the time he was seventeen, they were already calling him "Owney the Killer." At eighteen, he took over the midtown west side Gopher Gang and by the time he was nineteen, at least two murders were credited to him. When he was twenty, a group of rival hoods from the Hudson Dusters mob intercepted him and put five slugs into his wiry frame. But Madden lived, and at twenty-two was convicted of the murder of a fellow hood named "Little Patsy" Doyle.

Owney Madden's murder conviction came about this way: Madden had expropriated a moll by the name of Freda Horner from a minor member of his gang. While Madden was in the hospital having an overdose of lead removed from his gut, the girl returned to her original love, Patsy Doyle. When the patched-up boss returned to the mob, Patsy was marked for death. Freda's best girlfriend was told to call on Patsy and tell him that Freda loved him alone and wanted a second reconciliation. They set up a rendezvous at an Eighth Avenue bar and within minutes after Patsy arrived, one of Madden's gang slipped in behind him and pumped him full of bullets. To get even, Freda, who was again living with Owney, turned state's evidence and Madden was sent up for ten to twenty.

When he got out, he was hired by Larry Fay, a milk and taxicab racketeer and backer of night clubs, who used his muscle to keep order in several of the joints in which he had an interest. Madden not only kept order, but took over the entire night club business in midtown Manhattan. Within a year of his release, he was the biggest man in the rackets in that part of town. He was involved in beer, rum, gambling, clip joints and night clubs. Madden didn't get where he was by being stupid, and he was one of the first to realize the value of cultivating the Broadway gossip columnists. It was good for his night club business to be mentioned in the newspapers. Ed Sullivan once remarked, "You just had to ask Owney for anything you wanted and you'd get it—protection, special favors, and that kind of stuff. It was like knowing the mayor to know Madden."

Actually, it was *better* to know Madden than to know the Mayor. Knowing Jimmy Walker, probably New York's most gadabout and gregarious mayor, was easier than knowing Ed Koch, but knowing Madden was a privilege reserved only for the "in" people of New York's café society, of which gossip columnists were considered the most "in" of all.

Madden first encountered Winchell in Spindal's barbershop on Broadway in the West 50's, which was patronized by Madden and his mob, as well as by various gossip writers. The barbershop in prohibition days was a traditional meeting place for gangland big shots and newsmen, and it was while getting a haircut that Winchell first made the acquaintance of speakeasy baron Owney Madden. Madden approached the columnist as he was being shaved and told him he read his column every day in the *Graphic*.

Winchell was happy to be recognized by Madden and gratefully accepted his warm handshake. Madden insisted on picking up Winchell's barber tab. There has always been a strong link between barbers, gangsters and newsmen. Some of the barbers who once shaved the gangsters and columnists actually moved into the night clubs later on and established shops inside.

One of the favorite barbershops for the gangsters and gossips for a while was the Hollywood Barbershop at Broadway and 47th Street. It was there that one of the last surviving members of the Schultz gang was gunned down, after Schultz himself had been murdered in 1935, and, of course, it is hard to forget the Park Central barbershop where Albert Anastasia had his last shave.

Knowing Madden was certainly an advantage to the columnists. Madden gave large, noisy parties at hotels and restaurants around town and Winchell was occasionally invited to them. He also accompanied Madden frequently to prize fights, wrestling matches and ballgames.

After this first meeting with Winchell, the two became so friendly that Madden would make it a practice to drop in at the *Mirror* office from time to time to see the columnist. Gauvreau wrote about it this way: "Big shots ambled in and out of our office to hear some of the gossip before it got into print and often to offer kindly suggestions. Charles (Lucky) Luciano, later to be convicted as an operator of a widespread vice racket, frequently sounded the keynote for smart Broadway reading. A familiar caller in the *Mirror* city room was Owney Madden, the leading racketeer of New York whom I had not met socially, and who conferred with people on my staff who were in closer touch with his affairs."

And in fact, Madden gave Winchell a fantastic inside look at the night life, opening the doors on many aspects of the seamier side of Gotham life which he would not otherwise have noticed. While touring the hot spots with Madden, all sorts of guys and dolls would court Winchell's favor by slipping him items for his column. Ultimately, as such things do, his intimacy with Madden was to get Winchell into trouble. But for the moment, he was basking in the glory of his newly accelerated celebrity.

Traveling around with Madden, Winchell became a trusted confidant and listened sympathetically to the gangster's complaint that the *Herald Tribune* never mentioned him without reference to the fact that he had a conviction for homicide. Winchell accompanied Madden to the offices of the Trib to register his complaint. However, it did no good.

Once, walking with Madden, Winchell admired a Stutz Bearcat roadster in the display window of an auto agency. The next day, Madden made a present of the car to him. Winchell demurred. "Listen, I can't take cars from a guy like you," he said.

Madden seemed hurt. "Why not?" he asked. "I'm in a generous mood. Go ahead and take it."

Not many people cared to tell Madden he was mistaken in anything, and Winchell began to wonder how vigorously he should protest. "But I'm a newspaper man! If I take anything from you, people will think I'm doing you favors," Winchell said, according to Thomas's biography.

Madden looked Winchell up and down contemptuously. "What the hell favors could a punk like you do for a big shot like me?"

Winchell was on the spot. If he took the Stutz from Madden, all the other hoods would figure that he was Owney's man. On the other hand, if he refused it, he might become the butt of Madden's famous temper. Finally he decided to accept the Stutz. It was his first car. He drove it for about a year and finally persuaded Madden to accept the $2,000 purchase price. Apparently Madden wasn't all that upset about being paid, and later, when Winchell got into a serious jam with the mob, he was even to help him out.

Louis Sobol took over the slot that Winchell had occupied at the *Graphic* with a great deal of enthusiasm and pleasure. Though his column lacked the oomph of Winchell's, it was informative and actually much better written. Meanwhile Hearst, observing with satisfaction the impact Winchell was having on the *Mirror's* circulation, sent one of his editors, Jack Lait of King Features Syndicate, to sound out Sobol as to whether he would be interested in coming over to the Hearst organization. Lait took Sobol to dinner at Billy La Hiff's Tavern, and laid the proposition on him. Would Sobol be willing to take his column from the *Graphic* to the *New York Evening Journal*?

Actually, Sobol had had a feeler a few days earlier from William A. Curley, who was editor of the *Journal*. Lait pulled a long folded piece of paper from his pocket. It was a contract. He suggested that Sobol look it over and, if he found it agreeable, they could consider the matter settled then and there. Sobol, one of many on the *Graphic* who had a strong feeling that the lurid tabloid was on its last legs, grabbed the contract like a peregrine falcon hitting a pigeon. On the next day, he submitted his resignation to the *Graphic*, which had not, in his case, taken the precaution of signing him to a long contract. Two weeks later, on June 1, 1931, he started his long association as gossip columnist on the *Journal*.

But his departure from the *Graphic* was not without impact on the history of Broadway columnists. It started another gossip columnist on the road to fame. Ed Sullivan, whose position as leading sports writer on

46

the *Graphic* seemed shaky at the time because of feuds with the top echelon in the Macfadden organization, suddenly found himself allotted only a few inches of space in the paper. He was giving serious thought to quitting, but it was the Depression and jobs were scarce at the time, so he hung on reluctantly. When Sobol left, Sullivan was summoned to the head office and told he was off sports for good and that he had been assigned to handle Sobol's Broadway column.

Sullivan's entire life had been dedicated to the sports scene and he had always resented Winchell's (and Sobol's) type of column. He protested strongly but he was given an ultimatum: accept the assignment or leave the *Graphic*.

Sullivan started his new column on June 1, the same day that Sobol started his in the *Journal*, and he launched it with a blast. Some people say it was simply an attempt to grab attention on his first day as a gossip columnist. Others say that he was expressing the bitterness he felt about his new assignment.

He led off this way:

> "I charge the Broadway columnists with defaming the street. I have entered the field of writing that ranks so low that it is difficult to distinguish any one columnist from his road companions. I have entered a field that offers scant competition.
>
> "The Broadway columnists have lifted themselves to distinction by borrowed gags, gossip that is not always kindly, and keyholes that too often reveal what better be hidden.
>
> "Phonies will receive no comfort in this space. To get into this particular column will be a badge of merit and a citation—divorces will not be propagated."

The column certainly had its impact on Sullivan's fellow gossipers. Sobol, who had given Sullivan a warm send-off in his last column before leaving the *Graphic*, felt that the diatribe was directed at him. The next day, Sobol, from his position on the *Journal*, parried back, commenting in regard to Sullivan that "empty vessels make the most sound." He also labeled Sullivan's efforts "the ennui of his contempt-oraries."

On the following night, Sullivan was in Reuben's Restaurant and ran into Winchell who was with Lou Holtz and Jim Quirk, editor of *Photoplay*. Sullivan went over and sat with the three men. Winchell at first didn't say a word, but he was obviously sulking. Sullivan turned to talk to Holtz and then, according to Sullivan, Winchell cut in savagely. "Did you mean me in what you wrote in your column?" Winchell asked.

"No, not exactly," Sullivan said. "You know, the stage axiom of a big entrance."

"Well, Ed, as long as you've apologized to me, it's all right," Winchell said.

"I got so mad," Sullivan told the reporter doing a profile of Winchell in the *New York Post*, "I grabbed him by the knot of his necktie and pulled him over the table, right on top of the cheesecake.

" 'Apologize to you?' I said—'You sonofabitch, I did mean you and if you say one more word about it I'll take you downstairs and stick your head in the toilet bowl.'

"Winchell didn't answer me," Sullivan said. "I got up and left."

The feud was to simmer for some thirty-five years, with occasional flare-ups that made national headlines.

Winchell left Reuben's that night to go over to Texas Guinan's for a final nightcap. Texas hated to go to sleep, so she kept her place open later than anybody else did. Winchell needed someone to talk to and to cool off with, but that trip came close to costing the Broadway columnist his life.

7.

Vincent Coll, a young and ambitious hoodlum on the fringes of the mob, was doing well as a gunman for gang leader Dutch Schultz in uptown New York City. But he soon got in trouble when he went into business for himself and began raiding Schultz's beer drops and stealing the Dutchman's beer. This vexed Schultz and struck him as an insult to his dignity as a mob leader as well as a threat to his livelihood. Schultz's gunmen took the hint and went after Coll, determined to rub him out. Unfortunately, their aim was less than marksmanlike. They managed to miss Coll but instead killed his brother Peter. Coll thereupon organized his own gang and tried to erase Schultz. In this case, the result was more tragic; he missed Schultz but hit five children in a playground on East 107th Street, killing one of them. This brutal crime had the effect of making the public realize for the first time that the hoods they so glamorized and adulated were dangerous, bloodthirsty criminals. There was a surge of public sentiment for law and order. Coll was indicted and tried for the murder of the five-year-old boy. He engaged the best criminal lawyer in America, Samuel Liebowitz, who made mincemeat of the prosecution's case and produced a directed verdict of acquittal.

Coll was free, but he was still in big trouble. Even before he had taken a crack at Schultz, he had angered the Owney Madden crowd by kidnapping a mobster named Big Frenchie De Mange. De Mange was active in Owney Madden's night club network and Madden was not pleased when he was asked to cough up some $35,000 for the release of his chum. It was probably around this time that Coll earned the sobriquet of "Mad Dog," because his next venture was even more suicidal. He decided to kidnap Jack Marron, Madden's brother-in-law. Coll had first gotten the idea, some months earlier, of making a fast buck through snatching mob figures who could not complain to the police when he had kidnapped a slim, young Oklahoma bootlegger who was working for Madden. The Oklahoman's job was to visit the various nightclubs and make sure that everything stayed in line and there was no trouble. The principal trouble the Oklahoman had was with a tough bouncer, by the name of Toots Shor, who worked in a number of Madden's clubs. Shor and the Oklahoman took an instant dislike to one another and the Oklahoman was constantly trying to get Madden to bounce Shor himself from his organization. But Madden would only agree with the Oklahoman's protests and then move Shor to another club. In any event, Coll contrived to snatch the Oklahoman during a moment of inattention and held him prisoner for three days and three nights in a Bronx garage. He was finally freed when his wife came up with the ransom of 25 big ones. The Oklahoman was named Sherman Billingsley, and he was to figure importantly in Winchell's later life, but Winchell never learned of this story until the mid-sixties, after Billingsley had died. It was Billingsley's daughter Shermane who told Winchell about the kidnapping. In any event, Vincent Coll was in plenty of trouble.

He now had both Madden and Schultz out for his skin. Meanwhile these two mob leaders were at peace, having reached a delineation of their territory, with Schultz taking the uptown areas and Madden midtown and downtown.

Winchell did not join in the public hue and cry against gangsters following Coll's killing of the five-year-old. Instead, he held himself aloof from all the trouble and in fact printed only two inconsequential items on this event.

Winchell never took sides between the gangsters, and

he was friendly not only with Schultz and Madden, but with Big Bill Dwyer, Arnold Rothstein, Beau Weinberg and others of their shady ilk. But he also didn't distinguish much between the side of the baddies and the good guys, preferring a neutral stand.

On Saturday night, February 7, Winchell in his rounds paid one of his usual visits to Texas Guinan's place and Texas whispered to him an item she thought might look well in the Sunday paper. *The Daily Mirror*, as usual, hit the stands around seven o'clock the night before. It contained this juicy morsel:

> "Five planes brought dozens of machine gats from Chicago Friday to combat the town's Capone. Local banditti have made one hotel a virtual arsenal and several hot spots are ditto because Master Coll is giving them a headache . . ."

Anyone who had been following Coll's difficulties with the mobsters didn't have any trouble figuring out that there might have been some basis for the item. But they were surprised at the timeliness of Winchell's prediction. The ink was barely dry on the *Mirror* when it was confirmed by the rat-a-tat-tat of machine-gun fire at 12:45 a.m. Coll, who had been holed up in the Cornish Arms Hotel on West 23rd Street, was lured into a drugstore near Eighth Avenue. There he was riddled to death in a phone booth by a machine-gunner who was such a cool old pro that one got the impression he very well might have been imported from Chicago, as Winchell said.

When Winchell heard about the murder, his first reaction was one of glee. He rushed to the drugstore on 23rd Street and pushed his way through the crowd, saying, "I'm Winchell, I predicted this."

After interviewing the police on the scene, he rushed back to the *Mirror* feeling very gratified at his scoop. While he was there, he received a phone call. Nobody knows what was said to him, but the people at the office agreed on Winchell's reaction. "He was green," one of them said. People who were in the *Mirror* office that night got the impression that the phone call was either from Coll's killer or one of his friends. They suspected that the caller probably informed Winchell that he didn't appreciate this premature warning in the Coll matter and probably informed him that there was a fair chance Winchell himself might be rubbed out. Whatever was said, Winchell put down the phone and turned to a fellow reporter in the *Mirror* office and said hysterically: "They're putting me on the spot. They may be waiting outside. What can I do?"

This seemed to be the time to call in any due bills he had with Owney Madden and he phoned the gangster and asked him for advice. Madden told him to stay on the spot until he sent a couple of boys over to protect him. But Madden wasn't very happy, either, about Winchell's printed prediction and warned him that he must be careful never to do anything like that again.

Meanwhile, Winchell sat tight in the Mirror office and waited to hear from Madden. About an hour later, there was another call, apparently from Owney or one of his henchmen, and Winchell was told that the boys had been persuaded not to kill Winchell. According to information Winchell later got, Coll's killer (who, incidentally was never caught) was furious, but willing to listen to the arguments of someone as powerful as Madden on the local scene. Madden also got hold of Schultz and had him give Winchell's indiscretion a pass.

But despite their assurances, Winchell didn't leave the office until a couple of Madden's gunmen came over to escort him out. The gunmen, in fact, stayed with Winchell for at least four days, until he was satisfied that, at least, no one was immediately going to take a crack at him. But when Madden's gunmen left, Winchell called the police commissioner and asked for protection.

While his column for a long time thereafter carried very little about the mob, there was quite a bit in it about Winchell's fear for his life: "If only when my epitaph is ready," he wrote in one column, "they will say here is Walter Winchell—with his ear to the ground—as usual." Another item read like this: "If I had any moxie I would chuck the whole thing and go somewhere with her (Mrs. Winchell) and the children and laugh a little."

The Manhattan D.A. was so impressed by the whole performance that he called Winchell before a grand jury investigating Coll's untimely passing. Winchell hedged on the questioning, perhaps committing perjury, and said only that the tip had come to him in the mail anonymously. There was no way he was going to ruin so good a source as Texas Guinan.

But Winchell was still deeply disturbed and not at all sure that there wouldn't be repercussions. He finally decided to do exactly what he had suggested in his column. He chucked the whole thing and went to California with June and his two children. The column was suspended for six weeks and the diagnosis was, as announced in the paper, "nervous breakdown."

By the time of the Coll incident, Winchell had started a radio program which was showing signs of being successful. During his sabbatical, Louis Sobol took over the radio show and Paul Yawitz, later to be a Hollywood writer, did the gossip.

Even on his trips to Los Angeles, Winchell had a bodyguard assigned to him by the police. The word Winchell had regarding Coll's killer was that the man was still irritated, but was trying to control himself. Winchell was afraid that, now he was away from the protection of Madden and Schultz, their instructions might be forgotten. It would be seven years before Winchell made another serious play for underworld headlines. Winchell may have been running scared, but his fright was based on sure knowledge of much of what was going on in the city.

One night, during the temporary inattention of his New York City bodyguards, in Dave's Blue Room, a stranger beckoned Winchell away from a gathering of his cronies. Winchell, thinking he was going to get an item, sat down in the booth opposite the man who began to abuse him in colorful and vituperative language. Finally, the man muttered, "I'm going to kill you, you sonofabitch."

Winchell was terrified. He could see that the hoodlum was stoned, either on booze or dope and he remembered very well how his friend, gangster Arnold Rothstein, had been slain—shot under the table as he was talking to his killer. "Look," Winchell said, "I'm okay. Owney Madden is a good friend of mine."

"To hell with Owney Madden," the man replied. And it seemed no amount of talk was going to dissuade him.

Winchell, finally certain that it was curtains for him, said in desperation, "All right—go ahead and get it over with."

Thus confronted, the would-be killer's attitude seemed to change suddenly, and he slipped out of the booth and hurried from the speakeasy.

The next day, Winchell applied for a permit to carry a gun and ultimately carried one both in his jacket pocket and in his coat pocket, although he was never known to have fired either.

8.

Sullivan tried hard to fill Winchell's dancing shoes at the *Graphic* but he was not really temperamentally suited for the job of gossip columnist. Lee Ellmaker, who succeeded Gauvreau at the *Graphic*, realized the value of a top-notch gossip column, and despite Sullivan's initial disclaimer, in his first column, of any interest in "keyhole" journalism, Sullivan had to bite the bullet and admit that a gossip column without scandal was like an egg without salt. Three weeks after his sanctimonious debut, Sullivan led his column off with this item: "Grover Cleveland Alexander is back with his wife and off the booze." But underneath it all, the man who had come to New York to be the best sports writer in the city was seething with discontent in his new job.

He also resented some of the responses to the initial column from his former colleagues on the *Graphic*, Sobol and Winchell. Sobol had thought his remark about Sullivan being "the ennui of his contemptoraries" was clever, but he had a feeling that Sullivan would not take it well. This hunch proved to be accurate.

"I was standing in front of the theater at a premiere," Sobol recalls, "when I saw him charging toward me. He was really angry. 'I'll rip your cock off, you little bastard,' he said. Fortunately, I was able to duck out of the way while some other people held him back."

Shortly afterward, the two columnists patched things up, but Sullivan's feud with Winchell lasted for three decades.

The colorful *Graphic* editor Gauvreau had made the policy of the newspaper clear in a memorandum posted on the bulletin board at a point where it seemed that the *Graphic* might actually survive:

> "The circulation of the *Graphic* has reached the point where it is tearing the guts out of the presses. This has resulted from my policy of sensationalism. Any man who cannot be yellow has no place on the staff."

Macfadden, the health freak, tried to phrase the newspaper's attitude in loftier terms: "Every time anyone wants to condemn a story for its frankness they call it a sex story. That is no criticism at all. There's nothing wrong with sex stories. No romance ever existed that wasn't a sex story. No marriage is ever performed that doesn't involve a sex story. It is only prudery that points a forbidding finger at sex. You can't do anything about such an attitude. You can only lift sex to its proper dignity." However, many questioned whether the *Graphic's* treatment of sex and scandal actually added anything to the dignity of the stories. In truth, although Macfadden might have been an expert on sex in the raw, spinach and cold baths, he was hardly an expert in newspaper technique, and the fact that the *Graphic* was losing $9,000 a week was testimony enough to that.

Swallowing the bitter pill, Sullivan continued to give the *Graphic* what it wanted, plenty of scandal about sex and divorce. Some items from the following months:

> July 17, 1931. "Everyone who played a lead in *The Marriage Circle*, including Lubitsch, the director, has been divorced."
> August 8, 1931. "Abe Lyman's sister is returning from the Coast . . . without her hubby."
> August 13,1931. "Jean Malin belted a heckler last night at one of the local clubs . . . all that twitters isn't pansy . . ."

In January 1932, after less than a year with the *Graphic*, Sullivan published a self-critique on how well he had stuck to his initial credo: "Just twice in eight

56

months of Broadway columning have I linked a married man with a girl, both times through sheer ignorance of the tie that binds, and both times to my complete embarrassment when I learned of my blunders.''

Outwardly Sullivan's life seemed as discreet as Winchell's was profligate. Despite Sullivan's rigid exterior and apparently puritanical upbringing, he was as vulnerable as anybody to the temptations of Glitter Canyon. The difference between him and Winchell was that Sullivan kept his affairs strictly under cover. But his appetite in women was not terribly different from that of Winchell. They both liked flashy, show-business girls with long legs and curvy derrieres. Neither of them had any particular fetish about huge bosoms. What galled Sullivan was that in at least two or three cases, Winchell had gotten to girls that Sullivan was romancing before Ed did: one was a beautiful dancer, formerly part of a sister act, and the other, according to Bowles, ''a brunette singer with great legs who had a major supporting role in a Broadway musical.''

In the meantime, feud or no feud, keyhole journalism or not, Sullivan was stuck with the job. Following Winchell's lead, he tried to expand into other media. There was a short live radio program in 1930, which Walter Winchell later claimed he had arranged for Sullivan. The program was a bomb. If it's remembered at all in show business, it's because in one of his early programs, Sullivan introduced a young comic named Jack Benny to radio. Benny's comedy, however, did nothing to keep Sullivan's deadpan delivery on the air, and the show was cancelled weeks later.

Sullivan did make some money, although he never achieved much success as what Winchell later was to call a ''pointer.'' He got $3,000 for a two-week stint at the Paramount Theater introducing dancers, dog acts and comedians. But he worked for the money, since in vaudeville the routine meant five shows a day, each

57

who had some success at vaudeville emceeing, had an lasting about an hour. Nobody, however, was dazzled with Sullivan's stage technique. After all, Winchell, extensive background in show business which Sullivan lacked.

Sullivan didn't have long to nurse his discontent at the *Graphic*. The moribund tabloid, ailing since its start some eight years earlier, finally gave up the ghost in 1932 and went into bankruptcy. It died with $7 million in libel suits pending against it. A few weeks before it did, Sullivan got a call from Captain Joseph Medill Patterson of the *New York Daily News*. Patterson asked if Sullivan would be interested in moving his column over to Patterson's paper. Even the deadpan Sullivan could not help but break into a huge grin. *Would* he? The *News* was only the biggest paper in the country, with a circulation of over two million. That was the good news. The bad news was that the canny publisher offered him only $200 a week to start with, some $50 less than he'd been getting on the *Graphic*. But think of the audience, and think of Walter Winchell's reaction! Winchell had coveted the *News* spot practically since he had started with the *Mirror*. Of course, even with the *News's* two million circulation, unless Sullivan acquired enormous syndication, he still wouldn't equal the voice of Winchell, who ultimately achieved a syndication of a thousand papers, in addition to his radio audience.

But Sullivan could well feel his star was on the ascendant.

Exactly three years after he wrote his first Broadway gossip column, Ed Sullivan reviewed his accomplishments: "Just how well I've lived up to my promises of 1931 is difficult to tell . . . My platform against gossip hasn't a single plank left in it, for in the course of a week I run two full gossip columns. The reason I do it is because the readers demand it." (And he might have said so did his editor, although publisher Joseph Medill Patterson never really had the heart for that sort of thing.)

In his first year at the *News*, Sullivan received only

one memo from Patterson. It was about a column Sullivan had written concerning Samuel Goldwyn's "newest discovery," Anna Sten. Goldwyn had put a huge advertising and publicity budget into touting her charms. Sullivan wrote that Anna Sten bored him. The fact was that Miss Sten also seemed to bore the public; but next day there was a Patterson memo on Sullivan's desk. "I do not say that I do not agree with your opinion. However, I am deeply disturbed that any writer of mine would recklessly jeopardize the professional career of a young actress."

Sullivan was touched by the memo. "I read the memo and reread it. And as the meaning sunk in, I thought to myself: Here is indeed a great man." (Sullivan apparently did not take into account the fact that Goldwyn, who was spending a fortune on advertising for Miss Sten, might have given the great publisher a nudge.)

What really irked Sullivan was the fact that he was never in Winchell's league as a gossip columnist, and he knew it. A recent biographer of Sullivan, Jerry Bowles, in his book *A Thousand Sundays* said "he (Sullivan) simply lacked W. W.'s instinct for the jugular. Winchell was, as John Crosby observed after his death, 'a 14-carat sonofabitch.' Sullivan could be on occasion, but it was not his true nature."

Despite his personal animus toward Winchell, Sullivan had to respect his colleague's talents. It galled him even further when Winchell was called on to emcee various vaudeville and theatrical events that Sullivan followed in his footsteps there too. On the stage as well as in the newspaper he couldn't seem to come up to Winchell's excitement and glamour. Later, when Winchell got his start in radio, Sullivan tried again to follow him and there, too, he failed miserably.

"No wonder I was always tense and moody," Sullivan once told Robert Sylvester, the columnist. "I would have a radio show, have it cancelled, and then I would turn on my set on Sunday night and there he was. That staccato voice calling to 'Mr. and Mrs. America and all the ships at sea,' and me realizing that America was listening. I didn't even have the comfort of telling myself that he was lousy. He wasn't good. He was simply great. I would grow another small ulcer and start planning another radio show. I'd get it on. And someone would quickly get it off."

The rivalry between the two men even extended to their personal lives. Winchell's marriage had been rocky from the start and his open flirtation with the dollies, chorines, and glamour girls of the main stem was carried on in such an open fashion as to be a humiliation to his wife, June. Sullivan had met his wife Sylvia Weinstein in 1926 at a night club called the Casa Lopez, where the strolling musician was a young violinist named Xavier Cugat. The columnist was instantly struck with Sylvia's dark good looks and asked the club's press agent to introduce them. Sylvia's father was a New York real estate man who had made a bundle in the real estate boom prior to the great stock market crash, in which he ultimately lost it all. In her own estimation, she was the original Jewish-American Princess at the time. Sullivan's family, according to biographer Bowles, was less than happy over his romance with a Jewish girl, but Sylvia's family seemed quite content.

In any event, they married in 1930, but not before Sylvia tried to pacify the Sullivan family by agreeing that the children, if any, would be raised Catholic.

9.

The move to the *Daily Mirror*, with the clout of Hearst syndication behind him, had made Winchell one of the most powerful journalistic voices in America by 1932. But his private life suffered severely under the peculiar demands of the Broadway beat. The world of what Winchell called the "glitterati" held little fascination for his wife, the former June Magee. Perhaps her earlier experience in show business taught her all she wanted to know of the ways of the Rialto.

At first, she tried to keep up with Winchell. She accompanied him to play openings and on his rounds of speakeasies and dance halls. But it was not amusing to be left alone at the table while Winchell table-hopped in pursuit of gossip tidbits. June began to go home without her husband earlier and earlier and ultimately stayed home altogether. They soon fell into a contrasting night and day lifestyle. By the time Walter got home, June had been asleep for hours and, once home, Winchell was too keyed up by his exciting activities to go right to sleep. By the time he did doze off, June was having breakfast.

One obvious solution to fill her otherwise empty life, was children. But because of Winchell's erratic lifestyle, they were at first unable to have a baby of their own and June finally persuaded Winchell to allow her to adopt one. Winchell, concerned with his wife's increasing restlessness, and himself fond of children, agreed. In those days there was much less red tape about the process, and June adopted the child of a show business friend who had gotten in trouble.

The Winchells took possession of baby Gloria in 1926

61

when she was only one day old, but when they took her to the doctor for her first routine checkup, they received distressing news. The baby had a faulty heart valve and was not expected to live for more than a few years. June, by this time, having held the baby and looked into its drowsy blue eyes, could not believe the news. She assured the doctor that her tender, loving care would counteract the congenital cardiac problem. Despite this problem with the baby's health, the Winchells were a happy couple when they brought little Gloria back to the apartment they had taken over Billy La Hiff's Tavern on West 48th Street.

Now that June was preoccupied with the baby's care, Winchell felt free to spend even more time covering his beat, and his column began to show signs of an incipient problem that, to some extent, went with the job. Winchell was girlcrazy, and one of the ways he paid for his promiscuous roving was with plugs in his column. Though he assured June that these mentions were harmless favors to struggling chorines and models, it became painfully obvious that Winchell was collecting bedmates the way some people collected stamps. Acquaintances became concerned over the brashness with which he announced his conquests in the column. Here's a sample from the *Graphic*:

"Nursed the sheets till late, being weary from a strenuous tear the night before, having hoofed at a White Light place with Bobbie Folsom and other charming wretches. So to breakfast with Lovey Kent, who is as sweet as her Christian monicker . . .

"Up betimes and broke fast with a baby doll from Artists and Models . . . In the rain to keep a rendezvous with Mary Thomas who coryphees for a living . . .

"In the hay till noon again, and hastened to keep a rendezvous with Eula Youngblood, as lovely a cowgal as Oklahoma ever bred . . ."

Winchell had been told by some of his literary friends that he was a latter day Pepys, and he had taken the trouble to read the British diarist's work and to emulate,

62

at times, the elegant, if archaic style of the colorful English diarist. (He was not actually the first to evoke this parallel between New York columnists and Pepys. Franklin P. Adams had, for some years, carried a feature parodying the seventeenth century Britisher.)

Glimpses of Winchell's less-than-placid domestic life began to creep into the column, too:

> "Lay late, and began the day with a quarrel with my sugar, whose door I didn't mean to slam as I departed. It seems I am luckier in the dice house than I am in hers. So with heavy heart to my Broadway and upstage all whom I encounter."

At least some of Winchell's reputation as a news gatherer came from his seemingly uncanny ability to anticipate what he called "blessed events." And in 1929, he scooped everybody with a report of his own. June Winchell gave birth to a baby girl who was named Walda, after her seldom-home father.

The arrival of the new child, and Gloria's frail health, served to separate June even more from the affairs of her husband. Now that Winchell's salary at the *Mirror* had risen to $300—big money in those times—the Winchells were able to afford to send June and the children to Florida for the winter months. This gave Winchell even greater opportunity for making whoopee. In fact, H. L. Mencken, something of a student of Winchell's work, said, "Winchell, if he did not actually invent whoopee, at least gave it the popularity it enjoyed." Mencken seemed to think that the actual word might have originated in an old cowboy song he heard somewhere, and attributed its origins to English literature of the fifteenth century. Piqued, Winchell asked Will Rogers if he had ever heard the term "whoopee" used among cowboys. Rogers answered: "Well, Walt, I've heard 'em holler 'Yippee!' and maybe some of the boys on the range knew the word 'whoopee,' too. But they certainly didn't know what to do with it until you came along and showed 'em."

Winchell gave his answer in the column some months

later when the Ziegfeld show "Whoopee" became a hit with Eddie Cantor, and then a movie: "They contend whoopee is older than Shakespeare. Well all right, I never claimed it, anyhow. But let 'em take making whoopee from me and look out!" Winchell was being given serious credit for his neologisms and was sensitive about any implication that he had not originated them himself, although, in fact, many of them were fed to him by his growing corps of press agents. Among the expressions to which he gave birth: For having a baby; "blessed event," "getting storked," "preparing a bassinet," "blessed expense," "bundle from heaven," "baby-bound," "infanticipating": for love affairs; "on the verge," "uh-uh," "on fire," "that way," "cupiding," "blazing," "man-and-womaning it," "Adam-and-Eveing it": for getting married; "middle aisled," "Lohengrinned," "welded," "sealed," "merged": for breaking up; "renovating," "telling it to a judge," "straining at the handcuffs," "wilted," "have phfft," "this and that way."

Even lexicographer Wilford Funk was impressed by the new slang Winchell was coining or at least publicizing. In 1933 he listed Winchell as one of the ten most fertile contributors to American argot. His friend Mencken, in *The American Language*, reported a long list of words that Winchell used in his columns that he felt were destined to become part of the language:

Chicagorilla (gangsters)
Joosh (Jewish)
pash (passion)
shafts (legs)
debutramp (debutante)
wildeman (homosexual)
heheheh (mocking laugh)
moompitcher, flicker
　(moving picture)
radiodor (radio announcer)
messer of ceremonies
Mary Magdaléne
phewd (feud)

giggle water (liquor)
dotter (daughter)
Park Rogue
　(newspaperman)
Hard Times Square
intelligentleman
fooff (pest)
Hardened Artery, Bulb Belt,
　Baloney Boulevard
　(Broadway)
reviewsical
　(musical revue)

Interestingly enough, in the light of history, almost none of this ephemera has become part of the English language, with the possible exception of "shafts," "giggle water," and "flicker." Still, how many columnists have contributed even that much?

While Winchell's quips and quiddities delighted the literati and the hoi palloi, they had apparently only an irritating effect on *Mirror* executives. After a short stretch on the Hearst paper, Winchell found himself in trouble not only with his old enemy Gauvreau, but with Arthur Kobler, the editor who had first brought him over to the paper. Kobler, in fact, was so shocked and frightened by the "Mad Dog" Coll murder that he exiled Winchell from his city room and barred him from any part of the *Mirror* building except for his own office. However, aware of Winchell's enormous personal circulation, Kobler took great care to stay within the bounds of his contract. *Time* magazine reported:

> "Every move by Kobler and the *Mirror* is carefully considered, lest it give Winchell the supreme satisfaction of breaking his contract. The instant that should occur, Winchell would skip three blocks downtown to Joe Medill Patterson's big little *Daily News* . . . The *News* offered Winchell a thousand dollars a week for a Sunday column alone."

In fact, Capt. Patterson went so far as to tell Winchell once: "Anytime you want to come here, you're welcome. Ed Sullivan owes his job to you. If you gave up your column, I would get rid of Sullivan."

The year 1929 was a year of good news and bad news for America in general and for Winchell in particular. A few days after his return from his California nervous breakdown following the Vincent Coll affair, Winchell received a call that opened exciting new horizons. The call was from William Paley, head of CBS. "I would like you to meet Mr. Gimbel," Paley said, "who is in the department store business. I think you can slant your style of reporting for the radio, and Mr. Gimbel is willing to be the sponsor."

10.

Winchell rode his success hard, once he started hitting the big time in 1929 on the *Mirror*. In 1930, he went back to show business by making a Vitaphone short film called "The Bard of Broadway," with Madge Evans. His take was $1,750. That year, with his *New York Mirror* salary now contracted at $500 a week, his publisher, Arthur Kobler, who hated him with a purple passion, voluntarily gave him a raise, doubling the figure, plus syndication money. But even at $1,000 a week, Winchell was expanding his horizons.

In the beginning, despite his growing ego, Winchell didn't think he was suitable for the radio medium. "I talk too fast," he said. Certainly he was right by the standards of radio at the time, which was attracted to deep, soothing, resonant voices, reading with the solemnity of a death notice. Walter had always talked in a rapid-fire, off-the hip fashion. A member of the family said, "We figured he talked funny because his mother used to tie his arm behind his back to cure him of being left-handed." Winchell had radio offers before and rejected them for this reason. He was not only uncertain about his voice, but not sure that the public would accept a Broadway column wired for sound. But Paley was persuasive and Winchell, despite his misgivings, allowed himself to be signed up for a local newscast.

Paley's hunch proved uncannily right. Within a few months the show, entitled "New York By a Representative New Yorker," was a resounding local hit. Radio audiences were intrigued by Winchell's crackling delivery and copy that was racy and colorful, compared with most of the fare available, in those fledgling days of radio. (Although Winchell was credited with originating the breathless, machine-gun fire type of delivery on radio, actually he had been preceded by Floyd Gibbons, who was clocked at 217 words a minute.) A few months after the broadcast was started, it came to the attention of George Washington Hill, the eccentric and advertising-conscious president of the American Tobacco Company. Hill instantly grasped the appeal of the Winchell delivery, called the producer of American Tobacco's program "Lucky Strike Magic Carpet" and told him, "I want Winchell on my next show."

Within 24 hours, Winchell signed a contract for a thousand dollars a week. Oddly enough, his chore on the Magic Carpet was not to deliver news but to introduce a series of famous bands scattered around the country, which were the principal feature of the program. In that early radio era, listeners were impressed by the electronic leap from city to city. Winchell's job was to introduce the bands in his staccato, electrifying manner, with a phrase that soon became a popular tagline, "Ohhhkkkaaayyy, Aaammmerrriccca!" As he gained confidence, Winchell began to add tidbits of entertainment news to the program and invented his famous tag-line: "Good evening, Mr. and Mrs. America and all the ships at sea!"

The program was given extensive promotion by American Tobacco, with billboards, posters, radio spots and newspaper ads. In less than three months, Winchell had become a national celebrity. Just as he had been the first to launch a gossip column, he was the first of the columnists to extend his influence into another medium. But the others were soon to follow.

And Winchell, now that he had a national forum, began to look around for broader horizons. Shortly after the successful launching of his broadcast career, the country, in October of 1929, was hit by the greatest financial disaster in its history and from that point on, Winchell began to show an interest in affairs ranging far from the Great White Way. Perhaps the gradual realization of the enormous power he now wielded affected his conscience—and his ego.

The appearance of columnists, particularly Broadway columnists, on the stage was at least partially based, as Abel Green of *Variety* pointed out in his book *Show Biz*, on "the ability to entice top talent as 'guest stars' at no cost to management."

Obviously, syndicated columnists had a way of influencing talent with their ability to provide national publicity. Both Winchell and Sullivan were able to cash in on this. The future for this particular gift was still to come, because vaudeville went completely out of business within a few years.

In 1931, Winchell accepted his first professional stage booking in ten years—a $3,500-a-week engagement at the Palace, following vaudeville appearances by fellow journalists Heywood Broun, Floyd Gibbons, Mark Hellinger and Harry Hershfield.

Winchell reviewed his own act for *Variety* and called it "another freak attraction." Wryly, he commented, "This sort of headliner is too anemic for the best-known music hall. His appearance is oke—he has a natty tone about him. He can be heard in the last rows, too. But he is hardly big-time material. He simply won't do . . . Winchell should have known better and should stick to columning."

Many of his growing coterie of enemies would agree with Winchell's self-evaluation, but in fact, Winchell's dynamic quality transferred quite well to the stage. Winchell did not take his own advice and that year signed on with two network radio sponsors, Lucky Strike on NBC and Geraldine Hair Tonic on CBS. He even converted one of his column features, "Things I Never Knew Till Now," into a popular song with music by Al Van.

In 1931 a pair of independent song writers, Abner Silver and L. Wolfe Gilbert, paid tribute to his growing grip on the popular imagination with a song entitled, "Mrs. Winchell's Boy."

11.

In the years following the 1929 stock market crash, America reached its lowest point, possibly in the history of the nation, in terms of morale and confidence. But in a perverse way, this national despair proved a boon to the columnists of the country, the apostles of viewpoint and opinion. People were desperate to know what the future held for them, and clung desperately to any signs of optimism. Winchell, and such top syndicated columnists as Walter Lippmann, Westbrook Pegler, Heywood Broun, Franklin P. Adams and Arthur Krock were read avidly for some signs of relief from the country's dire situation. Perversely, the public took a great interest in the foibles of the very wealthy. Stories of what showgirl got diamonds from what playboy were read avidly. Gambling grew in popularity until the number of dice, card and wheel games was at its greatest height since the early 1920s. It was, as Winchell's biographer, Bob Thomas, said, "a grand time to be Walter Winchell."

"His tempo was one that America had chosen for itself in the early 1930s: frantic, furious, with a faint underlying air of desperation. He and the nation were going steady despite his many detractors. People read and listened to Winchell, they wanted to believe what he reported . . . His voice on radio was infectiously optimistic, indicating that good things were coming after the long, punishing months of the Depression."

While Winchell's popularity continued to grow at an enormous rate with the public, he also added almost weekly to the number of enemies that he made, sometimes on purpose and sometimes by accident. With the exception of the unwritten code between columnists

69

against revealing their personal foibles, Winchell couldn't resist a good item, even for friendship. One friend who was visiting him once, playing with Winchell's young child, was told that there would be an unfavorable item about him in Winchell's column in the morning, even though he was supposed to be one of Winchell's best friends: "Walter," the "friend" said, "you're not a man, you're a column!" Winchell smiled as though flattered.

The time came when Winchell finally got a hot item on Sime Silverman who was not only an old friend, but had given Winchell an important leg up in his early days, by feeding him tidbits from *Variety* before that theatrical newspaper hit the stands. Silverman, who seemed to be happily married, was then carrying on an affair, according to Lyle Stuart, with one Renee Davies. Renee was one of a remarkable group of sisters, all of whom were mistresses of prominent publishers. The most famous was her sister Marion, who was known throughout the nation as the mistress of Winchell's boss, William Randolph Hearst. Those in the know felt that Silverman's wife was well aware of her husband's unfaithfulness, but like many wives, she kept the secret to herself and hoped that the flirtation would pass. According to Lyle Stuart, Winchell published a blind item about the affair, using Silverman's real initials so that anybody could be certain who the "show business trade publisher" was. Sime kept a room on the fifth floor of *Variety's* offices where he would occasionally dally with the Davies woman. Everybody on Broadway knew about it, even Jimmy Durante who once, as a gag, had a small neon sign placed outside the fifth floor which read, "Chateau De Layem." Winchell reported on this practical joke also. Silverman complained bitterly to Damon Runyon: "I don't mind his ingratitude. I enjoyed seeing him get started. But apart from any personal considerations, isn't there a vein of decency in him?"

Silverman made one try at finding that vein before barring Winchell from *Variety* offices permanently. He stopped him in the street one day and said: "Winchell, you've got a girlfriend now, haven't you? How do you think Hattie felt when she read that drivel in your column?"

Winchell started to alibi, "I didn't mean you, Sime—"

"How would June like it if I ran an item on the front page of *Variety* advertising your extramarital affair?"

Winchell tried to laugh it off. "You go ahead, Sime. You do that. She knows the score anyway."

Silverman turned on his heel and walked away from Winchell in disgust.

In another incident reported by Stuart, a famous comedian came up to Winchell in Lindy's and poured a pitcher of icewater over his head. "You're so hot about my personal life," the comedian said, "I thought this would be a good way to cool you off."

Winchell never mentioned the comic again in his column.

When Winchell delved into the field of dramatic criticism, he had a tendency to sometimes sacrifice critical coolness for a good quip or a *bon mot*. Early in 1932, he reported a supposed dialogue between George S. Kaufman and Groucho Marx. According to Winchell, Kaufman said to Marx: "What do you think of Earl Carroll's 'Vanities'?" And Marx replied: "I had rather not say. I saw it under bad conditions—the curtain was up."

About a week after this item appeared, Winchell attended a party at the Central Park Casino given by A. C. Blumenthal, the theater owner and producer, and his wife Miss Peggy Fears. It was a celebrity-studded affair and Winchell was sitting at the table with Mayor Jimmy Walker, film star Pola Negri and actress Billy Dove. One of the guests was Earl Carroll who, up to this point, seemed quite a good friend of Winchell's. Some years earlier, when Carroll was tried for perjury for denying that there were nude girls present at a bathtub party that he hosted, Winchell had avoided the chorus of sanctimonious criticism which had hit the producer.

Shockingly, Carroll actually was sentenced to Atlanta Prison for refusing to admit that his show was obscene. However, since Carroll's release and his return to Broadway, Winchell had frequently given the producer's shows a severe roasting. On this particular night at the Casino, Carroll seemed to feel that his cup was full. When Winchell approached the table, the producer stood up and, looking at Winchell, said, "Walter, I wonder if you can take it. We've been taking it from you for a long time."

Winchell nodded agreeably and said, "Go ahead. It's okay."

Carroll impaled the columnist with an icy stare and said, loud enough for all present to hear, "I want to tell you that you are not fit to associate with decent people. You don't belong!"

According to Stanley Walker, the famous editor who described the incident in his book, *The Night Club Era*, there was a hush that fell over the whole room for at least five minutes. Carroll, having delivered his bomb, bowed himself out of the Casino. As far as is known, the two men never spoke to one another again. The incident didn't end there, for when Carroll had finished his diatribe, the owner of the restaurant, Sidney Solomon, stood up. In a loud voice he announced that not only did he agree thoroughly with the sentiments of Carroll, but he felt the same way about Mark Hellinger who was also sitting with the group. He turned to the Broadway columnist: "You're just another flashy bum like your friend Winchell over there. Everything I said about him goes for you, too."

Hellinger didn't take this insult with the same equanimity that Winchell had. He doubled up his fists in anger, and said to his lady companion, "Watch me sock that bird one to maintain my self-respect."

Winchell overheard Hellinger's threat and complicated the situation by calling over: "Say, Mark, when did you develop self-respect?"

The next day, both Hellinger and Winchell wrote their versions of the affair. Each claimed he had a scoop. And now that it was public, the incident refused to die, and spread the feuds that it had engendered even further. Marlen Pew, who was editor of *Editor and Publisher*, wrote an editorial about it: "These are the creators of the 'new culture' which circles about the Broadway column, babbles an audacious brand of illiteracy, sets up a new concept of decency in human relations, and has as its bugle-call the Bronx razz."

Hellinger found Pew's comments "cute." Winchell, as usual, felt that the remarks were aimed directly at him. It's true that he had been criticized several times in the past by Pew for not checking easily checkable stories. He had already started referring to Pew as "Marlen Pee-yew." A little later Pew wrote: "I hear that Broadway columnists hold regular meetings in midtown hotels nowadays to discuss various topics of their trade.

"Inevitably, this will lead to the writing of a code of ethics. What an interesting document it would be! I daresay they will tell us just what 'news' is. Evidently American journalism has long had a very limited view of the possibilities of what may and what may not be said in print. No doubt the new code will make it clear why a guess is as good as an authenticated fact in news columns.

"And, too, we may learn just how far a reporter may peek behind the curtains of private lives. At some early meeting, the boys might take up the grave implications in a line of type which recently appeared in Winchell's column, as follows: 'The best known film magnate attempted suicide last week.' "

Pew objected seriously to the innuendo against the unnamed producer. He felt that such anonymous accusations could easily "work much wrong and give considerable pain." Pew felt strongly that the item "contained no truth but was one of those spontaneous hunches that may easily pour from an undisciplined brain onto a permanent printing surface when stirring copy is feverishly needed and nobody is reading the manuscript."

He concluded his attack this way: "I have no stomach for the job of regulating journalistic morals of the white light paragraphers, being perfectly ready to let Broadway sewage find its own way to the sea."

Winchell took up the cudgels, as was his habit, against Pew, and never let up on him for many years. Yet, oddly enough, the usually thin-skinned columnist seemed remarkably tolerant of the insult to which he had been submitted by Earl Carroll. "Carroll was certainly entitled to his scolding of me. I had treated him pretty mean for many years," he said.

Winchell's humiliation must have been all the more galling when he noticed that Sullivan had been standing by and had witnessed the entire event. "I guess it was the most ignominious night in Winchell's life," Sullivan later said.

But Winchell was less kind than that to other enemies. One of his principal targets was fellow columnist O. O. McIntyre, who also wrote for Hearst. McIntyre, although he did not specialize in the type of gossip for which Winchell had become famous, was actually his predecessor as a Broadway reporter, and was noted for his folksy, down-home approach, as opposed to Winchell's brittle, slangy delivery. Winchell actually took his feud with McIntyre so seriously that he went to Hearst himself in an effort to get his fellow columnist fired, but the publisher refused to take sides.

Another early enemy among the columnists was vitriolic, right-wing columnist Westbrook Pegler, who pilloried the Broadway columnist in a parody which ran in the *New York Evening Post*, done in the manner of one of Winchell's features, "Portrait of a Man Talking to Himself." This, too, remained a life-long feud, never to be resolved.

Winchell's background as a slum child made him sympathetic to the poor of the nation. Too much of America was beginning to resemble the tenement corner at 116th Street and Madison Avenue where Winchell first learned about cold and hunger and insufficient medical care. But Winchell, who had never in his life voted, still clung to a certain neutrality which he felt was most suitable for his job as a reporter. During the 1932 election campaign between incumbent Herbert Hoover and Governor Franklin Delano Roosevelt of New York, Winchell wrote:

> "I do wish the various parties would stop submitting their ballyhooey to me about their respective candidates. I don't like any of them—and won't devote any part of the column's praise to them. I don't care whether Roosevelt wins or Hoover loses. I know too much about politics to care."

But in the first months after the election, Winchell was too distracted by a personal tragedy to pay much attention to politics. In December of 1932, just before Christmas, his adopted daughter Gloria died of pneumonia. Both Walter and June were at their child's bedside when she died. It was the first time they had been together in months. Friends say that Winchell never fully recovered from this tragedy. Years later, there would be tears in his eyes whenever he would discuss it. After Gloria's death, a reader sent him a cheap costume ring as a token of remembrance. Except for a wristwatch, it was the only piece of jewelry he ever wore.

Despite his avowed political cynicism, Winchell was one of the very first to sense the potential menace of the Nazis. While his understanding of international politics was dim at best, the Nazis' overt antisemitism and brutality struck an angry chord in the columnist. Biographer Bob Thomas says, "Undoubtedly what motivated him at this time was not a political axe to grind, but a very personal hurt. His most vivid memories of his childhood were the beatings he himself, a skinny underprivileged kid, had received from the neighborhood bully on the corner of Madison Avenue and 116th Street.

In his ten years as a newspaper reporter, Winchell

had learned to understand people, to recognize character from a chance remark. He watched the Nazis with interest for a few months—from a distance of 3,000 miles—and then made up his mind how he felt about them. "No different from some of the gorillas who hang around Broadway. Only these guys speak a foreign language and wear uniforms," he said.

While Winchell felt a strong hostility toward the Hitlerites early on, he was not yet aware of them as a potential international menace. He tended to think of the dictator as one more of the "baddies" he had known for so long along Broadway. In March of '33 Winchell broke a story in his newspaper column in which he described a photograph which had been given to him by one of his informants which he said showed representatives of the American Ku Klux Klan attending a Nazi conference in Berlin.

This, Winchell stated, was proof that the Klan and Hitler's Nazis are one and the same.

But Winchell had not been able to put that item on the air and he resented it. In fact, witnesses said that Winchell and the radio station censors almost came to blows during discussions of the script. He noted the conflict with an additional item in the column: "I could have made the point (about the Klan) on the air Sunday night. But those in charge of the skies struck it out for fear of offending whatever Nazis may have been listening in."

Winchell's political consciousness was undoubtedly raised by an incident which took place in Miami shortly before the inauguration of President-elect Roosevelt, who had decided to visit the city of Miami at the same time that Winchell was taking what was to become his habitual winter holiday in the sunshine state. Waiting for the Roosevelt procession in the bandstand of Miami's Bayfront park in a front seat was Joe Zangara, a 33-year-old native of Calabria, Italy, one-time bricklayer troubled with headaches, ulcers and periodic incoherent incidents.

At 9:30 in the evening, Roosevelt's open automobile

stopped before the bandstand where some 20,000 cheering Floridians and visitors had gathered to see and hear him before he took a train back to New York. Roosevelt pulled himself up on the car's folded-down cloth top and addressed the crowd with one of the informal little speeches for which he had become so well known. The crowd cheered as Roosevelt slid back down into his seat. Chicago's Mayor Anton Cermak, an old friend of Roosevelt, was sitting in the bandstand listening to the speech. Roosevelt beckoned him down to the car and said, "Hello, Tony."

"Hello, Mr. President," Cermak answered. After a brief chat, the mayor turned to walk away. As he did so, a man rushed up to hand Roosevelt a long telegram which the president-elect began to read. As he did so, Zangara stood up on the wobbly bench of the grandstand thirty-five feet away from the president, pulled a pistol from his pocket, and aimed it in the general direction of Roosevelt's touring car. There was a series of loud, startling shots. The first one hit Margaret Kruis, a Newark showgirl, in the head. A second bullet drilled into Mayor Cermak's belly; he crumpled to his knees. Blood oozed through his white shirt, making a narrow rectangle, parallel to his belt. Lillian Cross, the wife of a Miami physician who was standing near Zangara, managed to push his shooting arm into the air, but Zangara's fingers kept working the trigger. There was another report, and Mrs. Joseph Gill, wife of the president of Florida Power & Light staggered down the bandstand steps, grievously wounded in the abdomen.

Bang! Still another shot, and blood spurted through the white hair of William Sinnott, a former New York City detective who was vacationing in Florida. And now still another shot nicked the forehead of Russell Caldwell, a Cocoanut Grove teenager.

The whole thing was over in five seconds. The crowd roared, "Get that man!" And within seconds, Joe Zangara was buried under a waving pile of arms, legs and bodies. Roosevelt, who was by now behind a barrier of Secret Service guards, stood up, and his clear voice rang out strongly above the din. "I'm all right! I'm all right!" The convertible started out of the crowd of packed people. Somebody jumped on the running board yelling: "Mayor Cermak's shot!"

Roosevelt told the chauffeur to stop the car.

"Bring him in here!" the president-elect said. "Put him in my car." Roosevelt held Cermak in his arms as the car streaked away to Jackson Memorial Hospital behind shrieking police sirens.

In the memorial park, police threw the would-be assassin into a waiting car, the same one in which several of his victims were being loaded. Police drove the car first to the hospital where the wounded were unloaded, and then to Miami's new skyscraper jail where Zangara was stripped and safely locked up on the 28th floor.

Winchell, about this time, had dropped into the Western Union office in Miami to file his column to the *Mirror*. While there, he overheard a conversation. "It was four shots," one man said to another.

"No, it was five," the other man said.

That was all Winchell needed to hear. He ran to the police station and asked the desk sergeant where the police might have taken an arrested gunman. The sergeant suggested that he try the jail. Winchell hurried to the new county building and told the elevator operator to take him to the 28th floor jail. When he saw that the operator hesitated, Winchell handed him a dollar and the operator agreeably slammed the door shut and let Winchell off on the jail floor. There Winchell was blocked by the Chief of Police, but within a few minutes, he had flattered that official with tales of making him famous on front pages of papers all over the world. The chief was impressed and told what he knew about the man in his custody and his attempt on the President's life. He even let Winchell speak to Zangara a few minutes before other newsmen or even the sheriff had arrived at the jail. Winchell was thrilled. He had a real scoop this time, and a big one.

About the time that Winchell was leaving, Sidney

Skolsky, a *Daily News* columnist and a good friend of Winchell's, arrived at police headquarters, but was barred by the police. Angry, Skolsky shouted, "Hey! I'm a newspaper man, too. Ask Winchell!" But Winchell looked at Skolsky with blank eyes and told the police, "I never saw this man before in my life." Skolsky didn't get in.

Meanwhile, Winchell raced to the Western Union telegraph office, typed out his story, handed the copy to the telegraph operator, and returned to the Roney Plaza Hotel, thrilled by his day's work.

There was no question that, by any standards, but especially for a Broadway columnist, it was an exceptional newsbeat. But there was an anticlimactic ending to the story. Winchell's copy had been placed in a pile of other dispatches waiting for transmission of the Western Union wire. Steve Hannigan, a p. r. man who handled publicity for the city of Miami, was helping the other reporters with their later stories. He glanced over the Winchell story and recognized the exclusiveness of the quotes Winchell had gotten in his conversation with the would-be assassin. Hannigan copied the quotes out for the use of Associated Press and other news outlets.

By the time Winchell's scoop reached the news desk of the *Mirror*, its exclusive quotes were all over the country. Editor Gauvreau was not impressed.

"Play down the Winchell story," he told the make-up editor.

Winchell was furious at the treatment his scoop received at the hands of his old enemy, but Gauvreau's next move nearly sent Winchell into a screaming fit.

"You'll have to pay the eleven dollars' telegraph charges for that Miami story," Gauvreau told Winchell on the phone. "You know the rules: when you're out of town, you're billed for telegraphing the column."

Winchell was so angry that he went directly to Hearst with another one of his frequent complaints about Gauvreau, but Hearst repeated the answer he always gave to Winchell: Winchell would just have to get along with his fellow Hearst team members. (Some years later, on one of his rare visits to the *Mirror* office, Hearst went up to Winchell, introduced himself, and handed the columnist the eleven dollars, saying, "This is long overdue.")

In fact, Hearst was probably more in agreement with Gauvreau, deep down, than he was with Winchell, whose column he had never actually liked, though he appreciated its value as a circulation-builder. "Winchell seems to satisfy the whims of the younger degeneration," Hearst once told Gauvreau. Young people weren't interested in the truth, Hearst added. They weren't willing to listen to anything unless it was new and amusing enough to hold their attention.

But the Zangara affair, if it was a failure as a scoop, was the beginning of the most important relationship in the columnist's life—with President Franklin Roosevelt.

12.

Though the Zangara scoop did not get the news attention that Winchell wanted, it still added substantially to his growing legend. Winchell absolutely glowed when Damon Runyon, the veteran reporter whose approval Winchell had sought from the start, wrote an entire column in praise of Winchell. Winchell had that column copied and carried it around, showing it to all who would look for years afterwards.

With his growing syndication and the impact of his radio program, Winchell was beginning to be seen and heard everywhere. Magazines were even writing features about him in which he was described as "Little Boy Peep." In addition to the movie and vaudeville appearances he had already made, the Winchell image was augmented by a new play produced in 1932 called "Blessed Event." The leading character in the play was a high-powered, unscrupulous Broadway columnist, and the title of the play was a good clue as to who that character was supposed to be. The first night at the Longacre Theater, the audience spent almost as much time trying to see Winchell's reaction to the drama as they did watching the play. One viewer said that Winchell had "squirmed and blanched" at this parody of his nosy habits, but Winchell's friend Woollcott demurred. "Nonsense!" he said. "Winchell's emotions at 'Blessed Event,' if any, were probably an ingenuous and gratified surprise at finding himself, at 35, already recognized as enough of a national institution to be made the subject of a play. If he squirmed and blanched, it was because he, and he alone, knew that the two large and unsmiling men occupying seats behind his own, were Central Office plainclothesmen, assigned by the uneasy police commissioner to see that Winchell should come to no bodily harm."

Later, "Blessed Event" was made into a Warner Brothers movie starring Lee Tracy as the Winchell-type character and Dick Powell as the crooner he was supposed to have victimized. Tracy later made a career of playing this fast-talking type of newsman. But Winchell didn't get a cent out of the play, and began to think that it was perhaps time to cash in on the Winchell legend himself.

On one of his trips to California, he made the acquaintance of Darryl F. Zanuck who had just left Warner Brothers to form the Twentieth Century Company. Winchell ad-libbed an idea based vaguely on the story Runyon had done a few years earlier—the famous triangle between a gangster, a chorus girl, and in this case, a popular singer, rather than a columnist. Zanuck thought the idea was great and offered to give Winchell $25,000 for a treatment. Winchell submitted the idea under the title "Broadway Through a Keyhole," and Zanuck accepted it with delight. The picture went into production almost immediately, featuring the tragic crooner Russ Columbo, Constance Cummings and Paul Kelly. Almost as soon as it was in production, Winchell's fellow Hearst columnist Louella Parsons leaked a blind item indicating that Winchell had based his tale on the courtship of 46-year-old Al Jolson and 18-year-old Ruby Keeler.

The singer had met Ruby when she was a chorus girl in Texas Guinan's night club. Ruby had a lovely body and shapely legs. Jolson fell for her hard, and falling for Ruby was dangerous. Ruby Keeler had been keeping steady company for almost two years with a gangster named Johnny Irish who happened to be Italian. But according to Hollywood columnist Sidney Skolsky (and how he knows this is a mystery) Ruby was a virgin when she married Jolson.

Jolson at that time was considered the king of Broadway through the talking pictures he had made, "The

82

Jazz Singer" and "Singing Fool." "The Jazz Singer" grossed $5 million, big money for that time. Ruby was flattered by Jolson's attention, but Johnny Irish was less than thrilled. He warned Jolson, "Stay away from my girl, or else you'll get it!" But Jolson ignored the warning. Furthermore, he was more convinced than ever that he wanted to marry Ruby. A showdown was inevitable and a meeting between Johnny Irish and Jolson was arranged at the Sherry-Netherland where the singer stayed whenever he was in New York. On the day of the appointment, Johnny Irish rapped on Jolson's door and the jazz singer, with some trepidation, opened it. It was a raw, sleety afternoon, and Irish entered the room, crossed the window and stood watching the rain slashing down Fifth Avenue. His hand began massaging his belly. "It's weather like this," Irish said, "makes the bullet wounds in my stomach hurt."

Jolson heaved a sigh of relief. He realized the gangster knew he'd lost the nubile Ruby. Irish turned to Jolson and said, "I want you to take good care of her. If you mistreat her or I hear that something is going wrong with the marriage and she's not satisfied, all she has to do is get word back to me and I'll kill you."

"That's something you don't have to worry about," Jolson said, according to Skolsky. (Skolsky found this all out when he was assigned to do a picture which really was based on the Jolson-Keeler romance.)

On July 19, 1933, Winchell took his wife, June, on one of their rare public excursions together. He was leading her down the aisle of the Hollywood Legion Stadium, a popular Friday night gathering spot for the film crowd who came to see the boxing matches. As Winchell and his wife neared their ringside seats, Jolson rose from his own seat beside Ruby Keeler and stopped the columnist in the aisle. There were words spoken between them in an undertone and then, suddenly, Jolson aimed a blow at Winchell which scraped the columnist's neck. Another swing caught Winchell in the back of the neck, knocking him down, according to the United Press report of the incident. With that, Jolson returned to his seat and Winchell continued to his, while the packed house broke into cheers. Jolson got a big hand from the Hollywood crowd when they left the stadium before the boxing was over.

Later, when questioned by newsmen, Winchell denied that there was any intentional parallel between his story and Jolson's romance, but Jolson was not to be mollified.

"When my wife read that Winchell had sold that story, she couldn't sleep," Jolson told the UPI. "She became hysterical. I was so sore about it that when I saw him come down the aisle, well, I just smacked him down a couple of times."

This was not Winchell's version of the matter. He gave his story to the Associated Press. "A bunch of gorillas hired by a major studio were supposed to have been at the fight last night to give me a shellacking. But they didn't show.

"True, the scenario Jolson took exception to was about a gangster and a chorus girl, but it's not about Jolson and his wife.

"Jolson hit me once, and that was on the side of the neck. The guy who sent me down hit me from behind, and I know who it was and who hired him to do it."

Winchell also denied a rumor started "by snakes in the grass that the war was purposely started by the publicity department of the Twentieth Century Company," but Zanuck was delighted by the publicity and gave Winchell an additional $10,000 for his story. Winchell added a postscript to his version of the fracas: "Anybody else who wants to emulate Mr. Jolson can do so, but we're warning them that they will have to wait their turn in line."

A couple of days after the Hollywood Stadium encounter Jolson, still seething with anger, told the press that he was willing to meet Winchell in a duel over the matter of honor. Winchell said that he'd be glad to take Jolson on "anytime, anywhere, with anything."

As the challenged party, according to the Code Duello, Winchell had the right to name the time, the place and the weapons to be used. Jolson said that Winchell had named all the conditions but had stipulated that the duel would have to be public, for charity, and for a ten dollar fee. Jolson showed Winchell's reply to several of his friends, and they decided that it seemed likely that the only dueling which would take place would be with printers' ink. However, both parties swore to the press that the disagreement was not a publicity stunt. Winchell had, in fact, been carrying on a mock feud with orchestra leader Ben Berney on his radio show along the lines of the one later carried on between Jack Benny and Fred Allen.

One of the columnists covering the great punch-out in Hollywood was Sidney Skolsky, who had been sent by the *Daily News* to Hollywood to cover the increasingly spicy gossip of the film community.

Al Jolson remarked after the incident: "You can sing 'Mammy' for a hundred years, wear your poor old kneecaps out on splintery stages, and talk on the radio till you're hoarse as a bullfrog, but you have to sock Winchell before you really become famous."

13.

The early thirties was a time of terrible stress, which pushed American life to extraordinary extremes. It was a time of great leaders and dangerous zealots like Zangara.

When Repeal came in 1933, the speaks, which had been languishing during the Depression anyway, converted into night clubs. At first they lost a certain panache by the disappearance of the little peephole in the door through which patrons whispered their secret password, "Joe sent me." Now that they were converted into night clubs, the speaks had to have talent to lure trade in. But a few, notably Sherman Billingsley and John Perona of El Morocco, tried to hype the patrons' anxiety as to admission by deliberately making it difficult to get in, asking for reservations when the house was empty, or mythical memberships.

And people did fight to get into these self-designated "exclusive" clubs, even at a time when the hit song of the year was Yip Harburg's "Brother Can You Spare a Dime?" But it was a grand time to be Walter Winchell—or any other Broadway columnist. His tempo echoed that of the American thirties—frantic and furious, with a faint air of desperation. People read and listened to Winchell and wanted to believe what he reported. Living on the thin edge of poverty themselves, they wanted to hear the doings of the glittering conspicuous consumers. They were thrilled to read about the $250,000 coming-out party that multimillionaire Henry R. Doherty threw for his daughter Helen. As a token of her esteem, Helen gave each of her dozen closest friends a custom built Ford. In fact, it was a time when the public, tired of the drabness of their daily lives, were particularly fascinated with the doings of "Society," all of it grist for the mills of the columnists. The public had no way of knowing that many of these so-called "socialites" were given free drinks, meals and presents just to dress up the clubs for the suckers.

Winchell lost one of his blood enemies at the *Mirror*, Arthur Kobler, who was replaced as editor by Hearst's intellectual editorial sharpshooter, Arthur Brisbane. But he was hardly better off. Brisbane, like Kobler, took an instant dislike to Winchell and his column.

"I don't understand a word of his jargon," the new publisher complained to Gauvreau. "I'm always worried, for fear he will land us in a pile of trouble. He annoys me. There's that feverish restlessness of an excited mind about him that interrupts my work when he pops into my office. Yesterday he pulled out a bagful of clippings from his pockets, things people were writing about him (probably Damon Runyon's column praising his Zangara scoop) and he wanted me to read them! Does he think we're working for *him*?"

Brisbane's hunch had a certain truth to it. Before Winchell completely devoted himself to praising the New Deal, Mrs. Roosevelt was quoted in a remark that was unfavorable to gossip columnists. Winchell, as always, took this personally and reacted with a joke that made fun of Mrs. Roosevelt's malocclusion. Roosevelt's supporters were furious, but Roosevelt himself apparently didn't keep a grudge against Winchell, judging by his later actions. Of course, books written in the last few years giving a revisionist view of this seemingly idyllic presidential marriage might indicate that Roosevelt himself wasn't all that crazy about his wife's looks, in view of his long and somewhat overt affair with his personal secretary and others. But hostile though he might be, Brisbane, like Kobler, could not deny that Winchell's column in the paper was responsible for at least a third of the circulation of the failing tabloid.

During this period, Brisbane would fly into inexplicable rages. He developed a hatred for Mickey Mouse, a comic strip that was Gauvreau's favorite acquisition. Brisbane said that he would ultimately prove to Gauvreau that "this member of the rat family had no humor and was a waste of space."

Gauvreau was loyal to his rodent pal. "I decided that if I had to fire Mickey Mouse, I would walk out with him."

But Brisbane stuck to his hatred and periodically would shout at Gauvreau, "Throw that rat out!"

Gauvreau was never sure if he was talking about the comic strip or the columnist.

Winchell really seemed to have entered a new phase of his life in 1933 or so, with the Roosevelt administration. Aside from his idealized worship of the president, Winchell had also taken up the cause of John Edgar Hoover, who had recently been appointed head of the revamped Federal Bureau of Investigation.

After the repeal of Prohibition, the gangsters and gunmen spawned in the dry era launched a crime wave across the states that hadn't been known since the desperado era of the far west. Local law enforcement officials found themselves helpless against the bold, fast-moving criminals and Winchell, frequently regarded as a friend of the bad guys, found himself lined up solidly behind the G-Men, as the FBI agents had once been called by George "Machine-gun" Kelly, just before they captured him. In fact the expression, while coined by the hoodlum, was actually made popular by Winchell.

Winchell became so preoccupied with his new career as a social commentator that often as much as a third of his column was given over to national affairs. Not the least of it was a running vitriolic commentary on the doings of the newly enthroned Nazis.

At first Winchell's comments on the Nazis were simply his usual wise-guy chatter. For instance, his earliest criticisms of Hitler were based on charges that the dictator was a closet queen. Winchell compared

Entrance to The Stork Club, "The New Yorkiest place in New York," according to Winchell

Hitler to Broadway's "Lavender Patrol." In a column in March 1933 he quoted an alleged cable he had received from the mustachioed dictator: "Cable, March 26. Berlin. To Walter Winchell, care of the Paramount Theater, Bklyn: What are you doing over the weekend, would you like to spend it with me, I think you're cute. Love. Adolph Hitler."

A few months later, he jibed: "Hitler just turned down the last chance to enter a beauty contest because he found out that the first prize was a free trip to the Bronx. Henceforth this column will call him Adele Hitler."

The attacks, to Winchell's delight, were actually noticed in Germany. A month or so after Winchell's Bronx item, a Berlin newspaper ran his picture in three columns on the front page. The caption said: "A new hater of the New Germany." The *Volkischer Beobachter* said that Winchell was "the New Germany's American menace because he tells such unconscionable lies about the Führer in the American newspapers. His listeners and readers are morons."

So irritated were the Germans who at that time still thought they they might be able to enlist both the English and the Americans against the Eastern Europeans, that Hitler actually sent for a copy of Winchell's film "Wake Up and Live" in order to see for himself what the columnist looked like.

Winchell was delighted at the Nazis' reaction: "These bastards are vulnerable," he said. "They can't be the supermen they claim. They wouldn't squeal so loud if they were."

Naturally, William Randolph Hearst, Winchell's boss, was not terribly excited by his columnist's new tack. In the first place, Hearst rather admired Hitler, and in the second place, he was afraid that this slightly more serious tone might scare off readers. But Winchell had not, of course, given up his night club and gossip beat. Shortly before the repeal of Prohibition, Winchell had been told by Texas Guinan, "There's a nice feller named Sherman Billingsley, a country jake from Oklahoma, who has a new restaurant. He has been taking $10,000 a month for nine months out of the sock to keep it alive. Give it a look like a good little boy.''

Since Guinan was one of Winchell's favorite informants, even though one of her tips nearly got him killed, Winchell checked out the Billingsley place which was called The Stork Club and, eager to please Guinan because Billingsley treated him like a Ruritanian crown prince, he put his first rave for the club in print. ''The New Yorkiest place in New York is the Stork Club!'' Billingsley later admitted that after the Winchell plug, ''I started banking $10,000 a week.''

Billingsley was one of the first to realize the value of currying favor with the columnists who could provide him with the essential free space that could mean the difference between success and failure. Billingsley was well aware that a couple of lines in a column like Winchell's were worth more than a whole page paid-for ad in the *New York Times* or the *Daily Mirror*, and while he never took a paid ad in his entire career, he became famous for the lavishness of his gifts. In the case of Winchell, ultimately this even extended to providing him custom made Knize suits and of course all the food and beverages that Winchell and his friends could eat and drink.

Shortly after he met Billingsley, Winchell established what was to become his permanent headquarters, at table 50 at the Stork Club.

One midnight, as the columnist was finishing his dessert at the Stork, there was a phone call. Winchell picked up the phone, always available at his table, and a voice which he recognized as that of one of Owney Madden's top aides, said, ''Stay where you are. You will be called again in twenty minutes!''

A few minutes later, the phone rang and Winchell again recognized the voice of Owney's colleague: ''The big boss wants to see you in Miami Beach.''

Winchell knew very well that the only big crime boss

in Miami was Al Capone. "What does he want to see me about?"

"He wants to talk to you for the papers."

"Okay!" Winchell said, aware that he was either being set up for a hit or a scoop.

14.

Winchell was excited about the contact and even Gauvreau was aware that Capone had never before granted an exclusive interview for the newspapers. Both Gauvreau and Winchell knew that if Capone didn't like what the *Mirror* published, there could be trouble. Gang leaders were notoriously sensitive about what was written about themselves. Gauvreau himself had once been threatened with death by Owney Madden over something he had published, which perhaps explained his extreme nervousness about having such people around his city room. Winchell and Gauvreau both had heard the stories about gangsters and entertainers who had been kidnapped, beaten, or cut up in pieces and left in packages around Chicago, because they had offended the volatile Italian bootlegger from Brooklyn. (This was still before Repeal.)

Winchell waited in Miami for three days to be contacted by Capone's hoods, and then finally, one morning, two beefy envoys in dark suits arrived at his hotel and silently escorted him into the back seat of a chauffeured limo. Winchell, wedged between the massive shoulders and backsides of the Capone hoods, tried to lighten things a little by quipping, "I feel like a tube of toothpaste."

His joke was greeted with complete silence and the hush continued until the car arrived at Capone's strategically located island retreat. The Capone mansion was huge and white, decorated with cupolas, spires and ornate balconies, but Winchell was unable to appreciate the esthetics of the Capone architecture when he noticed the entrance guarded by still another pair of oversized yabbos. The columnist was nervous as he was led in complete silence past the two lounging guards, through a thickly carpeted room, into the sun parlor where Capone sat behind a desk, while two more guards sprawled in corner chairs. The Chicago gangster rose courteously when Winchell was ushered into the room. The columnist was surprised at his height. He was much taller than he looked in photographs, about six feet, with heavy, sun-tanned arms and cold, dark eyes in a doughy face.

Capone spoke in the soft, husky tones that we've all come to identify as those of a genuine Godfather: "I am glad you could make it, Mr. Winchell."

"Glad to be here," Winchell said, somewhat untruthfully.

With the social amenities disposed of, Capone got down to business about the purpose of the meeting. While he spoke, Winchell's eyes roved curiously about, recording details for his story. He noticed a gun on the desk and several small pictures on the wall behind Capone. One was of George Washington, the other of Abraham Lincoln.

Capone soon made it clear that he was bothered by the spate of unwanted publicity to which he had been subjected. "I don't like those phony inside-stuff writers who claim to know me. If you ever meet them, give them a punch in the nose with my compliments. It's a big laugh to read the things I'm supposed to have done and said. A bigger laugh is those movies about me. Where do they get those ideas? I also hate the damn newsreels that sneak pictures of me. How do those things look to my family?"

Capone not only was convinced that Winchell had the power to restore his reputation, but based on Owney Madden's recommendations, felt that Winchell would show discretion in doing it. But in the end Winchell wrote a noncommittal piece describing his adventures and crowing over his scoop, while doing little to salvage the Chicago bootlegger's tarnished reputation.

By this time, Winchell was so well established in the Stork that once, when he simply remarked that the summer New York heat wave was "murder on my sinuses," Billingsley ordered air conditioning for the Cub Room, where Winchell preferred to sit, although it was not only a novelty at that time, but extremely expensive. Somewhat later, Winchell complained casually that the lack of privacy in the barbershops he attended was becoming annoying. Billingsley had a private barbershop built at the Stork Club which was to be open for Winchell and other columnists, as well as favored friends, and even recruited one of Winchell's favorite barbers to man it. Word began to go around that Winchell actually owned a piece of the Stork Club, he seemed so at home in it, but all of his biographers seem to agree that he didn't earn any of his money that way, nor did he have any business relationship with Billingsley. Other columnists as well as Winchell gave the club a good press and were given favored treatment. While Winchell was still feuding with Sullivan, and to a lesser degree with Sobol, Winchell refrained from throwing his weight around and having his two colleagues barred. It is possible, too, that he didn't want to put Billingsley on the spot. But that year the feud with Sullivan was exacerbated.

At the time, Sullivan was touched and depressed by the plight of the unemployed.

"I'd seen Barbara Hutton around town," Sullivan recalled, "and I'd been impressed with her decency. I got the idea that maybe she could help make a better Christmas for some people . . . sort of like a Fairy Godmother. I wrote her an open letter in my column saying I'd observed the nice way she treats people, and I remembered that when I was a kid and things were bad, the Fairy Princess would wave her wand and everything would be all right.

"So I asked her if she would brighten up a few Christmases by throwing a big Christmas party for the poor kids."

Actually, a reading of the words Sullivan used in his open letter to Miss Hutton seemed less benign than he has indicated:

"An open letter to Princess Mdivani . . . The unreality of your existence must be boring, Princess. You have a husband who has little or no relation to everyday life. I read that he has bought himself a new string of polo ponies and that after the polo season has ended, he will hunt tigers. I believe it was he who insisted that a band be flown across the English Channel to play tango music for one of your parties.

"With people in distress all over the world, such reports create a sinister undertone . . . I have heard grim and resolute men say some nasty things about your husband, Princess . . . I would dislike to turn him loose along the waterfront of New York, or the South Side of Chicago. They might do some dreadful things to him and make it impossible for him ever to play polo again. I have heard underworld chieftains speak about him and his apparently callous disregard for human suffering . . .

"So in asking you to distribute one thousand Christmas baskets to the poor of New York, I . . . believe this is a . . . grand opportunity to wipe the slate clean . . .

Come on, Princess, what do you say?

Sincerely,
Ed Sullivan"

A good many people thought that Sullivan was not showing the best of taste in using this somewhat blackmailing approach toward Barbara Hutton. *The New Yorker's* Talk of the Town Department complained: "We think the time has come for someone to do something about Broadway columnists who write open letters to people for money, etc."

Winchell was as furious about the Talk of the Town item as he was about the column, because he felt that any reference to columnists would more likely be taken to mean him than Sullivan. Winchell says that Barbara Hutton phoned him a few days after the item. She wondered what he thought she should do.

"Wouldn't you say," he reported that she asked, "it is a form of blackmail?"

Countess Barbara Hutton Haughwitz-Reventlow

Ed Sullivan, columnist and entertainer, on the set of his "Talk of the Town" television show

"You said that, lady, I didn't!" Winchell says he told her.

That afternoon, he put a full report of the phone conversation in the column. The way Sullivan recalls it, Winchell "called me every name he could get away with. I don't know whether he was sore because I got the idea first or because he felt that Babs Hutton was personal property.

"Anyway, what he didn't know was that even before his column hit the street I'd received a check from her for $5,000. We threw the biggest and best Christmas party you ever saw."

Of course, it is possible that the $5,000 was sent by Hutton to Sullivan after speaking to Winchell before the column came out. Anyway, the rift, which had never been entirely healed between Sullivan and Winchell, was now deeper than ever. "He kept sniping at me," Sullivan told the *New York Post* some years ago, "calling it blackmail every time he talked about it.

"The party was so successful that the following year Barbara Hutton phoned me from London and sent another check for $5,000. We had an even better party . . . but Winchell was madder than ever. I've never spoken to him since."

That statement was made in 1952, when the *Post* was engaged in a blood vendetta with Winchell. The *Post* said that Sullivan was actually eager to go on record as yielding to no man in his dislike for W.W. "His column is just an extension of his vaudeville act," Sullivan told the *Post* reporters. "He's the kind of guy who'd do anything for a hand."

By 1934 the nation was so depressed by the economic situation, that divorces could hardly be afforded even by the wealthiest people. Only sixty were reported in 1934 from Hollywood. But the Depression had a positive effect, oddly enough, on the nation's reading habits. A survey in 1933 showed reading the most popular recreation, followed by radio. Films, which obviously cost more, rated third. People seemed desperate for information, which was perhaps why they turned to reading, and this hunger worked to the benefit of those self-appointed pundits, the newspaper columnists. Winchell, Walter Lippmann, Westbrook Pegler, Heywood Broun, Mark Sullivan, Franklin P. Adams, Arthur Krock and others were pulling top dollars on the nation's newspapers.

John Perona, an ex-bootlegger like Billingsley, had opened a place in 1924 on West 49th Street and Sixth Avenue. In those days, Perona was a recently-emancipated busboy from Chiaverno in the Piedmont. He quickly built up a reputation for having good food as well as unwatered liquor. He began early on to attract an international clientele, which included Luis Angel Firpo, the Argentine heavyweight, and others. Perona prospered in his 49th Street locale until 1929, when the Rockefeller interests bought up the neighborhood for the complex of skyscrapers that was to become Rockefeller Center. Perona got $10,000 for his lease and with this windfall opened up a joint called the Bath Club at 35 West 53rd. In 1931, he was doing so well that he needed larger premises and he established a future capital of café society at 54 East 54th Street. At the time, people in New York thought the stroke a bold one, since East 54th was considered a desert wilderness. Taking the hint, Perona christened his new cafe the El Morocco, quickly shortened to "Elmo's" by the regulars. Perona hired Vernon MacFarlane to decorate the place. MacFarlane elected to decorate the banquettes and chairs with blue zebra stripes, surrounded by imitation palm trees. It is not known whether it was planned that way, but the zebra stripes baffled newspaper caption writers who often would have liked to leave the location in which celebrities were photographed a mystery. Billingsley had tried to get around this by prominently placing his large Stork Club ashtrays on the table, but these could often be cropped out. The simulated zebra, however, was clearly identifiable and everybody knew it spelled "El Morocco." MacFarlane extended his desert motif, using French Foreign Legion-inspired uniforms for the doormen.

El Morocco quickly established itself after Prohibition as a principal rival to the Stork for café society. It was in El Morocco that the Duchess of Windsor finally wore a crown, one of the cardboard favors distributed by Perona on New Year's Eve. The King of Cambodia and the Crown Prince of Norway were frequent visitors to El Morocco, as were Erich Maria Remarque, Cesare Siepe and Vladimir Horowitz. But El Morocco had no prejudice against rich, distinguished or interesting Americans. Errol Flynn brought his child bride Beverly Aadland there to ritualize his last birthday. "It's taken me fifty years to learn that I need a psychiatrist."

Because of his open friendship with Firpo, Perona's place became the target of many nightclubbing champions. Gene Tunney and Rocky Marciano were always given ringside tables, and Max Baer was allowed to give hotfoots to his friends without interruption. Later on, Ingemar Johansson became so fond of the club that only the fervent protests of his managers restrained him from dancing at El Morocco all night before his unhappy return match with Floyd Patterson.

Actually there was something about the jungle mood of El Morocco that seemed to affect the machismo of visiting males. While it's true that wherever men gather and liquor is sold, fights are a hazard, El Morocco seemed to attract more than its share. Its first front-paged fracas took place after the New Deal was installed, when an outraged conservative squirted seltzer into the face of Jimmy Roosevelt, the president's son. For years, it was believed on Broadway that the social season was not really launched until the first blow was struck in anger at Elmo's. (In later years the habitués changed the familiar nickname for Elmo's to Elmer's, which still exists today on the East Side as a private club.)

El Morocco became so well known as a battleground for bluebloods that one Social Register scion, quarreling with another on the sidewalk outside the club, is alleged to have said: "I dare you to step inside with me." But the fights were usually short and harmless and quickly broken up by the resident personnel. Once there was a telling blow struck, and it was delivered by none other than John Perona himself, who slung a stabbing right hook to the nose of a New York industrialist whose insults apparently left no alternative response. As a result, Mayor Fiorello LaGuardia suspended El Morocco's license for 48 hours. A few days earlier, the Little Flower himself had resisted an attacker with a couple of punches on the steps of City Hall, but regarding Perona's pugnacity, the mayor declared that public brawling simply had to stop.

Macoco, the Argentine playboy, is said to have never missed a night at El Morocco when he was in America. Once taken for a Brazilian, he was asked, "Well, what's the difference anyway between a Brazilian millionaire and an Argentine millionaire?"

"Oh, about eight million," Macoco responded diffidently.

Regulars at his table remember hearing Macoco scoff at rumors that his ex-wife, Kay Williams, was to marry Clark Gable. "She can't marry Gable," he reasoned. "He has false teeth."

Miss Williams asked columnist Leonard Lyons to convey a counter-message to Macoco. "False teeth? So what?" she demanded, before removing her own bridgework.

As was the case in the Stork Club, visiting entertainers often offered impromptu and free performances for the distinguished guests. Such stars as Danny Kaye, Ethel Merman, and Judy Garland were known to perform at the drop of an olive. El Morocco played host to presidential candidates and princes, powerful capitalists and Soviet envoys. Once Krishna Menon playfully dumped ice cubes down the bare backs of Indian dancers appearing there. Film executive Jack Warner got up and tried to be a stand-up comic. Darryl Zanuck, a frequent visitor, never accepted change. "I can't stand coins except at the box offices of my movie theaters," he explained.

While there still appeared to be plenty of money for

people to spend on wild night life, the country was at the moment in the throes of the worst economic disaster it had ever seen.

Noticing the increasing appeal to readers of the columnists, papers which previously had left such mundane material to the tabloids began to be interested in gaining some of this circulation for themselves. When J. David Stern bought the *New York Post* in 1934, he decided that what he needed to jazz up the then-conservative journal was a gossip column—like Winchell's, only tasteful. Out of 500 applicants for the job, Stern picked Leonard Lyons, a young lawyer who for years had been peddling anecdotes and jokes to the various Broadway columnists, particularly Winchell, Hellinger and O. O. McIntyre. Lyons, born Leonard Sucher in 1906, was the son of a sweatshop worker who died when the boy was seven. He attended the High School of Commerce, City College (at night) and St. John's Law School from which he graduated in 1928. Unfortunately, a year later the stock market crash more or less wiped out the future for young beginning lawyers. To help his failing income, Lyons began sending column items to Winchell and the others. In 1930, he was finally hired for the magnificent sum of $15 a week to write a column called the East Side News for the English language section of the Yiddish newspaper, the *Daily Forward*. Years later, Lyons pulled out of his file a letter dated June 19, 1930. It read:

"Dear Mr. Sucher:
  You might as well know, you know, that your *nomme de guerre* is Leonard Lyons. Now don't complain; these things are fated.
                    (signed) Sympathy,
                             Nathaniel Zalowitz"

Zalowitz was a kindly man who was then editor of the English language section. It wasn't much of a job or much of a salary, but in those days it was quite an accomplishment to break into the newspaper business at all. The column, like all Broadway columns of the late

20s and 30s, was more or less modeled after Winchell's, offering quips, rhymes, aphorisms about broken hearts and electric light bulbs and the like. After six months, the *Forward* folded the English language section and Lyons was out of journalism. His law practice was at least bringing him some sort of a living. However, he still wanted to be a columnist. People say that Leonard wanted that job more than anybody had ever wanted such a job, before or since. It took him about four years to find his spot and many times during those years a lesser man would have said the hell with it. His ambition was bolstered by a high school girlfriend of his named Sylvia Schomberger, later to become his wife, who told him that he wrote such newsy letters full of social chit-chat that he definitely had a future as a columnist.

In pursuit of his ambition, Lyons wrote regularly to the publisher of every periodical from the *Times* to the *Racing Form*, outlining ideas for columns. Every letter was rejected with polite regrets. Lyons would spend much of his time calling on various editors with sample columns and a scrapbook of items he managed to have published. The editors would refuse to see him or tell him to go away. But Lyons exacted a minor revenge. Every time a sample column was turned down, Lyons would say, "Just wait. I'll get this all into print!" Then a week or two or even several months later he would return with a handful of clippings from Winchell, Hellinger, Louis Sobol and other big-shot columnists, demonstrating that his work had indeed appeared, piecemeal, in print and frequently with credit.

To be a contributor to the gossip columns in those days was a miserable experience. In the first place, the contributions were all voluntary and no payment was made. If he was lucky, the contributor might get a credit line. Lyons flooded the columnists of the day with rhymes, puns, topical jokes and other trivia—but with no gossip. He reaped a giant harvest of credit lines, but no checks. Mark Hellinger, who later went to Holly-wood and became a major producer, was one of those who accepted Lyons's items gratefully. Lyons, even then, specialized in the short paragraph, short-short story with a surprise switcheroo ending, kind of like a condensed O. Henry. Hellinger, who usually devoted an entire column to one story with a snappy ending, used Lyons's anecdotes as fast as he could get them. Naturally he did not put Lyons's name at the head of his column, but he would sneak his name into it somewhere so that the aspiring columnist could at least prove that he had submitted the items.

"It all happened before you could say 'Leonard Lyons,' " Hellinger would start one of his stories, certainly to the bafflement of the uninitiated reader. In one particularly pathetic story Lyons wrote for Hellinger, a man was sitting at his desk thinking about suicide: "He noticed a letter signed 'Leonard Lyons.' Who was Leonard Lyons? He didn't know." At that time nobody knew.

Occasionally the columnists, although tight-fisted with money, would give some of their busiest contributors prize fight tickets, second-night theater seats and other freebees. Occasionally there would even be a due-bill dinner at one of the night clubs. Lyons got to see his first Broadway show as a result of the generosity of Art Arthur's column in the *Brooklyn Eagle*, to which he had contributed some items. On their first big night out, Lyons and Sylvia, to whom he was by then married, went to see the musical "Sailor Beware" and to the Village Barn, one of the first of the crazy night clubs that were then in vogue.

When the *Post*'s Stern hired Lyons in 1934, it was probably in part because his column, though awkwardly written, and certainly not newsy, managed to list a lot of famous names and maintain interest with the shortness of its items. In the beginning, except for the few people he had met while gathering his scrapbooks, Lyons had no real contacts at all. But he discovered that you could get a lot of information by simply walking right up to a star and introducing yourself—particularly if you had a column on a New York paper. At the time he got the job, at the age of 28, Lyons had never been in a night club, nor had he been in a speakeasy during the dry days. To some extent his column was *sui generis*, the first in a long time that didn't make use of the three-dot system. Winchell seemed to find this gratifying.

"You're the first columnist to come along who doesn't copy me," Winchell wrote him during his first week on the job. In the beginning, Lyons had diffidently approached Winchell, to whom he had contributed a number of items, and asked him what he should call his column. Winchell thought for a moment and then on the tablecloth of table 50 in the Stork Club, he wrote the words "The Lyons Den."

"It takes a long time to get your name on the top," Winchell later recalled telling Lyons. "They usually put it somewhere in eight-point type, and here you have your name in the title."

Winchell, who later had a falling-out with Lyons, as he did with almost every Broadway columnist, always had the belief that it was Sylvia who designed Lyons's future. "I don't want to be married to a law clerk," Winchell says she told her husband. "That's too dull. I want you to make like Walter Winchell and do a column and put things in the newspaper so we can get free tickets to all the shows and movies and go to fancy places like the Stork Club and never have to pay checks." Winchell's wry comment: "They came from Rivington Street—but never left it."

About a month after Lyons started, he was introduced to Jimmy Cannon, then a friend of Winchell's, and a sportswriter on the *Post*. "I'm Leonard Lyons. I just started on the *Post*," Lyons said. According to Winchell, who was sitting at the table, Cannon replied, "Screw, bum. Come back when you have a reputation." Winchell says he told Cannon, "*You* screw, bum. *You* come back when you have a reputation."

Lyons had a slight, spidery frame and the face of an underfed sparrow hawk; he was almost as tiny and unprepossessing in appearance as Sobol, the *Journal*'s star. As a result, everybody was giving him advice in the beginning. Damon Runyon graciously offered three hints: "One, never let them give you a desk, because they'll always know where they can find you. Two, get as mad as you want, but never get off the payroll. And three, keep your by-line in there every day. Otherwise, your readers might miss it—or worse yet, they might not." This advice was given to him also at table 50 in the Stork Club. While he was listening, a head waiter brought Sherman Billingsley a $25 check issued by a stranger and asked if this would be acceptable in payment of the bill. As a result, Lyons got another little tidbit for his column and perhaps a bit of advice.

"Sure," Billingsley told the waiter. "A night club owner should always okay a $25 check from a customer he doesn't know. It's a cheap gamble. If the check bounces, you lose only $25. If it's good you've made a lifetime customer."

From the beginning, Lyons made it a point to emphasize that he was not interested in the usual gossip—rumors of marriages, divorces, pregnancies and adultery. As a result, many celebrities who might appear with the most flamboyant and obvious mistresses in public places, were reassured that if Lyons approached them with a question it would concern their professional life and not their questionable companion. This made for relaxation and the sort of confidence that brought in many good anecdotes for Lyons's columns. Certainly Lyons seemed one of the most unlikely of night club habitués. Unlike Winchell and Sullivan, he had eyes only for his wife and family, and never took a drink, confining himself to coffee while doing his rounds. Lyons also always claimed that he researched every item in his column and did not accept handouts from press agents. This may be a slight exaggeration, but in any event, he seldom had any press agent write his entire column as Winchell often did. And though he often twisted or missed the point of some of his best stories, he seldom got the names and facts wrong. *The New Yorker,* in a profile on Lyons, said:

"At any rate, in justice to Lyons, it should be said

106

that as often as not, when he appears to have garbled an item, he had been faithfully and accurately reporting a fundamentally garbled situation or epigram. We must ask ourselves what Dr. Johnson's reaction would have been if, while the Doctor was still in the process of recuperating from a tough night at the Cheshire Cheese, Boswell had turned up with a verbatim transcription of the evening's proceedings?"

One of the problems was that since Lyons never took a drink and had not much experience with those who did, he was not always aware of it when some of his informants were a bit tiddly. This occasionally led to trouble. The *New Yorker* profile on Lyons commented, "It's a safe guess that by closing time, Lyons is, in the strict medical sense of the word, the only sober patron in the places he visits. In a milieu which is a vast orchestration of alcoholic overtones, such a man must invariably miss certain subtleties. Gross manifestations of intoxication, like falling down on the floor, or starting to box with Ernest Hemingway, he can recognize. But occasionally he has failed to take into account the alterations of personality and purpose that are likely to set in between the third and sixth scotch and soda."

Once Lyons ran into a prosperous dress manufacturer at a night club in the company of a somewhat passé singer.

"Here's an item for you, Leonard," the manufacturer, somewhat the worse for wear, offered. "The little lady's going to have her own night club. I'm going to build a brand new one especially for her."

"Can I use that?" Lyons asked, pencil poised above his notebook. (Others would not have asked.)

"Of course. We want you to. We want everybody to know!" the manufacturer explained.

In the sober light of day, several hours after this item had been put before the public in "The Lyons Den," the manufacturer telephoned Lyons in a panic. "My God, Leonard," he croaked. "What have you done to me?"

"But you *told* me I could use the item," Lyons answered, sincerely baffled.

In one way or another, the story had a happy ending. The manufacturer, who knew that the singer had many admirers who dated back to the days when anybody who ratted on a gentlemen's agreement got his kneecaps broken with a baseball bat, decided that maybe he'd better back her in the night club, after all. The night club struggled along and finally was sold at perhaps a considerable loss. In any event, it changed hands many times and years later, Lyons cast a proprietary eye on its now glittering facade and remarked, "I built this."

Shortly after he was engaged by the *Post*, Lyons was picked up to be distributed by the King Features Syndicate, the same Hearst outfit that distributed Winchell. Since Lyons's politics were, if anything, more opposed to those of Hearst than Winchell's then were, he was uncomfortable with this association, but a buck is a buck and he soon began to pick up papers. Not without working his tail off, though. He lost 14 pounds in his first week at work, between his worry about his responsibilities and the lack of sleep engendered by the job's peculiar schedule. The link with Winchell became even closer, and Winchell began to regard him as his boy. One reason was that since Lyons had no use for the juicier bits of gossip, he often turned them over to Winchell, whereas Winchell in turn would either listen critically to gags that Lyons planned to put in his column, or occasionally feed him one of his own extras that was not spicy enough for the Winchell column.

The mid-Manhattan beat, pulsating with night life, was far more glamorous then than it is today. There were night clubs, roof gardens and such late-night restaurants as Lindy's—all places frequented by the famous and the notorious. A typical columnist's beat, and a limited one at that, would include the Stork, El Morocco, 21, Moore's, Sardi's, the Plaza, the Diamond Horeshoe, the Latin Quarter, Café Society (up and downtown), the Famous Door, the Cotton Club, the Paradise and uncounted others. Many of these have since closed, especially the large, garish clubs. You could select certain places if you were interested in certain types of items. Sportswriters were to be found at Toots Shor's, radio and big businessmen at the Barbary Room, the international set at El Morocco, and the Stork Club set at the Stork Club.

Other ports of call, less easily defined, included the Versailles, the 18 Club and Reuben's. While it was reported by many that Winchell and other columnists were not welcome at 21, the owners of 21 have consistently denied this, and the columnists have supported this denial.

As the roundsman for the *Post* readers, Mr. Lyons began to accumulate an impressive list of sources, many of them from the worlds of art and law, rather than show business. In an evening, he might pass time with Jim Farley, Ethel Merman, Helen Hayes, Justice Felix Frankfurter and the Duke and Duchess of Windsor, who were introduced to the Stork Club by Lyons. Lyons was on particularly good terms with literary types. On George Bernard Shaw's 90th birthday, the notedly reclusive playwright and author granted Lyons an exclusive interview, to which he naturally devoted an entire column with a big plug line on the front page.

One of the best bits of advice for which Lyons himself had no use, but which served as an anecdote for one of his columns, was given to him by a nationally known songstress who was acquiring beautiful memories one night in the candlelit Champagne Room of El Morocco—until the darkened corner where she sat was suddenly illuminated by the flare of a brandy flame from the crêpes Suzettes she had ordered. All eyes were immediately drawn to that corner, where the songstress was discovered supping with a married gentleman.

"I've learned my lesson," she confessed. "Never order crepes Suzette when you're out in a dark place with a married man."

Lyons differed from Winchell not only in the format of his column, but in his temperament and reaction to certain situations. When Lyons, who had run a number of Jake and Lee jokes concerning the famous Shubert brothers, was barred from their theaters, instead of sneaking in wearing a beard as Winchell had, he decided to make a legal issue of it. After all, it would be a shame if his education in the law went for nothing. Alexander Woollcott had already made a test case of the matter some time before, and the courts had upheld the Shuberts. Everybody had assumed that that was that. But when Lyons himself was barred, he refused to take it lightly. First, he checked to make sure that he had in fact violated a law. Then he decided to go about getting the law changed. One night, on his rounds, he met a State Assemblyman, Irwin Davidson, in Lindy's. Davidson agreed to introduce a bill making it illegal to refuse any sober, decent ticketholder to a theater, and he did. But the measure got sidetracked and buried in committee. This stalling went on for several years. Finally Davidson got mad. It happened that he was much in demand at the State Legislators' annual banquet as a teller of Jewish dialect stories—sort of an upstate legislative Myron Cohen. Davidson told the boys in Albany that unless they went along with his bill, they'd have to get another boy when it came to funny story time. The strategy worked, and the bill passed. The Shuberts instituted a test case and carried it right up to the United States Supreme Court, which supported the new law. Justice and Leonard Lyons had triumphed.

Everybody from then on could attend Shubert productions at will, as long as they didn't throw stink bombs or take pictures of the actors *en deshabille*. Aside from this distinction, Lyons is probably the only columnist ever to be cited in a judicial opinion. In the case of *David Katz* vs. *Horni Signal Manufacturing Corporation*, the problem was whether a man could sue for infringement if it turned out that when applying for his patent, he had not really understood the scientific principle on which the patent was based. In writing his opinion, Judge Jerome Frank of the Circuit Court of Appeals said: "It is immaterial whether a patentee correctly understands how his device operates." In a footnote to the decision he added, "Leonard Lyons reports that Marconi said of the radio he invented: 'Only one thing bothers me: why do you suppose this thing really works?' ''

Being a Broadway columnist, Lyons learned, was like living in a pressure cooker. But there were plenty of aspiring young journalists who felt that, what with one thing and another, it was nice work if you could get it, and several of them were about to blossom on the Broadway scene with considerable impact.

15.

By 1934 Winchell was beginning to develop into a New Deal ideologue as well as an international political pundit. He no longer boasted of his sexual conquests in the column, although this did nothing to slow down his private activities. But now, for the first time, he began to introduce a certain number of homey scenes involving his wife and child. For the benefit of his readers, he would describe the growing-up process of Walda, his surviving daughter, and quote her remarks at length. He would describe, for instance, how it felt to hold her hand. "Walking on the street with a warm, little hand clasped in yours," he wrote, "is a thrill only a daddy knows. Your child is clinging to you, so dependent and trusting—so safe with your firm grip to guide her. There really isn't a more thrilling thrill than that of a little girl's warm hand in yours as you swing along. Have a baby and start living."

In October 1934 he introduced a new feature in the column called "Mr. and Mrs. Columnist at Home." This was devoted to cozy little views of the Winchells' homelife and from that point of view would segue into the gossip scene and the international world.

Winchell's remarks were printed in italics and June's commonsense, prosy answers were printed in ordinary roman type. For example:

"How's the baby? I haven't seen her for days. Is she well?"

"Yes, she's fine. She's growing too fast—too fast."

"I met some man who said he met Walda at Bea's—and that she threw him with one of her words. He asked her to go with him to an ice cream parlor and

she politely told him that she couldn't go with him but that she 'appreshe-shated' it very much. She's a stylist like her pop.''

"What's going on downtown—besides the Lindbergh case?"

"That Vanderbilt woman is in the courts—messy stuff. Swell for the papers. Fighting over custody of her daughter, Gloria.''

"Yes, I know. Dorothy told me only last night that the child and Walda had been playing together in the park for weeks."

"Really? Well, we've finally gone social I suppose.'' (The Winchells then were living in an apartment on Central Park West, having moved from a flat they had previously occupied over Billy La Hiff's Tavern, a popular location for columnists and press agents. Sullivan once occupied the same quarters.)

"Poor Walda. She has her little aches. Dorothy told me that when Walda and the Vanderbilt child, who is nine, first met, Walda went up to her and said: 'What's your name?' and she replied: 'Gloria.' Walda's bottom lip started to quiver and her chin dropped—but she steadied herself—and never mentioned the incident to Dorothy or me, poor thing." (The point of this was the recent death of their daughter and Walda's adopted sister, Gloria.)

"Yes, I know. I've received several lovely poems from people about that line I ran the other day—about 'Gloria would have been eleven.' One came from a Cleveland newspaper woman—a lovely thing.''

"Don't run them—none of them—don't do it!"

"Okay, honey—I won't . . . I know.''

There was an undeniable poignancy to the strength of June's protest and one felt that it was real. Of course, his having published the anecdotes about Gloria and her protest probably did nothing to keep things settled at home. And gradually June's unhappiness about having these family dialogues aired to the general public began to be visible in the text itself. Here's another example which was only a few days after the one cited above:

"Did you read that column I did about you and . . ."

"Don't you mention that thing—do you hear?"

"What's the matter—what was wrong with it?"

"I said don't mention it to me! I threw it down three times—although it got me so curious, I had to pick it up each time and finish the darn thing. Don't put me in the paper—don't make me say things I didn't say. People will think I'm silly or something. Walda, come here. Be careful what you say in front of Daddy—he'll put it in the paper!"

"Oh, cut that out. Everything I said you said, you said! Maybe not on the same day, but you said those things. It's a good idea for a column, and I'm going to do it every now and then—and what do you think about that? It's intimate, personal, inside stuff about us—and several people have written in to say they liked it. Get me some orange juice."

"Nevertheless leave me out of it. Don't make me a character . . ."

Despite his male chauvinist approach to marriage, Winchell apparently did listen to his wife, because he discontinued the Mr. and Mrs. Columnist at Home series shortly after this, and at the same time announced an upcoming blessed event for Mrs. Winchell. This apparently didn't please his wife either, so he retracted it, although in fact it was true. A wag suggested that if the child were to be a boy it should be named Reid Winchell, and if a girl, Sue Winchell. But Winchell's long time mock critic Ben Bernie topped both of these ideas by suggesting that the child, whatever its sex, be named Lynch Winchell. There were plenty on Broadway who agreed with the sentiment, if not the name.

To retain the personal touch, Winchell turned his attention more and more to his Friday column written over the signature "Your Girl Friday." The column, however, was written by Winchell himself, and gave him a good chance to pat himself on the back for some particularly trenchant item or in a subtle way to make corrections or retractions without actually admitting having made an error. Also, it was a way of showing to the public the courage he was displaying in fighting Nazi and right-wing elements. And there was some truth to this, as there was an increasing burden of hate mail and some actual threats. A typical item from Girl Friday (remember that it's supposed to be Winchell's secretary that's writing notes to him):

"When they (the fifth columnists) start to knock you—as the saying goes—it's a sure sign you've got them worried. Don't stop going after them—the people who matter are saying that you're the one who can do it best. You've been in bigger fights, mister, and this is one you can't possibly lose."

Winchell was, by this time, at the high point of his career. His columns were printed in over 450 newspapers. He was the most listened-to news commentator in the history of radio. For a number of years his Sunday night broadcast was the most widely heard radio program in America—not just *news* program but *program*. It outranked the broadcasts of the most popular comedians, dramatic shows and music variety programs.

It was not unusual at club meetings, union meetings or social gatherings, for someone to say, "It's almost nine. Let's hear Winchell." And for fifteen minutes, everything would stop while the radio was turned on.

Ultimately, *Time* magazine even carried his picture on its cover. Getting your name in Winchell's column became a goal to which some people would almost devote their lives.

A debutante (Winchell called them "debutramps") held a party at Jack White's 18 Club on 52nd Street to celebrate her getting her name in Winchell's column.

"You've finally broken in, kid," her escort said, in proposing a toast. "You've made it. Are you happy?"

"Oh, I'm the most," she said. "The very most."

A press agent named Art Franklin reported that a manufacturer had offered him $5,000 if Franklin could secure a one-line mention of the man's company in Winchell's column.

Popular songs often had lines like "Winchell linked me with you," and "I didn't know we were through, I didn't know that I'd be blue, then Winchell Reno-vated us today."

Roosevelt early on realized the value of Winchell's column and after his attention was drawn to several favorable mentions in the *Mirror* he decided that Winchell would make a good sounding board for new policies. At a strategy meeting of top New Dealers, the President explained that he could use the column to feel out public sentiment toward a project before the project was actually officially announced, by means of planting a few rumors in Winchell's column.

Robert Sherwood, one of Roosevelt's ghost writers, and a Pulitzer Prize-winning playwright, objected strongly. "Winchell," he said, "is a man who dwells in cabaret cellars. A little gray mouse, always hunting for cheese."

But Ernest Cuneo, one of the President's close advisers, became a link between the White House and the Winchell column. Roosevelt, ever the master manipulator of men, knew how to get what he wanted. A little flattery, he knew, would go a long way and he wrote a letter to Winchell thanking him for his support. He followed this with a phone call in which he commented laughingly on a gag Winchell had published. It was enough to make Winchell a lifelong fan of FDR's.

It soon became a regular custom at White House press conferences for the President to ask Winchell to remain after the others had left. This not only gave Winchell some excellent items, but enormously enhanced his national prestige as a journalist. Getting the nod from FDR, Winchell would present himself at Roosevelt's private office where he would amuse the President with the best jokes and spiciest gossip that he had accumulated since his most recent visit. Roosevelt always enjoyed the chats and inquired about Winchell's wife and family.

It was during these tête-à-têtes that probably the first links were forged in the chain between the gossip columnists and the power of the president. Examination of documents revealed later by the Sunshine Law indicated it was not an uncommon practice in Washington for columnists to swap juicy tidbits about legislators or other D.C. figures in return for insiders' column items. It was a two-way street and a valuable one to both.   But no other columnist had an in to the administration like Walter's.

This was strengthened the following year when he became a friend and close associate of J. Edgar Hoover. Hoover's agency was just then struggling to get on its feet after years of obscurity, and the attention and publicity that Winchell gave to the G-Men was valuable to Hoover who was constantly struggling for a bigger budget from Congress and more latitude for his operatives, particularly in the political arena. From the beginning, Hoover made it clear that he was interested not just in catching gangsters, but in pursuing subversives and involving himself in the espionage scene. The association between Hoover and Winchell was to be a long one and valuable to both men.

Winchell first made the acquaintance of Hoover by means of plugs in his column and occasional telephone calls. Even before he had met Hoover in 1934, when Winchell went to Chicago for a stage appearance, he wound up with two G-Men assigned as his bodyguards. He hardly needed them, because mob friends had sent three gangsters to protect him in the Windy City and the Chicago Police Department had sent two of its finest detectives. Actually it tended to be an embarrassing situation for all. The G-Men got onto Winchell's train at a Chicago suburb. They told Winchell that they had been assigned to him by J. Edgar Hoover because of threats against Winchell by pro-Nazi elements.

In Chicago certain independent gangsters were running a protection racket for high-salaried stage and night club entertainers. The G-Men said that Hoover had tipped them off that Winchell might be hit by these same gangsters and ordered to cough up protection money, and said they were there to protect him from that, too. But when Winchell and the two Feds got off the train, three gangsters walked over and introduced themselves to Winchell. These were the two Fischetti brothers, cousins of Al Capone, and later to become famous members of the Chicago mob, and the third was an anonymous gunman. The G-Men, who were from the local Chicago office, recognized the Fischetti boys and glared at them venomously. Winchell explained to the federal officers that these people were acquaintances of his and that he was in no danger from them. The Fischetti brothers and their crony were allowed to take Winchell aside and explain the situation to him.

It seemed that Lucky Luciano, who had become the head gangster in New York when Owney Madden was sent back to Sing Sing as a parole violator, had telephoned them to watch over Winchell while he was in Chicago—in fact, to protect him from the same independent protection racket that the G-Men were concerned with. Winchell explained that he was already covered by the Feds, but the Fischettis were stubborn men.

"We're not leaving you," the Fischettis maintained. Their orders came from Luciano and they did not want any trouble with Charlie Lucky.

Reluctantly, Winchell introduced the five bodyguards to one another and they nodded frigidly. Winchell started through the station with the five men trailing him, and he wasn't out of it before he was approached by two more bodyguards, sent by the Chicago Police Commissioner. They also were bound and determined not to leave him. So during his entire week-long visit to Chicago, Winchell led a seven-man parade of bodyguards. Even one of Winchell's best friends, Damon Runyon, who happened to be in town at the time, could not get into the dressing room because either the G-Men, the Chicago mob guys or the police detectives—he didn't know which—pushed him out into the street.

At a party for Winchell at a Chicago nightclub, the seven-man detail naturally went along. The atmosphere grew tense. One of the Fischetti brothers fixed one of the police detectives with a stony glare and said that someday he was going to kill him. The detective was sitting across the table. He kept his temper while the Fischettis went on making slurring remarks about the G-Men, to the unconcealed glee of the police detachment who privately held no brief for federal law enforcement agents.

The Chicago affair went all right, but Winchell's closeness to the Federal Bureau of Investigation was to result in embarrassing moments during his coverage of the Lindbergh kidnapping trial—and afterwards.

16.

Winchell returned from his well-escorted trip to Chicago impressed by the fact that the chief of the bureau himself had assigned two men as his bodyguards. He wrote polite bread-and-butter notes to all the people who had helped him, to the Chicago Chief of Police, to Lucky Luciano and to J. Edgar Hoover. Hoover, who was still in the process of jacking up his department's publicity campaign, had been following with great glee all of the gratuitous plugs which Winchell had been inserting in his column for the FBI. He wrote back, inviting Winchell to come and visit him at the bureau if he was ever in Washington. Winchell, aware that the man could be an incomparable source of material, agreed and journeyed to the Capital with a close friend and Broadway press agent, Curley Harris. Harris and Winchell got the grand tour of the headquarters, including a look at all the recent bloody mementos of FBI battles, such as the guns that had been used in the capture of Dillinger.

Winchell asked some questions in a guarded tone about the still ongoing search for the kidnapper of the Lindbergh baby and came away with this column item:

"The Federal men are convinced they will break the most interesting crime on record—the Lindbergh snatch."

A few weeks later, New York police called in local crime reporters and tipped them off confidentially that one of the gold notes that had been part of the Lindbergh ransom had been handed to a Bronx gas station attendant who had been suspicious enough to write down the purchaser's license number. The police warned editors that publication of this information might drive away the man who was spending this money. All of them agreed not to publish it until an all-clear was given, in order not to interfere with the course of justice.

Winchell, not one of the headquarters police set, heard of the information several days later—possibly from Hoover himself. In any event, he did not feel bound by any pledge given by other reporters. On Sunday, September 16, Winchell announced the facts in his radio broadcast, touching off a tremendous furor in the world of New York journalism. Gauvreau, Winchell's old enemy, happened to be off that night, and in any event was not inclined to listen to Winchell's program, but he shortly got an angry call from the editor of a competitive paper informing him that Winchell had broken the embargo. Gauvreau was attacked on all sides by police officials, other editors and federal agents who felt that he could possibly have blown the entire case. Inspector John A. Lyons of New York Police Headquarters was appalled by the release of the information. He had been working patiently on the case, guided by a map showing the spots where several other gold notes were appearing. Pins were slowly forming a circle in the Bronx, indicating the focal point from which the criminal was probably operating.

Incidentally, the idea of using gold notes as part of the ransom payment was not one of J. Edgar Hoover's; it was the suggestion of Treasury men who had been consulted on the case. It happened that on Saturday, September 15, the day before Winchell's broadcast, Walter Lyle, a gas station attendant, had noticed a suspicious ten-dollar gold note passed to him by the driver of a Dodge sedan. On a hunch, he jotted down the license number of the car. It was this break which was to send Bruno Hauptmann to his death in the electric chair. Since the banks were closed on Saturday, Lyle didn't put the bill into the bank until the following

Monday. There, a bank teller checked his list and verified the fact that the certificate was part of the ransom money. Fortunately, Hauptmann was apparently not one of Winchell's radio listeners, nor a reader of his column which trumpeted the same news on Monday.

Gauvreau said that he was so distraught over Winchell's leak that he didn't sleep for 48 hours. On Tuesday, the following day, Hauptmann was trapped with $13,750 of the Lindbergh gold notes through the license number noted by Lyle. It was a fantastic break for Winchell, who took full credit for solving the crime. He even tried to persuade the gas station attendant that it was the broadcast and the item in the Monday column that made him suspicious of the gold certificate, but of course Lyle had noted the number before either of those became public.

Kobler, the publisher of the *Mirror*, who should have been deeply concerned by this breach of journalistic etiquette, seemed strangely unconcerned, and a month later Gauvreau was to discover the cause of his indifference. Hearst had foreclosed on loans Kobler took to finance his purchase of the *Mirror*, and was turning the paper over to one of his most dashing of Hearstlings, Arthur Brisbane, a columnist and editor of considerable repute.

The Lindbergh case had everything a sensational paper could want—famous names, attractive people, an innocent baby and above all, Hauptmann, a German villain at a time when the nation was just getting up in arms over the atrocities of the Nazis.

Brisbane, the new publisher, who like his predecessor took an instant dislike to Winchell, had already been displeased by some of Winchell's anti-German and anti-Nazi items. He issued a memo to the whole Hearst chain, apparently with the agreement of William Randolph Hearst, who was known to be pro-German:

"We may be accused of railroading Hauptmann. Let us give the public the impression that the judge is handling the case. We are constantly referring to the prisoner as 'the German.' If he were Irish, we would not drag in the Irish, if he were Jewish, we should not drag in the Jews. THE GERMANS ARE THE LEAST MURDEROUS OF ALL RACES. Their average in murder is much lower than ours, on the average by about ten to one. Emphasizing that Hauptmann is a German is an insult to the German people, and Mr. Hearst wants these insults stopped at once.''

But Hearst's strangely conscientious attitude for a publisher who had always encouraged the most scurrilous of scandal journalism, did no good.

The Hauptmann trial at the quaint courthouse in Flemington, New Jersey, became a circus. Distinguished sob sisters of the Hearst chain, Adela Rogers St. John and Fannie Hurst, handled the women's angle. Winchell, who already had a reputation of having an "in" on the case, and in fact was closer to Hoover than anybody else, left Broadway's limelight for the scene of the trial.

Gauvreau commented somewhat sourly, "His dread of falling into obscurity had landed him into row A, seat 5 in the court room where, daily, he contributed his own voodooism to the performance. Each piece of incriminating evidence he claimed to have predicted months ago, but he was not crowing about the part he had played in the episode of the ransom certificate . . .''

Justice Thomas W. Trenchard, an elderly and tired gentleman who had never before been exposed to this flood of press coverage, was overwhelmed. For the first time, the press was allowed to bring in still and movie cameras, as well as recording equipment, and although they promised earnestly not to use the equipment when the court was actually in session, the reporters simply ignored these assurances.

Winchell, meanwhile, covered his bases with Hoover, who didn't seem to mind the journalist's premature release of secret information. Winchell called the Director of the FBI and told him that he had known of the arrest of Bruno Richard Hauptmann an hour before the information was released to the press. He explained that he could have printed the story in the last edition of the

Mirror, but he was willing to withhold it—if there was a chance of arresting Hauptmann's confederates. Hoover was grateful, and Winchell sacrificed the scoop, but not without exacting a considerable measure of gratitude from Hoover. Later Hoover wrote Winchell a letter on official stationery, in which he told about a speech he had made to a newspaper editors' convention in Washington about the press's part in the Hauptmann case.

"I pointed out, without of course mentioning the name specifically, how a well known columnist had refrained from printing a truly national and international scoop in the Lindbergh case for 24 hours, in order not to harm the investigation which was being conducted in that case.

"Of course you know who that person is. The entire speech is 'off the record,' but I thought the editors should know that there was at least one columnist who put patriotism and the safety of society above any mercenary attitude in this profession. With best regards I am,

Sincerely,
"John"

Winchell was delighted by the encomium and framed the letter. He always kept it in a position of honor in his office.

The trial was an absolute picnic for Winchell, who had always doted on being a real reporter but had not had much chance to cover extensively a national news event. Others attracted from the news and literary worlds included Edna Ferber, his old friend Alexander Woollcott, Arthur Brisbane, the publisher of the *Mirror*, Kathleen Norris, Damon Runyon and others.

But according to Bob Thomas, Winchell's biographer, Winchell himself was the most important person at the trial. Jurors were asked by the defense, "Do you read Walter Winchell's column?" If they said they did, they were excused with cause. Certainly the case was a high point in Winchell's career and in establishing his credentials, such as they were, as a topflight newsman. He would let loose a broadside of predictions, hints and "scoops," and then pick the ones which had turned out to have some truth to them and herald them as major exclusives.

Meanwhile, his tie with Hoover became closer than ever, and they became social and drinking buddies, attending prize fights together, and posing for photographers in nightclubs. Hoover, in fact, appeared not averse to making something of a fool of himself. One picture, taken at a later period, showed the head G-Man of the United States holding a toy machine gun and wearing a paper hat at the height of a New Year's party at the Stork Club.

The story behind the picture was amusing, if embarrassing. Unknown to Hoover, who was not very well acquainted with the New York criminal set, one of the guests at the party was a notorious gunman named Terry Reilly, with a police record as long as the Stork Club menu. Some of the guests at Table 50 thought it might be funny to have Reilly pose for the photographer with the same toy machine gun Hoover had used. They pleaded with him to do this, but Reilly refused. In the first place, he was not in favor of such frivolous goings-on involving his profession. Also, he was well aware of the point of the joke that the photographer and others planned. In the relaxed atmosphere of the Stork Club party, Hoover was anxious to intervene in the argument and see good will prevail. He had been successful, only minutes before, in persuading Winchell and Louis Sobol to shake hands, ending a feud between the gossip writers that had gone back several years. Now he urged Reilly to go ahead and pose with the gun, but the gunman was stubborn—and embarrassed. He and most of the other guests at the party knew that he was at the time out on parole for extortion and impersonating a G-Man. He left the group without Hoover being aware of it, and Hoover continued to enjoy the special privileges he was being given by Billingsley at the behest of Winchell.

Only minutes before, he had been to see the private Stork Club barber shop upstairs which was presided over by a barber who, in his salad days, had shaved Owney Madden, Dutch Schultz and Lucky Luciano, as well as Winchell, Sobol and Sullivan. To St. Clair McKelway, the *New Yorker*'s observer of the Winchell scene, it seemed symbolic of an era. "Barbers, gangsters, gossip writers, political cynicism, café society. Subtract gangsters and all G-Men. Take away political cynicism and put in patriotic hysteria. Barbers, G-Men, gossip writers, patriotic hysteria, café society. A whistle and a bang and a hey-nonny-nonny and a happy new era for Mrs. Winchell's little boy Walter."

But there was something nagging the chief G-Man. Amongst all the favorable publicity and laudatory articles, some of which he was writing himself, there had grown a persistent rumor that not only did Hoover have no background as a criminal investigator, but in fact he never actually made an arrest himself. Seeing the flood of publicity which had resulted for certain of his agents as a result of their dramatic arrests, the chief determined that he was going to take a prominent part in the next major FBI bust. The accusation of Hoover's incompetence was all the more galling because it was brought up in a rather rude fashion by Senator Kenneth D. McKellar in the course of an FBI appropriations hearing. In fact, it was McKellar's viewpoint that all the ballyhoo for the bureau, including permitting news cameras inside of it and planting articles in various magazines "hurt the department very much, by advertising your methods."

Another senator, Senator George W. Norris of Nebraska, not terribly pleased with Hoover's record, added fuel to the fire: "Mr. Hoover is doing more injury to honest law enforcement in this country by his publicity-seeking feats than is being done by any other one thing connected with his organization . . . A detective who advertises his exploits every time he gets an opportunity, who spends the public money to see that they are spread over the pages of the newspaper in flaming headlines will in the end be a failure in ferreting out crime . . ."

But Hoover, who had never gotten so much attention in his life, was convinced that he was doing the right thing for himself and for the bureau. He continued his aggressive publicity at full speed. The next week, in fact, he posed for an autographing session with Shirley Temple, showing her the workings of an FBI machine gun.

His break came in 1936, shortly after the heated Senate appropriation hearing. Public Enemy Number One was Alvin (Creepy) Karpis, who was identified by Hoover as "Public Rat Number One." Karpis had already escaped one elaborate FBI trap in an Atlantic City hotel by slipping down the fire escape in his underwear. He'd also escaped another ambush in Hot Springs, Arkansas. G-Men finally pinned him down in a Canal Street rooming house in New Orleans. They instantly contacted the director and kept the hideout under surveillance until Hoover could grab a plane south to take part in the final collar. This added greatly to Hoover's dramatic image and tended to squelch those who said that he was not a real, red-blooded cop. But FBI old-timers state that it was Norman H. McCabe who actually put the arm on the fugitive. There was a slightly embarrassing moment when it was discovered that none of the hot-shot agents had thought to bring any handcuffs, and Karpis's wrists had to be tied behind him with one of the agents' neckties. Fortunately, Hoover had long ago instituted a policy that all agents should wear neckties, so there was no lack of haberdashery for the job.

The following day, the papers carried gigantic pictures of the arrest of Karpis with Hoover figuring prominently on the scene. Former FBI agent William W. Turner, in his book, *Hoover's FBI*, was less than impressed by Hoover's grandstand play, especially since Hoover seemed, knowingly or unknowingly, to be hobnobbing with close cronies of the biggest and most dangerous criminals in the country and spending a lot of time catching relatively harmless individual banditos: "While all eyes were riveted on the blazing chases of Pretty Boy Floyd, Babyface Nelson, et al., the Mafia and its allies were quietly building a criminal cartel preying on the nation. Compare John Dillinger with Vito Genovese. Public Enemy Number One was jaunty and dashing, with a streak of wildness, a kind of Douglas Fairbanks of the crime stage. The Mafia boss of bosses, on the other hand, shunned publicity, was personally inconspicuous, and lived modestly in the suburbs, his name only whispered among the 'soldiers' of the Mafia."

But if Hoover didn't recognize the importance of the Mafia, other arms of government did. As early as 1931, the Wickersham Commission, appointed to investigate crime under the Prohibition Act, recommended "an immediate, comprehensive, and scientific nationwide inquiry into organized crime," in order to "make possible the development of an intelligent plan for its control." Other governmental law enforcement agencies such as the Bureau of Narcotics, the Alcohol and Tobacco Unit and the Internal Revenue Service's Intelligence Division, all fought silently against the crime syndicates, but they never publicized their exploits and therefore they never got public support to increase their allocations of funds. The FBI had cornered the crime-fighting market with the help of Broadway columnists like Winchell, Sobol and Sullivan, who praised them to the skies while hobnobbing with the very criminals that the FBI should have been pursuing.

17.

Two of America's most powerful men realized the value of cultivating Broadway columnists as well as more distinguished members of the press. One, as mentioned, was Franklin Delano Roosevelt; the other, J. Edgar Hoover, who was just beginning to make a glamour department out of the Federal Bureau of Investigation.

In the early thirties, the FBI was just a stepchild agency of the Justice Department. Hoover had been appointed in 1924 and had basically been busy cleaning out corruption in the bureau itself, trying to depoliticize the agents, many of whom were political appointees. Hoover insisted that federal investigators have law or accounting degrees, as well as knowing how to act and shoot fast. But in 1932 the Bureau was still in a chaotic state. After the repeal of Prohibition, there was a crime wave of machine-gun-equipped desperadoes that surpassed in violence and scope anything short of the bad old days in the Wild West. Local police were completely unable to compete with the new criminals who had learned how to drive fast cars and use automatic weapons. Walter Winchell was one of the first to see the value of playing up the glamorous exploits of the feds. In the first place, he could do so without in any way offending some of the high-up gang members with whom he was so close in New York. Hoover's men basically occupied themselves with Midwest stick-up men and burglars who had nothing to do with the sophisticated organized crime on the New York scene.

At that particular time, it was not hard to dramatize the operations of the FBI. Two incidents which took place on June 17, 1933 and July 22, 1934, served to set the pattern for crime enforcement's new tough guys. In June 1933, Frank Nash, a mail robber who had escaped from Leavenworth only to be recaptured three years later, was delivered to Kansas City under a heavy guard, on his last lap back to prison. A phalanx of FBI agents and local cops escorted Nash from the train to the auto that was taking him to prison, and climbed in beside him. There was a back-up car with two officers in the rear. None of the cars left the curbside. Three notorious members of Nash's gang, Charles (Pretty Boy) Floyd, Verne Miller and Adam Ricchetti suddenly materialized with submachine guns in hand and demolished both cars and their occupants. All together, five people died, including Nash. In July 1934 America's Public Enemy Number One, John Dillinger, decided to take in a gangster flick at the Biograph Theater in East Chicago, accompanied by two women friends—or at least Dillinger thought that they were friends. One of them must not have been all that friendly since it was she who had tipped off the Federal agents as to Dillinger's whereabouts. Fifteen FBI men, headed by a handsome, 31-year-old agent named Melvin Purvis, who had newly been appointed head of the Chicago Bureau, were waiting for him. Spotting them as he emerged from the theater, Dillinger made a run for a nearby alley, trying to draw his gun as he fled. But before he could even raise the pistol to firing height, he was dead, one FBI bullet through his side and another through his head. The newspapers exulted in the dashing FBI exploit and Purvis was lionized by the local papers. The stories were picked up and flashed around the country and for a while Purvis was Public Hero Number One. The publicity glorifying the lawmen was a watershed point in what had up to then been the era of the Jesse James-type of anti-hero, a time when hokey biographies of bad men played by George Raft, Edward G. Robinson and Humphrey Bogart were filling the movie houses. Even then, the FBI was criticized for being trigger-happy and cowardly by some newspapers. Winchell and several other columnists came to the bureau's defense. In October 1934, the bureau and Purvis added to their fame when they ambushed Pretty Boy Floyd on an Ohio farm. The *New York Times* headline for the day told the story:

**PRETTY BOY FLOYD
SLAIN AS HE FLEES
BY FEDERAL MEN
Melvin Purvis Leads
Officers in Shooting
Down Outlaw**

Bandit Falls in Flight

**Unable to Use Pistols
After Ignoring Purvis's
Order to Surrender**

Long Sought as Killer

**Oklahoma Desperado Blamed
for Kansas City 'Massacre'
in which Five Died**

Purvis and the FBI came in for nationwide acclaim, and "Baby Face" Nelson was elevated to the role of Public Enemy Number One. This, by the way, was not yet an official designation. It would be several years before the FBI would hit upon the publicity device of listing its ten most wanted criminals. It was largely an unofficial designation by national consensus, probably, however, authenticated by the FBI. John Hamilton, a surviving member of Dillinger's gang, was voted Public Enemy Number Two. Purvis did his part in helping the FBI get proper credit. He told the AP: "The killing of Charles Arthur (Pretty Boy) Floyd brings to a close the relentless search and effort on the part of the Department of Investigation of the United States Department of Justice.

"The search was directed by J. Edgar Hoover, Director of the Department from Washington, and I have been in constant contact with him by telephone and

131

telegraph. Mr. Hoover has been particularly anxious, as have we all, to bring about the apprehension of this and other similar hoodlums.

"Mr. Hoover and all the special agents were particularly interested in Floyd because he killed one of our men in the Kansas City massacre of June 17, 1933."

Hoover, though somewhat irked by being upstaged so consistently by his blond and handsome bureau chief, still began to enjoy the spotlight of public attention to which he had not been previously accustomed. William Turner, a former FBI agent, describes his reaction in his book, *Hoover's FBI*: "Foppishly dressed, he showed up frequently at Manhattan night spots and sporting attractions, such as the Melrose Games and boxing matches. Something of a *poseur*, he was photographed signing an autograph for a curly-locked Shirley Temple, firing a machine gun, biting into a 'G-Man sandwich' at Lindy's, and chumming it up with such luminaries as ex-Oklahoma bootlegger Sherman Billingsley, maestro of the Stork Club, Toots Shor, Jack Dempsey, and Walter Winchell who hardly let a column slip by without a Hoover anecdote."

Other press friends who were in Hoover's coterie at one time or another included Quentin Reynolds, Ed Sullivan and Heywood Broun. Reynolds once had the temerity to put on the chief with a gag line: "Edgar, I think it's about time you were told that Mrs. Broun has been receiving threatening letters," Reynolds told the FBI chief.

"What!" Hoover said, leaping to his feet. "We'll get right after that. Have you any idea who's sending them?"

"Yes," Reynolds said, smiling. "The grocer."

Witnesses said that Hoover took the gag in good grace and in fact indications are that at this time, still feeling his way to national power, he would allow himself to be kidded in a fashion that definitely went out of style at a later date. He also found early on that the gossip he picked up from such people as Winchell, Billingsley, Broun and Reynolds was very useful in Wash-

J. Edgar Hoover celebrates New Year's Eve at the
Stork Club with Cobina Wright, New york society girl

ington. FDR's Attorney General, Francis Biddle, would tell how Hoover used to regale him with spicy exposés of the actions of other cabinet members which he had learned on his trips to New York. "Edgar was not above relishing a story derogatory to an occupant of one of the seats of the mighty," Biddle recalled, "particularly if the great man was pompous or stuffy."

But early on, Hoover began to see that these tidbits of gossip, or at least some of the more damaging ones, could be used to manipulate the cabinet and Congress into increasing what was at that time a relatively paltry allocation of funds to the bureau.

In those days, somewhat more innocent in some respects, no breath of scandal ever touched Hoover himself. There were no comments on his obvious federal free-loading, the fact that the government picked up all of his nightclub and racetrack tabs and paid for his holidays. Nor was it possible to connect him with any of the attractive ladies he met during the course of his nightclub tours. His name at one time or another was linked by some gossip columnists with Ginger Rogers's mother and with Cobina Wright, Sr. but there's no evidence he ever dated them or any of the others seriously. In fact, his most frequent date was Clyde Tolson, who shared a house with him to the end of his days and seldom, in fact, left his side.

Not everybody believed that Hoover at first actually engineered the enormous spate of publicity that erupted for the FBI in the early thirties. Jack Alexander, author of a *New Yorker* series on Hoover in 1937, theorized that the ballyhoo was at first "a spontaneous phenomenon," that the director not only didn't stimulate it, but in fact he "refused to cooperate with movie companies and fiction writers in the gathering of material or supervising of production." But after the Kansas City massacre, Hoover decided that a crusade against violent crime was needed. "Someone had to become a symbol of that crusade," Alexander commented, "and the director decided that because of his position it was plainly up to him."

134

Drew Pearson, who was close to Hoover at the time, revealed some years later that Hoover, once he got the idea, approached Homer Cummings, Roosevelt's first Attorney General. Cummings thought the idea of the crusade was interesting, and he had a small dinner party for a group of Washington newspapermen, including Pearson, at which he asked them whether they thought the FBI needed a public relations program so that the FBI's image of efficiency would be sufficiently potent that no kidnapper or bank robber would dare to challenge it. The correspondents agreed and recommended Henry Suydam, then Washington correspondent for the *Brooklyn Eagle*, who was appointed a special assistant to the Attorney General and, as Pearson put it, "performed so spectacularly that within a year he had transformed Hoover, previously a barely known bureaucrat, into an omnipotent crime buster whose name was familiar to every American." In fact, Suydam did such a good job that Hoover, learning the ropes of the publicity game, decided he didn't need him anymore, according to Pearson.

Once committed, Hoover plunged into the job with vigor and singlemindedness. There emerged a torrent of magazine articles, newspaper serializations, books and movies extolling the heroics of the G-Men, and the columnist who didn't want to miss inside bureau leaks had better run an item or two every week if he wanted to continue to bask in Hoover's favor. The director also used the opportunity to express his resentment of the competition for newspaper space he had been getting from Melvin, now known as "Little Mel" Purvis. The bureau had all of a sudden become too small for two such flamboyant personalities and obviously it was Purvis who had to go. He wound up in Hollywood, heading up a sort of junior G-man club sponsored by Post Toasties called the "Melvin Purvis Law and Order Patrol." Later his name was all but expunged from official histories of the bureau.

The FBI was at first not involved with the notorious kidnapping of the son of Charles Lindbergh, the trans-

135

atlantic flyer, which took place in May of 1932. But the furor stirred up by the crime caused such national antagonism to the quickly-growing crime of kidnapping that a law was passed making kidnapping in which state lines were crossed a federal offense. In 1934, two years after the kidnapping in which the two-year-old Lindbergh child had been killed within days of his abduction, the FBI became closely involved in the search for the kidnapper, and Winchell, who held the seat closest to the top of the FBI among columnists, was privy to a good bit of private information concerning that search which ultimately caused deep concern to his employers.

18.

It became clearer than ever that the light and amusing, tension-relieving paragraphs of the gossip columnists were giving the public what it wanted—a few laughs, a diversion from the grim times, and word of the intimate goings-on among the rich. Lyons had gotten a good start at the *Post*, but some of the higher-ups felt additional spice was called for. They summoned a new boy in town, a meek-looking, mild-mannered sleepy-eyed reporter from Ohio named Earl Wilson. Wilson brought sex to the Broadway column in a different way; instead of spilling the beans about the private shenanigans of the well-to-do, he made himself at home in the dressing rooms and bedrooms of the sex symbols of his time and gave a lush and glowing report of their physical attributes in a style that was both breezy and mocking. Fellow columnist Louis Sobol said of him, "He has a bizarre but eminently readable style and his subject matter is usually of the eyebrow-lifting type. Wilson has discovered anew the allure of feminine anatomical prodigality. He will devote an entire column to Mae West's capacious bust, Gypsy Rose Lee's unadorned torso, Betty Grable's exciting underpinnings . . . He has become the Peck's Bad Boy of journalism and is reaping heavy rewards." Wilson, unlike Winchell and Sullivan but like Sobol and Lyons, was a family man and not only referred frequently to his wife (who he characterized as the B.W. for "beautiful wife") but insisted on taking her on most of his rounds, with certain exceptions. Another colleague, Sidney Skolsky, christened Wilson "the Boswell of the Brassiere."

There was something engaging about Wilson's ob-

137

vious goggle-eyed embarrassment about the kind of confrontations involved in his business.

"On my very first sally into a nightclub," Wilson recalled, "I was gravely embarrassed by the low neckline of a girl who sat across from me. When she leaned over to talk to me, as she did frequently, I choked, turned red, and jerked my head away. That night I met innumᵉrable girls, all of them with low necklines and bulging busts. I learned that this was the standard equipment of the lady nightclub-trotters, and I had to steel myself to it. When I go into a nightclub, I go there in pursuit of information—at least that is the story I tell my beautiful wife."

Prior to his appointment to the job for which he created the title "saloon editor," Wilson had been, as he says, "a blameless rewrite man and feature writer, interviewing talking dogs, two-headed cows, Broadway actresses, and guys in East Orange, New Jersey, with an invention that will take the shine out of your pants."

Working strictly a day shift, he had not had much chance to be exposed to the screwballs and celebrities who inhabited saloon society.

"Now it was all open to me," he reminisced in his book, *I Am Gazing Into My Eight-Ball*. "The free whiskey, the ringside seats, the courteous bows of the proprietors. I loved it, and even if it makes me some kind of a moron, I must say I still do."

Actually, Wilson confesses, he got the idea for using the title "saloon editor" from a press agent named Will Yoland. At first the advertising department of the *Post* was a little afraid of it as being too flippant to the clients who took ads all around Wilson's page. "A nightclub editor can run his job so that he winds up feeling like a business manager to a prostitute," Wilson observed. "He pimps for the advertising department. He dumps into the paper all the sugary handouts written by the press agents, explaining how wonderful so-and-so is down at the Club El Burpo, and of course the Club El Burpo is overjoyed and takes out another ad."

But Wilson prided himself on the fact that while he

might have "pimped a little for the advertising department," he did write his own copy. Wilson was intrigued by the somewhat racier nature of the conversations he was hearing now that he was out of the talking-dog circuit. On one of his first rounds, he overheard Thyra Samter Winslow, a fellow night personality, discussing someone she had recently met. "They always said about him," said Thyra, "that after his mother got married, he was no longer a bastard, but he was still a sonofabitch."

Wilson's coups did nothing to irritate the grey eminence of columnist Walter Winchell. They were all outside his ken. On his second or third night out, Wilson scooped the nation by being on the scene when Jules Brulatour, an eminent man-about-town and husband of platinum blonde Hope Hampton, fell on his fanny to a gale of laughter from the surrounding celebrants. Alert to a hot news story, Wilson trailed the playboy to the men's room where he was recovering his aplomb.

"What happened?" Wilson asked him, his pencil poised, in the same voice he would have used if a cop had been murdered or a congressman had been caught taking a bribe.

"I fell on my prat!" Brulatour replied, succintly and loudly.

The next day, Wilson reviewed the pratfall instead of the new show at La Conga. The editors didn't seem to mind; the column was getting amused and favorable comment. They added, however, to be on the safe side, a third of a column at the bottom devoted to the usual three-dot type gossip. When Wilson took his job as saloon editor, his predecessor on the beat, Dick Manson, told him, "In six months you'll be a drunkard, you'll be bankrupt, and you'll be divorced. You'll also have ulcers. They talk about fine food on this job. Christ almighty, I live on hamburger sandwiches."

However, in some way, Wilson seems to have avoided these menaces of his trade. Although he was not a teetotaler like Lyons, he had "a couple of drinks along the way, but not enough to keep me from working afterward.'' The new boy on the block got a big hand from the other columnists already on the scene; Leonard Lyons of the *Post*, Louis Sobol, Ed Sullivan, even Walter Winchell. Lyons often gave Wilson tips that he could not use in his more sedate column.

"Winchell overwhelmed me with his kindness and was constantly encouraging me.'' The first time Wilson met Winchell was at a theater opening.

"You're doing a good job,'' Winchell said, "and you're not giving the racket a bad name like some of them are.'' Winchell went on to say to Wilson, "If there's anything I can do for you, just command me.''

Later, Wilson said, Winchell sat at his table in the Stork Club, and, in his left-handed stroke, actually wrote out items which he gave to the afternoon-paper columnist, items which probably would break before Winchell could get them into his own column.

Ruth McKinney, who later won fame with her play, "My Sister Eileen,'' helped Wilson to get settled into life in New York. With her famous eponymous sister, she helped Wilson to find his first New York digs, a rooming house in Washington Square, and it was there that Wilson quickly found Rosemary Lyons, a lovely secretary from East St. Louis, Illinois, and spent very little time persuading her to marry him. Later the family was enlarged by the addition of a son, Earl Junior, known as "Slugger,'' who later became a writer of revues and songs; and a much-ballyhooed miniature schnauzer, as well as a resident and apparently satisfactory mother-in-law, all of whom featured with some frequency in Earl's down-home-type column.

In his pursuit of pulchritude, Wilson naturally ran across that eminent collector and famous asbestos heir, Tommy Manville. Manville had, by this time, made himself a nuisance with all his paranoid publicity-seeking with most of the men of the beat, but Wilson was still a fresh face. Besides, he felt that the negative attitude of the other reporters toward Manville was unfair. "It would be like a White House reporter refusing to report Roosevelt for the last twelve years because he disagreed with his politics," Wilson observed.

By the time Wilson got involved with the gadabout Manville, nightclubs weren't as eager as they once had been to have him at ringside, and people were complaining that the quality of his wives was not as high as it had been, although Wilson personally felt that numbers six and seven, the Misses Billy Boze and Sunny Ainsworth, were "lovely young ladies." Wilson was present when the growing anti-Manville feeling had its first genuine expression at a nightclub called the Coq Rouge, operated by one Frank Bonacchine.

Manville and a party of five had arrived late, and then the playboy protested loudly because his reserved table had been given up. He was asked to wait in the bar. "You haven't got a table for Manville?" Tommy said pugnaciously. "Well, other places have a table for Manville." After a few more words, he stormed out. Bonacchine was advised by a friend that he had perhaps made an error, but the nightclub manager disagreed.

"Tommy Manville," he commented, "is one guy I don't like. He doesn't drink (Tommy at that time was on the wagon, and drank mostly Coca-Cola), and he doesn't spend money at a place—maybe two or three dollars. I would let some of my customers insult me, but not Tommy Manville. He's a jerk."

Wilson soon learned that Manville, with all his millions, was as greedy for publicity as a struggling young stand-up comic. When the war came, he was overcome with patriotic sentiment and called in newsmen, asking if it would be proper for him to get married with the war on. Would he get bad publicity? And would he get a *lot* of publicity? The reporters informed him that they didn't think he'd get very much publicity and that it would probably all be bad.

Wilson trailed him around the nightclubs on the night of his seven-hour, kissless marriage to Sunny Ainsworth, seeking column copy. Manville sat at his usual table at El Morocco with the bodyguard who always accompanied him, and started blubbering over the fact

141

that Sunny had left him. A photographer suggested that he pose for a picture sitting with another man. The caption would be, "Tommy Manville wifeless on wedding night." Manville was delighted with the idea, but just as he was getting set to pose for it, Sunny herself walked in cold sober, and marched up to the table. "What's wrong with you?" she asked him. Manville looked crestfallen. Instead of embracing his new bride for whom he had allegedly been searching all over town, he turned sadly to the photographer and said, "I suppose that ruins our shot?"

And then the unpredictable Manville suddenly turned, ducked, and ran out the back door of the club, leaving his bride sitting there. Later, when Wilson asked him what the idea of this was, Manville pointed out that it made a better story that way. Now, Manville felt, this wasn't just a column item, but a true front-page story. And it turned out to be, although Wilson felt, "It seemed like a strange thing for a man to be thinking about on his wedding night—even on his seventh wedding night."

But as bland and cheery as Wilson's approach was, he, like all Broadway columnists, managed to make enemies in time and get involved in venomous feuds. However, about the same time that Wilson blossomed on the scene, another brash youngster from the wilds of Chicago erupted on the scene like a ripe boil. Mortimer was his name, and poison was his game.

19.

Lee Mortimer got his big break when the *Daily Mirror* in 1932 decided to put out its first Sunday edition. Winchell's contract with the *Mirror* had stated that if they were ever to put out a Sunday edition, Winchell would be paid for a column in it, *pro rata*. This meant that he would get one-sixth of the thousand dollars weekly he was then collecting, or about $170 for the Sunday column. Since the *Daily News* had already offered him a thousand dollars to do a Sunday column alone, Winchell was understandably less than overjoyed at the new Sunday chore. And since he was not on good terms with either Arthur Kobler, the publisher, or Emile Gauvreau, the editor, a predictable spat erupted.

Winchell, still burning over the fact that the *Mirror* was making him pay for his own photographer and for all his phone calls, even for the daily papers, refused to play ball. Kobler had a good idea of Winchell's ego and weak spots and countered by engaging for $100 a week a young man, originally from Chicago, named Lee Mortimer, who was then working as editor of a weekly New York hotel throw-away called *Amusements*. Kobler always resented the extra money Winchell was making from his movie, vaudeville and radio commitments, and tied the new reporter to a deal whereby any outside earnings would be split fifty-fifty with the paper. He also included an option on Mortimer's services for five years, but reserved for himself the option of firing the young columnist at will.

Mortimer, nee Mortimer Lieberman, grew up in Chicago during the period when the Windy City was dominated by one of the most flamboyant schools of journalism in American history, and seems to have been infected by that spirit. Among the rowdy and unconventional journalists rattling around the Loop in those days were Ben Hecht and Charles MacArthur, who later became authors of the quintessential journalists' play, "The Front Page"; Walter Howie, who served as the model for the tough city editor in that play and later was editor of the *Mirror*, among other papers; and Jack Lait, editor of the King Features Syndicate at the time Mortimer joined the paper.

Mortimer's family, a well-to-do middle-class clan—his mother was Swedish—moved to New York in 1922 when Mortimer was eighteen. Mortimer briefly attended NYU but dropped out shortly to join the staff of the *Bronx Home News*, covering club parties and the police beat. His former night city editor said of him, "He was one of those wise-guy, flippant kids who wanted to be in on everything. He didn't associate with the other boys. He was conceited, aloof."

Mortimer left the Bronx paper to take a job with Heywood Broun—a job he got, by his own account, by barging into Broun's office and "pestering him for days." He told Broun he'd work for nothing. Broun at first refused, but finally gave in. In those days Lee Mortimer was a political liberal and was impressed by Broun's forthright, leftish stands. Other idols of his at the time were H. L. Mencken and George Jean Nathan, who were making a big hit with their magazine, *The American Mercury*.

In 1925, Mortimer married a pretty, red-headed neighbor girl named Gerry Pascal and, probably for financial reasons, he decided he no longer could continue to work for Broun for nothing and rejoined the *Home News* at a salary of $35, five more than he was getting when he quit. It was during those struggling years that Mortimer got a chance to renew a slight acquaintance with Harry Hershfield, who had been one of Broun's clique. Hershfield lived across the street from Mortimer's parents' apartment on West End Avenue, and when, during their broke period, Mortimer and his wife moved in with his parents, he and Hersh-field would walk their dogs together. Mortimer realized that Hershfield was influential, and began to cultivate him. He sent him cards on holidays, gifts on his birth-day and wires on his anniversaries. His hunch that Hershfield would be useful turned out to be valid, because after some months of this treatment Hershfield introduced Mortimer to Donald Flaum, who was the owner of *New York Amusements*. Flaum, who owed Hershfield some favors, gave Mortimer a job, actually three jobs. He was to do interviews with guest celebrities on the radio, serve as drama critic, and as editor of the paper. It was about this time that the columnist stopped calling himself Mortimer Lieberman and adopted the name Lee Mortimer, although he did not change it legally until 1942.

But Hershfield wasn't through doing favors for the wistful young Chicagoan. One day he took his young friend over to the office of Jack Lait at King Features, whom he had known for more than a quarter of a century. The *New York Post* in a profile of Mortimer said: "Lait, like Hershfield, succumbed to Mortimer's youth-ful earnestness, deft apple-polishing, personal service and eyes-on-the-stars ambition. He called A. J. Kobler, publisher of the *Mirror*, and suggested Mortimer as a replacement for Walter Winchell in the new *Sunday Mirror*." Winchell had finally closed out his arguments about the *pro rata* pay with his sworn enemy Kobler. "I'll tell you what I'll do about that Sunday column, Mr. Kobler," Winchell was reported to have said. "If you'll promise never to speak to me again, I'll do the Sunday column for nothing."

"You're on," Kobler retorted.

"Start it right away."

But Winchell felt the pang in his pocketbook, and reneged. It was then that Mortimer was hired.

Lait and his fellow Chicagoan soon became close friends. The King Features editor was a heavy drinker and didn't mind accompanying the new columnist on his nightly rounds of the clubs and bars, but Mrs.

Mortimer was not thrilled with either Lait's company or the endless round of drinking which frequently ended with the Mortimers half-carrying Lait back home, where he would rouse his patient wife at four a.m. and demand black coffee. She divorced Mortimer less than a year after he took on the nightclub column, saying only: "He liked Broadway. I didn't."

Mortimer didn't seem to be devastated by the departure of his childhood sweetheart. His tastes were becoming more show-businessy and exotic. Shortly after Gerry Pascal left him, one Patricia Whitney became the second Mrs. Mortimer, but for some reason the marriage was kept secret for almost five months. The story finally broke in the *Journal*, possibly leaked by Jack Lait. The afternoon Hearst paper ran it this way:

"Lee Mortimer, a Broadway reporter, half of whose stories are about silly runaway main stem midnight marriages, got scooped on one of his own yarns when the news broke that he and Patricia Whitney, brunette chorine at Paradise, were secretly married in Jersey City last November 27th after a gay party in a Broadway hot spot.

"Patricia was one of the thirty American chorines summarily ejected from England last year by the British Home Office, after the local chorus girls decided that American beauties were too much competition.

"The bride gave her age as 25. Her home is Rochester."

This marriage apparently never jelled from the beginning, although it was several years before the Mortimers officially split. When they did, Patricia got an annulment on the ground that the marriage had never been consummated.

Shortly after Mortimer took the job on the Sunday *Mirror*, Winchell, seeing that the paper shortly reached a circulation of 600,000, and unhappy at not being able to reach this audience, gave in and agreed to do the column for the *pro rata* figure. Mortimer, however, was carried on the paper as a Broadway reporter and occasional fill-in columnist. It was during this period that Mortimer, in search of a more clear-cut identity (he was a pale young man who had a tendency to fade into the woodwork), decided to emulate his idol George Jean Nathan, who had made it a practice to always appear in public with an exotic Oriental companion on his arm. If Nathan could do it, Mortimer thought he could also, and launched himself on a chase of Oriental sex thrills which was to be his trademark for the rest of his life.

20.

The Daily News was the biggest paper in America. But despite the relative popularity of the Sullivan column, it always irked Capt. Patterson that his gossip pages seemed to lack the vivacity and power of Winchell's column. An attempt was made to spice up the Broadway page one year after Ed Sullivan joined the *News*, by adding a second Broadway column by a feisty young entertainment reporter named Sidney Skolsky.

Meanwhile, while most business was going to the dogs, Hollywood was thriving in the mid-thirties, and Hollywood columnists were beginning to attract almost as much circulation as Broadway columnists, dealing as they did with figures often much more nationally known than the denizens of the Great White Way. Capt. Patterson at the *News* decided to replace Skolsky opposite the Sullivan column with John Chapman's column of Broadway, and send Skolsky to Hollywood to see if he could make a stab at cutting into the vast circulation of Louella Parsons, the Hearst Hollywood reporter. It was Patterson's idea, anyway, that reporters who stayed too long on one beat became too devoted to their sources and therefore unable to be hard-hitting. He planned to send Skolsky to Hollywood for a while and then rotate him back to Broadway and send Sullivan to Hollywood. But when Skolsky finally got out in the sunshine and went from being a night person to being a day person (he was, incidentally, allergic to sunshine and had a lot of trouble during his first months there, but finally, under medical treatment, was able to learn to stand the Hollywood sun), Skolsky found, to his amazement, that he liked it, and kept making excuses for not coming back to New York. Sullivan had no objection to this, because he had very little interest in leaving New York. Finally, in 1937, for some reason, Capt. Patterson ran out of patience. He sent Skolsky a wire telling him to get his tail back to the city, and told Sullivan to pack his sunglasses and bathing suit for the trip west. Skolsky issued what he called his "official statement":

> "The *News* assigned me to Hollywood for a year to do a column. I have been here four years. The *News* wanted me to return to do a Broadway column. I believe that Broadway columns are as passé as Broadway. Therefore I have resigned. They got me wrong. I love Hollywood."

Skolsky got his wish. He was fired by the *News* and stayed in Hollywood, working for a time for the *Mirror*. Skolsky soon discovered that Broadway wasn't the only place where back-biting and internecine feuds were part of the panorama. Louella Parsons and Hedda Hopper already had their well known feuds, some of them real and some of them make-believe, but they were not as damaging as the one that started between Skolsky and the immortal "Lolly" at the point where Skolsky left the *News* and joined the Hearst chain. The ex-New Yorker immediately got off on the wrong foot with Louella. All newcomers to Hollywood, especially rival columnists, were expected to seek an audience with the Great One in the hope that she would bestow her approval on them, much in the fashion that Winchell's favor was curried in New York. Skolsky, aware that he represented the second largest paper in New York, the *Daily Mirror*, and was already a person with considerable experience in the field, felt that he had to make no obeisance to so-called Hollywood royalty. On Friday, he turned in his column "Hollywood Is My Beat" for the Monday paper which came out Sunday evening. His first column was kicked off with one of his familiar subtitles, "The Gossipel Truth." On Sunday evening around 6:30, Skolsky went out to pick up the *Herald Examiner* which carried his column locally. On the front page, he was shocked to see a big headline: GARBO TO MARRY STOKOWSKI! Beneath it, "Exclusive story by Louella Parsons." The story told how Garbo and Stokowski met, how their romance had developed, and their plans to marry. It was certainly hot front-page news in Hollywood, if not in the entire world. On page 26, the first line in Skolsky's column was like a slap in the face to Louella: "Garbo will not marry Stokowski."

Parsons was furious. It didn't matter that Skolsky had no advance knowledge of Louella's story; she was determined to get the New York upstart. She called Hearst, to whom she had a practically open wire, and falsely accused Skolsky of being a communist. Skolsky's vociferous denials did no good when Hearst confronted him with the accusation. "Louella said that, and that's it, Mr. Skolsky," Hearst informed him. Skolsky pleaded desperately. "Are you sure she didn't say 'columnist'? You know, she has a difficult time pronouncing words."

"I know what she said," Hearst snapped. "You'll work out your contract, and when we're through with you, you'll be nothing."

Skolsky pulled his column out of the *Examiner*, but finished working out his contract in the *Mirror*, where it ran "about the size of a postage stamp." Following that, he was out of work for about eight months, until he finally resumed his career for the *New York Post* and its syndication service.

About three months after Louella Parsons had accused Skolsky of being a communist, he walked into Chasen's, a well-known Hollywood rendezvous, and saw Louella sitting in a booth with Alva Johnson, an influential magazine writer whose profile of Louella had appeared in the *Saturday Evening Post*, and Margaret Ettinger, a powerful press agent and Louella's niece.

Alva and Miss Ettinger, old friends of Skolsky, greeted him cheerily and asked him to join the group, but he shook his head and waved off their invitation. Ettinger was persistent. "Come on, Sidney, sit down," she called.

"No, no, I don't want to," Skolsky insisted, in a version of the incident he reported in his book *Don't Get Me Wrong—I Love Hollywood*.

But Ettinger persisted in her plea.

"No, no, I don't want to," Skolsky said. He knew there'd be trouble if he got too close to Louella. But his two friends kept insisting. Finally he gave in and slid into the booth next to Louella. He soon realized that neither Maggie Ettinger nor Alva Johnson had any idea of how Louella had sabotaged him in the Hearst syndicate, although he thought that Maggie, at least, should have known. Skolsky talked with his two friends back and forth across Louella, who did not participate in the conversation.

"She sat there, silent, looking as she always did, as if she was stone," Skolsky wrote. Sidney didn't address a single word to Louella, but no one seemed to think that was unusual. The conversation went on this way fifteen or twenty minutes, and then Louella turned to Skolsky.

"I didn't know you were such a nice man," she said. "If I'd known you were so nice, I wouldn't have told Mr. Hearst you were a communist."

"Jesus Christ! That I was a communist?" Skolsky wrote. "I saw red! My impulse was to get up and smack her, but I knew I couldn't hit a woman, especially in Chasen's. I didn't know how to get rid of my hostility."

Finally Skolsky had the answer. "Ouch!" Louella hollered.

"What are you doing there?" Maggie and Alva asked, surprised.

"I just *bit* Louella. She knows why," Skolsky answered.

Louella, for once, remained silent. Skolsky, amazingly enough, finished the food he had ordered before saying goodnight.

At Ciro's, two or three nights later, Louella's husband Doc Martin approached Skolsky and asked him what had happened between him and Louella the other night. Skolsky told "Dockie," as he was called, that he had bitten his wife.

"And I'll tell you something else, Dockie," he added. "I had the tooth removed."

Ultimately, as in the case of many columnists' feuds, Skolsky reached an armed truce with the powerful Hollywood columnist.

"Whatever revenge and release I had derived from biting her was soon forgotten. But I still take pride in what is far more important for a reporter. I was right. Garbo did not marry Stokowski."

Meanwhile, Sullivan was shipped to the Coast and a dapper, new young columnist named Danton Walker who had covered music, nightclubs and general utility jobs on the *News*, was appointed to be the new Broadway columnist, replacing Sullivan.

Meanwhile, the Captain promised Sullivan that he could come back to New York after one year in tinsel land.

Danton Walker was recuperating from an attack of bronchitis at his sister's home in Brooklyn, when he first got word of the new assignment from Captain Patterson. The message came via a particularly anxious Broadway press agent. "By that uncanny instinct which makes them what they are, he had somehow surmised that I was about to come to him with the most important contact in the newspaper field," Walker remembers. The press agent was extremely cordial and merely claimed that he had heard Walker was not feeling well and he had come to pay his respects. As a token of his esteem, and a get-well present, he had brought a tiny portable radio, one of the first of its kind. Somewhat puzzled, Walker accepted the gift absentmindedly, hacking and wheezing with the remains of his bronchial infection. Several hours later that afternoon, his sister received a phone call from a man on the *News*. "Have you heard it yet?" he asked excitedly.

"Heard what?" Walker's sister asked.

"That your brother is to be the new Broadway columnist on the paper. It's in Louis Sobol's column this afternoon!"

So the first event in Walker's career as a Broadway columnist was to be scooped on the story of his own appointment by another Broadway columnist. As his first gesture on the new job, Walker wrote to all of the other then-functioning contemporaries in the field, Winchell on the *Mirror*, Sobol on the *Journal-American*, Lyons on the *Post*, Ed Sullivan and even Hy Gardner out on the *Brooklyn Eagle*, asking their advice and suggestions for a novice in the profession. His second gesture was to write a column in the nature of a farewell in response to Skolsky's statement, reminding him "that so long as there was a show business, there would always be a Broadway."

Walker was very different in personality and background from most of the others, being of a fairly well-to-do Anglo Saxon family, well educated and something of a dandy. He astonished his fellow columnists by showing up for his first night's rounds in the nightclubs in a tuxedo. Despite the fact that he had worked in various capacities for the *News* for five years, he was still not used to the flood of effusion, importunities and offerings of favors that greeted him in his new post. He accepted them all with equanimity, which surprised the press agents, nightclub owners and show business people who were vying for favor.

"Why is it," he wondered, "that after getting a Broadway column you are considered a pretty regular guy if you still speak to your mother?"

Patterson had given him a terse summary of what he expected of him: "I want the column to be witty, informal and informative, and not just made up of a lot of 'puffs.' I want the Broadway of Katherine Cornell as well as the Broadway of the hatcheck girls. And don't pull your punches—but don't get us into any trouble."

Walker learned that before his appointment, but when it was already rumored that Sullivan was to leave the Broadway beat, the *News* had received no fewer than 5,000 letters written by aspirants for his job. But Capt. Patterson was known as a man with a whim of iron, and he had taken a liking to the style and personality of the natty new Broadway scribe. He seemed to like Walker's column from the start. However, he handicapped him in the beginning, possibly because he was uncertain whether Walker would find the right direction for his column, by instructing him to insert after the last line of his column the words, "Help! Help!" followed by an invitation to the readers to give their opinion of Walker's efforts. There was a variety of responses to this humble query. Some wrote in praising the Broadway columnist for this unusual display of humility. On the other hand, another 500 letters suggested that Walker eliminate the "I" from his typewriter. Several wrote in saying: "If you don't know your business by now, why don't you give up?"

After a couple of days of this barrage of critical mail, Walker carried his appeal to the Captain and was given permission to drop the line. But in the end, it was Patterson, in Walker's own estimation, who kept him from achieving the kind of spicy column that Winchell was dishing out.

"On the assumption that the *News* wanted the type of hot stuff being ladled out by Walter Winchell, I had dwelt too frankly on a society scandal involving a member of an auto magnate's family. In the same column was another item to the effect that James Moffatt had been slapped with a subpoena by an unidentified woman who thought she had some sort of case against him. In the latter item, there was no indication of sex, but Mr. P. jumped to the conclusion that there was."

Walker was summoned to a meeting of the managing editor, the city editor, the Sunday editor and Capt. Patterson himself.

"I will not have a scandal on this paper," Patterson thundered. "Gossip, yes, but not scandal." He turned to Walker and made his point clearer. "There's a fine line of distinction, and it's up to you to find it."

Harvey Duell, the managing editor, tried to back Walker up and protect him against these vague definitions of his job. "It seems to be a matter of who gets there first with such items," Duell said. "The other columns . . ."

"I am not interested in what appears in other columns," Capt. Patterson roared. "I am not interested in what appears in other papers; I am only interested in what appears in *this* paper."

Then, softening, he turned to Walker, who was considerably daunted by this response to his first couple of scoops. "This automobile thing—it might cost us some advertising, and as for this other line, don't report the extracurricular activities of a man unless you see him coming out of a brothel."

"I don't get around much to the brothels," Walker murmured defensively.

"Who is this Jim Moffatt?" Patterson queried. "Is he a bum?"

Walker and the three editors looked at the Captain in astonishment. Moffatt was the former United States Housing Administrator and the publicity he had received in recent months would have been enough to fill an entire newspaper. Patterson, when he was told who Moffatt was, commented in a somewhat mollified tone, "This may sound snobbish, but I don't want such items printed about respectable people. If it's about a chorus girl or a bum, okay."

Of course, this went completely against the Winchell dictum, which was, the bigger they are, the harder you hit them. And the severity of the Captain's views left Walker puzzled and shaken. After all, the tabloid had based its success largely on scandal in the news pages. A *New Yorker* profile on the Captain quoted him as saying, "The *News* built its popularity on legs. When we got the circulation, we put stockings on the legs."

He had also gone on record as saying that any situation involving sex, murder or money was potentially a good story; if it included all three, you hit the jackpot. The Captain also laid down another strict rule: "Just because a man writes under his own name doesn't mean that he is free to express an opinion or a policy that is in disagreement with his newspaper. A newspaper should express one viewpoint, not the viewpoints of a lot of people. If I were Roy Howard (publisher of the conservative *World Telegram*) I would fire Heywood Broun and Westbrook Pegler." (Both men had expressed opinions highly divergent from that of the *World Telegram*.)

Of course, Walker, unlike Winchell, didn't come to the paper with a following of hundreds of thousands of readers, so he did not have much of a weapon to answer the Captain with. Besides, as mentioned before, Capt. Patterson took a much closer view of his paper than did Hearst, who owned entire chains, of which the *Mirror* was only one of the links.

So strict were Patterson's views on the personal life of his staff, that he once fired Phil Payne, managing editor of the *News* in the twenties, for consorting openly with Peggy Hopkins Joyce, a notorious glamour girl of the period. Payne was later restored to his job, but was warned to avoid being seen in the future with notorious women in public.

A few days after getting his new assignment, Danton Walker was in the Stork Club when someone pointed him out to Peggy Hopkins Joyce as the new Broadway columnist of the *News*. She requested that he be brought to her table at once. Joyce, nee Marguerite Upton, daughter of a barber in a small Virginia town, had made a career of her marriages to a series of rich men, followed by sensational divorces and generous settlements, all of which made front-page news. She was known, quite rightly, as one of the most beautiful women in the world. Slim and lithe of body, some said she had the face of a madonna—exquisite skin, deep blue eyes, and a wealth of golden blonde hair, casually worn. Nobody could guess from this genteel appearance that she had a reputation as a man-eating huntress. Walker was introduced and sat down briefly at her table, as Peggy Joyce began sizing him up.

"I can give you a lot of news," she said demurely. "Why don't you invite me out sometime?"

156

"Why not just tell me some news of yourself—now," Walker answered.

"I haven't been very well of late—but you won't print that, will you?"

"No."

"I have taken up new thought—but you won't print that, will you?"

"No."

"Are you married?"

Walker answered that he was not.

"Are you a fairy?"

Walker said that he was not that either. And at that point, he suddenly realized that Peggy Hopkins Joyce's hand was giving his knee a significant grope under the table.

"Then call me Monday and ask me out for dinner, won't you?"

Walker murmured that he would consider her offer, and continued his rounds. During the course of the evening, he did pick up an item about Peggy Hopkins Joyce. After he had left the Stork Club, Miss Joyce, in a whimsical mood, had bribed the attendant in the gents' room to let her come in and powder her nose. It was a small item, but somewhat racy. However, the next day, when he got to the paper, several reporters of long standing on the *News* reminded him of what had happened to the managing editor for spending too much time in public with Miss Joyce and Walker, still shaky at his new job, decided not to take up her invitation.

"Being a Broadway columnist, I learned," Walker wrote in a later book on his experiences, "was like living in a pressure cooker. About two hours a day was required even to *open* my mail; phone calls came at all hours, even to my apartment, from cranks, press agents, and publicity-seekers of every ilk. I was forced to switch to an unlisted phone number. So many inquiries reached me by every avenue of communication asking about my background and other information about how I happened to get the Broadway assignment—the 'unknown' who had suddenly been cata-

157

pulted to this dizzy elevation . . ."

Walker's style on the job did seem unusual, such as wearing evening clothes to theater and nightclub openings and running a serialized autobiography in his somewhat lightly read Saturday column, describing his experiences in the theatrical profession. In traveling about the continent with his international connections, Walker began to take his column far from Broadway. On a holiday visit to Nassau, he was introduced by a public relations man named Charles Ventura, later to become a New York society editor, to a couple who were probably the hottest gossip column items of that and the previous year, the Duke and Duchess of Windsor. The Duke, only the year before, had abdicated the throne of England as King Edward VIII, to marry the woman he loved, the American divorcee, Wallis Warfield Simpson, now the Duchess of Windsor. Rumors going around the world were that the duke, regarded as somewhat of a nincompoop by most people who knew him, had been somewhat enthralled and taken in by the trappings and philosophy of Hitler's increasingly powerful Nazi Party. Prior to going to meet the duke and duchess, Ventura also introduced Walker to Sir Frederick and Lady Jane Williams-Taylor, grandparents of Broadway's newest glamour girl, Brenda Duff Frazier, whom Walker had already met in New York. Lady Jane had been a newspaper woman herself before marrying Williams-Taylor, head of the Royal Bank of Canada. She had a certain interest in gossip.

"I hear you are going to interview the Duchess of Windsor tomorrow," she said slyly. "Ask her about Goering. I understand she was a friend of his."

And the duke, of course, when he had abdicated, had finally been appointed Governor-General of the Bahamas, a position in which the Royal Family felt he could do little harm. The next day, the duke's equerry, Captain Drury, briefed Walker about how to handle his interview with the duke, who at that point had not yet given any interviews on the job. Trying to be fair, Walker hinted that it might possibly come up in the conversation that he would ask the duchess about whether she knew Herman Goering. The captain wearily assured Walker that it probably would come up, and apparently he had gotten his none-too-bright Governor-General aside and given him a clue on how to handle the matter. When it came up, it was handled so adroitly that Walker said he was unaware that Captain Drury was doing the prompting.

"The British know how to do such things," he remarked.

As they were chatting over a few cocktails, the Duke seemed to bring up the subject out of nowhere. He remarked that yes, in his official capacity, he had been required to meet Goering during a government tour of Germany, at which the duchess interposed, "But he didn't give him the Nazi salute!"

At this point Walker perhaps missed his great chance, because he knew all along it was not really Herman Goering with whom the Duchess had her friendship, but Joachim von Ribbentrop. Walker avoided making the viceregal couple uncomfortable, in favor of getting a longer and more impressive interview, which in fact lasted about two hours. Remembering how the duke looked at that point, Walker said he seemed "a rather pathetic shade of the fair-haired boy who had been England's 'best traveling salesman,' beloved all over the world."

"We all were slightly embarrassed, I think," Walker recalled, "when in commenting on world affairs, he preceded a remark with a line '. . . When I was King of England.' "

There was something most touchingly naïve about the remark, coming from this slim, blond, ex-monarch. Walker, like so many others, however, was captivated by the duchess.

"She was forthright in her remarks, and her deep blue eyes, her best feature, looked directly at you, giving the impression that she was exclusively interested in *you*, and all you had to say. She was dressed simply, but with great style; her skin was clear and clean, almost devoid

of makeup—as if freshly washed with soap and water—
and her light brown hair was brushed back, exposing
large, but shapely ears.''

Walker was a bit new to the royalty beat, or he might
not have been so desperately impressed with either of
the royal couple. Bessie Wallis Warfield Spencer Simpson grew up in what might be called humble circumstances in Baltimore where her widowed mother tried
to make ends meet by dressmaking and sponging off her
more well-to-do relatives. Ultimately her mother supported young Wallis by working as a hostess at the
Chevy Chase Country Club. But she realized the importance of a good upbringing to a young girl—the only
way to make a good marriage. She saw to it that her
daughter attended the exclusive Oldfields Boarding
School and that she made her debut at the Bachelors'
Cotillion.

Wallis's first husband, Earl Winfield Spencer, Jr., a
naval officer and something of a drunk, took the future
duchess far away from home to the Orient. There they
separated, and the young and beautiful Wallis Warfield
Spencer hung around for a while in Peking, supple-
menting her monthly alimony with earnings from poker
games, at which she excelled.

Ernest Aldrich Simpson, Wallis's second husband,
was something of a wimp, but had access to infinitely
more money than the ex-naval officer. He moved her to
London and introduced her into his own circle in which
the then Prince of Wales relaxed with his mistress, the
Viscountess Franes, formerly the American Thelma
Morgan. Unfortunately, Thelma was not impressed
with the Prince's somewhat lackadaisical attitude
toward sex, and had an ill-advised fling with Aly Khan,
the rising young playboy.

Mrs. Simpson, who found the young prince very
attentive and fascinated by her, seized her moment and
stepped in, while Ernest Aldrich Simpson, who knew
when he was out-classed, tactfully stepped aside. Not
that it was an easy row to hoe. The prince, according to
at least several sources, was reputed to have the smallest

The Duke and Duchess of Windsor with Elsa Maxwell

reigning penis on the Continent. But love conquered all, some said, with some pretty fancy boudoir work that Wallis had learned in the Orient. Of course, Walker was not privy to any of this, since he was relatively new to the international gossip business.

During the several hours of the conversation, Walker maneuvered delicately to get what information he could, without putting the royal couple on guard or making them hostile. He was, however, able to elicit from the duchess the fact that the reason the Windsors had never returned to England was clearly because of the opposition of Queen Elizabeth, the wife of the duke's brother, George VI. This in itself was enough of a scoop to justify the whole trip. But as he was taking his leave, being escorted to the gate by Capt. Drury, he was shocked when the royal couple's equerry said to him in a leisurely British drawl: "Of course you know, you can't *quote* His Highness."

Walker left in a state of shock, and all the way back on the plane to Miami he pondered the situation. The contact was an extremely valuable one. On the other hand, what was the use of such a contact if he couldn't report the news? Finally, he hit on what he thought was a brilliant way of handling the matter. He wrote up the story in the form of a monologue in which he himself did all the talking, but in which it would be obvious that his conversation was based on what the duke had personally said. At the very end, he put in a disclaimer that he hoped would cover the situation: "I have enjoyed this visit very much," he quoted himself as saying, "and next time, I hope to get permission to *quote* Your Highness."

The editors of the *News* were pleased with the column. The *News* was then running all three of its major Broadway columns, Sullivan, Walker and John Chapman's, side by side on the Monday page. This page had no advertising, but each Monday, one of the columns had to sacrifice some of its space for a strange little feature still appearing in the *News* called "Ching Chow Says . . .," a cartoon of a pigtailed Chinaman uttering an abstruse piece of Oriental philosophy, which some believe to be in the paper as a tip-off to the next day's number. The cartoon took up about half a paragraph of space. When Walker air-mailed his column to the *News*, he underlined his instructions to the managing editor that the copy go in exactly as he had written it, particularly the last paragraph. But when he picked up his copy of the *News* in Miami that Monday, he was shocked to find that the last paragraph, his explanatory tag about not quoting the Duke, had been preempted by Ching Chow. Furthermore, his column was somewhat put in the shade by a big story on page 3, the important news page, about the Duchess of Windsor, in which two female reporters stated unequivocally that the duchess had visited Miami the previous week under the pretext of getting an impacted wisdom tooth treated, but had actually gone to get her face lifted. This Walker knew for a fact not to be true. Remembering how he had sat for two solid hours facing the woman a matter of inches away in brilliant tropical sunlight, he would have sworn on a stack of Bibles there were no scars or evidence of any facial operation. But the editors of the *News* brushed off his protests with the explanation that their story came directly from the plastic surgeon who claimed to have performed the operation, and that was that. Obviously, there was no way that they were going to over-research a good story.

Walker was beginning to learn the ropes. What mattered in the world of scandal and gossip was getting there first with the best tidbits about the most important people, in a way that at least *seemed* credible. He also found that there was a world of people in New York who would fawn upon him and flatter him and give him the red-carpet treatment for only one purpose—*publicity*. In the immortal words of Jimmy Durante: "Everybody wants to get into the act."

"Romance for publicity, marriage for publicity, murder for publicity—yes, even suicide for publicity," Walker wrote. "In too many cases, suicide is the result of the exhibitionist. The man who sits on a sixteenth-story window ledge threatening for two hours to jump, while crowds gape at him from below, is enjoying the front-page stories he is going to make before, instead of after, the fact. Many a disconsolate dame takes the precaution of phoning friends after swallowing a lethal dose of sleeping pills, far enough in advance to be rescued in time for the next editions, possibly hoping that the publicity will net her a movie contract.''

While Walker didn't have the syndication that Winchell and many of his colleagues had, he still was columnist for the largest paper in America—in command of a circulation of two million readers. Publicists estimated that each line in his column was worth about a thousand dollars to them.

''A Broadway columnist,'' Walker wrote after some years on the job, ''has in the public eye become a rather legendary figure who's supposed to prowl the nightclubs until dawn in the company of a gorgeous blonde, sleep all day, and by some sleight-of-hand trick get a daily column written. To many he is a composite of a prophet, private eye, father confessor, trained seal, unemployment agency, unpaid promotional mouthpiece, and an instrument for award or personal vengeance, whose power to make or break is so great that his opinions are eagerly sought after—and bought, if possible.

''Actually, he is only a free-lance reporter with a special beat—the world. His column is, in effect, a one-man newspaper, of which he is both reporter and editor, working within the framework of his particular publication and subject to its policies. (A caveat ignored by some, Winchell in particular.) Anything that is newsworthy rates space in his column, whether it concerns entertainment, vital statistics, politics, or crime. But whatever he prints must be fresh news, exclusively his and he is working in a fiercely competitive field. It is the proper function of a Broadway column to *print* hearsay—news before the fact and straws in the wind. Often the course of events has been altered by the mere appearance of a tip-off in a Broadway column: the situation was correctly forecast *at the time.*"

(Actually some people estimated that a Winchell scoop on the Duke and Duchess of Windsor, in which he hinted that the duke was about to abdicate for the woman he loved, inspired British newspapers, which had been timid about discussing this delicate subject earlier, to bombard the duke with questions and actually push him over the line in making this important decision.)

Walker felt even more than some of the other columnists that his beat should extend into the international area, especially during the war crisis which was clearly approaching. "Broadway columns, I believe, more nearly reflect the public's taste than anything published in a newspaper, and generally speaking, are far more potent than the editorial pages. Many newspaper readers turn first to the Broadway columns and many of them read nothing else in the paper.

"Merely because a column is headed 'Broadway' is no reason for not scooping the Washington columns months in advance concerning, for example, a Chief Justice's resignation from the Supreme Court. Franklin Roosevelt, the most publicity conscious president we ever had, was an avid reader of the Broadway columns himself and deliberately used them as a sounding board of public opinion."

Walker felt in the pre-World War II period that it had become just as important to report what was going on in Europe and Asia as who was romancing whom in the Stork Club. Certainly it was true that his column and many others paid more and more attention to such cosmic events, and his work was certainly highly appreciated in some fields. In a compendium called *The Columnists,* published in 1944, a writer named Charles Fisher said: "The easy off-handed familiarity with which Danton Walker handles the names of the great, reads their minds and outlines their futures has a paralyzing quality which sometimes make the Messrs. Winchell and Lyons look like diffident amateurs."

The power and privileges of the Broadway columnists

offered many temptations: "Do we get offers of tips on horses, or the market—or of intimate favors from *artistes*? B-r-o-t-h-e-r! St. Anthony himself was never more tempted, nor in as many forms. A space-peddling columnist can pay off the butcher, the baker, the land-lord and the furrier—for the little woman's mink—but not many of them do," Walker wrote.

Walker's brashness, his somewhat snooty attitude, and perhaps his unwillingness to kowtow as abjectly to Winchell as the senior columnist would have preferred soon resulted in open warfare between the two colum-nists. Danton Walker was added to the ever-lengthening list of Winchell enemies. "Winchell and Walker are not pals," Fisher wrote in his book *The Columnists*, "and the cutting references they make to one another are presumed to keep Broadway and the distant clients in a dither." Not that Walker had that many "distant clients," since he only appeared in about a dozen paper aside from the *News*.

Shortly after Walker's column started, O. O. Mc-Intyre, the dean of Broadway columnists and until then Winchell's chief nemesis, died in 1938, and Winchell became the undisputed leader of the field and most syndicated of all columnists.

Meanwhile, Ed Sullivan soon discovered that the hills of Hollywood held no allure for him like the canyons of New York, and began to pester his editors to be returned to the bright lights of Broadway. Twice Capt. Patterson suggested that Walker switch with Sullivan and allow him to return to New York while taking on the Hollywood assignment himself. But Walker de-clined on the premise that he had not really established his position on Broadway and would be considerably weakened transferring himself at that point to the West Coast. Finally, after several years of dithering, a satisfactory switch was arranged for the moment. John Chapman took over Sullivan's stint, while Sullivan returned to Broadway, picking up where he had left off, except that his column was now called "Little Old New York."

"Since it was about the same people, places and things covered by my column, 'Broadway,' there was bound to be a conflict," Walker observed.

Time magazine considered the situation novel—a newspaper pitting one columnist against another, possibly to divide their power. But the probable reason for the policy was not to divide the power, but to double up their big guns against the competition. By now, every New York paper had at least one Broadway columnist, except the *New York Times*. Even the subdued and rather elegant *Herald Tribune* had assigned Hy Gardner to cover that area in a fashion as suitable as possible to their relatively conservative format. And now the stage was set for the entry of one of the most controversial and dramatic members of that flashy fraternity— America's first *female* Broadway columnist, Dorothy Kilgallen.

21.

In 1938, O. O. McIntyre, the dean of Broadway columnists, died, and his column "O. O. McIntyre's New York Letter," a highly successful effort, syndicated by some seven hundred papers, died with him. Louis Sobol, who had been doing his "Voice of Broadway" as sort of the second-string New York columnist, was moved into McIntyre's spot, and told to do a more general column as McIntyre did, rather than the many-itemed gossip column he had been doing before. Louis was regarded as one of the sweetest guys on Broadway, but certainly didn't have the venom and drive that were needed to make a vivid impression on that hard-hearted street.

At first, Sobol's former column, "The Voice of Broadway" was dropped altogether for several months. But the advertisers, nightclubs and restaurants who depended on the constant mentions in the typical gossip column finally applied so much pressure that the *Journal* decided to give in and called in Dorothy Kilgallen, who had been doing a brilliant job as a reporter, and had recently covered the coronation of George VI in England, to take over the "Voice of Broadway."

Sobol described her debut in a *Journal* feature story:

"At 25, Jimmy Kilgallen's little girl had moved into the esoteric circle dominated by the male sex. Walter Winchell, Ed Sullivan, Danton Walker, Lucius Beebe, Leonard Lyons—and of course this reporter.

"It was a new world for her. Heretofore her cast of characters had consisted of men and women on trial for murder, arson, political chicanery; of state and national dignitaries . . .

"As a Broadway columnist this slender, wide-eyed, deceivingly naive in attitude and soft-spoken mannerisms female reporter was to find herself mingling with a new set of characters. Under her columnar microscope queer little bugs twisted and crawled— racket guys, grifters, phonies, creep janes, society fops, chorus girls, pimps, overdressed jezebels and their rent-payers. Her daily copy was to bristle too with names like Tommy Manville, Billy Rose, Brenda Frazier, Prince Serge Obolensky, Elsa Maxwell, Dan and Bob Topping, Peggy Joyce . . ."

According to Sobol, Kilgallen, despite her extensive background as a reporter, was still a bit shy with these celebrity types and prudish concerning their habits, and even a bit awed by the famous names with whom she came in contact. But in a few short years, Kilgallen herself was to become a celebrity, along with the rest of them. In fact, Dorothy arrived just in time for the dawning of a new era, the café society era.

Oddly, she told an interviewer some years later that she had not been even interested or favorably inclined toward this sort of thing. Leo P. Wobido, a Jesuit priest, wrote in a Catholic magazine called *The Queen's Work*:

"One of her pet peeves was chatter columns, and she positively resented her boss's proposal that she take over the *Journal*'s Broadway column . . . She thought to herself as she turned in her sample stint, 'Well here's the column that will end all Broadway columns.' "

The town was full of excitement due to the hype for the New York World's Fair which was to open the following year. There was frantic activity, as if in anticipation of the war that was clearly on the horizon, in the fifty or more top-rated expensive nightclubs functioning in downtown Manhattan. As Lee Israel, Kilgallen's biographer, put it, "Each of these places had a press agent; each of the press agents beat the drum for his unique attraction. The Stork Club had special dollar debutante lunches. Sarita was charming snakes at the

Onyx Room. Brenda Frazier, the most celebrated debutante of the time, whose fan mail exceeded in quantity that of most Hollywood stars, was in the snakelike conga line at La Conga. The Arthur Murray Dancers were demonstrating the Lambeth Walk at the Savoy . . . there were acrobats flying from the tabletops, balloon nights, performing seals, society singers, rhumba bands, swing music, and a profusion of celebrities who helped pull in the paying customers.''

Swirling around in all this social broth were politicians, models, actors, debutantes and the rich who had previously stayed at home and enjoyed their social life in private. Now somehow they were all anxious to have their pictures taken at El Morocco, the Rainbow Room and the Stork Club. As Miss Israel put it, ''Without the Broadway column, the town would have been all dressed up with no place to go.''

Despite her demure appearance, Dorothy was no stranger to these purlieus. By the time she got the job as The Voice of Broadway she had been seen out in the nightclubs almost every night with an endless stream of eager swains. She knew a lot of the people who would become sources for these columns she now had to do—the debutantes and lounge lizards whom she ultimately designated in her column as ''the East Side crowd'' and the ''lunch bunch.''

The important thing to the bunch at the *Journal* was that Dorothy's writing had enough snap and bite to it that she had at least a chance of becoming a competitor of Walter Winchell's—something the rest of what he called his ''imitators'' had not quite succeeded in doing. The Hearst ballyhooers splashed her piquant though notoriously chinless photo across the front pages and touted their new acquisition. Dorothy Kilgallen: THE FIRST AND ONLY WOMAN BROADWAY COLUMNIST.

Contrary to her statements to the Jesuit priest, Dorothy seemed to love her glamorous new job, and had an endless supply of escorts and lady friends who trailed around with her on her rounds, delightedly gobbl-

Dorothy Kilgallen, "The Voice of Broadway"

Lee Mortimer
of the Sunday *Mirror*

Louella Parsons, queen
of the Hollywood gossips

ing up the freeload food and drink. "We would all have a beautiful dinner, a marvelous table," Rosemary Cox, one of her socialite companions remembered, "and there'd be no bill. We were freeloading. But we all liked her."

With her friends, Dorothy was cheerful, generous and surprisingly gentle. But her columns were another thing. She showed a tart enough tongue and a vicious enough vision to be the first of the new columnists to really give Winchell a run for his money.

22.

Kilgallen had barely found her bearings in the Big Apple when Winchell dazzled the street with some of his typical flash and filigree involving a mob member named Louie "Lepke" Buchalter. His was a dread name in New York. Lepke was deeply involved in narcotics, industrial extortion—and murder. He sat on the board of the national Syndicate which was a melding of the leadership of the dominant Italian and Jewish gangsters of the country. When Thomas E. Dewey began his racket-busting career in the late thirties, Lepke's was one of the prize scalps he sought.

Lepke got the word that Dewey was on his trail, and disappeared from the scene. For two years, he strolled around the New York streets undetected by Dewey's investigators, disguised only by some added weight and a mustache. In August 1939, Dewey, frustrated, tagged Lepke as "probably the most dangerous criminal in the United States" and put out an open call for his capture. To squeeze information from many rats that may have been willing to squeal, Dewey even put up a $25,000 reward for Lepke's capture dead or alive.

Gradually the heat on Lepke and other internal problems in the Syndicate caused many of his best friends, such as Meyer Lansky, Albert Anastasia and Bugsy Siegel, to feel that he was too hot to have for a friend. The word spread through the mob that Lep was kill-crazy and nervous, and even those who had no legitimate reason to be worried felt threatened. Lansky passed the word to the law enforcement people that a deal might be made for Lepke. He could be turned over to the feds and put away on a narcotics rap. Then when the time was ripe, he could be sprung. He might be through as a racketeer, but he had stashed away plenty of loot and would not starve. Big Albert Anastasia felt the answer should have been the one Dutch Schultz offered back in '35—to knock off Dewey himself.

Meanwhile, the boys in the mob put their idea to Lepke, and this aroused fear in him. Lepke knew very well the unwritten law that any man can get hit if he does not cooperate for the good of the organization. Lansky had enough clout with the Syndicate to order Lepke put to death if he didn't play ball. As Lepke hesitated, Lansky, at the right moment, sent in one of his prime killers, Dimples Wolensky, with his newest bright idea. A deal could be made with J. Edgar Hoover. Hoover would guarantee Lepke would remain in federal custody and his cooperation would be taken into account if he were convicted on the narcotics rap. Hoover, with no small thanks to publicity garnered from Winchell and the other Broadway columnists, by now had a big national reputation. While his forte was hardly organized crime—in fact he denied that there even was such a thing—Hoover was by now a national hero.

Lepke reasoned that if you couldn't trust Hoover, you couldn't trust anybody. According to crime reporter Hank Messick, a deal was worked out with the FBI, different from the one that became public shortly thereafter. Louis S. Rosenstiel, an important liquor industry executive who was a friend both of the mobsters with whom he had associated when he was a bootlegger and of J. Edgar Hoover—he founded the J. Edgar Hoover Foundation and made large contributions to it—was the go-between who made arrangements to surrender Lepke. The deal was that the FBI promised that Lepke would not be turned over to New York State. According to Messick, Hoover never learned of this deal, but the high-ranking aide who made the deal with Rosenstiel was later given a top job in the liquor business lobby in Washington.

Winchell, realizing the drama of the fact that Lepke

174

had been named America's most dangerous criminal, had been broadcasting appeals for him to surrender for several weeks by this time. On August 21, 1939 a phone call came to Winchell at the Stork Club, and an authentic-sounding voice that made Winchell's heart leap into his throat said simply, "Lepke wants to come in."

When he caught his breath, Winchell asked, "Does he trust me?"

"Yes."

"Okay," Winchell said, "I'll get in touch with Hoover."

Winchell hung up and called the FBI director in Washington. Hoover agreed that he would give Lepke asylum in a federal prison and hopped right on a plane for New York. But then the whole deal stalled for two weeks. Lepke's agent kept calling Winchell and making excuses, and Hoover grew impatient and irritated, even with his best pal Winchell.

"Here he is, the biggest hot air artist in town," Hoover remarked bitterly to Winchell.

There was another phone call, and this time Winchell laid down the law, what with the heat he was getting from Hoover.

"If Lepke doesn't surrender by four o'clock tomorrow afternoon," he warned, "Hoover says no consideration of any kind will ever be given him."

Six o'clock the following evening, Lepke's go-between phoned. Buchalter would surrender himself, but only if Winchell were present.

"Why me?"

"If he's with you, he knows they won't start shooting."

Winchell turned to Irving Hoffman, the press agent who was his close friend and major contributor. "Come along with me," Winchell urged.

"Hell, no," said the nearsighted and nervous press agent. "I'm a coward. Besides, I'm so blind I couldn't tell if it was Lepke anyway."

The Lepke henchman now told Winchell to get a borrowed car and drive to a Yonkers theater. When he arrived there, a stranger stepped out of the bushes and told Winchell to drive to 19th Street and Eighth Avenue. Here still another stranger entered the car and told Winchell that he should telephone Hoover with instructions to wait at 28th Street and Fifth Avenue between 10:10 and 10:20. One of Winchell's guides now took the wheel of the car and drove to a spot near Madison Square. Before he stepped out, he handed Winchell a *mezuzah*, a metal-encased religious symbol which is sometimes fastened to the doorways of jewish households.

"When you see him (Lepke)," he said, "give him this."

Winchell nodded his agreement. A few seconds later, a man in dark glasses stepped out of an alleyway, hurried up to the car, took off the dark glasses he was wearing and threw them into the street, and climbed in. Winchell instantly recognized his old acquaintance, Louis Lepke Buchalter. When Lepke gave him the nod, Winchell sped off to the corner where Hoover and his ever-present sidekick Clyde Tolson were waiting. Winchell stepped out of the car and walked over to where the two men were waiting. (Some people later said Hoover was alone, but this was not the case.)

"Mr. Hoover," Winchell said, "this is Lepke."

"Glad to meet you," Lepke said, somewhat untruthfully.

"Let's go."

Naturally, the Buchalter adventure made major headlines, and by some strange happenstance the timing of the capture coincided exactly with the *Daily Mirror*'s deadline. If Winchell had anything to do with that, who could criticize him? After all, he was a newspaper man first and a law enforcement agent second.

In any event, the nationally publicized capture was a feather in the cap for everybody. A major criminal was caught, Hoover got his publicity, and Winchell got his. Even Tom Dewey was satisfied, although he did not get his hands on the noted gangster. At least, his focusing the limelight on him had resulted in his capture.

But this was to be almost the last involvement with

major crime figures for Winchell. The signs were getting ever closer that a war was in the offing with Nazi Germany, as well as Japan, and for the next few years, Winchell trained his sights as much on national politics as they were on gossip—some say with considerable prompting from FDR's close colleagues in Washington.

23.

With the appointment of Dorothy Kilgallen, the entire cast of the columnist corps was complete. There were to be only minor revisions to the clique—if a group so disparate and so constantly at war with one another could be called a clique—until the great gossip era had ended. The canonization of the elite group of Broadway scribes was assured by the naming of a sandwich for Dorothy Kilgallen. She was the fifth Broadway columnist to be granted this meaty accolade. At $1.10, the Dorothy Kilgallen was the most expensive sandwich on the Reuben's menu, probably in deference to her status as the only distaff member of the tribe. The others, in descending order, were the Walter Winchell, 90 cents, the Ed Sullivan, 85 cents, the Danton Walker, 85 cents and the Louis Sobol, 60 cents. Oddly enough, with the exception of Kilgallen's sandwich being more expensive than Winchell's, the order of precedence was roughly the order of influence that the columnists had at that time.

Leo Lindeman of Lindy's famous restaurant was also given to naming sandwiches for celebrities. In honor of J. Edgar Hoover who often visited in the wee morning hours with Walter Winchell, Lindy named Hoover's favorite sandwich—raw chopped meat with condiments, a variation of steak tartare—after the FBI chief. Until the old Lindy's folded, it was still on the fare as a "G-Man Sandwich." After breakfast, Lindy often would try to take some of his guests along for some small entertainment. Frequently he would take Hoover, Marlene Dietrich, Doris Day or Jerry Lewis to the penny arcade next door where they would play a few

178

sets of ping pong.

Kilgallen, very shortly after she started "The Voice of Broadway," became recognized as the number two gossip power in the city. She alone had the ability to emulate Winchell's racy style and the toughness to strike about with her gall-laced verbiage regardless of where the whiplash fell. Therein she had the secret of success as laid down by the master, Winchell.

It was the dawning of the era of café society, and it was from café society that these gossip columnists earned their daily bread. According to Lee Israel, the biographer of Dorothy Kilgallen, "Café society was a *shiddoch* (marriage) between the rich and the restaurants, a co-mingling therein right out in public, of old wealth and new money, and both of them with the talented, the exceptionally amusing, the extraordinarily attractive."

Edith Wharton, in describing the changes that were taking place in this Roosevelt New Deal era, wrote:

"Though my parents were much invited and extremely hospitable, the tempo of New York society was so moderate that not infrequently they remained at home in the evening . . . The New York of those days was a place in which external events were few and unexciting, and little girls were mostly to 'be happy and building at home.' "

According to *Fortune* magazine, which occupied itself with the subject, the blooming of café society was cued to a third generation of wealth which was finally bored with Newport and to the rise of high grade speakeasies in the twenties, all of which ultimately evolved into the posh nightclubs of the thirties. *Fortune* also blamed the Depression, and claimed that the days of hunger marches and breadlines made elaborate dinner dances in the great houses "vulgar, if not dangerous ostentation." The rich decided, *Fortune* concluded, to entertain on their Long Island estates far from the madding crowd, or less elaborately in public hotels and restaurants. "And thus slowly, compounded of many different elements, at the outset unconscious of its own development in the obtrusive presence of noisier events, café society was born," *Fortune* concluded.

The poor, the discouraged and the downtrodden seemed to enjoy being exposed to the foibles of the rich, the giddy, the degenerate. Jerome Zerbe, former publicist at El Morocco and later a prominent society photographer, described the people he photographed this way: "These were the people whose houses, one knew, were filled with treasures. These were the women who dressed the best. These were the dream people that we all looked up to and hoped that we or our friends would sometimes know and be like."

Mary Anita Loos, the niece of the Anita Loos who wrote *Gentlemen Prefer Blondes*, got a job as press agent for one of the posh clubs at the time, Fefe's Monte Carlo. She was a close friend of Kilgallen's and in writing about her caught the feeling of the time:

"It was one of those heedless, luxury-glutted times that usually happens before a disaster. We were rushing headlong into war. Everything was excessive. Glamour was the word. Everyone was competing to be glamorous. And newspaper people, especially, were treated like royalty."

What Dorothy did, which was unique, was to fashion herself into a glamour girl. She was the first newspaper woman to put on her dancing shoes and get around with various escorts and *make* a personality out of herself. If she had been a little younger, she undoubtedly would have had facial work done and corrected her weak chin. She had a very good figure, marvelous black, curly Irish hair, beautiful eyes and a startling complexion.

She became, in a sense, the pulse of café society. Most of the society editors were older and most of them were gay. (The most influential and daring at the time wrote under the name of Cholly Knickerbocker in the *Journal-American*. He in actuality was a newspaper man named Maury Paul. The other columnist who oc-

180

cupied himself mainly with society was Lucius Beebe.) She was young and she was fresh. She'd accrued a certain amount of prestige and publicity on account of her news coverage for Hearst. When she got into writing her column, she ran with and reported on the younger people. To some extent, she was accepted by them. And she mixed café society, society, and show business—which was the first time that was done. To the extent that she dealt more with the newer names and the fresher ones, Dorothy was able to score a jump even on her principal rival Winchell and certainly on Lyons, Sobol and Wilson.

It was a time when names that seemed to have been invented only for their activities on the café scene were becoming common. Among the socialites, Brenda Diana Duff Frazier was certainly the most commonly talked about, and to some extent the most legitimate, in that she had a genuine society background and was heiress to a three and a half million dollar fortune. "Heiresses" could be anything from genuine socialites to mobster's molls like Virginia Hill, who was first mentioned in the columns as a prominent "ham heiress." This was the same Virginia Hill who later told a Congressional committee that she attributed her unwonted popularity with famous mobsters to the fact that she was "the best cocksucker in the world."

Other socialites prominently mentioned in the columns were Cobina Wright, Jr. and Lenore Lemmon.

Kilgallen moved easily among these frothy young creatures and developed her own contacts, to which generally speaking the other columnists were not privy. Meanwhile, Winchell increasingly disdained the café society scene in favor of his new hobbyhorse, the political scene. He became embroiled in a vicious verbal shootout with Charles Lindbergh, about whom he had written so feelingly during the kidnapping episode. Winchell now used his full energies to discredit the onetime hero, because of his public statements that England could not win against Hitler. When the actual fighting began in Europe, Winchell became even more involved and stepped up his personal war against isolationists.

He had become a really important ally for the Roosevelt administration not only in combatting isolationists, but in sampling public opinion on future measures. In 1940, when Roosevelt was contemplating running for a third term, Ernest Cuneo, who had become the President's contact with Winchell, came to New York and said to him, "Run an item on the air that Roosevelt is considering a third term."

Winchell did so. The next week, Cuneo suggested, "Run that item about the third term again."

Winchell complied again. Three weeks later, Cuneo made the same request. "Jesus, Ernie, I'll sound like a stuck record!" Winchell protested.

"Don't worry," Cuneo reassured him. "Run it."

Three weeks later Cuneo came back to Winchell and gave him one of the great exclusives of all time: "Now you can broadcast the third term campaign as a fact."

White House advisors had been using the Winchell broadcast to check public reaction and when the mail that had come into the White House, stimulated by the broadcasts, proved overwhelmingly in favor, Roosevelt became convinced to seek the presidency once more.

Winchell's increasingly vociferous pro-war and pro-Roosevelt campaign began to seriously irritate William Randolph Hearst, who was against both now, although he had been pro-Roosevelt in the beginning. (By this time Winchell's combined radio and newspaper audience exceeded fifty million, according to various pollsters. By that year also, he was estimated to be the highest-salaried American with an annual income in excess of $800,000.)

Winchell's campaign against the isolationists and his diatribes against the pro-Hitlerites earned him plenty of enemies and made his sponsor, the Andrew Jergens Company ("with lotions of love") worried about their $5,000-a-week hotshot. They tried to curb Winchell's heated attacks on Nazis and isolationists, but Winchell refused. The power he wielded on the radio audience could be demonstrated when in 1945 Winchell advised listeners to sell stocks so they would not be stuck when the crash that he expected came. Apparently based on this single radio item, the market broke. Winchell himself was shocked by the effect and decided that he should be a bit more cautious about his financial prognostications in the future.

On the positive side, that year he was the originator of the Damon Runyon Cancer Fund, and in the first year collected $5 million for cancer research. The fund is still going strong.

Sullivan, his constant rival, in the same year tried to compete with the Heart Fund, which was a worthy cause, too, but never reached the financial successes of Winchell's Damon Runyon Fund.

Despite Jergens' worries about Winchell's forthright stands, it stood behind him and in fact gave him a 50 percent raise from $5,000 to $7,500 a week. Subsequent sponsors, Kaiser-Frazer and Richard Hudnut, added $12,500 to his weekly take, bringing him up to $1,000 a minute, which was the highest compensation ever paid on radio.

Once the United States was in the war, Winchell didn't let up in his enthusiasm for our role in that giant conflict. Abe Lastfogel, Marvin Schenck and Howard Dietz took up an idea started by Winchell and staged a Navy benefit show in Madison Square Garden. Boxes cost a hefty $1,000 apiece and ordinary seats started at $16.50 each. Sales of ads for the 55-page souvenir program brought in $35,000 alone. This one benefit performance raked in $142,000, an all-time record at the time for any one-shot theatrical performance.

In addition to having the ear of the President, Winchell, as mentioned, was on a first-name basis with America's top cop, J. Edgar Hoover, as well as top underworld figures like Frank Costello. Celebrities were his breakfast cereal and he knew them all, whether their names were found in the Blue Book or on a precinct blotter. Movie stars and industrial czars sought his favor, and models and show girls were thrilled at his invitation to dance the foxtrot that was named for him, "I

Want to Be in Winchell's Colyumn, la-de-da-da-de-da-da . . .'' The ultimate honor for an associate was to spend the hours before dawn with Winchell playing cops and robbers by chasing down police calls in his custom Ford which was equipped with an official police two-way radio.

"In the pre-war days around the Stork, Winchell was the most exciting man in the world to us," a middle-aged matron who had grown up in Billingsley's posh playpen commented. "When I first began dating the man I later married, Winchell said we were 'closer-thanthis.' When we married, he called it 'a slight case of merger' and when I became pregnant, he said we were 'infanticipating.' When the baby arrived, he noted that we had joined 'the mom-and-population.'

"When the marriage soured, W. W. told the world we had 'the Mr. and miseries' which quickly developed into 'the apartache' which led to our 'sharing separate teepees.' It was only a matter of time until we 'Renovated' and disappeared from the columns as though we had never existed.

"Strange as it seems, we got a great sense of importance out of being recorded by Winchell in this fashion."

Although the five leading columnists and their lesser colleagues often maintained a public air of cameraderie and friendship, they were all extremely thin-skinned and had a tendency to turn the slightest abrasion into a major feud.

Hy Gardner, who wrote a quiet little column on the *Tribune*, commented, "The competition for the grist necessary to such an elaborate mill does not breed love and brotherhood among the columnists. Their demeanor toward one another at feeding time, which is quite late in the evening, may have a superficial cordiality. But underneath is the spirit of a number of very hungry intimates of a very crowded zoo awaiting a very small piece of meat."

Of course, columnists were not the only people that were thin-skinned, and on occasion—though rarely—a

Broadway scribbler would feel the brunt of his own effusions.

Winchell at one point was strolling from table to table, making his rounds at Lindy's, one of the late-night spots frequented by columnists after the nightclubs had closed.

A tall buxom woman entered the restaurant and walked directly up to the columnist from behind. She spun him around on his heels. Winchell stared at her, flabbergasted and a bit frightened.

"Winchell, do you know me?"

"What the hell . . . ?"

"You don't know me, do you?"

"All right, so I don't know you. So what?"

"So this," she said, swinging a lively right hand and slapping him in the face with all her might.

Winchell rocked back on his heels and stood there, gaping at her, stunned.

The woman turned on her heel and left.

Leo Lindeman, the owner of the restaurant, rushed over, deeply upset. "Walter, I like you. You're a nice boy. But I told you I'll have absolutely no fighting in my establishment."

"Who is she?" Winchell muttered.

"That's Nita Naldi," someone said who witnessed the event. Naldi had been the heroine, some years previously, of some of Rudolph Valentino's best pictures. Suddenly Walter remembered. He had written not long before that Nita Naldi was broken down and living in a sanitarium in France, and had hinted that furthermore she was taking dope.

"Jeez," Winchell mumbled, rubbing his reddened cheek, "I'm lucky she didn't kill me. I'll get that bitch."

It was about this time that Winchell, at the peak of his powers, according to his own memoirs, was approached by big boss Ed Flynn of the Bronx, then national chairman of the Democratic Party, and asked via Sherman Billingsley whether he would consider running for Congress. At first Winchell didn't believe that the message passed to him was true.

"Sherm," he said to Billingsley, "you're making wiz me zee joke, no?"

"It's no joke," Billingsley said. "Flynn asked me to ask you. He's the most powerful politician in town, you know that."

"Guarantee it?"

"Flynn said you couldn't possibly lose. He has this town sewed up."

"You mean they don't count the votes for the other fellow? Please tell Mr. Flynn I said thanks for the compliment, but I do not prefer politics to the newspaper craft."

Winchell was understandably cynical: "I've known too many politicians who stay in office taking orders from Murder, Inc., what is left of the Capone mob and other gangsters."

Winchell, however, made no mention of the person who had the most influence with the Democratic Party and was a frequent contributor to its coffers, Frank Costello, to whom he remained loyal throughout his career.

Robert Sylvester, a part-time Broadway columnist, estimated that the theater of war in which most encounters involving the Broadway columnists took place was basically confined to a group of about three restaurants in midtown Manhattan—Vincent Sardi's, Toots Shor's and Jim (Dinty) Moore's, plus two nightclubs, Sherman Billingsley's Stork Club and John Perona's El Morocco. "Within these unhallowed walls," Sylvester commented, "was a café society born and nourished. Here social and professional reputations were made and broken. Here came the debutantes who would be tomorrow's social leaders. Here came the princes and aristocracy from far-off lands. Here came the post-college young men who would soon take over dad's big business.

"And here to sort them out, were two men without education or social background of any kind—except, perhaps of the suspicious kind—each of whom sat near a guarded door at the entrance of his establishment and decided, on reason or whim, which applicant was 'fit' to enter. The applicant admitted on any given night may be a no-account loafer who just happened to have the right friends, and the applicant denied might just as easily be a pillar of his community and the trustee of ancient wealth.''

Though they had these elements of snobbism in common, Sylvester noted, ''the confusing truth . . . is that there could not have been two nightclubs more dissimilar than the Stork and Morocco.'' The dawning era of café society furnished a perfect arena for the success of both of these social arbiters and arena is the operative word, in view of the elaborate fisticuffs which periodically brought both of them to the attention of the general public.

24.

"Walter made me a multimillionaire after his first column plug," Sherman Billingsley told Bob Thomas, Winchell's biographer, and if anybody should have known, it was Sherman. For over two decades, Winchell laid down a barrage of publicity that made the Stork Club the most famous nightclub in America. "Such treatment held the promise of enormous profits for Sherman Billingsley, and he was the kind of man to take advantage," Thomas observed.

The Stork Club's Cub Room, of course, was the center of the "Winchell news service" which was centered on Table 50, Winchell's office and throne. For more than thirty years the columnist held court there and a fascinating throng of people would pass through, stopping by to pass Winchell news or exchange jokes. Many of them were the leading newsmakers of the era.

Grace Kelly told Winchell about her engagement to Prince Rainier in the Cub Room. Lana Turner and Artie Shaw announced their divorce there. Clark Gable was there with two of his wives, and Elizabeth Taylor with four of her husbands.

Ernest Hemingway told Winchell that after a two-hour dinner discussion with Spencer Tracy, one quotable line emerged. It was Tracy's: "Sometimes I think life is a terminal illness." (Hemingway evidently agreed, in view of his later actions.)

John Steinbeck approached Winchell there one night to congratulate him on his stand on intervention in the European conflict. "We all think you are doing a fine job for your country. Don't stop. Your enemies are the enemies of your country."

Winchell once wrote an item about Joseph P. Kennedy when he was still a favorite of the New Deal. The item said, "A top New Dealer's mistress is a mobster's widow." The street knew that the "top New Dealer" was Kennedy who was then SEC Commissioner. Kennedy handled the matter in his own way. He was a good friend and business associate of Winchell's close friend, Frank Costello, with whom he shared the import license for Ambassador Scotch. Through Costello, Kennedy reached Winchell. The father of Jack Kennedy was every bit as much of a swordsman as his son was later revealed to be. If there were going to be many blind items like that, his political future could be ruined. He persuaded Winchell to lay off in return for feeding him inside dope from the administration. After that Winchell never even commented on Kennedy's famous association with actress Gloria Swanson.

Winchell's wide acquaintanceship and numerous eager informants enabled him to accumulate enormous stores of secrets about the famous and infamous and to make some startlingly accurate guesses. He would keep the crowd that gathered around Table 50 fascinated by recounting unpublishable sex stories about the great and near-great. One of his unpublished stories concerned the little known fact that Dorothy Schiff, publisher of the *Post*, was carrying on an intimate affair with Franklin D. Roosevelt. According to one biographer, Winchell appeared to have a salacious anecdote about every prominent personality in contemporary America. The Stork Club phenomenon was actually a blend of Winchell power and Billingsley's extravagance, snobbery and sensuality. People came there to see and be seen. Billingsley once commented, "I found that a flock of celebrities made a café popular. People will pay more to look at each other than for food, drink and service."

By the late thirties, the Stork Club was an internationally recognized institution. You could look around the Cub Room and see Randolph Churchill, the Duke and Duchess of Windsor, Franklin Roosevelt, Jr., the aforementioned Joseph P. Kennedy, King Peter of

Yugoslavia, Lord Beaverbrook, the Shah of Iran, Winchell's close friend J. Edgar Hoover, Bernard Baruch, Jim Farley, and Andrei Gromyko, plus a galaxy of stars from the show business and sports worlds as well as the bright eager young faces of the preppies and debutantes who Billingsley encouraged on the theory that they would grow into company presidents and big-spending playboys. Billingsley also was aware that the presence of a pretty young face did almost as much to dress up the room as that of a well-known celebrity.

Herman Klurfeld, who became at an early age one of Winchell's only paid contributors, remembers vividly his first visit to Winchell at the Stork. The columnist was sitting at the table with the dramatically striking actress, Tallulah Bankhead.

"Lovely she was, but after more than a few drinks she was at her brassy, bitchy best," Klurfeld wrote.

"After shaking hands with me, she gushed, 'Glad to meet you, Herman,' then paused and added, 'Go fuck yourself.' "

"Pardon her French," Winchell said, trying to soften the impact of the remark.

Klurfeld also recalls Irving Berlin phoning Winchell at the table to sing to him his latest song in his inimitable raspy baritone. Winchell listened judiciously and then said, "It isn't one of your better ones."

The song was "Easter Parade."

"I remember, too, the melancholy sight of a liquor-soaked Westbrook Pegler being dragged out of the Stork Cub and dumped on the sidewalk while he shouted antiSemitic obscenities," Klurfeld wrote in his biography of Winchell. Pegler's anger with Winchell was part of a continuing feud that persisted for years. Winchell once published an item saying that Pegler and his wife had moved out of New York City because of kidnapping fears. (In fact, Winchell himself after the birth of his son Walter, Jr. in 1935 had moved to a 17-acre estate in Scarsdale, surrounded by a high iron fence, protected by armed guards.) Pegler somehow took the remark as an insult and retorted that the report was untrue. "Winchell could have determined that with one phone call," he said, and went on to call Winchell "a louse in the blouse of journalism." Pegler also added that in his opinion, Winchell was a "gent's room journalist."

The comments naturally deeply offended Winchell. He retorted by giving instruction in his column to his heirs that if he should die first and if a contrite Pegler should attempt to attend his funeral, that journalist should be summarily evicted.

The antiSemitic remarks might have in passing injured Billingsley, who in fact had a policy of allowing only very prominent Jews to attend his club.

A one-time Stork Club employee said that Billingsley had a list of his steady customers with the Jews marked by an X. Whenever Billingsley gave a party at the Stork, he restricted his invitations to no more than thirty percent Jews. Negroes, with rare exceptions, were barred. But Billingsley was clever enough to not broadcast his prejudices. Those close to the Stork knew about them, however, and so did Winchell.

One of his long-time associates, Ernest Cuneo, once said to him, "My God, Walter, how can you be pals with that Billingsley? You love Roosevelt and stick up for the Wagner Act—and he fights the unions. You're an enemy of prejudice—and he hates 'niggers.' You're a Jew—and he's antiSemitic!"

"I know, I know," Walter answered sadly. "But Sherman never lets me see that side of him."

Those who defend Billingsley point out that his snobbery was not necessarily racially motivated. "He just discriminates against poor people," his defenders were fond of saying.

Sherman's prejudices, however, were in the future to affect Winchell's entire career deeply.

After he established his home in Westchester, Winchell seldom visited it, preferring to spend most of his time in the city with his endless series of girlfriends. June, on the other hand, almost never came to the

Stork, which was the center of Winchell's universe. When she did come in, though, she often displayed flashes of her well known quick temper—but never showed any disloyalty in public to Winchell. On the contrary.

One night she was dining at the Stork with a friend when Ed Sullivan came to her table. He tried to convince her that though he was still feuding with her husband he had no grudge against June. Sullivan offered his hand. June spat in it. On another occasion at Table 50, Winchell's wife became bored with all of the gawkers who came and stared at the Winchell table. "I'll give them something to talk about," she said. She picked up an orchid on the table in front of her and proceeded to eat it, to the astonishment of the goggle-eyed tourists.

Although all of the other columnists knew about Winchell's extramarital affairs, and those of Sullivan and certain other columnists, too, there was an unwritten code not to write anything about it. But it was not always honored. Kilgallen once in her column mentioned that Winchell had been seen with an attractive girl.

"Dorothy," Winchell protested to Miss Kilgallen later on, "did you forget I am married?"

"No," Kilgallen answered coolly. "Did you?"

Wilson, who never did betray the columnists' code, described Winchell in the Stork in his heyday: "Writing notes in a bold lefthanded stroke, grabbing a telephone, stirring a drink, or eating a Winchellburger—(as the hamburger was called at the Stork Club in an attempt to boost Winchell's ego) he was the radio and journalistic oracle of the day, and you paid tribute to him when you passed Table 50 . . ."

Wilson also commented on having heard reports that certain tables were tapped or bugged and so were the ladies' and men's rooms, so that Billingsley could eavesdrop on conversations of the customers and pass some of the best tidbits over to Winchell for his column. In view of J. Edgar Hoover's close association with the club and later revelations of how Hoover's FBI *did* use overheard gossip to pressure people such as the late Jean Seberg, who was driven to suicide by gossip reports planted by the FBI, it seems not only likely that the rumors about the bugged tables were true, but that Hoover and his men with their expertise helped to plant them.

Certainly Billingsley was not above spying on his customers—or his help for that matter. One morning after everyone left the Stork Club, Billingsley summoned a crew of workmen in to replace the mirror behind the bar. The looking glass was replaced with a one-way, see-through mirror. Behind it, Billingsley had a movie camera set up, and beside this camera, for weeks on end, a special Billingsley security man sat with a notebook and pad, writing down the pecadilloes of any bartenders who were sticky-fingered or over-generous with the customers.

Once he got the hang of using a one-way mirror, several of those who knew him say that he also from time to time would install these gadgets in the men's and women's rooms to pick up whatever sexual or conversational tidbits that could be gleaned from this lavatorial supervision.

Billingsley encouraged the right people, the sort that made spicy gossip, by a policy that was simultaneously tight-fisted and generous. Although he was never known to spend a cent for paid advertising or publicity, he was extremely generous with souvenirs and gifts to the chosen people. "If I'm having a slow night," Billingsley once told columnist Bob Sylvester, "I start bringing out the gifts with both hands. I send bottles of perfume after bottles of perfume, and instead of a bottle of champagne to good customers I send a magnum. That way when those people go out they are not saying the next day 'Geez, it was slow in the Stork last night.' They're saying 'How does he do it?' I know what I'm doing with the gifts."

In those Depression years one of the most successful stunts offered by Billingsley was to release clusters of

193

balloons, many of which had hundred dollar bills in them, for which the lovely young debutantes and the dignified brokers and lawyers scrambled in a singularly undignified fashion. Other popular gifts were fireman-red suspenders, ties and cigarette lighters.

Another side of Billingsley's nature though, was revealed in his relationship to his help, where he was notoriously tight-fisted, and to his decades-long battle to keep his shop from being unionized. During a hearing over his attempts to beat the union out by the State Labor Relations Board, some of the testimony included a colorful memorandum which Billingsley had sent around to his waiters. It offered a glimpse of Billingsley's attitude toward columnists other than Winchell and other freeloaders. These were Billingsley's instructions:

"Attention to Waiters: When you are serving a house party that does not pay, don't even bother about changing the linen on the table or putting clean napkins or anything else on the table. In other words, save all you possibly can for the house when you're serving parties that do not pay—'cause they cannot kick if they do not pay."

Winchell himself was not shy about admitting the perhaps tarnished benefits of Billingsley's largesse, though he steadfastly denied the constantly reiterated suspicion that he was a part owner of Billingsley's place.

"In almost forty years that I knew Sherman he included me among the many newspaper people and others who could never get a tab . . . His gifts were many—rare liqueurs, Napoleon brandy by the cases. He gave many of us costly suits, via gift certificates to buy a $350 suit at Knize, a swank haberdashery on East 56th Street, New York City," Winchell wrote in his autobiography.

"I learned recently the fee for a suit there is $500, so I guess Knize has lost me . . . Billingsley gave away more costly gifts, souvenirs (sometimes motor cars) and gems purchased at Tiffany's and Cartier's."

Speaking of the sartorial splendor to which Billingsley

194

contributed, Winchell described himself this way: "People who know me well will tell you that I look like a Doll in my set-of-threads. Always in blue: navy blue suits, pale blue shirts, navy blue cravats, blue socks, and Baby-Boo eyes!"

The always-in-blue theme actually had been one of the things that Winchell copied earlier in his career from one of his predecessors, Mark Hellinger.

As time went on, Winchell began to patronize the Stork almost to the exclusion of most of the other nightclubs, with the exception of some of the late-night supping places like Reuben's, Lindy's or Dave's Blue Room. These stops were sandwiched between cruises late at night in his specially equipped police car, generally accompanied by three or four friends (generally press agents and often Damon Runyon), and sometimes celebrities he met in his rounds like Brenda Frazier, the fabulous debutante star of the late Thirties, John Gunther, or other journalists to whom he was anxious to show the "front page" side of his journalistic endeavors.

Generally when the car responded to the scene of police action it would consist only of police checking out a break-in, although once in a while the car would reach the scene of a holdup or a murder in time for Winchell to get what he called "a thrill."

This almost nightly routine was something of a pain to Winchell's friends and so he constantly had to recruit new members for the midnight cruise. Celebrities seldom attended more than once. Myrna Loy fell asleep the time she went. Actually it was possible to sleep in Winchell's police sedan since he seldom used the siren the police had authorized him to sound.

Sometimes, still unable to sleep after his tour of the police beat and the pastrami parlors, he would actually drive back to Westchester to visit his children. Lyons recalled this anecdote: "One morning he left Broadway at sunrise to drive to his Westchester farm. On the outskirts of Harrison, he came upon a group of fifty people, all with binoculars, focused on one spot. Winchell said: 'Reporters' luck, a news beat.' He rushed to the group and asked: 'What happened? How many hurt?' The spokesman assured: 'Nobody's hurt. It's the first yellow bobolink.' Winchell asked: 'What's that?' 'A bird,' was the answer. Winchell said: 'You mean that just to see a bird people will stay up until seven a.m.?' 'Not *stay up* until,' the spokesman corrected. 'We get up *before* seven.' "

Winchell's gratitude for favors was a one-way street. He expected endless thank-yous and servility from those for whom he proffered favors, but he'd be willing to double-cross even his best friend for a news item—and in fact did, if Billingsley can be regarded as his best friend.

Once Sherman was being given a hard time by a married socialite of whom he had once injudiciously become the lover. Unfortunately the socialite didn't seem to want to let go of the well-to-do restaurateur. When he tried to break off the affair, she would supply his newspaper enemy and others with "inside" stuff about his private goings-on. One night in the Cub Room Sherman was in a sullen mood about this lady. "I wish," he sighed to Winchell, "you would print what a tramp she is."

"Now look, Sherman," Winchell objected, "don't involve me in this. You know I don't operate that way."

Sherman was deeply hurt at this rejection by his friend, according to Winchell. He suddenly turned on the columnist and groaned, "Not you too!"

His voice, according to Winchell, was "hysterical and high."

"I just looked at him, astonished no little myself," Winchell wrote. "He had never talked to me that way before in all the four decades of our friendship."

"Just forget it," Billingsley said caustically. "I can get all the other guys [meaning columnists and newspaper execs] to do it for me. I can buy them all for a dime a dozen!"

"Gee, Sherman," Winchell answered, "thanks for not including me in that dozen."

So saying, Winchell got up and left. It was the beginning of a major rift between the two old friends. On this occasion, he stayed away from the Stork Club for almost three years.

Actually Billingsley had had an earlier run-in with his old pal when Winchell wrote an item linking Billingsley to a "prominent musical comedy star," thereby violating the ethic which most Broadway columnists honor more in the breach than the observance anyway—that they would not mention extramarital affairs of people who were still happily married or at least not contemplating breaking up their marriage.

Billingsley was furious at the revelation of his affair which was with Ethel Merman, but because of Winchell's great power he had to swallow the slight and pretend that it never happened. The item was generated on the occasion of Sherman's presenting the singer with an ostentatious diamond-encrusted bracelet engraved "From Sherm to Merm."

Probably the reason Winchell was somewhat cavalier in his attitude toward the affair was that he, in fact, never did get along particularly well with Merman. In her biography the singer had this to say: "I mentioned Dorothy Kilgallen earlier. I had a wonderful relationship with her, Leonard Lyons, Ed Sullivan, Hedda Hopper and Louella Parsons, as well as Radie Harris, Earl Wilson and Louis Sobol. But I can't say the same for Walter Winchell, who probably did more than anyone else to popularize the Stork Club. Sherman tried to keep us friends, but it was difficult.

"I had several run-ins with Walter and I never felt free to talk openly in his presence. If anything was said, there was always the danger that he would misconstrue or even destroy the meaning in some embarrassing way. As for a retraction? Please! Winchell never retracted. He was notorious for that. So when he was present, I always felt as if there was a scrim between us. Not that I was afraid of him, but he was a very difficult person to talk to. For a reporter he was not a good listener, either. He talked through you."

Naturally if Merman took a dislike to Winchell, she would have, almost by definition, to have had a favorable attitude toward his principal enemy, Ed Sullivan. One of the items Winchell ran that particularly annoyed Merman was one stating that Al Siegel, her arranger, claimed to have taught her all she knew. Merman blew her top and fired off a telegram of denial which, to do him justice, Winchell printed in his column:

> "DEAR WALTER,
> I'VE BEEN SINGING SINCE I WAS FIVE YEARS OLD AND I'VE BEEN TELLING THE TRUTH EVEN LONGER. AND I'M TELLING YOU THE ONLY THING THAT AL SIEGEL EVER DID WAS WRITE ARRANGEMENTS. HE NEVER TAUGHT ME ANYTHING."

Merman felt pretty good about that, since it was as close to a retraction as you could get from Winchell in his prime.

Sullivan, in discussing Siegel's claims, said that he had never taken much stock in such boasting. "Success is something apart from mechanical tricks," he wrote. "To be successful, a performer must have courage, determination, tact and all the allied virtues. Nobody can infuse these in the heart of another. And once a performer steps out on the stage, he is on his own."

Merman herself, although later not too happy with Sherman, did not deny the relationship: "I pride myself on being honest, and I'm not going to omit mentioning the affectionate relationship that existed between Sherman and myself . . . about my relationship with Sherman I'll only note that it was one of those times when I'd have been better off if I had listened to my mother when she said, 'Ethel, are you sure you know what you're doing?' "

Merman, however, admitted that she was impressed with Sherman's generosity, at any rate: "During that period of my life I drank only champagne. Sherman was always having replenishments delivered to my dressing room, so that I could have a bottle after the show. There were some eye-popping opening night jewels. And people still mentioned—some of them enviously—how Sherman had a catered after-theater supper for the entire cast of "Stars In Your Eyes" delivered to Boston during the tryout."

It wasn't only Merman that got this treatment, either. Radie Harris, columnist for the *Hollywood Reporter*, was living at the Algonquin and still talks of coming home at Christmas and having to pick her way through a living room which was piled with gifts from Sherman. Merman also made some good friends at the Stork, particularly J. Edgar Hoover and his constant companion Clyde Tolson. She remembered him this way: "Clyde was younger and very good looking."

On one of her opening nights, Tolson and Hoover sent a jointly signed telegram: "SINCERE GOOD WISHES TO YOU AND YOUR NEW SHOW. WE ARE SORRY WE CAN'T BE IN FRONT TO HISS—NO KISS YOU. TENDEREST REGARDS."

"Clyde undoubtedly sent it," Merman comments. "He had a wonderful sense of humor and was much easier to talk to than John. John was quiet and not easy to get to know. But since they were always together, Clyde kept things moving and we became good friends."

Merman recalls that during the New York World's Fair Sherman took her, Tolson and Hoover to dinner at the Italian Pavillion. Afterwards they walked around the grounds and when they came to the shooting gallery, Hoover and Tolson picked up guns and knocked off all the rabbits and ducks, one right after another.

It ultimately became well known on the Broadway circuit that neither Clyde nor Hoover were interested in women, but all Winchell ever said about his good friend was that he and Sherman never made it a policy to talk about the sex life of the FBI man. But that didn't mean they didn't talk about others. One night in the Stork Club, Winchell and Billingsley were sitting with Damon Runyon, who by that time had lost his voice to cancer and could only contribute to the conversation by writing brief but often flamingly vivid notes. Winchell and Billingsley were airing their suspicion that their respective girlfriends were being less than faithful. Listening to the two men fretting that they were being cuckolded, Runyon hastily scribbled a note: "Don't worry boys. Nobody ever ruined a good cunt by fucking."

Despite his cynicism, much of it probably caused by the constant pain he suffered, Runyon ultimately developed a genuine affection for his brash younger friend and even said that he found Winchell's rapid-fire talk engrossing: "I know of no man who is more entertaining than Walter when he is in the mood, nor one who has a greater store of experience from which to draw," Runyon once said.

Other literary figures, like George Jean Nathan and H. L. Mencken who were Stork Club regulars and fans of Winchell, admitted that they were overpowered by his personality. Once after a half-hour talkfest at Table 50, Klurfeld asked Nathan what Winchell had said.

"He said," Nathan smiled, "in several thousand words how wonderful it was to be Winchell."

Even St. Clair McKelway who wrote particularly vitriolic series in the *New Yorker* about Winchell in the late Thirties had to yield to a certain grudging admiration: "Winchell has a peculiarly bewitching personality. He has a lean face, full of alertness, with an expression of questing intelligence like a fox terrier. His eyes are blue and hard. He is consistently lively and restless; it is impossible to imagine him in repose. He has an enormous nervous energy, and the experience of watching him burn it up extravagantly is stimulating and sometimes touching. What he says may be uninteresting in itself, but his voice and manner are charged with an inner excitement which is communicable. One of his phrase-making friends calls him 'a thrilling bore.' When he is not talking, he sits forward with his head raised unnaturally in an attitude of intense awareness. His heel is apt to beat quick-time on the floor like a swing musician's, his gaze roves ceaselessly over the room, and his hands go on little fruitless expeditions over the tablecloth, up and down the lapels of his coat, in and out of his pockets.''

Even his cronies found Winchell amusingly self-centered in his conversation. Once Jimmy Cannon, the former sports writer and at one time one of Winchell's close friends, was at the Stork with a girlfriend, listening to Winchell deliver his monologue. After Winchell had talked for ten minutes without interruption, Cannon began to wonder if his girl might enjoy the evening more if she had another drink. Keeping his eyes fastened on Winchell's face in order to appear attentive, he whispered to his girl softly out of the side of his mouth, "Honey, you want something?''

Winchell stopped in the middle of his sentence and grabbed Cannon's arm. ''Jimmy!'' he said reproachfully. ''You're not listening!''

One man who spent an evening at Winchell's Stork table remarked afterward: "He was terrific. His conversation ranged all the way from Walter to Winchell.''

Here are Herman Klurfeld's notes on a typical news-and-ego-filled monologue:

"Cary Grant is Jewish gave the UJA $10,000 this year wonders why they don't approach him more often wonder why non-Jew Sinatra is solicited year after year but he is ignored I checked and discovered UJA didn't know Grant was Jewish how do you like that bitch the Duchess of Windsor, a few years ago Taylor Caldwell called her for a luncheon with fifteen others the duchess's secretary phones Mrs. Caldwell to ask what transportation she was using and Mrs. C. replied her husband would drive her over to pick her up the secretary said, 'I'm sorry Mrs. Caldwell your husband is Jewish and the duchess is Protestant and does not mix socially with Jews.' Mrs. Caldwell then exploded, 'Tell the duchess I am Dutch Protestant and I don't mix socially with prostitutes.' Bob Hope told me a funny about the fag who became ecstatic when he discovered his gums were bleeding how do you like the cheap-ass Justice Frankfurter at the Stork Club he received a bottle of champagne as a gift and told the waiter don't open it wrap it and I'll take it with me one for the oy-

201

gevalt department that Arthur Godfrey is a pain in the ass he knows damn well the Hotel Kenilworth restricts Jews but pretends it isn't so and he plugs the damn place on radio so does Paley know about it? Irving Mansfield tried to set him straight but Arthur blew his top and told Irving to mind his own business said he would stay where he damned please and didn't give a hoot in hell how anybody felt about it Godfrey can be a fuck Carl Sandburg walked into the Stork and Billingsley asked what does he do the schmuck never heard of him Paul Scheffer, a newspaperman tells everyone he writes Dotty Thompson's stuff maybe it's bullshit but she's getting more and more pro-Arab George Jean Nathan and H. L. Mencken are always telling me not to get so damn mad about things I tell them it's part of my act hell I don't get ulcers I give them Sinatra is in bad shape since the breakup with Ava wants me to help him get a job Meyer Berger gave me some items that drove the *New York Times* nuts I'm not worried about anything except tomorrow's column *I never ask J. Edgar Hoover about his sex life* I showed my son an FDR letter where the Prez asked about my son Howard Hughes never phones or mails news to me he has one of his people fly across the country and hand it to me in person he flew Steve Flagg from Hollywood to give me an item I couldn't use try not to talk to your bosses I've spoken to Hearst less than a dozen times usually on the phone the problem with having a mistress is not the screwing part it's having to eat dinner twice in one night.''

At his peak during those glorious Stork Club years, Winchell functioned as a king, a judge, a *caïd* to the various hangers-on and droppers-in. According to Klurfeld who was as close to him in those years as anybody, government leaders, Broadway and Hollywood stars, obscure entertainers, famous and unknown writers and composers—all came to Winchell for assistance. Sometimes he was called upon to iron out a problem between a nightclub dancer and a café owner or a dispute between White House aides. Quite often, in fact, he was a successful mediator. Once a Mafia chief sought to take over Billy Rose's Diamond Horseshoe Club. Billy came to Winchell for help, as did Sammy Davis, Jr., when underworld characters threatened him after he had rolled up mountainous gambling debts in Vegas. And Walter helped them. He once rescued Sinatra from agents who were grabbing seventy percent of his earnings, according to Klurfeld.

Billingsley, the benefactor of the poor, despite his hectic past as a bootlegger and mob enforcer, essentially hated violence, at least in his club, and was less tolerant of brawlers than any of the other club owners. Lenore Lemmon, one of the most prominent café society playgirls of the era, found this out to her sorrow when she got into a hassle with Marion Snowden, wife of Brad Dresser, a well known Stork Club swinger. The two ladies got into the altercation over the fact that Lenore had had a few dances with Dresser. Dresser brought Lemmon to the table and said, "I guess you know my wife."

"Sure I knew her," Lenore told newspapers, "Marion Snowden, the Standard Oil gal who was hitched to Prince Rospigliosi and Lou Reed and married Brad in Reno half an hour after her second divorce. I started to smile but she said: 'I don't want to meet her.'"

From this point things did not improve and before Lenore Lemmon left, her two escorts and several other bystanders met in a confrontation with Bob Topping and Put Humphreys who were at the table with Mrs. Dresser. The way Lemmon remembered it, "That Dresser dame swung wild and hit her own husband on the nose. And then somebody—I wish I knew who it was—came up behind and shoved me through the door. I landed on my rear license plate and got up and left with dignity."

But next day, Miss Lemmon said, she found that her knee and thigh were badly bruised. She was just examining them to see the extent of the damages when a telegram arrived from Sherman Billingsley. It said:

"SORRY TO ADVISE WE DO NOT NOW OR EVER WANT YOUR PATRONAGE AT THE STORK CLUB."

Asked about the telegram, Billingsley said, "I was gone then, but my manager called the police and had the whole bunch of them put out. Sure I sent the girl a telegram, and I sent one just like it to Nesbitt and some of the others involved."

The Stork Club press agent apparently hadn't gotten the word. He told newspapers: "Absolutely nothing happened here Wednesday morning. On my reputation as a press agent, the place was quiet as a tomb."

On another occasion, Ernest Hemingway, who had not apparently heard about the club policy on brawls, got into an unpleasant beef. According to the Stork witnesses, a lawyer walked up to the table at which Hemingway was sitting with Quentin Reynolds and other writers and remarked: "So, you're a tough guy."

According to the *New York Times*, "Hemingway sat meekly for a while as the visitor continued his taunts, but finally got up and knocked him to the floor." A friend of the fallen man and assistants in the club helped him to the street. For some reason Billingsley never enforced his rule on brawling against Hemingway in that particular case.

But if Billingsley's place was famous for its decorous behavior and generous favors, his principal opponent, John Perona of El Morocco, was almost the diametric opposite.

25.

Wilson defined it once in his book *The Show Business Nobody Knows*:

"What is a nightclub? was a question asked in the nineteen forties and the standard answer was: 'It's a place where the tables are reserved but the customers aren't.' "

Compared to the strait-laced, preppy atmosphere that Sherman Billingsley tried to engender, John Perona and his crowd at El Morocco were practically clowns in whiteface. Robert Sylvester said of Perona: "It is possible that he thought of himself as something of an amateur comedian. He guffawed louder than anybody when Woolworth Donahue, a playboy whose manic didos bored an entire generation of saloon-goers, crawled onto the hooded roast beef wagon and had himself trundled about the nightclub one late evening. He was hilarious when Michael Famer, one-time husband of Hollywood queens, had the men's room attendant bring articles to his prominent table so he could shave before dinner. He was even amused by the sight of heavyweight champion Max Baer crawling under tables with lighted matches to give friends a hotfoot.

"Such impolite gaucheries would have given Billingsley an immediate triple coronary attack. About the time Perona would be calling for another bottle of wine, Billingsley would be ordering more hot tea."

Perona was also much more likely to involve himself in some of the after-hours pugilism for which his place became famed, and was twice himself hauled before magistrates for walloping unruly customers with his fists.

Of course, Perona as well as Billingsley had to select his clientele, but his standards were a little more difficult to predict. The primary arbiter of who got past the entrance rope was a headwaiter named Carino who had a camera eye, an infallible memory and a genius for "dressing the room," which means placing a famous customer to the best possible advantage. Nobody knows why Frank Carino Beccaris was called simply "Carino," but it's part of the general mystery of Perona's operation. Elsewhere in the nightclub world, for instance, the classiest customers got the front table. But Perona and Carino had the idea that the best tables were not those that crowded the teeny dance floor where some overactive samba dancer might knock a glass of wine into milady's lap. So the curved, zebra-striped banquettes became the real celebrity-land. You might swing two or three times around the miniscule parquette allowed for dancing before you realized that the woman half-hidden by the curve of a wall seat backrest was Rita Hayworth, and that the thin woman several benches down was the Duchess of Windsor. Of course, with those zig-zag stripes, Perona had no need for the omnipresent logotyped ashtrays, which were the Stork Club's trademarks.

One of those who liked to make herself comfortable at Elmo's was Zsa Zsa Gabor, who in her first half-dozen years in America was first known as "Georgia" Gabor and then "Sari" Gabor. When she was still married to Conrad Hilton in the early Forties, she was known as Sari. Through her divorce and the massive battle with Perona which she claimed caused her to have a nervous breakdown requiring months of treatment, Zsa Zsa was battling through the gossip columns and the front pages, to become the Zsa Zsa of later celebrity. But she hadn't quite made it yet. As Sari she had the same talent for embroidering incidents in order to glamorize herself as she did later as Zsa Zsa. Once she showed up with a patch on her nose, which she told Earl Wilson was caused by being hit with a poker by a "jealous vife" in "Vashington." A little later, not getting

Café Society at El Morocco

much response to her original version, she elaborated on her story, telling Wilson that she went to Morocco "vith mine broken nose," showed a clipping about the "jealous vife," and got into an argument which brought about her ouster from the club—forever.

Wilson says that El Morocco told him that the broken nose had nothing to do with it. She'd gotten into an argument there with Perona and had thrown champagne into the face of a woman who sided with him. However, it was true that she was henceforth not welcome. Actually, it turned out that a plastic surgeon emerged to say that the patch was due to a 90-minute operation to straighten a bump on her nose. Sari was just making her story more interesting by rewriting it. Wilson says, "Perhaps she should have been a novelist instead of a glamour girl."

The Forties and the late Thirties were the times of the exotic playboy from Europe or South America. Perona's parlor was much more conducive to these aliens than was Billingsley's since Billingsley could not stand the look of anybody who appeared in the slightest way "foreign" to him. He once even barred a maharajah, saying that all "Indians" looked alike to him. He thought, in fact, that the maha was a resident of one of his native Oklahoman Indian reservations.

A suave, pencil-waisted, soft-spoken, dark-complexioned Dominican named Porfirio Rubirosa first gained his reputation in Perona's place. According to Wilson, "Girls melted in his arms when he danced body-to-body with them at El Morocco." Details of his love-making techniques were almost as well known on the nightclub circuit as the batting average of Joe DiMaggio. Rubi was known among his dancing companions as "big boy" and he danced in such a fashion as to make it clear why he had that reputation.

According to society columnist Igor Cassini, no mean lover himself, Rubi had his own special way to conquer a lady. Certainly not the intellectual or even the romantic type, he didn't waste time in conversation. "He went right to the point, or perhaps it would be more correct to sáy he made the lady get to it. An attractive English fashion editor told me of her first and unusual encounter with the famous Dominican lover. It was during a Paris dinner party, and Rubi was seated next to her. They had hardly exchanged a few words when Rubi grabbed her hand, under the table, and without preamble placed it on his hard cock. As she relates it, she was so stunned that she sat there frozen with that thing in her hand. It was a while, she guesses, before she politely withdrew. Rubi had made his move. From then on it was up to the lady, take it or leave it!''

According to Cassini, Rubi's secret weapon was "the perpetual hard-on.'' Whatever it was, it seemed to work, since his marriage roster was star-studded and gold-plated: first Flor de Oro Trujillo, daughter of Dominican dictator Rafael Trujillo; then Danielle Darrieux, French film star; Doris Duke and Barbara Hutton, two top money heiresses; and Odile Rodin, his last wife, an actress and model. In addition, he was involved in endless extracurricular affairs, including a hot one with the aforementioned Zsa Zsa Gabor, which obviously could not work out, since both were inclined to marry wealthy people, and neither had two nickels to rub together. In fact, Rubirosa managed to earn $100,000 by acting as paid correspondent for tobacco heir Richard Reynolds, when he was trying to get rid of one of his many wives. The wife, enthralled with Rubirosa's special techniques, had no idea that he had been paid to become her lover. Rubi himself had an explanation for this, which he told to Cassini: "If I think of the sound of money, I get excited.''

Incidentally, Cassini himself obliquely claimed to have the same talent as Rubirosa. He tells the story of his first wife Dara who was comparing notes on sex with her girlfriends on the Riviera when one of them raved about her current lover. "My dear, you would think it was made of bone!''

"But *isn't* it?'' Dara asked innocently.

Cassini said from then on his reputation was made. Be that as it may, Dara managed to tear herself away from Cassini ultimately to dally with Aly Khan. When he found this out, Cassini returned to his hotel room in a towering rage. "My bafflement only increased when I found a pair of Rubirosa's evening pumps in our hotel room."

Aly, of course, was another champion playboy and frequenter of El Morocco. Cassini, naturally curious in a personal way about Aly's charms, made a discreet inquiry as to what, besides money, he had to attract women, since he had been balding since early childhood and was developing quite a paunch before he was in his thirties. One of Cassini's column sources filled him in on the playboy's technique. Aly tended to disappear either before romantic action or at intervals. This was a tic so perplexing that one of his old flames quietly followed him to the bathroom and was startled to see the Khan "religiously splashing cold water on all of his pulse points and prick." But Cassini said the wealthy sportsman really had no cause to worry.

Maurice Messegua, a French herbalist who had been consulted by Winston Churchill and Konrad Adenaur, was summoned by the prince because some of his herbs were believed capable of producing increased virility. Messegua said that the prince was worried because he was making love, but seemed to have lost his appetite for it and felt this might be a sign of encroaching senility.

"May I ask you a question," Messegua said. "How many times a week do you do it?"

"Three times a day."

"With equal success and ease?"

"Absolutely."

"Perhaps," Messegua said, "I should come to you for advice."

In 1960, at age 49, Prince Aly Khan was killed at the wheel of his Lancia when it smashed head-on into another car in the Bois de Boulogne. With him was former French model Bettina, his last and longest love in a notable list that included Rita Hayworth, Kim Novak, Joan Fontaine, Merle Oberon, Gene Tierney, Irene

Papas and Zsa Zsa Gabor, along with a cast of thousands.

Ironically, five years later, within a few hundred yards, Rubirosa, an experienced driver, veteran of the Le Mans and Sebring, Florida, races, was whizzing through the Bois de Boulogne in his gray Ferrari. After a lavish dinner at the Tour d'Argent and a dancing session at New Jimmy's, he had driven his wife Odile home and gone out to the Calvados Club for a final nightcap. Headed home again, probably bombed, he hit a chestnut tree, exactly one half mile from the spot where Aly Khan had crashed fatally five years earlier.

Of course, wherever there are playboys there must be playgirls, and the late Thirties spawned a particular version of pulchritude which was to retain its vogue right into the war years. This was the society debutante, or, as Winchell called her, the "celebutante." Undoubtedly the champion of all these was a pretty, pale-faced heiress with arching eyebrows, shoulder-length brown hair, and staring eyes named Brenda Diana Duff Frazier who according to a committee that in 1938 selected the eleven most glamorous people, "made the American debutante the most attractive young woman alive." (The other glamour candidates were Orson Welles; the Duke of Windsor; Neville Chamberlain; Anthony Eden; Vera Zorina, the ballet dancer; Alice Marble, the singing tennis player; Countess Barbara Hutton Mdivani Haugwitz-Reventlow; Danielle Darrieux; Hedy Lamarr and Bette Davis.)

There is no question when it came to the debutante sweepstakes the 18-year-old girl who was heiress to a multi-million dollar grain fortune was the champion. Out of 400 debutantes that season, Brenda's newspaper linage outnumbered all of the others put together—and this, she swore, was without the aid of a press agent. Certainly nobody ever did locate a press agent who worked for the dark-eyed girl. Walter Winchell, who had been writing familiarly about her for months, met her formally in April 1938. He was so impressed that he not only coined a word for her, but he offered her a ride

211

in his police radio-equipped car.

Young Brenda was a columnist's dream, and according to the *New Yorker*, which went so far as to do a six-page profile on her that year, it was not a very long time after her debut "before a Broadway columnist was able to note that she'd been seen simultaneously with Bruce Cabot, Errol Flynn and Douglas Fairbanks, Jr., in the flesh." Actually, one of those she did date was later to reach greater notoriety than the ones mentioned in the columns—Howard Hughes, with whom she spent a good deal of time, mostly in Nassau, sailing in his yacht and cruising in his plane. All this and barely eighteen.

Despite this notoriety, Brenda, who was up until at least five a.m. in Elmo's, the Stork, or the Colony every night, surrounded by at least five or six escorts, did not like to be called a celebrity.

"I'm not a celebrity," she told E. J. Kahn, Jr. who interviewed her for the *New Yorker*. "I don't deserve all this. I haven't done anything spectacular. I haven't done anything at all. I'm just a debutante."

And it was true. While some of the other debutante celebrities were working for their bread as singers or publicists for various causes because their families had lost their fortunes in the tragedy of '29, Brenda was a genuine heiress, and therefore did not have to lend herself to crass commercialism. She spent all her time shopping for evening dresses and bouncing up and down on an endless series of amphetamines and sleeping pills to keep her slim figure that was so admired. In those days, nobody had yet heard of anorexia nervosa, but Brenda ultimately became so wrecked by her efforts to keep her weight down and her consciousness up that she had to be put away for a year in a sanitarium, suffering from what was described as "a nervous breakdown."

Eventually Brenda, after being courted by the most eligible men in the world, noblemen and movie heroes, financiers and playboys, married an ex-football player with the romantic handle of John (Shipwreck) Kelly, who planned to take her away from the dilletantish

Joan Crawford (left) and Brenda Frazier tête-a- tête at the
Stork Club

round of nightclubs and dieting which had become her habit. He bought a farm and Brenda shopped for gingham dresses and knitting needles. She bore him a daughter and for a time the bucolic life seemed becoming to Brenda, who filled out and gained color in her formerly corpse-white face. But she couldn't stand to be away from the fanfare and frivolity of the Great White Way, and after a few years she returned to the glamorous life she had been accustomed to. Somewhere in the late war years, the glamour just up and went—though not completely. She was still being pursued in 1953 by Roman playboy Pietro Mele, who tried to break down her door and beat up three cops in his efforts to spend the night with her. Brenda, who was 33 by that time, and again down to eighty pounds, said that Mele was just "a poor, unfortunate, hot-headed boy."

In the hearing for assault which followed, it came out that Mele had also once taken a poke at his beloved, in the bar of the Essex House.

But Brenda's reign as America's and possibly the world's leading glamour girl was short-lived, probably because, other than her patrician appearance and sparkling eyes, she did not really have enough scandal to offer the voracious gossip mills. Her habit of appearing simultaneously with five or six escorts on most occasions tended to minimize the possibility of real romance.

A more dramatic debutante who managed to keep her name prominently in the columns in those same years, either for tossing her shoe at a chandelier, or starting a riot in the Stork, was Lenore Lemmon. Lemmon had to work at being a debutante, singing and modeling, since whatever family money may have existed had long since evaporated by the late Thirties. But if the publicity was intended to get her the attention of wealthy suitors, it seemed to work. In the fall of 1938, when she was barely eighteen, Lenore was accused by Mrs. Joseph Paterno, Jr., of being one of the "so-called café society glamour girls" to whom her husband had suddenly become vulnerable. In a divorce suit against Paterno who was heir to a multi-million dollar building fortune, Mrs. Paterno said she might have forgiven one fling with these young butterflies of the night, or perhaps two, but not three. In the suit she named among her husband's sweethearts Patricia (Honeychile) Wilder, Jane Gilbert, a debutante of the previous year, and Lenore Lemmon, who Mrs. Pateron said had been entertained in her home and had used her toilet articles. As far as Miss Wilder was concerned, she said her husband was seen kissing the beautiful young debutante "while on the dance floor at El Morocco on election night." This hardly seemed likely to people who knew Paterno, because the year was 1940 and it was Roosevelt who was elected, hardly a favorite of the rock-ribbed Republican playboy. In any event, Paterno managed to avoid his problems with his wife temporarily by being drafted into the Coast Artillery, whereupon playboy Tommy Manville made the strange but generous offer of providing a loving home for Paterno's wife and child while he was in the service. Manville made the gentlemanly promise that he would maintain a proper attitude toward Beverly until the divorce was final. Columnists had a field day with that one too, because all a woman had to do was get her name in the papers to have Manville propose to her, or sometimes it was the other way around.

Paterno, interviewed at Camp Davis, North Carolina, said of his wife's suitor, "If he is the glamorous, romantic Manville that he seems to think he is, and the future candidate for Beverly's hand in marriage—as we say at mess hall—he is not the ideal family chaperone. But maybe he is now old gaffer Manville, genial shadower of vanished youth—as I read in the drill manual—and about as seductive as last Thursday's oatmeal. We will let the courts decide what he is."

Whatever decision was made, Manville never did marry Mrs. Paterno—one of the few he missed. Neither did Lenore marry Paterno, because a few months after Paterno left to join the Army, she eloped for a four-day honeymoon with Jacob L. (Jakie) Webb, the great-

great-grandson of Cornelius Vanderbilt and heir to quite a bit of his money. Webb, however, turned out to be an enormous disappointment. In the first place, during the honeymoon, Lenore said: "I found out that Jakie was tattooed from head to foot." Apparently this was not to Lenore's taste. Then it turned out that Jakie had paid for their honeymoon and subsequent pleasures with a series of rubber checks which neither he nor his family could make good on. That is to say, Webb couldn't, and his family wouldn't. Worse than that, Webb not only seemed to have no money despite being an heir to the Vanderbilt fortune, but spent a lot of time borrowing money from Lenore's wealthy friends. Within a month, Lenore separated from her disappointing husband, but columnists were by now on his somewhat eccentric trail.

After finally making good on the checks, Webb went into the Army, where he soon made the rank of technical sergeant, but soon after was confined to post for going AWOL. A few years later, he turned up in Reno wearing a captain's uniform, claiming to be a Flying Tiger veteran with 63 Jap planes to his credit and yards of ribbons on his chest. But his get-up so startled Army officials that he was locked up again for safekeeping. Then he went back into active service again, but not for long. In Hawaii he went AWOL again and was finally given a dishonorable discharge and a stretch in Lewisburg Penitentiary. All in all, not the best match Lenore could have made among her many suitors. Ultimately Lenore, once called by the *Daily News* "larruping Lenore" because of her front-page barroom tussles, married a British singer named Robert Hamish Menzies whom she finally divorced in 1953 when she retired, apparently from her former haunts and from the front pages. All of this seems to show that being a play*boy* is a lot more fun than being a play*girl*, although it may be said that at least Brenda and Lenore are still alive, at this writing, which is more than can be said for most of the playboys of their era.

But by now the drums of war were thundering in earnest, and people had perhaps a little less time for the didoes of the rich and privileged. Winchell, Kilgallen (who now had a radio show of her own and was second in rank only to the master), Walker, Sullivan and the others began to train their guns "over there."

26.

When Winchell first started his column in the *Mirror*, its content was a blend of ninety percent gossip to ten percent news. By the early 1930's, however, Winchell had begun to incorporate more and more anti-Nazi and political material in his column. Hearst was against this change. Broadway chatter had been selling very well on the newsstands and Hearst didn't want to do anything to change that. But basically he completely disagreed with all of Winchell's views on domestic and international affairs.

A head-to-head battle commenced between Winchell and Hearst which continued for at least six years. Hearst would kill material and send out instructions to editors on the various syndicated papers to take out anything controversial, and Winchell, who had an innate dislike for being told directly or otherwise what he should write, kept adding more of the material every time Hearst took something out. Besides that, he was seriously concerned about the rise of the new Nazi order. In March of 1938 Hearst, angry and frustrated, sent this message to the editors of all newspapers using Winchell's column:

"Please edit Winchell very carefully and leave out any dangerous or disagreeable paragraphs. Indeed, leave out the whole column without hesitation, as I think he has gotten so careless that he is no longer of any particular value."

Once that memo went out, Winchell began to have real censorship trouble with his out-of-town papers, as well as the *Mirror*. Many of the Hearst editors agreed with their boss, and were opposed to Winchell's views from the beginning, so that they had been cutting him even without Hearst's instructions for a long time.

Eleanor "Cissy" Patterson, owner of the *Washington Times-Herald* was a notorious right-winger and she thought nothing of slashing Winchell's column to the size of a postage stamp. It must be remembered that both Patterson and Hearst were notoriously pro-German in those pre-war years.

One whole column left out of the Hearst papers in 1938 was an account by playwright Lillian Hellman of the Falangist bombing of Madrid.

On Saturday, September 2, 1939, it appeared likely to everybody in the Western World that Great Britain was about to go to war with Germany. Winchell, deeply disturbed by this turn of events, decided to use what he felt was now his worldwide influence, to do something about this. He sent a cablegram to Prime Minister Neville Chamberlain as follows:

"MAY I RESPECTFULLY OFFER THE SUGGESTION THAT IF BRITAIN DECLARES WAR THE DECLARATION MIGHT BE WORDED NOT AS "WAR AGAINST GERMANY" BUT AS "WAR AGAINST ADOLPH HITLER PERSONALLY AND HIS PERSONAL REGIME." STRESSING THE FACT THAT HITLER DOES NOT REALLY REPRESENT THE TRUE WILL OF THE VAST CIVILIAN POPULATION OF GERMANY. SUCH DECLARATION MIGHT HAVE THE ASTONISHING EFFECT OF BRINGING THE GERMAN PEOPLE TO THEIR SENSES, ESPECIALLY IF SUCH DECLARATION CAN BE MADE KNOWN TO THE GERMAN PEOPLE AND INEVITABLY IT WOULD VIA RADIO AND OTHER CHANNELS. THIS IS MERELY A LAYMAN'S SUGGESTION OFFERED IN HOPES OF A NEW ERA OF WORLD PEACE."

Winchell printed the text of the cable in his column the next day without comment, but on the following day he wrote this in his column:

"If you read Monday's column this may interest you. At 2:33 a.m. September 4th the London Telegraph Agency flashed a dispatch reporting that Prime Minister Chamberlain had just read a proclamation to the German people via a French radio station, in which he stated that Great Britain did not declare war against the German people, but against Adolph Hitler and the Nazi regime . . . the suggestion was sent to the Prime Minister in a cablegram, acknowledgment of which has arrived.''

Whether it was true or not, Winchell was convinced his power had reached a new high and that Chamberlain indeed had acted as he did because of the Winchell cable, and for all anybody knows, he did. It was, in any event, an uncanny bit of timing and did much to add to the growing legend of Walter Winchell.

In prewar years, Winchell was gaining readers but making many important enemies among the people he called the "assolationists." His opponents were formidable. They included Senators Burton K. Wheeler, Robert R. Reynolds, Harold P. Nye, Theodore Bilbo; Representatives John Rankin, Clare Hoffman, Hamilton Fish. The isolationists trumpeted their attack against Winchell in Congress and at antiwar rallies throughout the land and he responded with attacks in his columns and broadcasts. When the isolationists formed the "America First Committee," Winchell taunted: "In union there is stench." Charles Lindbergh, formerly one of Winchell's great heroes, was one of the most outspoken America Firsters and aggressively pro-German. Winchell turned the full power of his hostility against the Lone Eagle: "Lindbergh wants the British to quit. Apparently he thinks everyone quits as easily as he does . . . he once quit America—remember? If he ever had a real reason to quit again, it is now.''

In 1940 when Roosevelt finally ran for his third term after feeling out the American public via the Winchell column, Winchell was the most powerful voice in favor of that candidacy against the Republican candidate, Wendell Wilkie. Lined up against Roosevelt, among important press voices, were William Randolph Hearst, Henry Luce, Roy Howard, Frank Gannett, the owners of the *New York Times* and most of the others who controlled what Roosevelt called "the one-party press."

Roosevelt defeated Wilkie in the Electoral College by 449 votes to 82, a victory that was bound to bolster Winchell's already high opinion of his influence. At any rate, Winchell had a better idea of the pulse of the American public at this time than did these prominent publishers.

By 1940 most of the other columnists on the Broadway beat were beginning to get on the bandwagon in terms of the war that was clearly coming, and the mood of the public called for more and more serious material. As Charles Fisher put it in his book *The Columnists*:

> "A report that Miss Greta Garbo puts sugar in her soup is no longer sufficiently startling in itself; it must be accompanied by an account of secret doings in the State Department, a view of next week's events in Afghanistan, and the latest breakfast *bon mot* of Winston Churchill."

Danton Walker, the dandified *Daily News* columnist who tended to be politically sympathetic at first to his isolationist boss Joseph Medill Patterson, nevertheless began also to carry more and more material about the upcoming conflict. In August 1941 he ran an item which said: "Mussolini is about to pay a visit to Austria 'to review Italian troops'—actually to confer with Hitler." Four days later the item was confirmed by front-page headlines all over the world announcing that Hitler and Mussolini were engaged in a five-day conference.

Walker himself wrote: "Long before the attack on Pearl Harbor, the Broadway columns—all of them—were trumpeting warnings to the American people, and if newspaper editors had paid more attention to these straws in the wind, the events of that day might not have been such a shocking surprise." As proof, Walker cites a couple of items from his own column late in '41:

> "October 27, 1941: The N. Y. K. (Japanese steamship line) will shut down within four weeks, virtually closing the Pacific trade relations between Uncle Sam and the

Nipponese. One of the top executives already has received his notice . . .

"December 1, 1941: U.S.-Jap relations are complicated by a feud between Emperor Hirohito and his military clique which actually ordered Special Envoy Kurusu to return home last Thursday . . . (and in the same column) Diplomatic relations with Germany will be officially severed by March 1st . . ."

But most ironic and galling to Walker was the column he wrote for publication on Monday, December 8th, which was written on Sunday morning, December 7th. It led off with these items:

"The War Department in Washington is seething over the disappearance of important plans from under the noses of high officials there last week . . . Japanese officials in the Capital have been offering their automobiles for sale . . . "Allied" troops are expected to take over policing of the Dutch East Indies following the outbreak of war between Japan and the United States . . ."

Walker was sending his column, as usual, up to the managing editor in short takes. The first two had already gone in and he headed the third paragraph with the line: "In the event of a surprise Japanese attack, you can paste this in your hat—"

"I don't remember what was to be pasted in your hat," Walker wrote, "because I had to rewrite the page. I was beginning on paragraph number four when I felt a hand on my shoulder—the managing editor's. He had come in from the city room with the last paragraph of the column.

"You'd better change your tenses here," he said. "We just got the flash that the Japanese attacked Pearl Harbor this morning."

Kilgallen, by now definitely the second most powerful columnist in New York after Winchell, paid less attention to the war for several reasons. One was that she largely agreed with Hearst's views politically. The second was that she was quite concerned that her new husband, Richard Kollmar, would be drafted. According to an old chum of Kollmar's, Edgar Hatfield, Kilgallen's new husband, "played every trick to stay out of the service and he did so successfully. He would tell female friends, if asked why he was not in the service, that he had a duodenal ulcer. Male friends would be told that there was something wrong with his scrotum."

"If war comes," Kilgallen frankly told a close friend of hers, "I'll do anything in my power to keep him out." Ultimately, Kollmar had the best excuse of all. Dorothy became pregnant with a child who was born on June 12, 1941, and called Richard, Jr.

Dorothy asked Maury Paul, the snooty social column editor on her paper, the *Journal*, to announce the child's birth in his "Cholly Knickerbocker" column. Maury Paul, who didn't think too much of Dorothy in the first place, and resented her scooping him on items he felt were strictly in his domain, demurred.

"You are *not* society, my dear," he hissed, "and I see no reason why your child should be mentioned in anything but a Broadway column."

Dorothy never forgave Paul for the slight, but since he was not long for this world anyway, that particular grudge died with its subject.

When the long-awaited war finally struck on that gloomy Sunday, Winchell was the only columnist to actually offer his services to the country. He had been a reservist in the U.S. Navy since 1934 and he sent a telegram to the Secretary of the Navy requesting instant active duty as a naval officer. He was 45 and his request for active duty was denied because of his age. But his offer to help the Navy full-time came to the attention of the Secretary of the Navy, Frank Knox, publisher of the *Chicago Daily News*. Knox, as a publisher, was aware of Winchell's potential as a Navy propagandist. On Christmas eve of 1941, Winchell was sworn in as a lieutenant commander on active service. His duties, which were limited to New York City, were to help spread the Navy message, and stage benefits for Navy relief. This in no way interfered with his columns or his radio program for Jergens Lotion. But Winchell had officer uniforms tailored to his measurements and wore them to the Stork Club on his nightly rounds. This infuriated his isolationist critics in Congress.

"The Navy should call Winchell to active duty or disenroll him," demanded Carl Vinson, Chairman of the House Naval Affairs Committee.

"Active duty?" Winchell replied. "The record shows that I requested it on December 7, 1941 and was granted volunteer active duty—without pay—on December 24th."

Cissy Patterson, his Washington nemesis, was quoted as saying, "There isn't a night goes by that I don't get down on my knees and pray that they take the bastard off shore duty and put him on a destroyer that will sink."

Kilgallen was affected by the war only in the sense that her father, noted Hearst journalist Jim Kilgallen, was shipped over to cover the Pacific for his papers the day of the Pearl Harbor attack. Thereafter, he saw action in the Mediterranean at the battles of Anzio and Casino, and elsewhere. Her husband Richard, tired of answering questions about his nonmilitary status, was at Dorothy's behest named Radio Advisor to the Chief Adjutant General of the Army.

Kilgallen's contribution to the war effort, beyond keeping Richard out of it, consisted mainly of her work for the Father Duffy Canteen which was named after the famous Broadway priest, Rev. Francis P. Duffy of St. Malachy's Church. Kilgallen, observing the work of Gertrude Lawrence, who would travel around in uniform and distribute sandwiches to soldiers patrolling the Broadway beat, enrolled a group of her own to do likewise. They formed a small group of women, as her biographer Lee Israel described it, "dressed to kill in tailored navy blues, snappy little caps and gold eagles on their shoulders."

Dorothy's group included Dorothy Gulman, a press agent and close friend, Gertrude Bayne, another press agent and close friend, and her sister Eleanor. The group would pick up sandwiches and coffee from Jack Dempsey's, the Latin Quarter, Versailles and Lindy's and distribute them to soldiers at their posts in various lonely spots in the metropolitan area. When their duties were over, Dorothy Gulman would take the unit to be entertained by one of her accounts, Dempsey's or the Barbary Room, where they drank champagne and gossiped. But pretty soon, the unit began to get so much attention for itself that the head of it protested and they quit en masse. After that, Kilgallen's patriotic feelings were expressed in other ways. According to Lee Israel, she began to send to the FBI all subversive communications that came her way. The first was an insane antiSemitic scrawl which accused her of following in the footsteps of "Jew Sobol" and "Jew Winchell" by her "daily hate of Hitler, which proves that you too play to the Soviet Marxist Jews!" She sent the note to Hoover at the FBI and the federal agency opened a dossier on Dorothy. According to Israel, "Dorothy would have liked to have established with Hoover the relationship that Walter Winchell enjoyed."

But the many unverified and credulous reports she poured into the FBI, none of which seemed to be verifiable, led them to dismiss her, according to the contents of her dossier, which was later made public, as "flighty and irresponsible."

No matter how big the war got over there, it was not enough to interrupt the constant eruption of internecine battles between the Broadway columnists themselves. A few months after the war started, a new feud arose between Winchell and Danton Walker. Walker wrote a blind item in his column on January 20, 1942: "One of the Navy's Lieutenant Commanders . . . hurled a bottle of ketchup at a heckler in Lindy's at 4:30 a.m. Monday, then fled into the street to call a cop . . . the offender was booked at the 54th Street Police Station."

The next day Winchell admitted that he was the Naval Officer referred to and that there had in fact been a "conk busting," but he denied everything else and, in fact, an investigation showed that no one had been arrested. He attacked the report as "carelessly itemed by the columnist who once fled from a girl playwright and hid in the Stork Club basement for an hour. The Lindy's free-for-all was started by a chump who now has six stitches in his head to remember it by."

But Winchell wasn't through with Walker. He followed up next with a taunt about "that whoopsy columnist's original job," and printed a letter that he had received saying that Walker "started out as a female impersonator in the Grand Street Follies . . . in 1925—sa-wish!" As people said in those days, "Don't fool with the Lone Ranger." When Winchell got mad, he really lashed out.

Walker responded with this item: "Lieutenant Commander Winchell has won his first engagement in the battle of Broadway with ketchup bottles at six paces . . . will the new slogan be 'Remember Lindy's!' in lieu of 'Remember Pearl Harbor'?"

For the next few weeks, the columnists kept sniping at each other. Details of the fracas were lacking. Winchell claimed that the bottle was thrown by somebody behind him and was aimed at him, rather than at the man who got hit, who was William Lipman, a Bronx building contractor. Lipman's wounds were in the end treated at Polyclinic Hospital and no action was taken by anybody except the columnists against one another.

Some years later, in its lengthy exposé of Winchell, the *Post* revealed the story behind the Great Ketchup Duel. Lipman had written to Winchell asking him why, as a Jew, he continued to plug the Stork Club. In his letter, Lipman commented critically on Billingsley's attitude toward Jewish patrons. Winchell never answered the letter, but ran into Lipman at about one a.m. in Lindy's by accident. According to members of Lipman's party, they began discussing the letter that Winchell had ignored amongst themselves. Winchell was standing nearby and presumably overheard the dialogue which was highly unflattering to him. The columnist walked over to another table, picked up a ketchup bottle and hurled it at Lipman. It was badly thrown; and when Lipman tried to catch it he was hit over the left eye. Winchell ran out and Lipman was taken to the Polyclinic, where stitches were taken. Meanwhile Winchell, apparently anxious to cover himself, had sought out his friend, Broadway detective Johnny Broderick, who showed up at the hospital and took Lipman to the West 54th Street Station. On the way over, Broderick disclosed that Winchell had called him at his home. When they arrived at the station, Winchell was already there with several of his friends. There was a long discussion in which Winchell charged that Lipman had been offensive and started the hostilities. Finally, after much charging and countercharging, both sides agreed to drop the matter. Winchell and Lipman were forced to shake hands and walked out together. As they were leaving, Winchell pulled out the small, pearl-handled revolver he always carried in his coat and said: "What if I had used this on you?"

Lipman replied: "Would that have made you a bigger man?"

Winchell found it harder to brush off the attacks of his enemies in Congress, who now put pressure on the Blue Network, a subsidiary of RCA, to censor the Sunday night broadcasts of Walter Winchell and his colleague and friend Drew Pearson. The network, pressured by various members of Congress, sent a memorandum to the two commentators not to make "derogatory or insulting remarks" about any member of Congress or "any other person holding any public office."

Navy Secretary Knox defended Winchell's position and said that while Winchell had made his remarks as an active duty officer, they were "not considered as scandalous conduct tending to the destruction of good morals." With the help of a liberal press which leaped to his defense and the general wartime dissatisfaction with isolationists, Winchell got out of that without any trouble. But his feud with Cissy Patterson in Washington became even more bitter. Patterson at the same time launched a vendetta against Drew Pearson, which was all the more poignant since Pearson was her son-in-law and, some suspected, either had been her lover or at least was a "love object" of hers.

"Whenever Cissy came to town," Winchell recalled, "she romanced me to take her riding in the car along the crime beat and tell her anecdotes and tales of the beautiful people and the not-so-beautiful gangsters who populate Broadway.

"She liked me so much," Winchell remembered, according to Ralph G. Martin in his book *Cissy*, "that when I brought my daughter to Washington, Cissy insisted we not return to Manhattan in a 'silly little old regular chair car' but in her private Pullman."

But in 1942 Winchell came to one of Evalyn Walsh McLean's parties with his friend J. Edgar Hoover. They were sitting with Cissy and Evalyn when the Washington publisher suddenly said to Winchell, "Why don't you quit looking under your bed for Nazis?"

"You mean, and finding them?" Winchell responded.

"I mean, your column, which is read only by servants down here, is becoming a bore the way you keep after the Nazis."

"Mrs. Patterson, why don't you get another boy?"

It must be remembered that aside from her genuine pro-Nazi or at least pro-German feelings, Cissy Patterson was a notorious and poorly-controlled drunk. She left the table and the party after Winchell's remark, and Winchell soon felt the brunt of her anger. His column was now not only frequently shortened, but relegated to the back pages, as was Drew Pearson's. At the same time, Cissy Patterson described him in print as "a middle-aged ex-chorus boy suffering from a chronic state of wild excitement, venom and perpetual motion of the jaw." She called him "a pop-gun patriot," and "a grimy clown . . . one of those whispery, furtive characters who used to pop up from nowhere to ask if we'd care to buy some spicy French postcards."

She went on to describe "that chamber of horrors he

calls a brain." Even in the privacy of her home, when she heard him on the radio, she would yell, "Turn that bastard off!"

In one headline in her paper, almost an inch high, she called Winchell a "cockroach."

Winchell counterattacked, describing Patterson in his column as "the craziest woman in Washington, D. C."

Cissy called her lawyer and said, "I want you to sue Winchell and I want you to sue him TODAY!"

The lawyer demurred, aware that there was no real case. "Do you want to talk about it?" he asked.

"No," Patterson answered, "because if I do, you'll talk me out of it."

The suit was exceptionally stupid, since Winchell's contract made him immune to damages.

"He is forever boasting that he is the American Hitler would most like to hang," Cissy commented. "In what respect does that make Hitler different from anybody else?"

Martin comments: "This vitriolic attack was probably triggered by liquor and drugs, but its source might have lain deeper. The isolationist gospel she preached had been loudly rejected by most Americans, her readers among them. She was exhausted and embittered by her long battle to change public opinion. She realized that she was engaged in a losing fight, and she did not like to lose. Her defeat was doubly galling because it represented a victory for Roosevelt. Cissy might well have turned some of her rage toward FDR's supporters. Perhaps it was this emotion that gave the hysterical tone to her attacks on Winchell and Pearson."

In August 1942, Elmer Hollander, a Pennsylvania Congressman, went so far as to demand that the FBI investigate "America's number one and number two exponents of the Nazi propaganda line—Cissy and Joe Patterson."

It didn't help Cissy's cause any that one of Winchell's enemies, rabble-rousing, antisemitic preacher Gerald L. K. Smith, nominated her to his personal hall of fame. Cissy was beginning to get increasing quantities of hate mail. A bomb was thrown into her newspaper building. And then, inexplicably, one day, set in the middle of an ad for a house in the classified pages of the *Times-Herald*, was the line, "SHIT ON ELEANOR JEW PATTERSON." This was ironic, since one of the principal charges against Patterson was that she was anti-Semitic.

According to Martin, her attitude toward Jews was "confused and complex. She had married a Jew; her former son-in-law was part Jewish and so was her granddaughter; several of her lovers had been Jewish or part Jewish . . . Herbert Swope, who had made her part of his family, was Jewish; Bernard Baruch whom she admired so extravagantly was Jewish; . . . yet her conversation was studded with all the derogatory cliches about Jews that she had picked up at so many parties from so many peers. She laughed delightedly at anti-Semitic jokes. And now her new concern was that Jews were the strongest backers of the war."

Winchell responded to Cissy Patterson's suit by informing his syndicate, King Features, that he would not renew his contract with them when it expired in November. He made it clear that his purpose was to get rid of Eleanor Patterson.

When renewal time came, King Features acceded to Winchell's pressure and eliminated the *Washington Times-Herald* from its list of Winchell subscribers. Winchell thus had performed a rather unique trick—he had fired his boss.

In 1943, her case came to trial, and she tried to drop it in return for a $25,000 settlement. But Winchell refused to pay a farthing. The case was dismissed by the court.

It was the heyday of Winchell's power, and when the war began to turn a little more favorable, he could be excused for overweening hubris. Almost weekly, he had messages from the President, thanking him for this or that chore. At one time, he ran into John Steinbeck who said he had a message from the President. "What was the message?" asked Winchell.

"Well," began Steinbeck, "I saw FDR and he told

Winchell (right) with Brigadier General Elliot Roosevelt and Mrs. Roosevelt (Faye Emerson)

Walter Winchell (left) in the Cub Room of the Stork Club with attorney Ernest Cuneo, General C.R. Smith, and Brigadier General Harold L. George

me to tell you confidentially that all your troubles in the Navy were being caused by the influence of Col. McCormick, Cissy Patterson and Capt. Patterson. They were out to discredit you, the President said. And they called on their friends in Congress to help. The President said to tell you, 'Thank God you came through in good shape.' "

On another occasion, Roosevelt told friends, when Winchell was under attack, "After the war, when Winchell's real story is told, it will show that he served his country well and faithfully—on important military missions and otherwise."

In the middle of all the wartime excitement there was a somewhat amusing sidelight when Emile Gauvreau, who had not been heard from in some years, sued Winchell over comments that the columnist had made about Gauvreau's best-selling autobiography, *My Last Million Readers*. Winchell had claimed that Gauvreau was unable to write and had hired a ghost to turn out all of his signed stuff. One of the amusing angles of the lawsuit, which was ultimately settled, was that the *Washington Times-Herald* was right in the middle of it, since the paper had published the column about which Gauvreau was suing. Whatever settlement was made, it couldn't have hurt Winchell, because as mentioned before, his contract with Hearst protected him against such suits.

In Roosevelt's last years, personal attacks on him by the lunatic fringe increased, and Winchell, who had a deep personal loyalty to the Chief Executive, became seriously concerned. One day, while Winchell was in the Oval Office, Roosevelt showed him a letter he received that morning from one of his sons who was in the service overseas. In the letter, the President's son wrote that he was distressed by the slanders uttered against his family by administration enemies in Congress. The end of the letter read, "Pop, sometimes I really hope one of us gets killed so that maybe they'll stop picking on the rest of the family."

"Will you please let me tell the people about this on

Sunday night?" Winchell pleaded.

"No, you mustn't," the President said.

"Please," Winchell begged. "Somebody has to explain the meanings of these attacks on your children. All four of your boys are a credit to their country."

"Walter, you never asked me for a favor. Don't start now. Please let that letter remain unprinted," Roosevelt said.

The next day Winchell tried to go around the President by appealing to Mrs. Roosevelt, but she was no help. "If he told you not to print it, don't do it," she advised.

The principal attack against Roosevelt's sons was the work of an isolationist Congressman named Lambertson. Shortly after the interview with the President, Winchell discovered that Congressman Lambertson's own son had registered as a conscientious objector with his draft board. Since Roosevelt had not said anything against the use of this story, Winchell put it on his following broadcast. The next day, Grace Tully, the President's secretary, called him. "That was some little trick you performed last night," she said.

"You mean I'm in the pup tent?" Winchell asked.

"Better get down here today," Miss Tully said.

"Did you hear it?" the columnist asked.

"Everybody heard it," Tully responded.

"Everybody?"

"I mean *Mister* Everybody!" Tully answered.

The next day Winchell proceeded directly to Washington and to the President's office. As he sat down near Roosevelt's desk, he noticed a newspaper clipping on it. It was a report of his own Lambertson radio story of that Sunday night.

The President pointed to the article, smiled gratefully, and said, "Thanks."

Once during the censorship dispute, when some controversial lines were eliminated from Winchell's script, the President, who was on a half hour later, broadcast the same information to the nation.

Winchell, according to columnist Leonard Lyons,

233

asked the radio executive who censored his script: "Did you hear that? He is saying the very things you would not let me say."

One of the executives replied: "Yes, but the President is on sustaining (not sponsored)."

Even during the war, Winchell didn't restrict his column entirely to politics. When the Olson and Johnson revue, "Hellzapoppin' " was produced just before the war, most of the drama critics wrote blistering reviews which normally would have killed the show. But Winchell had been at the opening, had enjoyed himself thoroughly and had given the show rave reviews in his column and on his radio program. The drama critics laughed at Winchell's taste, which simply made Winchell repeat over and over again that the show was "a dandy antidote for the blues," and "was worth the price of the ticket." As far as could be seen, strictly on the basis of Winchell's plugs, the show went on to play for five years, grossed $7 million, and made Olson and Johnson millionaires.

Toward the end of the war, another producer, young Michael Todd, whom Winchell called the boy wonder of the big stem, brought a show to Broadway, an expensive musical called "Up In Central Park." It opened to mixed reviews, but Winchell was extremely enthusiastic about the show in his column and on his radio program. On Monday after the broadcast, there were lines around the block, which continued until the show became one of the hits of the season. (Winchell's daughter, Walda, acting under the name of Toni Eden, was given a small part in the play, but quit after a few weeks.)

In April of '44 Winchell was saddened when his friend Damon Runyon underwent an operation that revealed that he had cancer of the throat and had to have his larynx removed. Five months later, he had additional surgery on his lymph glands, which were also cancerous. He knew he was dying. There was no time for him to learn to speak with an artificial voice box and he was from then on forced to communicate by writing voiciferous notes or going home and typing out his comments. It was out of this association that Winchell's most creditable enterprise, the Damon Runyon Fund for Cancer Research, grew.

Winchell's gloom over his chum's fate was exacerbated by the death of the President in April of 1945. Roosevelt had been probably the only person in the whole world, other than J. Edgar Hoover, in whom Winchell had complete faith. And something in the columnist seemed to crack with the death of his hero. From that day on, Winchell was a strangely changed man.

27.

"Walter Winchell executed a political about turn after the war. The move perplexed his followers, amused his enemies, and helped bring about his destruction . . . He was a unifying figure at a time when Americans sought desperately to be together—first to combat the Depression, then to fight the war.

"That changed. With the bewildering loss of the father-figure, Roosevelt, and the disillusion with a victory that brought no peace, the American spirit became fragmented. Walter Winchell contributed to that bewilderment and disillusion . . ."

(Robert Thomas in *Winchell*.)

For one thing, Walter Winchell and Harry Truman simply were two different men. Roosevelt, on the other hand, a sophisticated, adaptable, cosmopolitan, Easterner, a man of the world, appreciated Winchell's zippy style and his New York wise-guy manner. Truman, his homespun Kansas successor, was a different matter, although he did at least make a gesture of friendship when he invited Winchell for a private interview to the White House. Winchell's version of his break with the President was that he was offended by the President's use of gutter language during their talk. Winchell admitted that he was not above such salty expressions himself, but felt that it was not becoming to a president.

According to another Winchell version, Truman had attempted to exercise his Missouri charm on Winchell and had actually, to some extent, succeeded. But after he left the office, Winchell suddenly remembered leaving his hat (apparently Winchell had been willing to remove the ever-present lid in the presence of the president). As he opened the door to retrieve the fedora, he heard Truman say to one of his assistants: "I guess we pulled the wool over that sonofabitch's eyes."

In any event, they got off on the wrong foot. Winchell's advice about how to run the country's affairs was ignored by the president. After Winchell printed some material that the press had been given off the record, Walter became completely *persona non grata* with the testy Truman. "No man should consider himself more important than the president," Truman remarked. Winchell was stung and he began to snipe at the president, just as he would an ungrateful crooner. When Winchell ran an item saying that the president's daughter Margaret, to further her show business ambitions, had undergone a secret nose job, Truman exploded with anger.

When it was suggested that Winchell temper his criticism of Truman in light of the huge problems facing the president, he replied derisively: "Does he have to get out six columns a week *and* do a Sunday broadcast?"

Winchell's attitude toward the president caused a subtle shift in the constituency of his readers who were largely working class and middle-of-the-road liberals, both of whom strongly supported the new president.

At the same time, Winchell's relationship with his colleagues on the main stem was as stormy as ever. The long Winchell-Lyons friendship suffered a serious strain in the late spring of '45. Winchell had been planning to take his usual summer vacation from his radio show and had been discussing with network officials who would be his temporary replacement. Lyons wanted the spot badly, and took it for granted that his pal Winchell would recommend him.

Winchell, however, had a different idea. He suggested that three personalities should substitute for him in his weekly fifteen-minute spot. From a long list of names submitted to him by ABC Radio, Winchell chose only Frank Kingdon, an ex-college president, to handle the serious news side of the show. As far as the other two, Winchell told network officials, "It's up to you fellows to select and supply them."

Winchell was in California when he first heard that Lyons wanted the job, but by that time it was too late. The network picked Quentin Reynolds and Florence Pritchard as the other two replacements for Winchell. Lyons was upset and in *Variety* he charged that Winchell had double-crossed him.

After a certain period of strain, the long bond of friendship between the two prevailed. When Winchell returned to New York they resumed, for the moment, their nightly chit-chat meetings at the Stork. But some years later, in 1952, when Lyons was involved in a court proceeding in which he was challenged to reveal his sources for certain information, the relationship suffered a more serious rupture.

Lyons was threatened with contempt and a possible jail sentence for his refusal to talk.

Winchell, twitting the always-serious Lyons, wrote in his column that "jail might do Lyons some good."

In a column a few days later, he quipped, "From the Lyons Den to the Lyons pen."

Lyons was not amused by Winchell's jests and launched a series of counterattacks in his own column. The old controversy was renewed, only more savagely this time.

Lyons found it embarrassing to serve on the board of the Damon Runyon Fund which Winchell had founded and was a vice president of, and he formally resigned. This opened the way for some serious journalistic infighting, which soon degenerated into another Broadway feud, especially after Lyons told his readers that Winchell, the super-patriot, had never voted or even registered to vote.

Winchell rose to the challenge. Nothing was left to the imagination. Lyons was now on his "drop dead" list. Winchell wrote of his former pal: "The liar's den again affectionately embraced the Duke and Duchess of Windsor. Not all his former neighbors (on Rivington Street) and those around Lindy's have forgotten that news photo of the Windsors (in Berlin during the purge), giving the Nazi salute, standing alongside Hitler's murderers, Ribbentrop and Goebbels."

And so the public controversy continued ad nauseum.

Winchell managed to regain some popular esteem in 1950. The International Ladies' Garment Workers Union had put up a $25,000 reward for the capture of the man or men who had stabbed a certain William Lurye to death in a West 35th Street phone booth on May 9, 1949. A month after the reward was posted in a Sunday night broadcast, Winchell appealed to those who had information about the murderer to report it to him so that he could give to the Runyon Fund the $25,000 reward. Nothing happened until the following May.

Here is what Winchell said subsequently developed, as he wrote it in a column:

"I had forgotten the Cancer Fund angle when I was approached (a month ago) by people I had never met before . . . 'Would you be interested in bringing in B. M.?' said the party. (Benedict Macri was the principal suspect in the Lurye slaying.) 'He has been thinking over what you said on the radio last year. He feels that since he is being accused of taking a life—he would be doing a decent thing in coming in to you—so that the reward could save lives someday.' This speaker then arranged for me to discuss it with others . . . the conversations lasted from two to three hours for three nights in succession . . . that was early June . . . 'Besides the Runyon Fund angle,' I remarked during the first meeting, 'what else do you want from me?'

" 'Nothing,' said the spokesman, 'except maybe you would be interested in knowing something about Benedict Macri. He has never been in any trouble until this thing happened. He has never been arrested—not even a parking ticket or passing a red light. He has a wife and children. This might never get in the papers and we thought maybe you would write that.' "

There followed, as in the Lepke case, more meetings, more weird phone calls, and finally a rendezvous with a go-between in the mid-fifties which led to the surrender of Macri to the columnist at 20th Street and Eighth Avenue, the same neighborhood in which Lepke had turned himself in eleven years before.

Winchell got much mileage and kudos from the Macri surrender. However, Macri, who was a friend and close associate of the murdered gangster Albert Anastasia, ultimately beat the rap in the Lurye stilettoing. But the ILGWU gave the Runyon Fund $10,000 anyway. Macri went to work in Hazelton, Pennsylvania for a mob garment factory. But by this time, the whole brouhaha had blown over and Winchell had another feather in his cap.

In this era Winchell and most of the other Broadway columnists, following the lead of Senator Joseph McCarthy, developed a severe case of anticommunist whim-whams. Winchell had been booming McCarthy's cause and defending him against detractors since 1950, when McCarthy first started his wild-eyed attacks on what he said were homosexuals in the U.S. State Department. But he kept his enthusiasm for the Wisconsin Senator within bounds at first, until it bumped smack into an old question of Winchell's loyalty when McCarthy got up on the floor of the Senate and tore into Washington columnist Drew Pearson.

Pearson's crime, according to McCarthy, had been uninhibited attacks on "tail-gunner Joe." McCarthy demanded that Pearson's sponsor, Adam Hats, drop the columnist. It was a serious attack, and one that could cost Pearson quite a bit. The Washington columnist was hard-pressed for allies. Six years earlier, he and Winchell had stood together when they were attacked in a similar situation for criticizing Congressmen, and they had successfully thrown back the attack. Now, in the same situation, Pearson put in a strong appeal for Winchell's help. But Winchell, by this time, was in a situation where he could not afford to offend McCarthy. He turned his old friend down cold.

In return for his devotion, Winchell became the recipient of some of McCarthy's choicest confidences. Of course, this operated to McCarthy's advantage, since

240

everything he told Winchell was immediately put in the papers—without being checked.

McCarthy would often appear at the Stork Club and sit down at Table 50 to attend Winchell's nightly lectures on himself and pass along his latest tidbits about reds in government, show business and elsewhere. However, McCarthy was unreliable, sometimes even regarding his own personal life. On September 7, 1953, he tipped Winchell that he and his fiancée Jean Kerr were going to get married by the end of the month. A week later, Winchell had to make one of his rare retractions to announce that the engagement would not be announced after all. Four days after that, Walter was embarrassed to see the happy news of McCarthy's wedding in all the headlines. Winchell explained it this way: His column had been right on both occasions, he wrote. McCarthy himself had been his source. The lady had broken the engagement between the appearances of the first and second items; that was all. Then she had once more changed her mind—a woman's privilege. However, Walter never did understand why McCarthy didn't tip him off before the final news was broadcast to the world. Despite this double-cross, Walter remained loyal to McCarthy, even in view of many critical comments from his readers. At least he was now on a path that was pleasing to his Hearst bosses.

By this time, every Hearst columnist was firmly on the McCarthy bandwagon, including Dorothy Kilgallen and Igor Cassini, the new society columnist who had come to the *Journal* from the *Washington Times-Herald* where he had been a favorite of Cissy Patterson. Cassini was appointed to replace the late Maury Paul. He was much friendlier to Dorothy Kilgallen than Paul had been and although he himself was a Russian aristocrat refugee, he did not make such a high-hat distinction between social names and Broadway. In those years, people who were on the anti-red warpath were able to combine political and show business items when McCarthy turned his guns on subversion in Hollywood and on the Great White Way. The House Unamerican

Activities Committee announced: "Communism is rife in the entire film industry."

In the spring of '51, Winchell, after taking it relatively easy on his former show business colleagues, wrote, "Movie moguls will drop red-tainted performers quicker than you can say Joe Stalin."

The next month he followed up: "The explanation and crocodile tears by party deserters (in Hollywood) remind us to warn you all with this from the works of the talented Arthur Koestler: 'Do not trust any ex-Communist—including me!' "

Another item typical of the growing paranoia toward the alleged Hollywood Communist cabal: "Directors, scenarists and others named by the House Unamerican Activities group are having their dirty names deleted from film adverts. S'bout time."

In fact, Winchell's vitriolic attacks on what he perceived as U.S. Communists was so strong that it even brought about a truce with his archenemy, Westbrook Pegler. Now that both supported McCarthy, they met in friendship at the Stork Club, and Pegler for the moment forgot his characterization of Winchell as a "gents' room journalist."

Adela Rogers St. John, one of Hearst's chief writers and a confidante of his, revealed the big part that Hearst himself had taken in this smear campaign. According to Miss St. John, the House Unamerican Activities Committee had the services of the entire Hearst organization as an unofficial research source: "We had two floors of the Hearst Magazines building on Eighth Avenue in New York devoted entirely to the testimony and investigative answers we had gotten. The Hearst crew put all the material together— chiefly through a man named Jack Clements, who knew more about Communism than anybody else, and J.B. Matthews—and then the Committee got into it. Hearst forced that . . . out of this, of course, came the Hiss case and the breakup of the group in the State Department. We made one fatal mistake—and how could anyone have known it? We were looking for a senator to carry the ball. I went down and tried to get Millard Tydings . . . He said, 'Nooooo, noooooo, they'd beat you to death before you were through.'

"The only guy who would go was (Joseph) McCarthy. We didn't know he was a drunk. If McCarthy hadn't been an alcoholic the whole story would have been different, because he had the material but he kept blowing it."

To Dorothy Kilgallen's credit, she did not join wholeheartedly with the rest of the Hearstlings in their attacks on show business Communists. On the other hand, she did not exactly oppose the campaign. She wrote: "*Red Channels* (a newsletter purporting to list left-leaning actors and actresses) may have made some mistakes in linking innocent persons with Communism. And this, if so, is deplorable. But never let anyone tell you that it didn't hit a great many nails on the head."

As for Winchell, many of his intellectual and liberal former supporters were becoming increasingly distressed by his hysterical anti-red program. Some attributed sinister pressures to his unwavering support of the senator. After all, Winchell in earlier years had left himself open to many charges that he could be regarded as pro-Communist during his campaigns for intervention in the European war. One former FBI man who worked for McCarthy boasted "McCarthy doesn't have to worry about Winchell; we've got the goods on him."

Whether this referred to the columnist's political background or his personal life was not explained. Some of Winchell's friends said that the columnist privately hated McCarthy. One source quoted in a *New York Post* profile of Winchell said, "I've had many talks with him about his relationship with McCarthy and he always tells me to keep calm and says: 'Don't be a schmoe, how can I go for a man who defended the Malmady massacre?'

"But Walter was once charged with being a commie tool and I think his support of McCarthy comes from insecurity and an attempt to prove to the public that he is one million percent anti-commie. He is trying to build up a record of being anti-commie to answer bigots like Gerald L. K. Smith.''

Winchell's palship with McCarthy, of course, involved becoming friends with some other questionable colleagues of the senator, such as attorney Roy Cohn and his sidekick, G. David Schine. When Schine was attacked for using his influence to get passes in the Army, Winchell wrote: "Ladies and gentlemen, don't let the Communists get you fighting among yourselves . . . the real issues are the Alger Hisses, the Rosenbergs and all the submerged Communists among us who have given and are giving our secrets to Russia.''

Winchell even extended his friendship to the youthful neoconservative William Buckley, Jr.

In the course of his anticommunist diatribes, Winchell got into a serious shooting match with the *New York Post*, which he accused of being a nest of subversives. The *Post* responded with a 24-part series which raked every part of Winchell's career over the coals, but somewhat surprisingly gave a clean bill to his private life. Whether this was due to a lack of information or some form of journalistic loyalty was never disclosed. This feud with the afternoon paper exacerbated Winchell's rift with Lyons and also finally got him into a beef even with the amiable Earl Wilson. All this resulted in a savage lawsuit between Winchell and the *Post*, in which the *Post* sued Winchell and Winchell countersued for defamation of character. The *Post* claimed that Winchell's epithets for its editor James A. Wechsler tagged him untruthfully with the label of Communist. Winchell often referred to Wechsler as "Ivan Wechsler," called his paper "a presstitute," a "postitute" and "el pinko." Also he frequently referred to the paper as the *New York Compost*. During the trial, Winchell tried to claim that when he said "el pinko" it was a misprint for "el punko" and that "Compost" simply referred to a heap of dry and decaying leaves. In the end the court rejected Winchell's excuses and fined the Hearst organization $30,000. They also forced Winchell to publish a lengthy retraction of his statements that

Wechsler or his paper were Communists or sympathetic to Communism.

"If anything which Mr. Winchell said was so construed, he regrets and withdraws it," the retraction said in part.

"The *Mirror*, too, wishes to retract any statements which were subject to such construction . . ."

Winchell was also forced to broadcast the same language on his radio program on behalf of himself and his sponsors. In the end, Winchell's devotion to extremist right-wing views and his loyalty to the bigots among his friends, led to the scandal which brought about the downfall of the most powerful journalist in American history.

28.

In the South and in colonial empires, "planters" are people who grow cotton, copra or peanuts and walk around in broad-brimmed straw hats. But on Broadway a planter is something else. He is a press agent whose principal goal in life is to place articles about his clients in the various Broadway columns. In order to persuade said columnists to carry these plugs, the press agent must feed a certain number of "free" items, that is, interesting tidbits about people who are not clients of his. Many of the columnists actually had a formula by which they would reward the column planters. With Winchell, for instance, he would give the press agent's client one plug for every five free items that the press agent gave him. Despite their denials, all of the Broadway columnists to some extent are the tools of press agents, many of whom are more interesting and colorful than the columnists themselves. Wilson, Lyons and Hy Gardner of the *Herald Tribune* always claimed that they dug up their own material, and they did spend more time doing the rounds and personally interviewing their sources than some others, but just the same all of them at one time or another made use of these substitute wordsmiths.

Franklin Roosevelt said once: "No one has something to say five days a week." Commenting on this, Barry Gray, broadcaster and once briefly a *Post* columnist, said, "And so trash filled the Broadway columns regularly—tidbits from press agents, puffs for free meals from restaurants, plugs for ingenues (for free love—what other reason?). In short, it was a jungle . . ."

Some press agents actually made a fulltime career out of just placing items with Winchell. Among his inner circle of "bodyguards" was Ed Weiner, who later fell out of favor by daring to write a biography of his famous friend, and Irving Hoffman, mentioned earlier in these pages. Hoffman also had a small apartment in what had been the La Hiff building.

Columnists, especially Winchell, paid press agents not only for news items and gags but for clever word inventions as well. Many of the coinages for which Winchell became famous originated with press agents. Kurt Weinberg, one of Winchell's inner circle, once got five plugs for his clients by slipping Winchell a piece of paper on which was written: "NeWWsboy."

Columnist Earl Wilson freely admitted getting much of his word coinage from press agents. Gertrude Bayne, one of the few female column planters, once called Wilson and said, "Listen Earl, how about calling him Frank Swoonatra in your column just as a gag?"

Wilson took the suggestion, ran the item, and soon found the coinage being used in columns all over the country. "How do you like that for plagiarism!" Wilson commented, humorously.

If Winchell didn't like a gag submitted by a press agent he would say, "Try it on Sobol," or "Maybe Sullivan will buy it." If the joke did get printed by another columnist, Winchell cracked, "I see my rejects are ending up in the garbage pail."

Irving Hoffman, the bright, brainy, nearsighted cartoonist and writer, was the most important press agent in Winchell's life and the only one who dared to sass him back. Biographer Thomas believes that the friendship between Winchell and Hoffman was "perhaps the only abiding friendship that Walter was to know in his lifetime. Hoffman appeared to be the only person besides June Winchell who could tell Walter when he was wrong, and get away with it."

"Gossip columnists are the carpet-sweepers in the Hall of Fame," Hoffman had the nerve to say once to Winchell. And Winchell had such faith in his friend that he even let him enter the *Mirror* composing room and make changes in the column proofs. Of course, the association with Winchell helped to make Hoffman a rich man. Movie studios placed Hoffman on a retainer of $25,000 a year only because of his access to the chief columnist. Hoffman also represented corporations, producers and others who valued the good will of Winchell.

It was Hoffman who had one of the most brilliant p.r. inspirations in the history of that shady trade. When the King and Queen of England visited FDR in 1939, Hoffman suggested to his friends who had a pipeline to the president that FDR serve them hotdogs and explain to them: "Here we call them Coney Island Red Hots." FDR was amused and complied and the story was page one and also featured in newsreels. Hoffman represented Coney Island and his friend Nathan Zapkin was press agent for the frankfurter industry.

Winchell and the other columnists were able not only to get items fed to them but to get all sorts of services and freebies from the press agents who were so anxious to plant plugolas in their column. According to Lyle Stuart, ten years after Winchell had started his column, he wrote about himself in the *Literary Digest:* "I don't golf, fish, swim, fly in planes, play the piano, cook or even ice skate."

When a hanger-on asked him why he didn't learn to fish or swim, Winchell stood looking at the friend, tight-lipped, skeptical, narrow-eyed.

"Listen," he said finally with gruffness in his voice, "if I want to fish or swim, I don't have to learn. I'll send a press agent to do it for me." Then he turned his back and walked away.

Winchell's use of press agents was probably the most flagrant in that he seldom appeared in public without three or four of them surrounding him—he called them his bodyguards. Being among this select group was in itself worth a fortune to the press agents, because with its radio outlets and mass syndication his was considered the best column break in the country. Lyle Stuart, describing the situation, said: "The press agents scurry about to curry Winchell's favor. They shudder when he is roused. They wince when he burps. And many of them have secretly admitted that they despise him upon whom much of their livelihood depends.

"Without Winchell a press agent is 'nowhere' . . . and so they live in ulcerous anxiety that they will offend the man whose columns they fill." The general pattern for Broadway press agents was to submit their hot items in succession to the various columnists, selecting the items according to which would be suitable for a certain column, but trying always to get the big break in Winchell first.

Winchell, it must be said, always did them the courtesy of returning their items the next day if he was not going to use them, which left them free to submit the items to Kilgallen (second choice during most of the heyday of the columnists' power) or to Lyons, Wilson, Sullivan and so on down the line. On the other hand, Winchell was one of the few who used entire columns scripted by press agents and he would not consider an idea for a column on spec. The poor press agent would have to write the entire column and then submit it for the master's approval. Since most press agents are busy people (spending a lot of time convincing their clients that they are giving them a terrific buildup) these Winchell columns were often written by freelance writers hired by the press agents. Sometimes the freelancers were newspaper men (like Frank Farrell, later a columnist himself). Press agents paid varying rates for these columns, ranging from $50 or $60 each up to $300 if the column was actually used by Winchell. Winchell of course paid the press agents only in plugs, but it was well worth it. In those days of relatively uninflated dollars, a press agent could clear twenty-five or thirty thousand dollars a year just by having access to Winchell. The columnists would usually edit the material, zip it up and give it some of their own personal flavor. Since the writers were aware of the market they were writing for, there was usually very little revision necessary.

In addition, the columnists would collect several hundred items a week for their Broadway gossip columns. One of Winchell's strengths was the number of these short items he carried which packed a lot of information or misinformation into a small column. According to Bob Thomas, one of Winchell's biographers, many press agents suffered from a malady they called "the seven o'clock stomach." They claimed that their digestive systems would become upset as the time approached for the *Mirror* to be delivered on the midtown newsstands. They couldn't eat a bite or digest any food until they had scanned page 10. If there were no items mentioning their clients, dinner would be even a greater hazard. They knew that they'd soon have to answer angry calls asking, "Why can't you get me in Winchell?" The press agents made up their daily schedules to fit Winchell's. They knew just where he'd be at any given time and they submitted their material accordingly. Some sent copy by mail or hand delivery to Rose Bigman, Winchell's girl friday at the *Mirror*. A very rare few who had the real Winchell "in" were allowed to deliver material to his apartment in the St. Moritz. Some press agents would drop by the barber shop in the Taft Hotel where Winchell was shaved and trimmed every day at 6 p.m. and drop off items. Some even got themselves shaved twice a day so that they could accidentally be on the premises when Winchell was there. According to the owner of the barber shop, business fell off forty percent during the weeks that Winchell was out of town.

One of the problems was that Winchell's principal hangout, the Stork Club, was no-man's-land for column planters. Billingsley was openly hostile to press agents who tried to conduct business in his place, so most had to wait for Winchell's late night visits to Lindy's or Dave's Blue Room.

Wherever press agents got together, Winchell was likely to be the main topic of their conversation. Several of them were playing poker and began to tell little taunting jokes about Winchell as they dealt the cards around.

Jack Turman, one of the press agent players, gazed skyward and addressed the Great Deity: "Walter, I'm not listening!"

Once Winchell broadcast the information that Bette Davis was dying of cancer. She issued a detailed and indignant denial. That night, one of the press agents joined his friends in Lindy's and remarked, "If Bette Davis doesn't have cancer, she's in trouble!"

Winchell called the column planters his "field agents." Kilgallen called them her "spies." Lee Israel, author of *Kilgallen*, Dorothy's biography, was intrigued by the sexual metaphors of the press agents' lingo—*servicing, planting, scoring*. "Dorothy was a quirky number, easily tantalized and just as easily turned off. To succeed, a press agent had to apprehend her vagaries, her tastes, her sensibilities, what she liked, what alienated her, how to handle a spat, when to lay back, how to cajole, when to telephone directly and when, more wisely, to work through intermediaries."

Among those "servicing" Kilgallen in those days was Liz Smith who started out as a press agent, went on to become an assistant to society columnist Oleg Cassini who was now writing under the Cholly Knickerbocker byline, and ultimately today is the largest syndicated gossip columnist in the country, and probably the only top-rated one.

One of the press agents wrote of his columnist contacts: "They're all spoiled. I guess psychologically they hate to admit they couldn't exist without us. You can't write a column *six* days a week without a lot of *peepholes* feeding you information. If all the press agents died tomorrow, the columnists would have a hell of a time. It's *phiz*-ically impossible to be everywhere and check everything."

Very few of the columnists bothered to check the multitudinous items that poured across their desks. They enforced accuracy by the expedient of cutting a press agent off if they were fed a wrong-o. Walter Winchell would put them on his "drop dead list" for periods of from three to six months and sometimes forever, depending on the importance he gave to the wrong information. Kilgallen and the others used the same technique to keep their informants straight. Many of them avoided being accused of having something wrong by making up not only the item but the person in the item. Cassini in his gossip column actually made up the names of celebrities about whom he planted items and then would find to his mischievous amusement that he was getting other items from press agents about these fictitious celebs. One of these was "Stuyvesant Pierrepont" whom he had romantically involved with a French countess. Pierrepont challenged a rival to a duel and was seen wining an dining all over town. Eventually Cassini himself confessed the hoax. Another of his inventions was "Elliott Weems," a handsome, eccentric millionaire from Akron, Ohio who performed super feats with girls. Although "Weems" had no talent at all except for girls and spending money, invitations by the score poured into the office for him, and other columnists began to see him about town. Cassini decided to kill him off.

Cassini had to resort to these tactics because he was somewhat at the bottom of the list for press agent feedins. "In the beginning," he said, "I could not rely on them as much as I might have liked because of the pecking order. The best stuff went to Winchell . . . The minute Winchell discovered any one of them had given a hot item to a competitor, he would bar the guilty publicist from his column for months. In other words, because he was king he could hit where it hurt . . ."

As a result, Cassini was forced to do his own digging, to learn to be a good reporter. Cassini says that Danton Walker at one time carried so many press agent releases verbatim that as a joke someone sent him a tip about two people carrying a torch for one another. Walker ran it, only to discover to his horror that the names belonged to two male waiters, who didn't appreciate the joke at all.

If Winchell was the king of the columnists, then Eddie Jaffe was certainly the king of the Broadway press agents. Bob Sylvester devoted a whole chapter of his book *Notes of a Guilty Bystander* to Jaffe and the mob that surrounded him. Jaffe occupied a two-room apartment on the top floor of the building at 156 West 48th Street, which had once housed Billy La Hiff's Tavern. The quarters were famous for having sheltered such stars as Winchell, Ed Sullivan, Jack Dempsey, Damon Runyon, Toots Shor, Mark Hellinger and Bugs Baer. Jaffe was a small, wiry man with a shock of Brillo-like hair and a gift for making friends. Almost overnight, his apartment became a twenty-four hour hangout for a group that ranged from broken-down Broadway actors and entertainers to some very glamorous celebrities indeed. According to Sylvester, there was hardly a night—or even an afternoon—when a drop-in could not find there a Hollywood star, a noted beauty, a few hustlers and even some solid businessmen. Also producers, politicians, policemen and a rare few honest workingfolk. One of the reasons a lot of the men came around was that Jaffe's apartment served as a sort of home-away-from-home for pretty young actresses and out-of-work chorus girls, strip-teasers in the burlesque shows that were a major part of the town's entertainment scene at that time, plus any lonely or displaced female of whatever motivation. They hung around at Eddie's because he never demanded anything from them and was always helpful, sometimes even with a free publicity break. "Romance flowered at Eddie's," Sylvester reported, "although hardly ever for Eddie. In the midst of the gab, the raucous laughter, the tears and sometimes the hysteria, some pretty fantastic deals were launched in Eddie's pad . . ."

Once Eddie was doing publicity for a hillbilly guitarist and country singer. "Look," Eddie told this client, "you sing and play guitar and you are from Louisiana. Why don't you go down there, get up in front of those hicks, play your awful guitar, sing those songs, make a speech and run for governor. I can get you a lot of publicity and maybe a record contract."

The homesick folksinger liked the idea. It did get him

some publicity, and it also got him elected Governor of Louisiana. His name was Jimmy Davis.

One of the people who launched his career from Eddie's pièd-à-terre was Marlon Brando. "He was a difficult guest," Jaffe remembers. "He would take off his dirty socks, borrow a pair of mine from the top drawer and leave his dirty ones in the same place—as a reminder for laundry service, I guess."

Brando hated Jaffe's phone, which was constantly ringing. He would answer it by stating: "Mr. Jaffe's former apartment. Mr. Jaffe passed away this morning."

Jaffe couldn't care less. He once made a survey and found out that 63 percent of the phone calls that came to the apartment were not for him, anyway.

Singer Dorothy Dandridge met the musical director of "Carmen Jones" at Eddie's and landed a leading role in the film.

"Even when she was famous and playing the Waldorf," Jaffe remembers, "she would insist on coming to my joint after work and washing the dirty dishes. Indeed, we rarely had any other kind of dishes."

Rodeo cowboys also tended to hang around Eddie's place, which was quite near the old Madison Square Garden. One of Jaffe's clients (and some suspected, his secret lover) was Margie Hart, the stripper. Jaffe had even gotten a slick name for her trade from H. L. Mencken—ecdysiast, which Margie used for years to describe her specialty and which got her acres of space. In those glory days, Eddie's place might be used for any kind of deal. In one of the rooms, Jimmy Hoffa's lawyers and lieutenants hatched a deal that edged Dave Beck out of the top spot in the Teamsters Union, and edged Hoffa into same.

Julie Newmar, then an unknown, tall and buxom showgirl, in her campaign to turn all of Broadway on to health foods, was a regular at Jaffe's. While the tall, well-endowed showgirl was busy dishing up sprouts and wheat germ, Jaffe and other colleagues were trying to persuade a young man named Jackie Mason to continue studying to be a rabbi and stop trying to tell jokes because he had a horrible Jewish accent.

Often the approach of the press agents to the columnists was bizarre or masochistic. There was even an approach called "the weep." In this effect, the press agent would come to the columnist with a press release in hand and inform him that the boss would fire the bearer if the story wasn't printed, and that his wife needed another operation or even that the bearer himself might have some terminal ailment. One press agent went so far as to dress a small girl in old, tired clothes and send her to see the various columnists. "My Daddy's sick in bed again," this mock offspring would tell the columnists, "and Mommy said I should stay out of school today and help him get well by bringing you this envelope." Art Franklin, one of the master press agents and column planters, once had bandleader Cootie Williams for a client. Williams, after sending Franklin his fee every week during a long road tour, came back to the city and barged angrily into Franklin's office, complaining that he had received very little publicity for his money.

"Are you kidding?" Art asked. "Why, everybody in town is talking about Cootie Williams."

Cootie, mollified, was impressed. "What are they saying?"

"They're saying, 'Whatever became of Cootie Williams?' "

Oddly enough, Williams still kept him on.

One of the most prolific employers of press agents was Arthur Murray, the dance master, who insisted that his flacks keep planting Arthur Murray jokes in all of the columns. One day he fired a flack who had not succeeded in planting a gag for two weeks. The press agent asked Murray why his services were being terminated. "You have lost my sense of humor," said the humorless Murray.

29.

"Power is the great aphrodisiac," Henry Kissinger once said. Certainly that axiom worked for those Broadway columnists who wanted to avail themselves of the power of the press. Some were notoriously strait-laced and no breath of extramarital activity, even in that secret underworld of unpublished gossip to which they were all privy, was ever even hinted at. Wilson and Leonard Lyons took their wives with them practically everywhere and were considered the ultimate family men. Sobol, too, was considered of that blameless ilk. But others furnished the night folk with enough gossip to fill a column out of their own personal lives every day. The most flagrant in their sex activities were Winchell, Kilgallen, and Lee Mortimer, though others certainly must have indulged their powers from time to time.

Winchell had been flaunting his dalliances in print almost from the beginning of the column, as noted before. After a while he got the message from his wife June and avoided publicly bragging of his activities—in print, at any rate. Winchell would get favors from ambitious showgirls, singers, film starlets and the like. But as frugal as he was by repute, he often would patronize prostitutes. His friends couldn't understand why he was paying for something he could receive for a simple plug in the column. The answer was that he considered call girls safe, especially after one embarrassing Hollywood experience. Winchell walked out of a nightclub into a parking lot. A nude girl leaped out of a nearby car and rushed toward him, trailed by a photographer. Fortunately, Winchell spotted them and dashed back into the club for refuge. Later he said that he suspected some of the pro-Nazi groups he had been attacking of being responsible for the incident. For some time thereafter, he was extremely cautious about being compromised. One of his friends commented, "From now on Walter will get laid while wearing an overcoat."

But Walter continued his pursuit of women right up to his final days. He described it as "my favorite sport—bending, stretching, and coming."

Of course chippies, harlots and ambitious showgirls weren't the only women in Winchell's life. Once some of Walter's many enemies spying on him got a report that Winchell had registered for two bedrooms in one of the newest hotels in Washington, D. C. Everybody knew that June was not with him and there was much curiosity about the occupant of the second bedroom.

At about nine o'clock that night a very pretty young red-haired woman entered the hotel, got on the elevator and went directly to Winchell's suite. She was eagerly followed by spies out to get the goods on Winchell. They watched from around the corner as the redhead knocked on Winchell's door and was admitted a moment later. Now the spies knew something was going on. The question was to find out exactly what, and get proof of it. Around midnight the hotel informant rushed over to them and offered to sell them a hot tip.

"Room service has just received a call from Winchell's suite, from Mr. Winchell himself, to send up *two* plates of ice cream, *two* pieces of chocolate cake and *two* cups of coffee," the employee told them. For $50 one of the spies persuaded the room service waiter to turn over his apron and the food delivery cart.

The spy-waiter then walked into Winchell's suite, pushing the food order before him. He saw Winchell there in his shirtsleeves, slouched comfortably in an easy chair. The redhead was there too, in a negligee, lolling on the sofa. While the "waiter" arranged the dishes, the goodlooking red-haired woman walked over to Winchell and said, "Darling, you're wonderful and I love you." She leaned down and kissed him.

The waiter left Winchell's suite very happy. He felt he

had conclusive evidence of monkey-business on Winchell's part. He prepared an affidavit that night to be used in an attack on the columnist. But there was one thing wrong with it. The lady described in the affidavit as "young, well built, pretty and redheaded," was Walda Winchell, the commentator's daughter, who at 12 o'clock that night had become 17 years old.

Lyle Stuart was then editor of a weekly newssheet called *Exposé*. From information amassed for the newssheet, he wrote a biography called *The Secret Life of Walter Winchell*. According to Stuart, Winchell's reputation had become so notorious in regard to women by the late twenties, that Forenz Ziegfeld, the Broadway producer, used to warn his showgirls against dating any Broadway columnist, but especially Winchell. "He has the worst reputation on Broadway where women are concerned," Ziegfeld would say. "Any girl who wants to remain proper will not date Winchell." Wilson Meisner, the Broadway wit, phrased it differently. "There are two ways for a showgirl to become famous. Vertically and horizontally. If you're going to do it horizontally, it will be quicker if you know Winchell."

When he was too young to be cautious, Winchell would parade his women where they could be seen and admired. Every new woman was a buttress to his insecurity about his place in society and the world.

Winchell was not content with showcasing his women in the night spots, but would kiss and caress his companion in a possessive way so that the whole world could see that their relationship was more than a purely social one. Once, he even got into an argument about the size of his companion's bust measurement. He insisted that the waiter find a tape measure and then coolly measured her bust from several angles and opened her top buttons to prove that she wasn't wearing falsies. All of this activity irritated June Winchell exceedingly, and finally she refused to appear with him at all in public. Hellinger tried to warn Winchell: "A married man can't be running around too much, Walter. At least, not running where so many people can

Walter Winchell with daughter Walda at the Stork Club

see him."

Winchell made a half-hearted effort at discretion. He rented a top-floor suite at the St. Moritz Hotel on Central Park South (or perhaps was given the use of it in return for publicity). He would escort his lady friends of the moment through the lobby in the early morning hours and then send them home alone about noon that day. A few elements besides Hellinger's warning, though, caused Winchell to become at least a little more cautious. One was a rumor that somebody in the mob was going to try to blackmail him after framing him with a girl who was under the age of consent. Another factor was his knowledge that he had made many enemies and some of them might be imaginative enough to have private eyes follow him and record his romantic shennanigans. And in fact, an incident involving a fellow newsman confirmed Winchell's concern and caused him to move carefully, at least for the next few months. The newspaper man—we'll call him "Al"— was alone one day in the second floor walkup apartment he shared with his wife. His wife had left to take in a movie, as was her custom on Monday nights. About a minute after she'd left, somebody knocked on the door. Al, thinking his wife had returned for something she'd forgotten, opened the door without asking who was there.

The next scene took place in less time than it takes to describe it. A fifteen-year-old girl pushed past him into the room, ripped off her blouse and brassiere and began to scream: "Help! Police!" She had hardly gotten out the first cry when two policemen miraculously appeared, running up the stairs with their pistols drawn.

"This man tried to rape me!" the girl cried. Al was given two alternatives: either he could face the charge of attempted rape of a minor, or he could leave town within twenty-four hours. Al appealed to everybody for help, but nobody seemed to be able to do anything. Winchell, who was a close friend of his, was shocked. He called the police commissioner and the commissioner told him to "lay off" Al's case. He even went to Hearst executives, but they shrugged their shoulders, as if to say they were helpless. Somebody big had it in for Al, and there was nothing anybody could do about it. Winchell let the incident serve as an object lesson to him. From that point on, he would have his girlfriends rent a private apartment and then would abandon the apartment and the girl after a month or two. Sometimes he would continue to sneak them into the Moritz through the servants' entrance on 58th Street, but nobody ever actually seemed to get around to photographing Winchell ducking in and out with his various popsies.

The one thing Winchell did not worry about was being exposed by his fellow columnists. There was an unwritten law that none of the columnists, even those engaged in career-long blood feuds like Winchell and Sullivan, would ever expose his colleagues.

In his actual dalliances, Winchell usually managed to keep things light, temporary and without strings. But in the mid-Forties, as he approached the fifty mark, love came to Winchell in the shape of a tall, lushly endowed showgirl from Texas who possessed enormous charm and poise. Her name was Mary Lou Bently. She was 16 when they met. Those who know about such things agreed that she was definitely one of the best looking showgirls ever to hit Broadway, and her freshness at a time when showgirls were, as Lyle Stuart put it, "more tart than art," was like a breath of clean air from the Texas plains. Winchell was truly smitten. When they started going together, he temporarily abandoned Table 50 at the Stork for one at the Versailles where Mary Lou worked. He would tell press agents to whom he was displaying her for the first time, "I don't have to point her out. You'll know her. She stands out from all the others."

After years of discretion, Winchell finally once again put aside caution. Once more he walked right into the front door of the St. Moritz with Mary Lou and would be seen publicly with her in nightclubs, kissing, patting and caressing her, nibbling her fingers and once kissing the arch of her foot. "It's the first time I've ever really been in love," Winchell told a friend. "I never knew what it was like before. She's wonderful."

Meanwhile, Mary Lou herself was a bit more discreet and tried to ward off suspicion by officially rooming with Mary Dowell, who Winchell also helped to make famous as "Stuttering Sam" Dowell, calling her the "prettiest of the Texas skyscrapers . . ."

Naturally because of the columnists' code and the threat of Winchell's wrath, nobody dared to write any items about this romance.

Young Mary Lou seemed absolutely thrilled with the power and poise of her new boyfriend. Owners of the clubs where she worked treated her with extremely special consideration. Winchell, always afraid that he would be taken advantage of by a woman, actually spent very little money on her but Mary Lou hadn't been accustomed to much and besides, even without spending money, Winchell could expose her to a level of luxurious eating, drinking and presents which was overwhelming to the girl fresh from the Texas prairies.

Lyle Stuart saw Mary Lou Bently as representing Winchell's lost youth. "She was the gay era of Texas Guinan that would never be again for him. She was calmness and confidence, beauty and grace. Where he was a minority in a minority in a minority, she sprang from the heart of America and was cool and clean and untarnished by the lust and ambition that still burned deep in the heart of Winchell.

"She had no goal beyond feeding and clothing herself and enjoying herself. She had no goal but he knew he must work hard to the last day that he lived to retain the illusion of power and importance so dear to him."

But ultimately, as it must in these things, the hot flame of ardor cooled after several years. Finally Mary Lou stopped staying at Winchell's apartment and had him deliver her to her own. Then one night she refused to let him in. "What gives? I'm no stage door Johnnie," he complained.

"It's over, Walter," she said. "You know that."

"There's someone else?"

"Yes."

Winchell turned on his heel and left without even saying good night. He moped for a week away from his usual haunts. Earlier he had indicated that he was willing to give up the Bently girl, but the idea of her taking up with someone new rankled. He flew to Miami where he cried on Al Jolson's shoulder. (Their feud had been patched up years before.) "I don't understand it," he said. "The kid was crazy about me."

Winchell went so far as to hire a private eye to follow Mary Lou and find out who his successor was. It was a radio announcer named Frank Gallop, who remained her friend for several years before going on to other pastures.

Even two years after the breakup, Winchell felt a special proprietary interest in Mary Lou Bently. He discovered that she had gotten a job in Billy Rose's Diamond Horseshoe and he called Rose, who was also a notorious womanizer.

"Billy," he said, "I want you to keep your hands off that girl."

"I'm not interested in her," Rose protested.

"Just the same, I know your reputation. You lay off that girl."

As far as it is known, Rose did so.

In 1950 Mary Lou married an army officer and went off to live with him in Japan.

Oddly enough, Winchell seemed to have no animosity toward Gallop and did not knock him in the column. He even once okayed him to audition as an announcer for his own program. (But Gallop didn't get the job.)

Winchell didn't have a notorious public romance again until 1953. By that time, he had definitely passed the age where a young kid like Mary Lou Bently would have taken him seriously. He focused his attention on Jane Keane, part of a sister act of singers and comedians that had had a modest success.

Betty, one of the sisters, was the mother of a nine-year-old child by actor Frank Fay. She had been living with him for some years when she became pregnant and reminded him that he had once promised to marry her. But by this time Fay had become a devout Catholic and he claimed that in the eyes of the Catholic Church he was still married to his first wife, Barbara Stanwyck. The couple parted, but in later years when visitors asked who the child was Betty would frankly answer, "That's Fay's kid."

Winchell liked both Betty and Jane and at first had trouble deciding which one he would go for. Finally he chose Jane. He set about winning her over. Once before, he had joined a vaudeville actress in her bedroom, and after she had given in to him the first time, she told him frankly, "Walter, I want to get paid off in plugs for this."

This time Winchell launched his campaign by plugging the Keanes even before the request was made. In one two-month period, he gave the two sisters 21 fulsome plugs. It was an irresistible one-man campaign that would have convinced even the greatest doubting Thomases that the Keane sisters were the most exciting new act in show business.

"Every big-time talent agency is vying to sign Betty and Jane Keane who are killing the people in Vegas at the Sands . . ." one plug raved. Another: "Matty Fox sent those Keane girls a contract which their barristers are studying. 'At least a dozen TV films' annually for the 'Betty-Jane Keane Corporation.' Two weeks ago (before orchids here) they were a Sister Act. Now they're gonna be a corporation!"

On and on the plugs went, and certainly the Broadway cognoscenti knew which way the winds were blowing, although it may have taken them a while to figure out which sister was Winchell's choice.

In Beverly Hills he spent hours alone with Jane in her hotel room. Lyle Stuart, not a friendly biographer, claims that at the time Winchell was "a little old to do much of the usual thing, so mostly he did what was usual for him: he talked about himself."

It is not known where Stuart got his information from

but it would seem that unless Winchell himself told it to him, it would have had to have been from Jane Keane.

Others apparently gossiped privately about Winchell's talents. John Crosby, who had known Winchell fairly well and ultimately became one of his devout enemies and critics, said: "I saw Winchell give . . . venomous treatment to several aspiring young singers or actresses at Table 50—as if he knew no pretty girl would sit with him except to get her name mentioned in his column.

"Pretty girls slept with him for the same reason. I knew one young singer trying to get noticed on Broadway via Winchell's bed and she told me: 'It was terrible. The telephone kept ringing with items for his column.' "

Crosby concluded that Winchell was "truly a 14-carat sonofabitch, no doubt about it.

"He invented keyhole journalism, as unsavory a headstone as any journalist could wish for. He could sell 40,000 copies of some awful book with a single mention in his column. And did. He could ruin an actor's career by accusing him, probably falsely, of being a communist. And did. He looked like a cross between a weasel and a jackal and he was indeed a bit of both. He was the true father, not only in America but all over the world, of gutter journalism . . ."

While he was still carrying on with Jane Keane, Winchell had a casual but intense affair with another young up-and-coming actress, Marilyn Monroe. Not only had Winchell abandoned discretion by this point, but he often bragged freely about his sexual achievements. When he was in Hollywood, producers like Samuel Goldwyn and Harry Cohen provided him with willing and beautiful playmates whose performances he would describe to one and all afterwards. Oddly, he described Marilyn's talents as strictly "average." According to Stuart, he gave detailed descriptions of the anatomies of prominent movie stars. "Being an experienced reporter, he noticed everything, from the shapes of their nipples and vaginas, to their sexual aptitudes and proclivities. His knowledge of this subject was practically encyclopedic."

For a time he patronized Polly Adler's elegant "House Is Not a Home" along with other big names, including Nelson Rockefeller. Some say that the reason Winchell was so critical about Marilyn's talents was his growing preoccupation with the alleged red conspiracy. One of his items subsequent to his romance with Marilyn said, "Marilyn Monroe will be a *Time* Mag cover story soon. I can't imagine them digging up anything people haven't read before. Unless they name the authors, stage directors and others (so close to her lately) who are on government lists as informed reds, etc."

It was around that time that Winchell leaped to the defense of his friend, J. Roland Sala, who was handling the defense of accused socialite panderer Mickey Jelke. In a daring move to aid in Jelke's defense, Winchell delivered a girlfriend of his, Grace Appel, to the defense attorneys, at the same time arming Sala with a slip of paper advising what questions to ask. The lawyer drew from Appel the strange story that she had been in Joey Adams' apartment in the Waldorf-Astoria Hotel some years ago. She said that some men in the apartment asked Pat Ward to join them in what is commonly known as a gang bang. Grace, who was a childhood friend of Pat Ward, who stood accused of being the leader of a band of prostitutes being purveyed by Jelke, said she was shocked at the request. Pat Ward, however, couldn't seem to remember the incident, nor could anybody else. But apparently the purpose of the testimony was to indicate that Pat Ward was a loose woman before Jelke allegedly led her down the primrose path. All in all, it didn't do much good for the defense, nor did it bring Adams' name into disrepute. Adams denied the whole thing. Winchell seemed to feel that his gesture had been effective, however. He sat back smirking with satisfaction, until assistant district attorney Anthony Liebler began his cross-examination.

"Grace," he said, after some preliminary questions, "did you ever call my wife and tell her that you were in love with Walter Winchell and wanted to stay with him as his child?''

Winchell signalled violently to the girl, shaking his head so that she would answer no, and she got the message and answered Liebler's questions sobbing, ''No.''

After a few more questions, Liebler dismissed Grace Appel from the stand, walked over to Winchell and put his arm around the columnist's shoulders. ''Walter, I didn't intend any implication with that question. I just wanted to show the jury that the girl was a little, well, you know. She acted pretty crazy on the telephone.''

Winchell was extremely shaken by the question. ''What about my wife?'' Winchell blurted. (June had recently suffered a respiratory infection and was seriously ill.) ''She's dying and you ask a question like that. What effect do you think it will have on her?''

Liebler finally offered to write a letter explaining the source of his information, if it would help Winchell with his wife. Winchell accepted but was not completely mollified.

''She's almost dead,'' Winchell muttered. ''This'll kill her.''

Liebler assured Winchell he would make the letter plenty strong and would completely clear Winchell. Unfortunately Winchell, on the following day, ran a full-column attack on Liebler. Liebler told an assistant, ''If he's going to be that way about it, I'm not going to write his lousy letter.''

Winchell followed up with a series of attacks on the assistant DA whom he was anxious to ''get,'' and even put investigators on his trail to find any incriminating circumstances they might rake up. About his own part in the affair, he wrote in his column, ''The fact is that for a woman to say she loves Walter Winchell is no attack on her credibility . . .''

But the confidential report Winchell finally received on the private life of Anthony Liebler hardly filled the bill for Winchell. It had been prepared courtesy of a press agent who paid the investigator $100 a page for the six-page report, hoping to get an in with Winchell.

"How is it, Walter?" he asked as the columnist riffled through the pages.

"Nuts," Winchell said. "This Dutch bastard doesn't do anything but go home at night. He's been married eighteen years and all he ever does is go home."

It was a strange way of life, as far as Winchell was concerned.

Even more flagrant in his lifestyle was Lee Mortimer, who with *Mirror* editor Jack Lait, would fill in on the Winchell column when Winchell was on vacation. Lait and Mortimer, in the early Fifties, became notorious for a series of alleged exposé books called the *Confidential* series, full of information about sin and sex and crime in America's big cities, New York, Chicago, Washington and finally around the world. The information was about 30 percent accurate and the research often took no more than a few days.

Mortimer's third wife, Una White, a singularly beautiful Anglo-Indian girl, was one of the famed French Casino beauties. Later he told a newspaper that she had married him in order to stay in the country. The marriage, which lasted three years, was fairly stormy, as the bride herself told it. "I went to play a London engagement in 1939. When I got back to New York, people were talking. To me, about me, behind my back, to my face. Everywhere.

"It was a known fact that Lee was running around. He was playing about, mostly with Orientals. Everybody knew. And everybody whispered it to me."

She went to California the following year and got a divorce on the grounds of mental cruelty. The charges were true. Mortimer once showed up at the Stork Club with no less than four slant-eyed beauties on his arms, but left very quickly when Billingsley, Broadway's prime xenophobe, advised Mortimer that "four Oriental girls at a time are too many."

Mortimer became so involved that he was quoted as saying at a later time, "No white woman is worth marrying." By this time Mortimer's tastes were so well known that when Ann Koga, a 13-year-old Hawaiian schoolgirl of Japanese descent wrote to the *Mirror* asking if she could find a pen pal in the United States, the city editor turned her letter over to Mortimer. Strangely, Mortimer answered the teenager's letter and a correspondence developed. Some years later when the girl had become a journalism student at the University of Hawaii, Mortimer made a date to take her out in Honolulu. One year later she came to New York at his invitation and he got her a job as a chorine in a night-club show known as "Lee Mortimer's China Dolls." By this time, Mortimer was collecting for publicizing the nightclub and getting a percentage of the take. Ann Koga became Mortimer's personal agent on the premises. She picked up his take from the nightclub, served as his girl friday and also as his official hostess. By now his apartment in the Beaux Arts had taken on a pronounced Oriental flavor. An Oriental actress described it this way: "You might call it honky-tonk or bastard Chinese," she said. "He had Chinese wall hangings, a sunken living room, a library filled with books on Chinese and Japanese subjects. Veddy, veddy modern."

One of the other China Doll girls said: "He used to invite the whole cast up to his flat for parties. We hated to go, most of us, but we were afraid to stay away. After all, he did get us jobs.

"Ann Koga would extend the invitation. That was long before she became Mrs. Mortimer. Lee would serve drinks, usually champagne. Celebrities would drop in—Joey Adams, Milton Berle, Morton Downey. We'd have to yell we were starving, though, before Lee would send out for sandwiches. Then we'd eat and run."

Ann Koga married Mortimer in April of 1951. According to one article based on interviews with some of the girls invited to Mortimer's affairs, they were "strictly in the exotic orgy class." A guest described a typical Mortimer shindig this way:

"We went up to his apartment in the Beaux Arts Hotel, which is a fashionable place. But as soon as I stepped inside, it was like another world.

"The lights were very low, like a dark bar, and there was strong incense burning. We met Lee and he said he hoped I liked champagne, because that was all he ever drank or served.

"The place was filled with corny pseudo-Chinese art and furnishings, and most of the men were there without dates. There was a whole group of Chinese chorus girls from the China Doll, and when a new man would come in, Mortimer would sort of assign one of the girls to him.

"In no time at all, the guys were making like these were their *regular* girlfriends and nobody else was present—you know what I mean? The lights got even lower and the guys even freer with their hands in a big hurry.

"Finally I got tired of fighting off strange hands and left . . . But there seemed to be a lot of his girls who didn't dare to say no to the guests, even though they looked like they wanted to. And Lee kept wandering around, mauling one of the Chinese girls, and then another, and then another . . ."

It was about this time that Mortimer, who was having trouble holding readers to his column even with his bizarre and racy items, instituted a type of plug which nobody would have wanted. You might call it a telephone plug. To build interest in the column, he would put the names, addresses and phone numbers of the chorus girls that he was mentioning into the column. It got the reaction he wanted—the girls were deluged with pornographic suggestions, telephone propositions and amorous visits from all kinds of perverts and mashers at every hour of the day and night.

Dorothy Kilgallen was for many years the most proper of the Broadway columnists. Although she gallivanted around town more than most, she was usually accompanied by one of her woman friends, Jean Bach the press agent or others, in spite of the fact that it was well known that her husband was a notorious and prominent philanderer. But in 1952 she made the acquaintance of an up-and-coming 25-year-old crooner from the boondocks named Johnny Ray who had just scored his first hit with a song called "Cry." It sold two million copies for Columbia, making it the second biggest record in the company's history. Lee Israel, writing in her book *Kilgallen*, tried to catch the strange appeal of this unusual singer: "There was a Kol Nidre choke in his voice, and a demented revivalist abandon in his performance. He jumped, wept, thumped, whispered, knelt and contorted in a way that no white performer had done before."

At first, Dorothy treated the Johnny Ray phenomenon as something of a joke. But early in 1952 she covered his opening at the Copacabana and wrote, the following day:

"I have a terrible confession to make. A simply awful thing has happened to me.

"How am I going to say it?

"Goodness, it's too frightful, really. (Steel yourself, girl. Get it off your bodice for once and all.)

"All right. Here it is.

"I've come to just love Johnny Ray's record of 'Please Mr. Sun.'

"Now will anybody ever speak to me again?"

By this time Dorothy was not only famous locally through her "Dorothy and Dick" breakfast program, but she had become one of the permanent panelists of the network TV game show, "What's My Line?" She was also covering major crime trials for the Hearst syndicate which earned her even more glamour and reputation. But as she edged into her forties, Dorothy suddenly awakened to sexuality, and Johnny Ray was the unlikely recipient of her attentions—unlikely since he was regarded by many as an end-all alcoholic, constantly getting arrested for weird antics on the road and also suspected of being a homosexual. In 1951 he was arrested in Detroit for making an "indecent proposal" to a young man. He pleaded guilty, but the affair didn't get much public mention.

Kilgallen was so much in love with the young singer that she filled her column with plugs for him, to the point where the Hearst organization had to tell her to cool it off a little, that it was becoming too obvious. When her lover wasn't in town, Dorothy would constantly introduce his name into conversations with her friends and play his records in the background. By this time, her marriage had degenerated to the point where it was not even necessary to hide the relationship from Richard.

Meanwhile Dorothy would go so far as to join Johnny in his road tours, covering up by saying she was going to, say, Chicago to cover a bright new comic, Lenny Bruce.

Oddly enough, she did see Lenny Bruce, who was a friend of Johnny Ray, and Dorothy, noted for being one of the greatest prigs on Broadway regarding off-color language or humor, for some reason got a tremendous charge out of Bruce's act and remained an ardent follower of his during his trying years. According to Lee Israel, Dorothy by this time had not had any sexual relations with her husband for years, and even before that, their sex life had been far from exciting. "God, she was starved for affection," Johnny commented. "Sometimes I didn't know how to handle it."

They would often make love in his apartment during the afternoons when Dorothy was supposedly at the hairdresser, and generally on Sundays, after she finished her stint on "What's My Line?" Ray's place was always full of hangers-on and friends of all sexes and there was little privacy. They would have to make love in the bedroom or the den of his apartment, with everybody fully aware of what was happening.

When she was with Ray, Dorothy seemed to throw all caution to the winds. At a party given by a friend of hers, Harold Rothberg, they were seen by a press agent "lying on that double chaise of Howard's, giggling and fondling and boozing. There must have been ten other people in the room just as *amazed* and *embarrassed* as I was. But it didn't make any difference."

Danny Lavezzo, the owner of P. J. Clarke's, said that they frequently sat at one of the front tables and "necked in the corner with the whole world watching."

Jack O'Brian, certainly the only columnist who could outdo Dorothy in the staunchness of his Catholic ethic and opposition to smut, communism and adultery, finally violated the columnists' code by reporting with some disgust:

> "The *groping* of each other, and the *kissing* and the *necking*! two tables away from me. This is no hearsay. I observed it myself at El Morocco and the Stork. It turned out that while she criticizes other people, *Miss* Kilgallen is not too blameless in her own life."

Lee Israel estimates that a lot of this indecorous public behavior was due to the fact that Dorothy had begun to drink heavily and was unable to hold it as well as she once had. Johnny's own taste for drink did nothing to help the situation. They even went so far as to be seen publicly necking in the bar that Richard Kollmar had opened, called the Left Bank, and later in one of the rooms in her apartment, a risky thing they were driven to by the fact that Johnny had a homosexual roommate which made love-making something of a problem. Dorothy and Johnny could not make love in his apartment while Monty was there, and since he was there all the time, they often had to indulge in their affectionate displays either in nightclubs all over town or risk confrontation with Kollmar in her apartment.

In the middle of all this, Ray was arrested again for "accosting and soliciting" a policeman for "immoral purposes." The officer claimed that Ray had invited him back to his hotel for a drink and had made an indecent suggestion in the process. Johnny Ray said that all he had suggested was a drink. A jury of twelve women acquitted him, whereupon Ray actually fainted. The newspapers gave it a heavy play, except for the *Journal*.

Some years later, Ray became seriously ill, a weakness compounded by his endless pill-popping, chain smoking and drinking. He checked into Mt. Sinai Hospital, where Dorothy visited him as frequently as she was permitted. On one occasion, according to Lee Israel, "his high fever and forced celibacy had begun to take their toll. He (Ray) beckoned to her. She drew the curtain and climbed into bed with him. They were discovered by a nurse, who ejected Dorothy from the hospital."

It would have made a great item for "Voice of Broadway," but even without the benefit of publication, gossip got out and the word reached Dorothy's husband Richard. Finally it appeared that the whole mess would be aired in the press, when the *New York Post* announced a ten-part series—a profile of Dorothy Kilgallen, and it was obvious it would be a hatchet job. Her friends stood by with gritted teeth until the pieces appeared, day by day unfolding the foibles and peccadilloes of the *Journal* columnist, but not a word about her extracurricular love affair. Nobody was certain whether this was due to bad reporting, fear of lawsuits or the journalists' protective code.

30.

A prophet might have noted the first cracks in the Winchell pedestal as early as 1948 when he still seemed to be at the peak of his powers. At that time he was urged by Jack O'Brian and others to get into television. But Winchell turned down the suggestion. He had a nice thing going, spending six months in New York and six months at the Roney Plaza in Miami, and the biggest radio audience in America. At that time television was still in its infancy. It seemed silly to disrupt his life for a tiny audience in a medium that was yet to prove itself.

In June 1948, Ed Sullivan, who had less to lose, went on CBS with a new variety show called "Toast of the Town." Winchell thought his old enemy's stiff, unbending manner and lack of stage presence laughable. It seemed impossible that the show could ever last.

Just about the time that Sullivan was launching his show, Winchell had a serious beef with his long-time sponsors, the Jergens Company, which had introduced a new antiperspirant called Dryad. Winchell refused to handle the commercials for some reason and the argument degenerated into a serious breach. Ultimately Winchell talked himself out of a $390,000 a year contract, but then rejoined ABC at a higher figure.

The next incident, however, certainly has been marked by all historians of the Broadway scene as the beginning of the downfall of the king.

It all started on October 16, 1951.

Josephine Baker, the famous black American singer and entertainer who had become a star in the Follies Bergere dressed only in a bunch of bananas, came to New York on one of her rare visits for a stint at the

Roxy. Following the show, Miss Baker and two friends decided to drop in at the Stork Club for a late evening snack. Baker had been away from the States so long that she probably had not heard the stories concerning Billingsley's anti-Negro bias.

Josephine Baker entered the club with Roger Rico, French singing star of "South Pacific," and Mrs. Rico. They ordered crabmeat, steak and wine. After a long wait, Baker later said, waiters came to the table one by one to report there was no crabmeat, there was no steak, and there was no wine. Then, according to the singer, they got nothing but the silent treatment. According to Shirley Eder, the Hollywood columnist who was there that night, Winchell was present, but not at his usual table. Instead, he was at a small table next to the door.

"We saw Sherman Billingsley come into the room looking pale and angry. He stopped at Walter's table to whisper something into his ear, then he turned and left the room." When Josephine Baker came in, according to Eder, they saw Winchell wave to her and then leave the club. "I remember," Eder says in her book *Not This Time, Cary Grant!* "the service was not particularly good on this night, and we waited a long time for our food, and we noticed that Josephine Baker and her party were not served immediately. We also realized that Billingsley never came back into the room. This was unusual!"

Then, says Miss Eder, Miss Baker got up from her table not too long after her party had arrived and left the room. She was gone for some time. When she returned, there was much whispering and conferring in her party. Then they all got up and left. The Eders sensed that something was happening, but they didn't know what it was. It was obvious, however, that Baker and company did not receive the VIP treatment they were entitled to.

The scene shifts to Chandler's Restaurant, where Barry Gray, a long-time talk show host, had been running a successful program for some years. On that night in 1952, Baker walked into the room five minutes before

Barry Gray of MCA radio

Gray was about to go off the air. He recognized her at once and gathered that she would like to be put on the program, but he pointed at his watch to let her know that the time was practically gone. She nodded and made a sign to have him join her at his table when she was finished, which he did.

At the table, Josephine Baker told Barry Gray that they had waited for service at the Stork Club for more than half an hour and that she felt that she was avoided by waiters, captains and the management. She also said that Walter Winchell had been present at an adjoining table and had seen the whole thing. She was particularly angered by this, for he, she said, was "the great liberal—and did nothing to have his friend Sherman Billingsley intervene and see that I was accorded proper treatment."

Gray didn't know what to do. Winchell had been a friend of his and very supportive to him in his first job at WOR. He plugged the young radio commentator repeatedly and often would stop by in the late hours when Gray got off the air, in the company of Damon Runyon, and invite the tall young broadcaster to cruise the city streets with him, chasing police calls, and then adjourn to Reuben's for a sandwich, where, says Gray, "Winchell would talk, and I would listen, hanging on to every word."

Gray had gained on WOR the reputation for being an abrasive and controversial speaker. Once he had gotten in a hassle when interviewing Broadway publicist Ed Weiner, one of Winchell's closest friends and associates, who had made a snide comment about columnist Leonard Lyons. Lyons, a lawyer himself, threatened suit, and joining him in the hostilities were Dorothy Kilgallen, Ed Sullivan, and Danton Walker, among others. This probably spelled the end of Gray's close friendship with Winchell, who was lined up with Weiner on the other side. As a result of the spat, WOR decided to dispense with Gray's services and he was exiled to Miami for some years, where he worked out of the Copacabana nightclub with some success. On May 5,

1950 he returned to New York to start the show out of Chandler's.

Oddly, Winchell didn't seem to hold a strong grudge against Gray and when he was in Florida he would often drop into the Copa and give moral support, which Gray realized did not hurt with his boss.

He was not anxious to be on Winchell's D.D. list. "If Winchell disliked you," he said, "and wrote about it, the best thing you could do would be find a high window, or a handful of sleeping pills. Don't put it down—many a career ended, and a life, because of Winchell."

Gray realized that putting Josephine Baker on would infuriate Winchell. He hoped that he could stave that off by asking Winchell to come on and answer the charges himself. He called Winchell at home and later in Florida where he had gone following the incident. He was told that Winchell had left and could not be reached. He sent a telegram. He then asked Josephine Baker to return the following night with her attorney, Arthur Garfield Hays, and tell her story on WMCA. All day the town was buzzing with rumors about what would be said about the Stork Club incident. Reporters had already picked it up and it was front-page news and highlighted in Earl Wilson's column.

That night Gray introduced Baker and her attorney, and she told the story of her run-in at the Stork. She then lashed out at Winchell for his apparent indifference to her problem. The next day, Gray tried again to get in touch with Winchell and get his response, but with no success. Instead, Winchell had Ed Weiner and boxer Ray Robinson come up and offer a rather pallid defense, which mainly ignored the actual incident, but touted Winchell's extensive efforts in the cause of civil rights.

"When the program was over," Gray wrote in his book *My Night People*, "I was handed a copy of the *Daily Mirror* . . . The attacks on Baker had begun. She was accused of selling out to the Nazis when France was occupied by the Wehrmacht. She was 'a traitor to

279

America' because she lived abroad. And as I recall, he said her act wasn't too good in the first place.''

Josephine Baker asked for another shot on the Gray show to answer these charges. She showed the audience a medal given to her by the de Gaulle Free French Forces for her efforts on their behalf. She explained that she had gone to live in France, not because she didn't love America, but because she had been so well received as a performer there and like any entertainer, she had to go where the work was.

Immediately after Baker went off the air, Gray was called to the phone. It was Ed Sullivan. Sullivan, who was barred by his publisher from discussing Winchell in his newspaper column, asked Gray if he could come on the air to "defend Josephine Baker." Gray agreed and informed Sullivan that Winchell had been invited and would be invited again.

"It makes no difference—I want to talk about the lady, and tomorrow night if possible!" The poker-faced columnist and now TV star sounded really excited.

Gray wired Winchell yet again at the Roney Plaza and got no answer.

Chandler's was bulging at the seams on the night that Sullivan appeared.

Sullivan launched into a recital of his considerable record as a fighter for civil rights and against discrimination. As for Winchell, he pointed out that Winchell had frequently in his column repeated the words attributed to Voltaire: "I disapprove of what you say but I will defend to the death your right to say it."

"Josephine Baker said something of which he disapproved. I ask you—did he defend to the death her right to say it? No He didn't . . . In his megalomania, he was so burned up that this one voice had risen to question any particle of property or any area of which he was a friend, he called her a fascist, he called her a communist, he called her antiSemitic, and then capped it all by calling her anti-Negro."

Sullivan pointed out that Baker had, in a carefully documented statement, refuted each of Winchell's charges. "Charges," Sullivan said, "made recklessly and with great abandon.

"I say that he is a megalomaniac and a dangerous one.

"Now I say I despise him as a newspaper man," Sullivan continued his attack. "I say he's traduced every ethic of the newspaper world . . . When you picture yourself as Winchell pictures himself—and I've known him for a long, long time—when you picture yourself as a little Hitler, able to tell the big lie over and over again and ruin somebody who speaks up against you, I tell you then that man is in a dangerous state, and I tell you that a country which is exposed to his ravings and his rantings is in a more dangerous state."

Sullivan went on to rake Winchell over the coals, pointing out that the Broadway columnist could hardly understand Baker's situation in Europe since he knew nothing about the Continent, and had never been there, despite the fact that he set himself up as an international expert and an advisor to prime ministers.

"When I sit at a microphone and say I despise Walter Winchell, I despise him because to me he has become dangerously anti-American. He has joined up with the legions of character assassins such as a Senator McCarthy. He represents everything to me that is most hateful in power, entrenched power."

The Sullivan broadcast, and Gray himself, became the focal point of the greatest character assassination campaign that Winchell had ever launched, and he continued it for at least three years. Gray was called (and sometimes in the same column) a fascist, a communist, a heterosexual, a homosexual, a marital cheater, a deadbeat, a lousy broadcaster and unamerican.

Winchell used his word coinages to play some tunes on Gray's name. He was described as "Borey Pink," "Borey Yellow," "Borey Red," and "Borey Lavender."

"It was total war," Gray comments, "and Winchell was doing a first-rate job on all fronts."

The attack got results. Gray's 11 p.m. news program,

sponsored by Sealy Mattresses, was cancelled. Another contract with Channel 5 TV was also cancelled when it still had six months to run.

Winchell was pleased with his handiwork, but didn't seem to be able to let up on the subject. Through his loyal press agents, he pressured guests against going on Gray's program. Gray suddenly found himself the victim of a mass guest freeze-out. Sponsors began to drop off one by one, as Winchell's henchmen passed the word that the sponsorship of Gray made Winchell very unhappy. Winchell even attacked the station, saying that the WMCA call-letters stood for "We Make Communists Adorable."

This overkill had a reverse effect on Nathan Straus who owned the station. Angrily he proclaimed, "If Barry has *no* sponsors, he stays on the air!"

Not all the sponsors did drop out, but the character of the show was changed by the pressure. Celebrity guests who had appeared willingly on the Gray show admitted openly to him that they were afraid to take on Winchell: Danny Thomas, Jan Murray, Phil Foster, Jack Leonard, Sophie Tucker and others. Gray even found that when he went to Lindy's for a sandwich, conversations would stop, as everybody watched who would say hello to him. The only one who did was Danny Kaye.

He started to receive great amounts of crank mail, and once he was told by one of the Chandler's customers whom he believed to have mob connections that "a small contract" had been put out on him.

A few nights later, Gray and a writer friend of his, "Snag" Warris, left Longchamps Restaurant after a late night supper. Snag, who was to drive the broadcaster home, entered the car on the driver's side and Gray waited on the other side for him to cross and open the door. Then suddenly he heard the scuff of a shoe behind him and when he turned to see what it was, he was struck a heavy blow in the eye and went down, unconscious. Snag was still reaching for the door and didn't see what had happened, but he did see three men kicking something on the ground. Gray was being worked over, kicked in the ribs, groin, head and face, but was not really aware of it, because he was already unconscious.

Warris yelled, "What are you doing?" and leaped out of the car to help, but one of the men pulled a gun and said, "Stay out of this, you bastard!" All three then jumped into a car and took off.

Snag helped Gray back into the car, and took him to the police station to make a report. The next day, the *New York Post* carried a full front-page picture of Gray, complete with his wounds, cuts and bruises.

The police shrugged their shoulders and said they could do very little. They asked him if he knew of anyone who might want him worked over. Gray's replies gave rise to Earl Wilson's comment that "the suspect list has narrowed to 1,000." However, the police did assign a two-man bodyguard team to travel with him for a while. After three months he asked that the guard be removed, but the police then insisted that he carry a .38 caliber Colt to protect himself.

In the fall, Gray was to start a new series at Dumont Television in the old John Wanamaker Building. As he approached the studios at ten o'clock one night, three men came swooping around the corner. Gray didn't actually notice them, because he thought they were running for a bus. There was a stop on the next corner and he often saw people trying desperately to catch the bus before it left. As the men came opposite him, his back was to them. Suddenly he felt himself hit across the back of the head with a hard, metallic object, knocked down and again kicked repeatedly. He was left in a semi-coma on the sidewalk and the men left as swiftly as they'd come.

Again the police came and again the same questions and the routine, and a feeling of helplessness about catching any of the perpetrators. Gray moved out of town to Westchester, and the police would convoy his car to the first toll booth near the George Washington Bridge, at which point Westchester Highway Police would convoy him home. Local police would cruise the streets protectively afterwards, all night. After he almost accidentally shot a neighbor who came upon him in the darkness, Gray decided to dispense with the pistol.

Meanwhile, Winchell had still not given up in his attacks. He gave Gray's home address in New Rochelle, so that the hate mail now reached him directly at home. "There were threats by mail, strangers slowly driving past our house. In short, a period of harassment that one who has not been through it can hardly imagine!" Gray wrote.

His income dropped precipitously. The phone stopped ringing and the invitations ceased. And most disturbing to Gray was what he called "the total silence from Ed Sullivan's quarter and from Josephine Baker."

The silence from Sullivan was understandable, since it had been a long policy of the *News* not to publish anything about Winchell. But then Sullivan didn't even return Gray's calls.

Josephine Baker, though she is probably unfortunately best remembered now for the Stork Club affair, had her share of excitement. She lived through four husbands, scores of lovers (including Hemingway, Simenon, and Le Corbusier) and gained the attention or friendship of Castro, Collette, de Gaulle, Mussolini, Peron, Picasso, Tito and El Glaoui, the Pasha of Marrakesh.

Eventually, after moving his program to a series of restaurants, Gray made it a studio audience show in the station premises above Lindy's.

But for the first time it seemed as though Winchell himself was being hurt in this slugfest. His liberal friends had long since left his bandwagon during his McCarthy era hysterics, and had been waiting for a chance to take a crack at him for a long time. He was now feuding with everybody—with the *New York Times* and its publisher Arthur Hays Sulzberger; with the Pulitzer Prize Committee for never having recognized him even with a dunce prize; with his old editor on both the *Graphic* and the *Mirror*, Emile Gauvreau; with *Time* magazine; with the *New York Post*; with Leonard Lyons and Ed Sullivan as well as Barry Gray, plus the *New Yorker* magazine which had written a disparaging profile. Also with President Harry Truman, Drew Pearson, Elmer Davis and Arthur Schlesinger, Jr. He was at war with the book-publishing industry and with Bennett Cerf, in particular, whom he accused of lifting gags without credit. He had turned against the Democratic Party and opposed Adlai Stevenson viciously. And finally, he even got into a beef with Earl Wilson.

A writer for *Theater Arts* magazine commented, "The only columnist not in an active feud at the moment is Louis Sobol, who is too little, and Hy Gardner who is too insecure."

Actually the only one who didn't get into the squabble was Kilgallen, who contented herself with a few snide blind items about Baker. Of course, at this time Dorothy had other things on her mind.

Meanwhile an erstwhile publisher of raunchy silk-stocking sex magazines decided to launch a new gossip publication called *Confidential*, apparently lifted from the successful book series by Mortimer and Lait—without credit. Harrison however was clever enough to realize that if he started out with a fulsome plug for Winchell, he stood a chance of getting excellent publicity for his scurrilous exposé publication. His first issue featured a story called "Winchell Was Right About Josephine Baker." Harrison actually took the magazine to Winchell and showed it to him. On the following night on his network radio program, which was by now a television simulcast, Winchell held up his copy of the magazine.

"I'm telling you," Harrison told an *Esquire* reporter, "from then on this thing *flew*. That was what really made *Confidential*, the publicity."

Aware that they were on to a good thing, *Confidential* began to publish a Winchell-angled piece in every issue.

"We tried to figure out who Winchell didn't like and run a piece about them. One of them was 'Broadway's biggest double-cross.' It was about all the ingrates who Winchell had helped to start their careers who turned their backs on him and double-crossed him or something. We had one in every issue. And he kept on plugging *Confidential*. It got to the point where some days we would sit down and wrack our brains trying to think of somebody else Winchell didn't like. We were running out of people, for crissake!''

It wasn't long before people got the idea that perhaps Winchell owned a piece of *Confidental*, which was soaring to enormous circulation. Within its first few years, it reached almost four million copies per issue, which was the biggest magazine circulation in the country at that time.

(Ironically, Harrison had gotten his start as a teenage copy boy on the *Graphic* at the time that Winchell was working there on his first column.)

Of course, Harrison basked in the reputation of being a confidant of Winchell's. A columnist ran a story saying that Harrison had been taken for a ride by gangsters.

''It was a completely phony story, but when Winchell read about it,'' Harrison remembered, ''he was mad as hell and he called up and said, 'What's the idea of not giving me that story first?' I told him there was nothing to it, it never happened, but he didn't believe it.''

Harrison also managed to make a good contact with Lee Mortimer, with whom he conducted a mock feud for years. Mike Todd told reporter Tom Wolfe: ''He used to meet Lee Mortimer . . . in some damn booth. Both of them would get right in there in the same booth and talk, and Mortimer would give him stories, for crissake.'' Later they would sit in nightclubs and glare at each other balefully for public consumption.

The ''feud'' also gave rise to another important publishing venture. Lyle Stuart who had been, up to this point, an admirer of Winchell's stands in his more liberal days, had just launched a newspaper called *Exposé*. Its first issue sold only about 2,000 copies. But the next issue, which was devoted entirely to a hatchet-job profile on Winchell with a news peg of the Baker case, ultimately sold 150,000 copies.

In addition to rehashing the Baker affair, Stuart printed a number of matters that had not been covered by Winchell's more polite adversaries: Winchell's reliance on press agents and his extramarital romances.

Stuart's first order of 10,000 copies somehow became ruined in a bath of mimeograph ink at the newsdealers' union. Stuart borrowed some money and printed more. He actually delivered the copies to the newsstands himself.

Winchell couldn't ignore Stuart's attack. He sent his spies out to dig up whatever dirt they could on the brash young reporter. They found that Stuart had once pleaded guilty to an attempted extortion rap at the age of 19. But this didn't cut a tremendous amount of ice. Winchell got friends in the police department to help harass Stuart. A publisher of comic books for whom Stuart was the business manager found that his office was raided and Stuart was arrested on the grounds that the comic books were obscene.

"Attention all newsstands!" Winchell blared in his column the next day. "Anyone selling the filth of Lyle Stuart will be arrested in a similar manner!"

In an incident that seems shocking in retrospect, Stuart, when he stepped out of his home in North Bergen one day, was blackjacked unconscious by three men. Stuart managed to pick two of them out of a police lineup and they were convicted of assault. Nobody could tie Winchell to the beatings, yet they bore an unnerving parallel to the beatings that Gray had suffered.

But in many ways Stuart came out of it all better than Gray. One night on his television simulcast, Winchell held up a copy of *Confidential* that featured an attack on Stuart. "Read about this rat!" Winchell commented. Stuart went to court over it. He won $21,500 in the libel suit, which combined with his profits on *Exposé* enabled him to establish his own business as a book publisher.

287

The interesting thing about Stuart's attack on Winchell was it signaled the end of the Winchell era. People seemed to accept his report and were even anxious to read the worst about Winchell, once their hero.

Looking back on it now, it seems as though *"l'affaire Baker"* was both the high and the low point of the Broadway gossip columnist era. It led to deep rifts and animosities that never healed, some of which grew into even deeper feuds in the years to come.

31.

There is no reason to believe that if Winchell had taken his original television offer in 1948, he would have became a star. But what happened to Sullivan, a man with relatively little show business background and certainly no onstage personality, must have irked his long-time enemy no end.

"The Toast of the Town" was a hit with the public right from the start. The first show featured a couple of young comedians who had been recommended to Sullivan by his daughter Betty—Martin and Lewis. The two comedians were an instant hit, as were the other acts for which Sullivan in the beginning paid scale. Still nobody could quite understand why the show worked and why the audiences liked it. Certainly the critics and most intelligent commentators thought it laughable. CBS also was not impressed with Sullivan as a performer. Emerson Radio, his first sponsor, dropped the show after 13 weeks, but CBS began offering The Toast to other sponsors "with or without Sullivan." To his dying day, Sullivan never forgave CBS management for that slight. Remember, these were the days before Neilsens were available for precise measurement of audiences.

John Crosby, admittedly one of the most acerbic critics and the most intellectual on the New York scene, tore the show to shreds. He led off this way: "One of the small but vexing questions concerning anyone in this area with a television set is: 'Why is Ed Sullivan on every Sunday night?' . . . In all respects a darn hard question . . . and it seems to baffle Mr. Sullivan as much as anyone else . . .

"After a few opening bars of music, Mr. Sullivan, who is introduced as a nationally-syndicated columnist, wanders out on the stage, his eyes fixed on the ceiling as if imploring the help of God, and begins to talk about his 'very good friends.' Sullivan's 'very good friends' include virtually everyone in show business, several of whom are waiting in the wings to perform their specialty . . . If the dear friends are show people, Mr. Sullivan may request them, with rather steely insistence, to come up and amuse the folk. Mr. [Bob] Hope, one of the highest-paid entertainers in the world, obliged with evident reluctance and his opening words to Mr. S. were: 'The first thing I'd like to discuss with you is money.' Later when Jerry Colonna [one of Hope's second bananas] was persuaded (bludgeoned would be a more apt description) into joining Mr. Hope, the comedian remarked wryly: 'Remember this is for nothing.'

"Not all entertainers are as eminent as Bob Hope, and naturally there are many who haven't the courage to make such wisecracks about a man who has a nationally syndicated column at his disposal. One entertainer I know who gets from $1,500 to $2,000 a week in nightclubs was talked into doing his cherished routines—he only has three—on the show for $55. Mr. Sullivan is a persuasive fellow.

"If he has any other qualifications for the job, they are not visible on my small screen. Sullivan has been helplessly fascinated by show business for years. He has been in vaudeville, on the radio, and now on television. He remains totally innocent of any of the tricks of stage presence and it seems clear by now that his talents lie elsewhere."

Sullivan was furious about the Crosby blast and suspected that Winchell was in some way behind it. Certainly Winchell got on the bandwagon by accusing Sullivan of blackmailing performers into going on his show, an accusation which probably had at least some basis in fact, although Sullivan didn't see it that way. The issue was to be brought up time and time again

290

during the increasingly successful run of the Sullivan show.

Sullivan went so far as to fire an acid reply to Crosby in which he said among other things:

> "From every survey we've been able to make, the CBS Toast of the Town has the biggest audience in television and the most enthusiastic . . . Oscar Hammerstein II, a rather experienced hand in show business, has expressed his delight and amazement at our progress in a completely new medium and specifically praised "the professional polish, the pacing of the show and the entertainment value." Eddie Cantor after seeing the show on a television set, said that we were so far ahead of any program he's seen that he was dumbfounded at the potentials of a medium he'd disregarded."

The comments indicate not only the varied opinions of the Sullivan show, but the fact that '48 was really the infancy of television. There was a great paucity of material and there was no question that Sullivan's show, with its fast pacing and top talent, offered the best available TV variety show at the moment. He also denied blackmailing talent into appearing on his show. In any event, the union soon made that issue a moot one by adopting rules that prevented TV shows from paying talent less than the acts would normally get for a nightclub appearance. Talk shows were exempt.

However, the show was still not famous for spending a fortune on talent and this money issue wound up causing a major falling-out between Sullivan and Frank Sinatra, who had previously been good friends.

In the spring of '55 when the "Toast of The Town" was the leading show on television, Sullivan bought the rights from Sam Goldwyn to air 30 minutes of the hit musical movie "Guys and Dolls" as a sort of preview on the show. Sinatra was angered by this deal and said that he wouldn't approve of it unless Sullivan paid him $25,000. The two men had been friendly up to that point. When Westbrook Pegler attacked Sinatra for being a slacker during the war and for his connections with Lucky Luciano, Sullivan defended him vigorously.

Sinatra in return gave Sullivan a wristwatch with a note that said: "Ed you can have my last drop of blood." Now Sinatra criticized the Sullivan show and said that it paid inadequate salaries to its talent. Sullivan responded angrily in a letter to Walter Pidgeon, head of the Screen Actors Guild.

"I particularly resent . . . Sinatra's reckless charge that Toast does not pay performers. To date we have paid out over $5 million in salaries . . . Aside to Frankie Boy—never mind that tremulous 1947 offer: 'Ed you can have my last drop of blood.' "

Four days later Sinatra answered Sullivan's dig: "Dear Ed, You're sick. Frankie. P.S. Sick, sick, sick!"

Whether Sullivan was as bad as people said or not, he certainly had peculiar mannerisms on stage which made him the natural butt of comedians and critics. His stiffness and apparent stagefright engendered in some people a maternal feeling and others a fit of the giggles. One fan wrote: "It takes a real man to get up week after week—with that silver plate in his head."

Others warmly congratulated him for his triumph over facial paralysis, a twisted spine and olls. He was called by wags, "the unsmiling Irishman," "an artistic basket case," "the Miltown Maestro," and "Mr. Rigor Mortis." Some people called his show "The Toast of the Tomb." A rival producer said of Sullivan after the show had been successful for some years: "Sullivan has never lost his appeal, because he never had any to start with."

One of his great critics whose comments eventually caused him to be regarded by Sullivan as an actual enemy was the witty Fred Allen, who was genuinely appalled by the success of the no-talent columnist: "He's a pointer," complained Fred. "You can teach a dog to point. Just rub meat on the target."

This goaded Ed into what he considered a witty riposte. "Maybe Fred should rub some meat on his sponsor."

But there was no shutting up Fred Allen. He hit him

again and again with remarks. "Ed Sullivan will be a success as long as other people have talent."

Joe E. Lewis added to the assault: "Ed Sullivan is the only man who can brighten up a room by leaving it."

Carl Reiner, who refused to appear on the show for Sullivan's prices, said: "Love is like Ed Sullivan. You can't explain its hold on you, but after a while you take it for granted."

Henny Youngman's one-liner was: "In Africa the cannibals adored him. They thought he was some kind of frozen food."

Earl Wilson chimed in: "Ed Sullivan knows what the public likes and one of these days he's going to give it to them."

But at least one commentator had a remark that was nice as well as funny. Alan King said: "Ed does nothing, but he does it better than anyone else on television."

Sullivan, in an attempt to show that he had a sense of humor after all, finally hired a young impressionist, Will Jordan, who would go on the show and do imitations of Sullivan that were more like Sullivan than himself.

Time magazine, in a relatively friendly jibe, described him this way: "On camera, Ed has been likened to a cigar store Indian, the Cardiff Giant and a stone face monument just off the boat from Easter Island. He moves like a sleepwalker; his smile is that of a man sucking a lemon; his speech is frequently lost in a thicket of syntax; his eyes pop from their sockets or sink so deep in their bags that they seem to be peering up at the camera from the bottom of twin wells. Yet, instead of frightening children, Sullivan charms the whole family."

In the end, *Time* concluded: "No one likes Ed except his 35 million viewers and his ecstatic sponsor . . ." because Sullivan turned out not only to be an extremely effective television host, but a fantastic salesman for Lincoln-Mercury, his sponsor, which was in the end the bottom line.

Winchell, eating his heart out on the sidelines as his radio show gradually dropped in the ratings, could only strike out by boosting whatever NBC show went on opposite Sullivan's "Toast of the Town." To be fair, Winchell's failing radio ratings were not due so much to lack of talent or even to a somewhat lessened public regard for him, but rather to the general failure of talk radio in those years, and the rise of television as the new medium.

Sullivan's TV work was not all on camera. He had a strong idea about talent and exercised a firm hand in its selection. Sid Caesar and Imogene Coca, who were top attractions at the time, did a bit which got no laughs during rehearsal. Sullivan dropped them like a stone without a second thought. Dinah Shore wouldn't sing the material he had selected for her. She was off the show and never invited back. During final rehearsals, Sullivan would sit on a stool just offstage and give his final approval or disapproval to the various acts. It was agony for the talent agents who had to watch. He might call up an agent like Marty Comer who was one of his most frequent talent scouts and say to him, "What is this, Comer, amateur night in Dixie? Get that schmuck off my stage." The agents had no choice except to take their defeats gracefully and go back to the drawing board. Putting up a fight just made it tougher the next time.

According to Jerry Bowles, a recent biographer of Sullivan who wrote *A Thousand Sundays*, some of the clever agents actually learned to appeal to Ed's vanity. "More than once an untalented female singer-dancer got on the show because an agent whispered in Sullivan's ear that the girl really had the hots for him."

As he gained in power, Sullivan seemed to become as disputatious as his column rival Winchell in terms of involving himself in feuds. One of the most spectacular took place in 1953 when Arthur Godfrey got into a hassle with a young singer on his show named Julius La Rosa. La Rosa was fired arbitrarily from the Godfrey show and accused of lacking "humility." What Sullivan

294

didn't know was that the singer had been deeply involved with one of the McGuire Sisters, who were also on the show. The girl was married. Godfrey had warned him to break off the relationship but Julie had refused. This ended in a series of arguments and squabbles. At one point Godfrey ordered all of his people to take ballet lessons for some reason or other. Julie didn't show up for his lesson, nor did most of the others. Worse yet, La Rosa, who was one of Godfrey's personal discoveries, hired an agent to fight for more money. Godfrey considered him, as Winchell would say, "an ingrate."

One Monday morning in September, Godfrey brought La Rosa on the show just before closing. When the young tenor had finished his song, Godfrey said, "Thank you, Julie. And that, folks, was Julie's swan song." Godfrey had fired La Rosa on the air before an audience of millions.

Marlo Lewis, Sullivan's producer, heard of the incident and instantly got on the phone to Sullivan. Sullivan agreed to put La Rosa on his show for $3,000 a week, (more than he ever got on the Godfrey show) and it was well worth it for the publicity that resulted and the good-guy image it gave to Sullivan. In the years that followed, Sullivan continued to toss darts at Godfrey whenever the occasion arose.

The following year, the genial redhead fired Marian Marlow, a girl singer on the show, and Sullivan booked her for ten appearances. In '54 Godfrey, who had several incidents in which he was accused of being a reckless pilot in his private DC-3, was accused of flying recklessly at the Teterboro Airport and responding to the criticisms of the control tower with wisecracks. The control tower, after a low and erratic approach by Godfrey, had radioed to him to ask if his craft were out of control or in trouble. Godfrey replied flippantly, "No, that's just a normal Teterboro takeoff."

"That contemptuous reply to the control tower," Sullivan wrote in his column, "best illustrates Godfrey's major weakness, inability to apologize. But his time it has caught him in the backfire . . . Godfrey is sensational on a TV screen. But there's no place for sensationalism in flying. That is for the birds.''

Neither Godfrey nor Sullivan ever spoke to one another after that. There is no question about it. Old Stone Face was as good a hater as there was in the business.

On a humid summer evening, only a few months after the by then famous Josephine Baker incident, Ed Sullivan, his wife Sylvia and a young assistant producer from "The Toast of the Town" were in the Stork Club. Winchell as usual was there at Table 50 in the Cub Room. Sullivan, as he always did when he found himself in the same room with his rival columnist, asked for a table directly facing Winchell. Somehow Sullivan seemed to enjoy staring Winchell down in public places and never missed an opportunity to do so, although, according to Bowles, it "made his ulcer hurt and left Sylvia a nervous wreck.''

Sullivan was feeling his oats. Finally after all those years of sucking hind titty to Winchell, he was in a position of power. His top-rated television show made him at least as powerful, if not more so, than Winchell, and Winchell's actions in the Baker situation had certainly left his popularity on the downgrade. On this summer night, Sullivan was particularly hot under the collar with regard to his perennial rival. Winchell, at a Friar's Club roast in Hollywood only weeks earlier, had taken the opportunity to acidly criticize both Sullivan and Lyons at what was supposed to be a friendly trade affair. Sullivan lashed back in his Saturday column by writing, "Jack Benny, George Burns, George Jessel and other Coast performers who belong to the L.A. Lodge of the Friar's applied their own yardstick to Hollywood hokum this week. They permitted a visiting newspaper man to acknowledge the dinner in his honor by blasting other New York newspaper men. In New York, if such a bizarre, tactless thing had happened, Friars at the head table would immediately have disassociated the club from the guest slander of the newspaper men, who have been pretty good friends of performers. Apparently this didn't occur to Abbot Benny . . ."

Adding to the heat of Sullivan's feeling of anger toward Winchell on that particular night was the fact that the young production assistant with the Sullivans had worked for Winchell for a year. He told them that it was "the most miserable year of my life," and added, "Winchell was a truly evil man." The young producer was sort of a pet of Sullivan's and he resented the torture the young man had undergone working for Winchell.

Here's how Bowles described what happened next:

"Toward the end of the evening, Winchell got up to go to the bathroom. Sullivan immediately put down his glass, wiped his lips on the napkin, said, 'Excuse me,' and left to follow. Sylvia was distraught. She, like everyone else in the city, was aware that Winchell normally carried a revolver in his pocket. 'Follow him,' she said to the young assistant. 'Something's going to happen.'

"The assistant opened the outer door of the restroom gently and stepped inside. There was another inner door and he opened it slightly and peeked inside. What he saw was an extraordinary tableau. Ed Sullivan, the king of Sunday night television, was holding the head of Broadway's most influential columnist firmly in the bottom of a urinal and gleefully pumping the flush lever. Winchell was making noises which sounded like sobbing.

" 'I didn't do anything,' the assistant says. 'I just turned around and quietly walked out.' "

It was part of the fun and games in that era in which the power structure of the great columnists was beginning to come apart at the seams.

32.

> *"Anybody can become angry—that is easy; but to be angry with the right person, and to the right degree, and at the right time, and for the right purpose, and in the right way—that is not within everybody's power and is not easy."*
>
> **Aristotle: Nicomachean Ethics**

With the weakening of the web of power that the gossipists had maintained since the early Thirties when Winchell launched his first column, there came an even greater wave of backbiting, vituperation and feuding, both within their own community and with the subjects of their gossip items. And these arguments, as has been seen, were not simply verbal set-tos, but often resulted in physical violence. One of the earliest principals in these classic feuds of the genre was the much-battered Lee Mortimer.

In 1947, when Mortimer was still feeling his oats as a lesser power among columnists, he began a feud with Frank Sinatra, then famous for being a skinny singer so lacking in strength that he had to cling to a microphone out of sheer weakness. The macho Mafia-oriented side of Sinatra had then, as yet, not emerged. For whatever reason Mortimer had, according to Sinatra, been "needling" him for two years in his column.

"He referred to my bobbysoxer fans as morons," Sinatra said. "I don't care if they do try to tear my clothes off. They're not morons. They're only kids." (In fact, most of these "kids" had been recruited and planted by Frank's press agents, including the afore-mentioned Gertrude Bayne, who had the inspiration of naming him "Frank Swoonatra," and providing the background for that nickname.)

In 1945, Mortimer had written a song and sent it to Sinatra with a pressuring memo suggesting that Frank plug it. Frank sent back a cold note saying it wasn't his type of song. Most commentators on these incidents feel that it was this rejection that triggered Mortimer's hostility. Anyway, came the magic night at Ciro's nightclub in Hollywood. Sinatra claims that Mortimer was heard giving his insult treatment in person and at the top of his lungs, including references to Sinatra as "a dago singer." Certainly Frank's claim that Mortimer used negative stereotypes in describing other races was justified by much that Mortimer had written. Reading his stuff, one easily got the impression that all Negroes were "white man haters," and "dope addicts," that the Irish were responsible for all corrupt government in the country, that Mexicans were a drag on the economy in the communities of the West and that Puerto Ricans were disease carriers.

Other patrons sitting near Mortimer, who was not famous for his ability to hold liquor, said that they had heard the columnist use terms about Sinatra's Italian origins that could start a street fight in most locales. Some offended friends of Sinatra rose to leave.

On the way out, they stopped at Sinatra's table and told him what they had heard. As loud as Mortimer's comments were, they apparently hadn't reached Sinatra's environs on their own volume. One of the comments about Sinatra referred back to charges the year before that Mortimer had made stating that Frank was hobnobbing socially with Lucky Luciano in Havana (a charge that was apparently true). Sinatra's explanation was that "somebody," he didn't remember who, introduced him to the exiled rackets boss in a casino there while he was having dinner and he had been pleasant, as any gentleman would. Later facts indicate that Sinatra had an unfortunate tendency to be introduced to these types of people and be photographed with them.

Mortimer was at the nightclub with a Miss Kay Keno,

one of the attractive Chinese women that it was his habit to appear with. Sinatra was present with Lenny Hayton, MGM musical director and husband of Lena Horne, and several other people. The two bumped into one another in the foyer as Mortimer was leaving the club. Sinatra apparently felt the time had come to take action upon the slur against his origins, and he expressed himself with a strong right to the chin that sent Mortimer to the floor and later to a nearby hospital for x-rays. There is some disagreement as to what preceded the one-punch encounter. Sinatra said that Mortimer had given him a sneering "what do you amount to" look and had repeated his slur on Sinatra's Italian ancestry.

Mortimer denied that he even knew Sinatra was in the place. (This was probably true, or he would not have said what he did in such a loud voice.) He said that, in any event, the singer "sneaked up behind" him and slugged him and that "three stooges" (not *The* Three Stooges) of Sinatra had held him on the ground while the crooner flailed away.

Sinatra retorted: "I swear on a stack of Bibles that nobody held him. It wasn't necessary. I guess you'd call it 'no contest.' "

The next day, detectives showed up at a radio station where Sinatra was rehearsing "Oh, What a Beautiful Morning," and turned it into a ghastly morning by hauling him into court to answer battery charges preferred by Mortimer. Mortimer complained of severe pain from injuries diagnosed as "a swollen left cheek, swelling behind the left ear and bruises of the right wrist." He signed the complaint, charging the spindly crooner had hit him without warning or provocation. Even then, Mortimer was extremely unpopular with his colleagues in the press and they all vied with one another to chip in for the $500 bail that was set for the crooner.

Mortimer, on the other hand, in answer to questions, admitted that he "needled" Sinatra in print because "I don't think he's a good singer and I've questioned his efforts to be a leader of youth."

As soon as he was released on bail, Sinatra took off

A youthful Frank Sinatra at ringside, Madison
Square Garden

for New York to be presented with the Thomas Jefferson Award from the Council Against Intolerance in America. It must be remembered that many of these people have changed their images and that in those days Sinatra, like Winchell in his early days, had been considered a fighter for liberalism and tolerance, a stance he never departed from until 1963, when he was offended by the fact that the Kennedys dropped him from their slate of supporters because of his alleged mob associations. Funny how that theme keeps recurring in Sinatra's life.

George Evans, then a publicity man for Sinatra, urged the singer to settle with Mortimer for fear that if he didn't, he would get himself blacklisted in the whole Hearst chain—including the columns of Winchell and Kilgallen. The singer glumly took his friend's advice and a few weeks later Mortimer appeared in court and read a prepared statement, saying in part: "I acknowledge that I have received satisfaction for the injury done to me. Furthermore, Sinatra has publicly acknowledged that I did not call him the vile names he stated I called him. Under the circumstances, it is not my desire to proceed further with the prosecution of the case."

But Mortimer was not one to forgive and forget. He nursed the incident for many years. As recently as 1960, he launched another blast at Sinatra in the *Mirror*. In part he said: "Thirteen years ago, come this Friday, Frankie Boy took a poke at me from behind, while two of his thugs held my arms. At that time and ever since, there has been a lot of confusion about what happened because some newspaper men who ought to know better are stooges of Sinatra and shake and shiver like female juvenile delinquents when the self-proclaimed newspaperman-hater deigned to look at them . . . Sinatra's cowardly attack on me came as a result of what I printed in the *Mirror* then and which some are only beginning to find out now: that he was surrounded as far back as the 1940's by reds, pinkos and weird left-wingers who made common cause of their adulation of him with the gangsters with whom he has always been associated . . ."

One of the reasons Mortimer wouldn't let the Sinatra story go was that it was a good one. It was about a big name, and he really had the goods on Frankie: "It is a matter of public record that Sinatra is the owner of stock in a Las Vegas gambling casino well known to be an underworld operation. But what is not a matter of record, though well known to everyone in the trade, is that Sinatra, who started life as a protegé of Jersey mobster Willie Moretti, has been chosen by certain interests to take over the entire amusement industry, beginning with the ownership of star acts, investments in nightclubs and casinos, motion pictures, TV and radio production, records, juke boxes, music publishing and what have you."

Sinatra never has gotten used to the fact that anything he did in public would make headlines. An Italian newspaper reported that he'd punched a photographer. Winchell questioned Sinatra on what had happened. Sinatra said, "The bum wouldn't leave me alone. He'd been trailing me for three days like a sneak. He was just a freelancer out for a fast buck, trying to get me at my worst if he could. So I flattened him."

"Frank," Winchell counseled him, "I wish you would stop hitting people. It makes it bad for guys like me on your team to fight for you."

"The creep was bothering me," Sinatra said. "When a guy bothers me I belt him."

So Winchell reported it that way and added: "This was—and always will be—Frank Sinatra."

Sinatra eventually fell out with Winchell but remained fairly friendly with Earl Wilson and Lyons. Kilgallen was another matter, about which more later.

Off the record, Mortimer's lawyer told the press that he'd been given $9,000 for the sock in the jaw. Mortimer had threatened to sue for $250,000 which would have been a record price for a one-punch bout. Later he told friends: "I got an easy $9,000 from Sinatra. Maybe somebody else would like to take a punch at me at the same price." If he had published that statement, he probably would have had dozens of requests, but in fact his offer was not taken up until a couple of years later, unless we count the case of Mrs. Peggy Flournory, an attractive Washington blonde who once tiptoed across the slippery dance floor of John Perona's El Morocco and clouted Mortimer across his ear. She was just upset about some comments Lait and Mortimer had made in their book *Washington Confidential* about her city.

Mortimer's next bout took place in the Riviera, a New Jersey casino and nightclub just across the George Washington Bridge. Again, Mortimer was on the receiving end.

It happened in the men's room of the nightclub on May 15, 1950. According to playwright Sidney Kingsley who witnessed it, "Some guy was punching Mortimer and had him down on the floor."

Mortimer explained the incident by saying that the mob had sicced goons on him because of his efforts on behalf of law enforcement. Later when questioned about the incident, he mentioned five mob names and said that a New Orleans Mafia boss who was in the club had reason to work him over because of an article he had written. He even brought in the sacred name of Frank Costello. He charged: "First they tried to buy me and then they tried to sue me. And then to have me fired and warned me off with a token beating." Nobody ever figured out who did the punching. The old gag about Mortimer was revived on Broadway: "They're looking for a hundred thousand suspects in the latest slugging of Lee Mortimer." Obviously inflation had set in.

Winchell finally had his most serious break with his old crony Leonard Lyons when the *Post* ran its 24-part diatribe pillorying Winchell. Winchell was convinced that his old friend Lyons had cooperated in the exposé.

According to those who investigated the situation, including Winchell-admirer Ed Weiner in his book *Let's Go to Press*, Lyons was apparently not guilty of this charge. But now the mild-mannered Lyons took up the cudgels against Winchell for his unjust accusation. Day after day, the two columnists exchanged verbal brickbats across their pages. A typical Lyons zinger was as follows:

"Trial note: In covering the Jelke vice trial yesterday, Walter Winchell reported that he was told that Pat Ward had named a well known newspaper man whose initials are twins. 'Oh, I get it,' wrote Winchell about the trollop and the newspaper man. 'You must mean L.L.' That was a lie."

Winchell, in his own column, naturally let Lyons have it with both barrels. "He (Lyons) has . . . attempted to damage the Runyon Fund with half-truths, untruths and outright lies—because of his festering hate against this writer—who did everything possible to help him make good when he started a column . . . the insiders around town know all this—but the ingrate probably never went to bed without ending his prayers with: And please let Winchell drop dead so I can get some new outlets . . . when I was ill, he went around telling the lice I was 'a very sick man' . . . he didn't mean I was sick with a virus . . . he has written letters about me (now in my possession) that would win a libel action and acquit me in a minute if I pushed him in front of a speeding truck. What is left of his conscience keeps telling him: you know very well you aren't chasing ambulances for a living because Winchell was born! You swiped Winchell's entire act but who hasn't? You are hateful for only one reason. It isn't because Walter couldn't stand you any longer on the Runyon Fund. You hate him because his column replaced yours in Washington. A horrible fate for a professional name-dropper.'"

Lyons hit back with this tidbit:

"Personal, to Police Commissioner Monoghan: I am about to write a series of replies to Walter Winchell's latest outburst against me—the one in which he concludes that he would be acquitted if he were to push me in front of a speeding truck. This therefore is public notice to you to pick up his permits and the pistol he carries, or else the City of New York shall be held accountable for any consequences. I write this not out of any concern for my own safety, but only because Winchell himself has indicated, were he to pull a trigger in all probability he would hit either an innocent by-stander or himself.''

Meanwhile the public had a field day with the feud. Many of them, tiring of Winchell's pomposity, cheered on the seemingly mild-mannered Lyons. *Variety* wrote, "There hasn't been much of this sort of newspaper stuff around of late. It's a fresh script daily . . . never a dull moment.''

Time magazine, which was both anti-Winchell and anti-Lyons from previous skirmishes, commented: "Whenever Manhattan's keyhole columnists tire of puffing their friends or scalping their enemies, they refresh their spirits by jealously skinning one another.''

Certainly it was true that it didn't take much to stir up a whirlpool of vituperation in those circles.

The mere hint of a slight could plunge Winchell into a savage vendetta with another columnist. One night Winchell was holding forth in front of the Club Abbey with a group of his usual followers. He noticed Louis Sobol approaching the club and hailed him: 'Hey Louis, I want you to hear this!' Sobol, who'd been captive to Winchell's notorious long monologues before and was feeling under the weather with the flu, answered glumly, 'You want me, you come over here.' And he continued on his way into the nightclub. That was enough for Winchell. War was declared. He began sniping at Sobol in his column and the thing turned into a full-fledged feud, to the point where the men didn't talk to each other for several years until the night on New Year's Eve when J. Edgar Hoover almost posed for those photos with Terry Reilly, the F.B.I. impostor. Hoover, who was obviously feeling very good that night, induced the two to make peace.

Genial Earl Wilson, after years of immunity, finally managed to hit a raw nerve in Winchell when he commented on Winchell's manipulating of ratings to make his failing television show look good. Wilson made the egregious error of correcting Winchell in print. Winchell hit back with half a column rebutting and belittling Wilson. He frosted the saloon society columnist for years thereafter and then inexplicably one night he ran into Wilson at a play opening and gave him a pass: "Some guys are giving the newspaper game a bad name. You aren't one of them."

Another old-time crony of Winchell's was Bob Sylvester of the *Daily News*. That friendship died in Lindy's one night when Sylvester was seated with a group of press agents. Winchell entered with his current flame and singing protegé Roberta Sherwood. He had discovered her in a tiny Miami boîte and had practically single-handedly pushed the *haimish*-looking singer, who always sang with a cardigan sweater pulled inelegantly around her shoulders, to stardom with a relentless campaign in his column and on the air.

As Winchell led Roberta toward the table, Sylvester cracked, "All right boys, everybody up. Here comes the queen." Winchell blew up at the gibe. "Bob, I'll never forget you for this!" And Sylvester became another entry on Winchell's D.D. list.

Frank Farrell of the *World-Telegram*, who was really an insider in Winchell's group—a close friend of his who even contributed whole columns under Winchell's by-line, finally felt the venom of Winchell's fangs. Farrell was in the Stork Club with Sherman Billingsley and a few others one night when Winchell was on holiday in Florida. Billingsley happened to make an unfavorable remark about the wife of Frank Costello. A few days later, Winchell called Farrell apparently in panic, and said: "Are you trying to get me killed?" Farrell was dumbfounded. He had no idea what Winchell was talking about.

"Costello's mad as hell about that crack about his wife. He thinks I said it," Winchell fumed.

"Why would he think that?"

"You said so."

"That's crazy. Who told you that?"

"Sherman."

Now Farrell blew up. He caught the first train to Miami, taxied to the Roney Plaza and encountered Winchell in his favorite locale, the putting green. "I flew all the way down here to tell you what I think of you," Farrell told his former friend. "After twenty years of friendship you're ready to convict me like a Hitler court. You're telling everybody what a bastard I am because of something I didn't do. If that's all I mean to you, you can take our friendship to the guy who made that remark about Costello's wife: that snake Billingsley."

Farrell and Winchell didn't talk for three years after that encounter. And then, again in an inexplicable mood of amity, Winchell said to his old friend, "Can we be friends? I'm sorry." Farrell agreed, but said, "I'll never shake hands with that other guy," meaning Billingsley.

As far as is known, Winchell never took the incident up with his friend Sherman.

Let's not give Winchell all the kudos for cantankerousness. Oleg Cassini, whose "Cholly Knickerbocker" society column had degenerated into something much more closely resembling a Broadway gossip column, got into a spat with Ed Sullivan during the McCarthy era. Cassini, a noted right-winger, had roasted Sullivan several times for putting on entertainers he considered to be leftists like Lena Horne, Larry Adler and Paul Draper. Cassini considered his attacks on Sullivan to be "perhaps not my finest hour." However, he seemed to get considerable gratification, if only in elevating his visibility by feuding with the columnist who had a much larger circulation. "The public response was overwhelmingly in my favor," Cassini said, recalling the incident. "And Sullivan, under pressure from Ford, his sponsor, and the network, had to drop them from the show." Eventually poison-pen columnist Westbrook Pegler and renegade communist columnist George Sokolsky joined Cassini in his assaults on Sullivan who, however, seemed to emerge without any taint himself.

As a result of the attacks by Cassini and others, neither Draper nor Adler were ever again able to earn a decent living in the United States and both went to live in Europe. But Sullivan was chastened and began to consult with Theodore Kirkpatrick, another notorious red-baiter of the era who published a newsletter called *Counterattack* which purported to identify all suspicious characters on the left. If Sullivan had any thoughts that one of his entertainers might be attacked on the grounds of being a red, he checked it with Kirkpatrick. In 1950 he even admitted the closeness of this liaison: "Kirkpatrick has sat in my living room on several occasions and listened attentively to performers eager to secure a certification of loyalty. On some occasions after interviewing them, he has given them the green light; on other occasions he has told them veterans' organizations will insist on further proof."

Sullivan added that he thought that *Counterattack* was doing "a magnificent American job." It was Kirkpatrick who later published the infamous *Red Channels: The Report of Communist Influence in Radio and Television,* which ruined literally scores of performers' careers.

The seething pot of shifting animosities was never allowed to simmer down. If it wasn't one thing, it was another. In 1956 the Sullivan-Winchell feud again erupted into headlines which took up the entire front page of at least one New York paper. At the time, Winchell was just starting an NBC television series on Friday nights. He stated in a *Look* magazine article that it was Sullivan's influence that had kept him off CBS. Winchell said that one day he had received a call from Frank Stanton of CBS. "Frank asked to see me and when we met I said, 'Frank, I turned you down to stay with ABC seven years ago. Now's your chance to turn me down. Would you consider me for things other than commentating—panels, quizzes, variety? I don't want to be off TV.' "

Stanton, according to Winchell, replied, "Don't

worry about a thing."

"I never heard from Frank after that," Winchell said. "I subsequently heard that when Sullivan learned about the talk he threw a tantrum. I guess Frank decided to leave well enough alone."

Sullivan replied with a blast in *Collier's* magazine, repeating the origins of his first big feud with Winchell, the Barbara Hutton affair. In the article he defended, somewhat inaccurately, his own record for liberality, although it was clearly a better one than Winchell's: "In the conduct of my own show, I've never asked a performer his religion, his race or his politics. Performers are engaged on the basis of their abilities. I believe that this is another quality of our show that has helped win a wide and loyal audience." Apparently Sullivan had forgotten all about his frequent conferences with *Red Channels'* Kirkpatrick.

Winchell, who at that time was making a last, desperate gasp to overtake Sullivan with a variety show of his own on NBC, conducted press conferences in which he devoted as much time to attacking his long-standing enemy as he did to puffing his own show. He accused Sullivan of being a talentless fraud, a copycat, a person of questionable morals. He even went so far as to state that Sullivan had "the big C"—cancer. (The accusation, though scurrilous, was true.)

The Winchell show, which had a modest success at first, ran rapidly downhill and was cancelled at the end of thirteen weeks. What put the final nail in the coffin was another intemperate right-wing Winchellism. It was during the 1956 presidential election campaign when Winchell on the program cracked: "A vote for Adlai Steverison is a vote for Christine Jorgensen." That was enough. Winchell's sponsors dropped the show.

By this time, Winchell was getting so sour he even finally broke with his old friend Billingsley. Billingsley, in the late Fifties, had become enamoured with his image on television. Irving Mansfield, a one-time Broadway press agent who had become a television producer (and husband of novelist Jacqueline Susann),

Sherman Billingsley interviews actresses Jinx Falkenberg, Dorothy Lamour and Anita Colby for the radio program that emanated from the Stork Club.

proposed a weekly show to be called "The Stork Club." Billingsley loved it. Winchell hated it. "Who needs it?" he asked his pal. But Billingsley had his own motives. He told friends, "If I could get on TV, that sonofabitch (Winchell) will be jealous of me."

CBS bought Mansfield's idea and went so far as to build a studio-type replica of the Cub Room on the second floor of the nightclub. Billingsley, trying to tart up his image for television, insisted on buying a grotesque toupeé that set the network back a thousand bucks. Winchell took the chance to dig at his friend about the hairpiece in his column.

Billingsley reacted with fury: "That sonofabitch—how about him calling me bald! He's bald as a billiard ball."

Winchell heard about Billingsley's comment and he was not exactly thrilled. Meanwhile Billingsley proved to be one of the greatest clowns—inadvertently—ever to appear on television. He was one of the most witless and inept hosts in the history of the medium, but somehow he managed to continue to attract sponsors because of the glamour of the environment. The show survived for three years.

Fred Allen was as appalled by Billingsley's ineptitude as an emcee as he had been by Sullivan. Billingsley, Allen quipped, was "the only man in television who needs a teleprompter to say hello."

One night Billingsley had as his guest a man described as the King of Persia. Billingsley asked him, "How are things in Cairo?"

Once, when interviewing a famous actress, Billingsley thought it would be a great idea to ask her bluntly how old she was. The actress mentioned an age that seemed right—to her, at least. But Billingsley couldn't let it pass. "I'd hate to be hanging since you were that old," he jested.

Some of Billingsley's stupid remarks were costly. Once he held up a picture of his old enemy, Toots Shor, and muttered something about Shor's debts. Unfortunately for Billingsley, Shor was watching the program and instantly had his attorney Arnold Grant—the recently deceased ex-husband of Bess Myerson—file a suit for $1,100,000 naming Billingsley, The American Broadcasting Company-Paramount Theaters, and The Stork Club. After four years of court battles, Shor accepted a settlement of $48,500 and a letter of "sincere regrets" from ABC. Billingsley's lawyer was Roy Cohn.

Billingsley was in seventh heaven while he had the TV show. Although his name was well known to the public through columns and occasional photographs, he was not exactly a household word. But now he was becoming one. He took producer Mansfield proudly for a walk around the block. People waved at him in recognition. "See—they recognize me!" Billingsley said. "They recognize me from the TV show. Half the people in New York don't even know what Winchell looks like."

Finally the Stork Club show went off the air and Winchell for the moment patched up his rift with Billingsley. But in 1956 the sore festered again. Winchell was at Table 50 one night with an account executive for Old Gold cigarettes, the sponsor of "The Untouchables" series, of which Winchell was the narrator. Billingsley had a deal with Chesterfield that the Stork's pretty cigarette girl was supposed to place packages of Chesterfields on every table, saying sweetly: "Compliments of Sherman Billingsley." When the cigarette girl came to Table 50 in the Cub Room, where Winchell was off on one of his nonstop conversations with Sherman, she dropped a pack of Old Golds in front of the ad man, smilingly saying: "Compliments of Elliot Ness." A cute, friendly gesture, but Billingsley blew his top.

33.

Winchell's very much on-again, off-again friendship with Sherman Billingsley suffered still another blow in 1956, when he discovered that Billingsley had cooperated with the *New York Post* in the scathing series that was written on him in 1952. As Winchell got the news, Billingsley had secretly contacted the top brass at the *Post* and made a deal: if they'd go easy on him, he'd help them prepare a blast at Winchell. The *Post* agreed, according to Winchell.

The series, in fact, contained much intimate information and even pictures that could only have come from someone really close to Winchell. Winchell, almost paranoid on the question of loyalty, suspected many of his close friends and even put some of them on his Drop Dead List on suspicion alone, but he never dreamed that his greatest crony might have been behind the leaks.

In 1956, when he learned what he believed to be the truth about Billingsley, he apologized to some of those he wrongly put in the doghouse. "I just have to be more careful about picking my friends in the future," he said. "If I couldn't trust Sherman, I don't know who I can trust."

There was some reason to believe Winchell's suspicions were true. The *Post* certainly did a diluted job on Billingsley and let him off the hook almost painlessly. By this time, the friendship had cooled even without the added burden of Winchell's discovery. During the previous year, he had hardly ever showed up at his usual table at the Stork. Billingsley, it was believed, resented Winchell's evenings in the haunts of hated

314

rivals like Toots Shor and John Perona. Winchell, on the other hand, found Billingsley's increasingly scornful attitude toward members of the press irritating.

In public, Sherman always told of his great respect for the columnists who hung around in his place, but in private, he would comment: "I can buy them all for a few neckties or a bottle of perfume."

At the same time, Winchell seemed to be losing his zip. The year after this split with Billingsley, a friend had the temerity to comment to Winchell, who was then 54, "Walter, you're getting old. Listen, we know you're the king and there's nobody like you. But who do you think can ever take your place? I mean, who would you say is the crown prince?"

The interlocutor began to run down the names of the other columnists. "Wilson?"

Winchell made an ugly face.

"Kilgallen?"

He held his nose. "There is no crown prince," Winchell interrupted. "They all stink."

Then the king walked away, obviously deeply annoyed. The friend who asked the questions was never again mentioned in Winchell's column.

But there was no question that Winchell, always perceived as the eternal winner, was beginning to get plenty of negative feedback. After his break with his drug sponsor, Winchell continued on television with Revlon but after a year the sponsor got caught in a battle with the ABC network and dropped the show. Revlon claimed that the network had shifted the show around as much as three times in one week and that it was making it impossible for Winchell's show to be a success. And it seemed that once Revlon dropped out, there were not many sponsors willing to take Winchell on.

While he was at liberty from show business commitments, Winchell decided to take another swipe at his lifetime enemy Sullivan, who was scheduled to open with a vaudeville show at the Desert Inn in Las Vegas in July of '58. Winchell pushed through a fast contract to headline in "Tropicana Holiday" at Monte Proser's

Vegas Tropicana, going back to his old trade as a song-and-dance man. He agreed to donate his salary of $37,500 a week to his favorite charity, the Damon Runyon Fund.

"But performers like Noel Coward and Marlene Dietrich don't make any more than that," Proser protested.

"I know," Winchell replied with a wink, "but they're not syndicated!"

The show was a modest hit. Proser's place pulled in enough people and publicity to make the sting worthwhile. *Variety*, reviewing the Winchell act, pointed out that the columnist had last appeared as an entertainer at the Palace in 1934, so that he could probably be reviewed in their department called "New Acts." *Variety* called the Winchell headline act a "unique and pleasantly novel show." Joe E. Lewis summed up the attitude of many first-nighters who were frankly expecting Winchell to "flop at the Trop," when he said, "I was a little disappointed—I *liked* the show!" "Tropicana Holiday" was scheduled to run until June 10th, when Sullivan started his gig.

Meanwhile, as though they sensed that their days of absolute power were drawing to a close, the columnists began to get even more savage in their feuds with one another and with the outside world.

Kilgallen had been swiping at Sinatra since the early Fifties. According to her biographer Lee Israel, Kilgallen's hostility toward the singer went back to the point early in Sinatra's career when Kilgallen and Lillian Boscowitz, wife of millionaire Hubie Boscowitz, and one of Dorothy's best friends, decided that they would play a joke on their husbands who were lunching at the Colony together. Kilgallen called Frank Sinatra's agent and arranged to have Frankie, on whom, according to Israel, she was decidedly "gone," accompany them to the restaurant. Walter Pidgeon was lined up to escort Lillian. Unfortunately the joke fell flat because the husbands had already been tipped off to the gag.

Richard Kollmar, Dorothy's husband, had telegrams and flowers in abundance delivered to Sinatra at the table and Richard and Hubie wrote their wives mash notes like, "What are you doing tonight, baby?"

The event made even the snobbish Maury Paul's column, largely because the Boscowitzes, who were social, were involved in it.

Years later, Dorothy shocked an audience of millions on the Mike Wallace Show, where she was sitting for an in-depth interview, when she implied that Sinatra had begun to attack her in public because she (Dorothy) had resisted Sinatra's sexual advances. Since Dorothy, prior to her involvement with Johnny Ray, was considered to be something of a prude, and since Frankie was known to make a pass at every femme within arm's reach, her claim could possibly have been true. Certainly Frankie, having been selected to be Dorothy's "gag" escort and having caught the feeling that she was very taken with him, might have been excused from making at least a desultory pass. In addition there was the fact that everybody in New York knew that Dorothy's husband Richard not only chased quite a few women, including prostitutes, around the tables of New York hot spots and into a number of boudoirs, but was also (possibly falsely) frequently accused of chasing young *men*. In any event, Frank did not start to snipe at Dorothy until she ran some unfriendly column items about him.

One ran:

"Success hasn't changed Frank Sinatra. When he was unappreciated and obscure, he was hot-tempered, egotistical, extravagant, and moody. Now that he is rich and famous, with the world on a string and sapphires in his cufflinks, he is still hot-tempered, egotistical, extravagant, and moody."

This was the time when Frank was madly in love with Ava Gardner, whom he described as "the most gorgeous creature who ever walked." When Ava left Frankie, Dorothy ran an item saying that a representative of the William Morris Agency had been assigned to look after Sinatra to keep him from "slashing his wrists."

Dorothy, in fact, began to hit at Sinatra so frequently that it was hard to tell just which item drove the singer into retaliation. This was a time when all of the other columnists at Hearst were also taking potshots at the Hoboken crooner.

When Sinatra finally decided to strike back, he did it from nightclub floors in New York and Las Vegas. He stopped inexplicably in between two songs, "Young At Heart," and "The Second Time Around" to tell his shocked audience that Kilgallen was "an ugly broad." He said she had a face like a chipmunk's and was commonly credited with originating the term "the chinless wonder." Strangely enough, these slashing attacks got laughs, first from his entourage and later from other people in the audience. The attack hit Dorothy where she lived. She was vain and sensitive about her looks, although she was not averse to zinging others with derogatory physical remarks. Her review of Madame Nikita Khruschev focused largely on the fact that the lady in question had fat legs. Kilgallen, when she heard about Sinatra's tirade, talked to her lawyer about suing, but she was advised that there was nothing actionable in the Sinatra attack.

Sinatra's abuse seemed to focus a latent hostility toward Kilgallen which had been developing during her appearances on the television show "What's My Line?" Before Sinatra mentioned it, there was never any reference to Dorothy's physical appearance. Now letters to Goodson and Todman, the producers of the TV show, demanded: "Get that chinless wonder off!"

Once, when Dorothy was attending a Broadway opening, an elderly bag-lady broke through barriers police had erected to hold back the crowd, came close to Dorothy and shouted, "Hiya, chinless!" According to her escort, Ben Bagley, a young record producer, Dorothy was so shocked that her hand began to shake.

Things were never good, to put it mildly, between Kilgallen and Sinatra after that. It was Dorothy who had first revealed what became an important fable in the celebrity folk idiom. Her column read: "Lana, Ava, having gay time in Mexico."

This was her lead item:

"Lana Turner and Ava Gardner who dashed off to Mexico together ostensibly to forget their man troubles, are the talk of Bill O'Dwyer's bailiwick. (O'Dwyer, the former Mayor of New York, had by that time been appointed Ambassador to Mexico.) The girls are really living it up South of the Rio Grande. Fernando (Lamas) seems to be taking his loss cheerfully, but Frank is giving pals the torch talk."

A week later, Dorothy struck again:

"Frank Sinatra is frightening his friends by telephoning in a gloomy voice, "Please see that the children are taken care of," and then hanging up. He called the next day to apologize blaming it on The Glass."

A couple of months later:

"Frank Sinatra, who tossed Lana Turner out of his Palm Springs house when he found her visiting his wife a few months ago, may make more blowtop headlines before long. Lana and Ava had plans to do some vacation chumming in Europe."

What really stung Sinatra is that the piquant tale was picked up by *Confidential* and expanded with much sexual innuendo. Even a less touchy character than Sinatra might have been put off.

Ever since Ed Sullivan's success on TV, the public's interest had begun to focus much more on the idiot eye than on the printed word. Jack Paar, who under a cloak of humility and sincerity was able to milk acres of print publicity by starting feuds with well-syndicated columnists, managed to strike fire with Winchell when he brought Elsa Maxwell, the famous party-giver, onto his

319

program as a guest. Maxwell had repeated the ancient charge that Winchell had never voted. Unfortunately for her that was no longer true—Winchell had apparently cast a few ballots since he was originally attacked on that count. He sued and forced Maxwell to make a public retraction. Paar took up cudgels for Maxwell and the story really built up in the prints—page-one treatment.

Winchell lashed out at Paar, calling him "an ingrate in action" (Paar was another whose success Winchell felt came from plugs he had given him in an early stage of his career). He wound up his attack on Paar saying, "It looks like they will soon change the title of the 'Tonight' Show (Paar was one of Johnny Carson's predecessors on the late night stanza) to the 'Tuneout Show.' "

Paar meanwhile managed to get more publicity, perhaps not so pleasing, when he walked off the "Tonight Show" following the deletion from his script of a mild joke involving a W.C.—a water closet. Paar stayed away from the show for 25 days. On his first night back he took off after Winchell again and also took a couple of swings at Dorothy Kilgallen. Because of Winchell's previous lawsuit, the references to him were deleted by the network though the ones to Kilgallen made the kinescope. But there was enough left about Winchell to bring him roaring to the counterattack, which probably did not displease Paar. What Paar said about Winchell was this: "Walter Winchell, the silly old man who under oath could not admit—*under oath*—that he writes his own column completely—sometimes days go by and he doesn't write them—has never said a word about me in a year and a half when I was here to defend myself.

"As soon as I left and he thought I was not returning, he started all sorts of vicious innuendo about the show, about payola, about my virility . . ."

In a following program he blasted Winchell for his girl-chasing activities which were fairly well known in the trade but not to the public.

Winchell came back: "The other day Paar told the New York press that I'm a senile old man. Now he says I'm a lecher. How could I be both?

"He's never forgiven me for catching him in a lie which he had to retract. That was when he permitted Elsa Maxwell to say on his show that she could prove Walter Winchell had never registered or voted . . .

"Paar has said that morally Winchell has no right to comment. As for my morals, I know I'm not as virginal as Paar is. But is anybody?"

And so the exchanges went on. Paar had conceived a hatred for the Hearst press when they hinted he was in Havana palling it up with Castro when actually he was in Honolulu. In one of his attacks on Kilgallen he accused her of using "novocaine lipstick."

When Elsa Maxwell came back on the show and announced she was going to Europe aboard a ship, Paar cautioned:

"Be careful on that liner. Don't get too near the railing because 'all the ships at sea' may have his own submarine . . . he thinks he's another state . . . he thinks he's Mr. and Mrs. America, but he's only a balding eagle . . ."

Winchell once had cautioned enemies: "Never fight a newspaper man; he goes to press too often." But now he had a new lesson to learn. You couldn't win against a television star like Jack Paar who could answer back every night before an immense national audience.

For the first time Winchell was no match. He was ridiculed into silence. But he got some satisfaction when Desi Arnaz arranged for him to be a narrator of a new show, "The Untouchables."

The series became a roaring success and Winchell referred to it as *his* show. He would call up producer Quinn Martin and tell him, "The U.N. thought we had a good show this week." (By U.N. Winchell meant not the distinguished international society but what he called the mobsters, "the Underworld Nobility.") "The Untouchables" ran successfully for four seasons until there was a reaction against TV violence and it was forced off the air. However it ran for a long time on reruns and Winchell became known to a whole new generation as the strange, exciting voice behind the crime series.

Having disposed of Winchell and possibly restless for more tigers to hunt, the weeping host of the "Tonight Show" decided to take on Ed Sullivan, thereby succeeding in making enemies of the three top columnists of the day.

The fight started in a spat over the fact that Paar was paying his people the union minimum of $320 for his late show, where Sullivan had to pay the full nightclub price. Sullivan discovered that several of his brightest stars such as Myron Cohen and Sam Levinson had been appearing frequently as guests on the Paar program for the minimum fee. He felt this was manifestly unfair and got in touch with the performers to explain his point of view. As a result, Myron Cohen cancelled a scheduled appearance on the Paar show in March, 1961. That night, Jack Paar read an open letter to Sullivan on the air. The letter complained about Sullivan's challenge and pleaded: "Ed, I don't have money to pay performers. This show is a low-budget freak that caught on because performers want to come on and want time to entertain people without the monkey act and Japanese jugglers waiting in the wings."

The studio audience, all devoted fans of Paar's, laughed. The situation escalated until Sullivan challenged Paar to a debate on the "Tonight Show"— without a studio audience, in order to be fair to both. Paar accepted. It was a slow week for news and the feud became the number one story in the country. Both Sullivan and Paar seemed to be enjoying the attention and publicity enormously. Then there was another exchange, and Paar announced that he was not going to bar a studio audience just because Sullivan was appearing on his show. He made some other stipulations and then said that he'd be willing to appear on Sullivan's show with or without an audience, with only one stipulation: "I don't want to be given four minutes and then have eight acrobats come in the middle of the discussion."

Sullivan had made his request because Chicago columnist Irv Kupcinet and *Herald Tribune* columnist Hy Gardner had gotten rough treatment from Paar's studio audience when they were invited on his show for a question and answer exchange. However, he agreed to waive his request and to go on before a Paar studio audience. The big debate was set for Monday, March 13. The entire country seemed to be waiting for curtain time. It was an event, incidentally, bigger than any of the presidential debates have been since. All along, the program had been planned as a debate, with an argument, a rebuttal and a summing-up, but at 2:30 p.m. before the show was to go on, Sullivan was informed by Paar's office that Paar wanted it simply to be an open discussion. Sullivan responded by telling the press, "Paar has simply welshed. As a matter of record, I challenged Paar to this debate last week. He specifically accepted the debate . . . I am ready to go on tonight and debate. If Paar wants to change his mind before four p.m. I will go on. Paar can now put up or shut up and his deadline is now four p.m. I have no further comment."

NBC responded within a half hour with a lengthy statement which stated in essence that "Sullivan had bowed out."

That night Paar opened with a fifteen-minute monologue in which he said, "Ed Sullivan has proved to be as honest as he is talented." He went on to say that he was disappointed in Sullivan "as a man," and that "He is afraid to appear on the show—not that he would be murdered, but that he would commit suicide in front of an audience . . . Everybody looks more interesting here, and if you had been here, Ed, you might have looked more interesting for the first time."

After some muttering about Ed's loyalty and his importance to show business and "the way he has used his column to beat people over the head who would not

323

come on his show," Paar decided to go even further in his attack: "Ed Sullivan is a liar. That is a libel. He must now sue and he must go to court—not like Winchell and Hoffa who sue just to save their face. The public is going to insist you go to court and under oath, I repeat, Ed Sullivan, you lied today."

Jack Gould in the *New York Times* called the whole incident a "highly distasteful brawl." His comment had some sobering effect on the two combatants. "The emergence of the dispute," Gould said, "emphasizes the almost incredible pressures that are a daily part of the TV life. The fierceness of the constant fight for survival in video is indicative of how the law of the jungle devours many otherwise sensible people, and directly affects what the public sees . . . If the people of the Congo think we have gone back to the playpen, they can't be blamed."

Sullivan via CBS sent out a final statement on the matter. He said that Paar's program had proved that his demand for a discussion instead of a debate was "only a cloak for exactly what he did last night: name-calling, a shocking indulgence in personalities, and a continued willful distortion of the true, true issue." Sullivan ended the statement by saying: "I will have nothing more to say on this subject." And the public end of the feud died just then.

Sullivan, however, did get in one last punch several years later when he told *Time* magazine that the best he could say for Paar was that he is "a thoroughly no-good sonofabitch."

There was another little flurry of publicity when Paar made an answer on Lee Bailey's half-hour interview program. He said among other things: "NBC has its peacock. I think that CBS now has its cuckoo." Sullivan apologized and the matter finally came to rest. Among other things, it simply was not possible to get the public as excited as it once might have been over a dispute between these two TV personalities. Besides, Sullivan was a sick man and the emotional strain of the Paar affair had not helped. He had had ulcer surgery

Ed Sullivan "clowns" with three French boxers

and was not recovering as quickly as doctors hoped, mainly because he still needed gallbladder surgery. There were other problems, too. By the early Sixties Sullivan's family, including his son-in-law Bob Precht, who had become producer of his show, realized that he was beginning to get senile. In 1966 he was diagnosed as having hardening of the arteries which affected his memory and his coherence. This no doubt led to some of the famous fluffs that were featured in the later years of his show. Here are some cited by Jerry Bowles in *A Thousand Sundays*: "Good night and help stamp out TV." (He meant TB.)

Introducing Rich Little: "Let's hear it for this fine young Canadian comic, Buddy Rich."

Wishing a speedy recovery to his son-in-law, Bob Precht, who was home nursing a cold, he said, "Best wishes to our producer, Bob Hope."

Once Bob Newhart, a frequent guest on the show, recalled Sullivan had a couple of French jugglers who spun plates on the top of sticks. "These guys do their bit, and Ed, for some reason or other, decides he wants to talk to them. So he calls them over. Now these guys are French and neither one of them speaks a word of English. 'Where're you fellows from?' he asked. They just look at each other. Then one of them starts to mumble something in French. 'No. no,' Ed says. 'Where are you from?' They're really panicked now and they're jabbering to each other and finally Ed hears the word 'Paris.' 'Paris, um, well, you give my regards to Marshall de Gaulle when you get back.' "

But Sullivan's show was by no means finished. It reached its greatest peak when he introduced a set of cuddly young lads from Liverpool who created the biggest sensation in the history of the show. They were called the Beatles.

34.

Sullivan had run across the Beatles on a trip to England when he found the London airport so jammed that the Prime Minister could not fly out to Scotland and the Queen Mother had difficulty arriving from Ireland because of the crowd of 15,000 kids that had turned out to greet the Beatles. Sullivan hated rock 'n roll but he knew crowds. He was impressed and signed the Beatles for three appearances at $4,000 each, even though they were at the time almost unknown in the States. A careful promotion campaign was prepared for their appearance. Brian Epstein, their manager, persuaded Capitol Records to release the Beatles' new single, "I Want to Hold Your Hand," to coordinate with the show. Capital Records agreed, impressed by the Beatles' forthcoming triple appearance on the Sullivan show, and five million stickers saying "The Beatles are coming" were printed and distributed, along with Beatles buttons and Beatles wigs. The record was released a month before the scheduled first appearance on Sullivan and by the end of the month had reached the number one spot on the record charts. The nation was primed for the debut of the Beatles.

The day they arrived at Kennedy airport was like a scene from "The Invasion of the Body Snatchers." By one o'clock on the day of the Beatles' arrival, there were 5,000 kids at the airport being controlled by 110 policemen. The chartered plane arrived at 1:20 p.m. and a huge roar went up from the crowd, which almost escaped the control of the policemen. Inside, there was a press conference that was like a scene in a madhouse, with members of the New York press corps pushing, shoving, shouting, and punching to get position.

The show was a vast success. There were 50,000 requests for tickets to the rehearsal and the show itself. Sullivan's introduction was: "Our city—indeed the country—has never seen anything like these four young men from Liverpool. Ladies and gentlemen, the Beatles!"

They sang "I Want to Hold Your Hand." Even Bob Precht, who had been opposed to the whole booking, had to say in the control room to nobody in particular, "Jesus Christ! This is the damndest thing I ever saw."

On Monday, Sullivan got fantastic news. The weekly Nielsen ratings, which had just replaced the Trendex ratings as a measurement for TV popularity, gave "The Toast of the Town" a score of 44.6 for the first show. Some 73,900,000 viewers are estimated to have watched it—the largest audience in television history to that time.

Sullivan was elated. It was the first time since his early successes seven years ago that he had topped the ratings. The top names continued to make news. Sullivan was again in the news when he fired Jewish dialect comic Jackie Mason for giving him the finger on the show. That feud also made big headlines for a few weeks, until it was forgotten and some years later Sullivan made peace with Mason and even admitted him on the show again.

Meanwhile, Winchell was again getting into a hassle with King Features Syndicate over the editing of his material—this time, not because it was too liberal, but because it was objectionably right-wing and savage and not acceptable to a good many of the subscribing papers. Winchell told King Features that he had had plenty of offers elsewhere. If he resigned from his contract there, he could always go to the *New York Post*, which had made him an offer.

Paul Sann, editor of the *Post*, put out a public statement completely denying Winchell's claim. He stated flatly that nobody representing the *Post* had made an offer of any kind to Winchell, nor had any intermediary been authorized to make one.

The statement was superfluous. The handwriting was on the wall. Toward the end of 1962 there was a printers' strike which put all of the New York papers out of business for 114 days. After the strike was settled, the *Mirror*, which had not been too healthy even before the strike, ceased publication on October 15, 1963. Not even ace reporter Winchell had known about the collapse in advance.

One of the *Mirror*'s top executives was reportedly in bed with a famed movie star when he learned of the paper's expiration. "Well," he said, "I've been fucked twice in one hour. One good. One bad."

Winchell was extremely shaken about the demise of the *Mirror*. "My flagship has been sunk," he said.

In the last edition of the paper it was announced that some *Mirror* features, including Winchell's column, would be published in the *Journal-American*. But at the *Journal*, Winchell had even more problems than he had when he was published in the *Mirror*. The editors slashed his copy mercilessly and at random. But it wasn't only Winchell's flagship that was sinking. The whole era that he represented was coming rapidly to a close.

In early '65, Ethel Merman, Sherman Billingsley's former girlfriend, was passing the Stork with Russell Nype, her singing co-star in "Call Me Madam" on Broadway. She knew that people had not been coming to the Stork for some time because, among other reasons, of Sherman's refusal to employ union help. Merman and Nype decided to go in to say hello for old times' sake.

"There was no one at the door," Merman said, recalling the days when you couldn't even get to the door without all sorts of pull. "Three people were sitting at a table—Eleanor Whitney, Freddie Backer, who became Judge Backer, and a gray-haired man who had his back to us. He jumped up. It was Sherman, but I give you my word of honor, I didn't recognize him until spoke. He was so old and stooped and thin.

"Except for a couple of waiters, we were the only people in the place. In the course of the conversation, I mentioned that Sherman had closed the Cub Room. He nodded and for a moment there was a flicker of the old Sherman. 'Yes. After you stopped coming,' he said, 'I only opened it so that you'd have a place to go.' That was only a part of his courtly charm. Of course he had closed it because nobody went there anymore."

In September, Sherman Billingsley underwent treatment for a heart ailment at Roosevelt Hospital. At the same time, on the same floor, Winchell was undergoing a checkup. It was his first hospital visit as a patient. Apparently neither man realized that the other was there.

Early in October, a sign was posted at 3 East 53rd Street: "Stork Club Closed. Will Relocate."

The two men never saw one another again, and the Stork Club never reopened. Billingsley died broke and in debt.

That same year, the *Journal-American*, which was also struggling for survival, had a drastic cost-cutting program. Winchell, Kilgallen and other columnists had their column frequencies reduced and salaries slashed.

The three short columns Winchell now had weekly took up less than half the space his column had occupied in the *Mirror*. Before the end of the year, Winchell had to release his only paid writer, Herman Klurfeld. He gave him no severance pay after 27 years.

On November 7, Dorothy Kilgallen finished her stint on the "What's My Line?" show. She was, as usual, clever, witty and quick-minded. She went to P.J. Clarke's with her friends Dorothy and Bob Bach, where they had a couple of drinks. Dorothy had her usual vodka and tonic. Then she left them for a date which the Bachs assumed was with a new lover she called "the out-of-towner." At one o'clock she appeared, a little bit high, at the Regency Hotel. The man behind the bar, Harvey Daniels, said hello to her. He did not notice that there was anybody in her company, which was unusual, and he did not see her leave. But nobody ever saw her again—alive. Kilgallen was discovered sometime on Monday sitting up in bed in her third floor master bedroom—dead. She had apparently been reading a copy of Robert Ruark's book, *The Honey Badgers,* which lay at her side.

Death was attributed to a heart attack. Ten thousand mourners attended her funeral and viewed her closed coffin. A week later, the heart attack verdict was reversed and a death certificate was issued which ascribed her death to "acute alcohol and barbiturate intoxication—circumstances undetermined." (Pills and liquor taken simultaneously.)

Milton Helpern, New York's chief forensic pathologist, said there was no way of knowing whether the death was suicide or accidental. After a lengthy investigation, Lee Israel, her biographer, determined that Kilgallen had taken at least 15 to 20 sleeping pills on the night of her death. When Israel asked the doctor in charge whether she had intended to kill herself, he "wiggled his hand iffily."

There was a rumor spread by Kennedy conspiracy theorists, of whom Kilgallen was one, that she was just one more in a chain of mysterious murders connected to the assassination of the president. Nothing was ever established to prove this point.

By this time, Winchell, at 68, was beginning to show his age; not only was he slower, but he was uncharacteristically gentle and accessible. He had dropped his mantle of toughness and unapproachability. At major trials, he would pop up in the press section, thin, silver-haired, affable, a ghost of himself passing along stray crumbs of news to any colleague who might be sitting behind him.

There had been much tragedy in his private life. His wife had been seriously ill with a respiratory problem for years and was forced to live in Scottsdale, Arizona where the dry air was believed to be helpful to her condition. His son had been a problem since childhood. As he approached his teen years, he developed a strange ondness for guns and bizarre pranks.

Once, as a young boy, he smeared himself with ketchup and lay down in the road near his Westchester home, apparently to get the reaction of passing motorists. When he was scolded for his behavior, he snapped, "If you were Winchell's kid, how would you grow up?"

Winchell's daughter Walda, of whom he was so fond, developed what seemed almost a hatred for him. When she was eighteen, she eloped against Winchell's will with a 29-year-old art student named William Lawless. Winchell was furious and what had made him even angrier was the fact that Ed Sullivan printed the news of the wedding first. Walda and Lawless never lived together and the marriage was annulled. Some years later she fell in love with a young man named Billy Cahn, of whom Winchell equally disapproved. They eloped without WW's OK. He subjected his daughter's boyfriend to an unmerciful probe and found that he had been jailed for six days in Florida in 1935 on a charge of vagrancy. Thereafter he printed item after item about Cahn, calling him a "con" or a "con artist." Cahn was a producer who had, among other things, produced "Toplitsky of Notre Dame." Winchell warned everybody important to have nothing to do with Cahn. He blacklisted anybody who disobeyed his orders. It made for a rift with his daughter that was really never healed. After several years, the marriage ended in divorce. Walda moved to California where she became the wife of a social figure, Hyatt von Dehn.

Walter, Jr. joined the Marines, hoping he would get to use his talent with guns, but he was discharged for being under age. He appeared in the news in 1963 when he was charged with pistol-whipping fifteen youths who had trespassed on the Winchell estate. Winchell seemed to be able to do nothing with the disturbed boy. On one occasion, Walter Jr. moved to Kenya where he tried to use his guns as a white hunter, without success.

Walter Jr. became friends with Gene Fowler, the editor and journalist who had been a close friend of his father's. Despite the fact that he had never been close to his father, Walter Jr. showed considerable family loyalty when he worked for a time as a radio newswriter—and even some skill. But there was a wistful quality to his notes. Once he wrote of his father, "Have tried to get him to go fishing with me for years, or play golf with some of his friends, but the only interest he's ever had is the typewriter and I don't press it anymore . . ."

In a letter to Fowler, he wrote: "When you say that 'everything you read about Walter is trash,' you couldn't be more right. The crap these people turn out would ruin anyone's digestion. The latest book by Ed Weiner missed the target again. Dad had always screamed: 'Don't prettify me!' . . . He's a champion, Gene, and there are damn few like him left around . . ."

But the gulf between Walter and his father widened. In '66 Walter Jr., who had increasingly been showing neo-Nazi sympathies, married a German girl without his parents' knowledge and his communications with his father ended. In 1967 Walter Jr. underwent psychiatric treatment at a hospital in La Jolla. He was now openly ranting and raving against the Jews and in favor of Hitler. But it was clear to those who read sadly about this that the man was seriously deranged.

He moved his wife and two children to Santa Ana in 1967 and applied for welfare relief, listing himself in his application as a freelance writer. On Christmas Day of 1967 he ended his life with a .38 automatic.

Winchell was completely crushed by the suicide of his son. He never quite recovered from it. He had barely time to get over this grief when his wife June finally succumbed to her long illness and died on February 5, 1970. She was buried in a cemetery in Scottsdale near her son.

Winchell was sick and tired, and so was the whole business to which he had devoted himself. He tried to syndicate himself without any luck, appearing in only a hundred papers toward the end. He was a victim of his own excesses, but also of changing public taste.

_et's face it," said Robert Sylvester in 1967. "The .line of Broadway meant the decline of the Broadway .lumn. Broadway was once a great, glamorous street. Now look at it. It's shoddy. You can't be the historian of something that no longer exists."

A press agent connected with Winchell told a *Times* reporter that although the public was still interested in scandal, a new lifestyle had taken over. "Look, you have glamorous unmarried stars now openly living with each other. You get people going on TV and talking about the most intimate things. You get magazine articles that are incredibly blunt.

"Everything's changed. No one's shocked anymore."

Winchell left New York for good after the death of his wife and son and shuttled between Los Angeles and Arizona. In Los Angeles he lived in the Ambassador Hotel, a lonely figure. The bounce had gone out of him. "I have stopped seeing everyone," he wrote Bob Thomas when he was asked to cooperate in a biography in 1970. "There is nothing I want to discuss about my career. I leave it to you historians to deal with."

In 1970 he was unable to attend the 25th anniversary of the charity he founded, the Damon Runyon Fund, because he was undergoing stomach surgery at the time. Gamely he sent a message to the fund that he was going to make a comeback as a columnist. He died of cancer, the ailment he had devoted so much energy to fighting, in March of 1972 at the age of 74 in Los Angeles.

Newsweek, never a friend of his, commented generously, "Whatever his occasional difficulty with the facts . . . Winchell was a major figure in twentieth century American journalism. He was a pioneer, not merely of the gossip column, but of a fresh approach to newspaper writing, and despite his blatant vulgarization of celebrity foibles, he somehow humanized his subject."

One of Winchell's contemporaries, Stanley Walker, while city editor of the *New York Herald Tribune*, paid him his finest tribute: "Winchell did much for journalism for which journalism has been slow to thank him. He helped change the dreary, ponderous impersonality which was pervading the whole press."

The name of the fund Winchell had founded in honor of his friend Damon Runyon was changed after his death to the Runyon-Winchell Fund. During Winchell's lifetime he had distributed over $32 million for cancer research, raised on behalf of the fund.

In 1971, after 23 years, Ed Sullivan's show succumbed to receding ratings and was taken off the air. In the words of one critic, "Sunday was cancelled."

After the cancellation of the show, Sullivan kept his hand in television by hosting variety specials, many of which were extremely successful. Nobody could figure out the secret of Sullivan's success, but his own explanation was blunt: "I am the best damn showman on television."

Sullivan, who had always had a close relationship with his wife of 43 years, Sylvia, drew even closer to her after the cancellation of his show. On March 16, 1973 Sylvia died from a ruptured aorta. She had seemed up to that point to be in near perfect health and looked much younger than her 69 years.

With her death, Sullivan plunged into a deep depression from which he never really emerged. On October 13, 1974, in Lenox Hill Hospital, Sullivan's stay on Earth was cancelled at the age of 76. He died, like Damon Runyon and his old time enemy Winchell—with whom he finally patched up his differences in those last years—of cancer. When he died, he was President of the Runyon-Winchell Cancer Fund.

Three thousand mourners showed up on a cold, wet, rainy day for his funeral. They included readers, television viewers, celebrities and friends. The last of the bigtime columnists was gone and the influence of the remaining Broadway gossips was waning rapidly.

Today we have Liz Smith, probably the most influential gossip columnist in America, who works for the *New York Daily News*, Sullivan's former paper. We have Miss Rona Barrett on television. We have various prominent gossips on the *New York Post* and in the *ington Post* and the *Washington Star*. But there no giants anymore. There is nobody whose single or whose sole support can make or break anybody. There is nobody who commands an audience of tens of millions every week. Theirs was a long era—sordid, vicious, violent, exciting, romantic, and colorful. There would never be anything quite like it again.